# WITCH-HU

# Trilogy

### By K. S. Marsden

To Chris,

Thank you so much
for supporting Children in Read
2022

Happy Reading!

K.S.M

# Malleus Maleficarum,

## maleficas ut earum hæresim, ut phramea potentissima conterens

# The Shadow Rises

## Witch-Hunter 1

**K. S. Marsden**

## Chapter One

Hunter knocked back his cold, expensive beer. He was sitting alone at an open-air bar in the middle of Venice. It was late in the night, or at least it felt late - the days and nights seemed to take forever to tick past. The dark canal flickered with yellow lamp-light, along with new fragments of colour.

Hunter eyed the fairy lights that the new owner had strewn across the trellis beams, a cheap way to create a 'youthful' environment. He didn't approve.

He looked around again, his gaze deadened as though he saw through the thin veil of these mortal amusements, and was not impressed.

Hunter Astley appeared to be a very normal guy, though one could never call him average. He ticked every box for the traditional English gent; in his mid-twenties, tall with black hair and classic good looks; he held an aura of charm and intelligence that was woven so appealingly about him; he had a confidence that was only partly to do with a large family fortune to his name.

Yet all this helped to distract people from looking too closely, to stop them noticing that scrutinising gaze and apathy to the mundane facts of life. Because under the veil, there were darker things to fear.

Hunter Astley was a witch-hunter.

Under the guidance of the Malleus Maleficarum Council, alongside other witch-hunters, Hunter worked tirelessly to eradicate witches and witchcraft, to prevent curses and black magic and to stop the witchkind gaining the hold and power over the unaware, ignorant world. The witches never stopped in their pursuit of power, so neither did Hunter and his fellow witch-hunters.

Except for now. Hunter was on holiday - against his own will, one might add. But the question was, when you know that evil magic is threatening everywhere beneath the surface, what does a witch-hunter do for a holiday?

Oh, he was bored. And in his bad mood, Hunter knew who to blame: James. Good old, annoying, interfering James Bennett. His colleague, who considered himself the brains of the operation, and was as loyal as he was irritating. The two of them had been working overtime since a big coop last Hallowe'en, and last winter had been the busiest they had ever known the witchkind. The increased activity had taken more of a toll on Hunter of course. When considering the two of them, it was Hunter that was the man of action and James was his back-up, his background researcher.

James had taken it upon himself to insist that Hunter needed a break now that it was spring. Ok, things were calmer now, and ok, the last job had nearly killed him. But only nearly, he was still alive. His arguments had been ignored and Hunter had finally agreed to take a week's holiday, especially as James threatened to lock up all the open cases and divert current issues to the others.

Although, when Hunter agreed to stop work for a whole week, that didn't stop him sneaking into his own office to slip all the Venetian files into his suitcase before he left. Not that it had been much use. The damn files hadn't been kept up-to-date and he was chasing ghosts. And no, ghosts didn't exist.

A trio of young women sauntering past dragged his attention back to the present. They were all beautiful, but the tallest of the three was particularly striking.

Hunter noticed that his weren't the only eyes that watched them cross the room, so he was an average guy after all. He smiled at the idea, maybe James was right, maybe he could enjoy a holiday.

When he raised his gaze again, the girls had gone. Hunter drained the last of his beer and made his way over to the bar. He leant against it and waited for the barman. He noticed her perfume first, a fresh scent that contrasted sharply against the alcohol.

Hunter looked up to see one of the girls standing a few feet away. With her heels on, she was almost as tall as Hunter. Her dark brown hair was tied back, and there was a proud tilt to her jaw. Hunter appreciatively inventoried the slim waist and long legs.

As though sensing his inspection, the girl turned on her heels to face him. Her hazel eyes locked onto him, coolly assessing him in return. Apparently dissatisfied, the girl turned away again.

Hunter inwardly laughed, not even a word passed between them and he had been shunned. His poor ego. He ordered a drink, and as he waited for his beer to come, he caught a male voice – one whose accent didn't hide the waver of uncertainty.

"… let me buy you a drink."

Hunter turned to see a very smart, suited type, leaning into the girl. His smile did nothing to disguise the fact his suggestion had been half a question. It almost reminded Hunter of how James was when he had to talk to beautiful girls. Honestly, Hunter felt a little sorry for men that floundered so easily.

He paid for his beer and found himself watching as the girl looked uncomfortable as the suit got closer. Her painted lips somehow managed to convey a pout and a sneer that spoke volumes against her silence.

The guy grew increasingly unsure at her stony silence and eventually slunk off.

Hunter smiled to himself, keen for the challenge. He moved towards her and finally spoke. "Scusi, signorina..."

Her eyes suddenly snapped onto him again, her frown increasing. "Scusa, non parlo l'italiano." She replied in perfect Italian.

Hunter smirked at her avoidance. "Great, neither do I! But it's good to know that you talk at all." He couldn't help but notice that she was even more beautiful close up. If one got past the fixed haughty glare, of course.

There was a twitch in her lips as though she fought down a smile. The woman turned to her friends. "Let's go." They obediently shifted away from the bar. "Good night." She said to Hunter and, making no excuses, left.

Hunter watched her retreating figure. What a strange, beautiful girl.

Hunter stood nursing his beer for a quarter an hour, before giving in to his dull mood and heading home. He weighed up the desire for company tonight, there had been enough female eyes turned in his direction this evening, including the waitress at the restaurant earlier. But it felt like too much effort. No, he'd much rather go back to his apartment, have a night cap, and see when the next flight back to London was.

Although it was spring, it wasn't cold. The late-night walk was actually pleasant as he moved away from the youthful hub and into the quieter streets. It was then that he heard a scuffle in the distance, followed by silence.

Hunter stopped, looking in the direction of the brief disturbance. It was most probably a cat, or something equally innocent. But that niggling feeling in his gut grew, calling to him. Damn it, was he getting withdrawal symptoms from work? Looking for trouble where there was none to be found? The utter silence made his senses tingle; his instincts kicked in and took over. He made his way quietly in the direction of the noise. Down a shadowed path to where a heavy door was ajar. Hunter stood against the gap and heard people moving inside, he began to see the weak light of candles as they were lit by two flitting figures.

Hunter reflexively lifted his hand to his throat, closing his fingers around the comfortable weight of the protective amulet. Next, he knelt down and retrieved the small gun strapped to his calf, thankful that he had gone against his colleague's advice, that he had decided to remain armed.

Standing tall again, he slipped inside, pressing the door shut behind him. The large room was lit by a hundred candles - some witches were overly keen on the traditional touches. There was a makeshift altar, a long table covered with black silk, and a young woman strapped to it. She struggled sluggishly against her bonds, her breath fast and frightened. She was probably drugged, but at least she was alive. For now.

Hunter shifted around the edge of the room, keeping to the shadows. His eyes widened as he recognised the victim – the girl from the bar…

Her identity was confirmed when her two friends entered the circle of candlelight, bristling with excitement.

"P-please… please, you can't…"

Hunter could hear the girl's slurred pleas, her focus strengthening as those she considered friends came closer.

Hunter kept his own breathing low and steady, his gaze moving to a tall man with greying hair, although his face was unlined. He carried the knife, holding it up with reverence.

As he drew up to the altar, Hunter knew he had to act. There was no time to assess hidden dangers. He stepped into the light, trying to look as confident as possible. "Stop! Fermo!"

They all turned, shocked at the unwelcome man that had interrupted their ritual. Hunter rushed to speak before they caught up with the situation. "I charge you to stop. I am Hunter Astley, by the Malleus Constitution you will surrender now to my authority to be bound and registered. If you refuse to come quietly, I am empowered to take any means necessary."

Oh, it all sounded quite grand and official, and if he had had back up they might have turned themselves in harmlessly; but one Hunter against three put the odds in their favour.

"Assalire." *Get him.* The man ordered. "Subito!" *Now!* He barked as the two girls hesitated.

Ah, perhaps they were new to this game, Hunter thought, briefly giving him hope. But hope and desperation were put out of his mind as his body moved almost instinctively into action. He felt the charm about his neck heat up as it absorbed attacks

15

from all three. He took aim with his gun and fired a single shot...

*****

The brown-haired girl woke up in a large bed with soft sheets, an early morning breeze rippling through the white cotton curtains and filling the room with cool and pleasant air.

"Good morning." Hunter said gently as he stood in the doorway, waiting for his guest to wake up. "How are you feeling?"

The girl sat up sharply, but then groaned, pressing her hand to her aching head. "Where am I?"

"Still in Venice, in my apartment. My name's Hunter by the way." He smiled politely. This was usually the part where people thanked him.

She frowned, a certain intelligent harshness returning now that she was fully awake. "Why? You had no right to take me anywhere. What did you do, drug me?"

Hunter waited patiently for her to finish, a slight smirk at how easily people forget what was hard to believe. "It's nice to feel appreciated for saving your life," he replied calmly and innocently. "I'll put on some coffee, come on through when you're ready."

He walked into the main room, smiling as he did so.

The girl sat dazed for a moment, then slowly slid out of the covers and stood up. She was still in last night's clothes, the smell of smoke and alcohol clinging to them. She didn't hesitate for long and Hunter heard her bare feet padding into the very luxurious open plan apartment. She stood next to the sofa, watching Hunter suspiciously in the small kitchen.

"So last night was real? I mean, what happened, and why?"

Hunter didn't reply immediately, but brought through two cups of steaming coffee and invited his guest to sit down. "If you don't mind me asking, had you known those girls long?"

The girl shrugged, "A few days, they were at the same hotel as me. I was on holiday alone and they were friendly, inviting me out day and night. I thought they were ok."

"It was their job, to gain your confidence. But they were going to kill you, to sacrifice you, last night. They were witches." Hunter glanced up as he finished speaking, watching her carefully after this revelation.

"Witches?! As in 'fire burn and cauldron bubble'? You've got to be joking."

"No, I am completely serious," he replied with an apologetic smile. "Witches are real, and to be blunt, they're all black-hearted, evil... I'm sorry you got involved. If we were in England I could offer you something to erase the memory - but as it is..."

"Are there a lot of witches?"

Hunter shrugged. "Depends on what you mean by lots? There are too many in my opinion. If I tried to put a number on them, perhaps ten thousand worldwide." He paused to drink his coffee. "Does that surprise you?"

"I don't know; it's not something I've previously considered." The girl replied quickly and rather sharply. "But I suppose if you count all the fortune tellers and-"

"No." Hunter broke in with a rue smile. "All those harmless, normal people that play with the idea of using magic - they aren't witches. Witches are an entirely different breed of human, at least one parent has to be a witch; you can't become one by wanting it. And they don't waste their power telling fortunes at fairs either. Instead, they create illnesses and plagues; they torment victims with illusions and nightmares; they can bring storms, fires and floods. They do all this and more, for their own gain, or sometimes just because they enjoy it.

"Their powers are only limited by their strength - they gain a temporary boost from draining the life from victims; that is why they perform sacrifices, their thirst for power is insatiable. Sorry, I don't mean to frighten you."

The girl sat there quietly for quite a while, naturally taking time to comprehend all this. Finally, she spoke with an obvious scepticism. "So... if those girls are witches, and I was the sacrifice - what does that make you?"

"A witch-hunter."

She raised a brow. "A witch-hunter named 'Hunter'? How very original."

18

Hunter sighed. "You're a very pleasant, friendly character, aren't you? So, you know about me, do I get to learn your name?"

"Sophie Murphy." She replied without hesitation. "What... what happened to the girls - I mean, the witches?"

Hunter paused. "The two female witches weren't very powerful creatures. They agreed to be bound. But the male witch that was in charge was executed on site."

"You killed him?" Sophie's voice shook.

It sounded bad, but people just didn't understand. "He wasn't willing to cooperate; I hope you don't mind." Hunter replied with a certain bite. Oh yes, he could act the hero and save her and get away unscathed, but he must do it without killing violent witches? Sure.

"So... bound? What does that mean?" Sophie asked more quietly, helpfully shifting the focus.

"Oh, it means they submitted to arrest. Then their powers are 'bound', effectively removed so they can never use them again. The witch serves time in prison, same as any convict." Hunter replied, giving the brief version of binding. The witch-hunter's handbook devoted about three dreary chapters on the subject. "You've got nothing to worry about from those girls, they're powerless and it may be a lifetime before they're free."

They were interrupted as the door flew open. A young man entered, slamming the door behind him before turning to glare at Hunter.

"You couldn't do it, could you? You couldn't go even two bloody days without looking for trouble?" A thick Yorkshire accent shouted out as he turned to throw down his coat and two bags in the kitchenette. "You call me up at 3 in the mornin', and it's me that's gotta fly out and clean up. I've already rang the Italian branch of the Council, we've got a meeting with 'em this afternoon - they're not happy, Hunter - you know the rules. You notify them if you're operating or hand it over to one of theirs."

Hunter sat back, appearing unfazed by this little outburst. When the young man had finished, he spoke quite coolly. "Sophie, this is my colleague, James Bennett. James, this is Sophie, the girl that would have been sacrificed by the time I had followed the proper lines of authority." Although he spoke calmly enough, there was a hardness in his tone.

James reined back his frustration as he held out his hand to shake Sophie's, while giving her an appraising glance. "Sure, spurred on by a bonny face." He muttered to no one in particular.

There was no denying the warning in Hunter's voice this time. "Just take her statement, Mr Bennett."

It took half an hour for James to take down everything Sophie had to say, then a further hour for her to answer his unending questions into every tiny detail. Finally, he sat back, closing his notebook.

"Right, thank you, Miss Murphy. I'll get this all typed and copied for the Council... ah, there's just one more thing."

He reached into his briefcase, and after ruffling through many stuffed-in papers he pulled out some sheets and handed them to Sophie. She took them hesitantly, glancing down at the thick paper covered in text.

"It's a non-disclosure contract," he explained, leaning over so that he could see the writing he already knew by heart. "I'm sure you can understand, it's to protect you and us from... well, other witches finding out, or idiot interference."

"He means the media and general stupidity of the human race," Hunter added as he hovered about the formal conversation.

Sophie looked between the two of them and back down to the contract. "So, signing a piece of paper is supposed to guarantee my silence. I can see some flaws there."

"It legally and, ah, otherwise binds you to silence over the subject," James said seriously. "You will be unable to speak of it to anyone outside of the Malleus Maleficarum Council. Speaking of which, we'll organise you a contact for when you get back to England in case you want help, memory modification or the like."

Sophie continued to stare at the contract with an emotion resembling disgust. "And if I didn't sign it?"

Hunter leaned in, deadly serious. "We make sure you don't talk. As we said, it's for your own protection. I suggest you sign."

Sophie slowly picked up a pen and scrawled her name at the bottom of the page. James swiftly snatched it away from her and stuffed back in his briefcase. The three sat in silence for a few minutes before Hunter stepped up. "I'll see you out, Miss Murphy."

As he opened the front door for her, Sophie gazed up at him questioningly. "When do I see you again?"

"If everything goes to plan?" Hunter replied, leaning against the open door. "Never."

## Chapter Two

Spring was warming to summer.

Amongst the rolling hills and the green pastures of the English countryside in the picturesque village of Little Hanting life went on as normal. It was a quiet, sleepy place, with fields of cows and rattling tractors. There were old stone houses built in clusters. The grandest of which was Astley Manor, set in a large estate. No one could remember a time when there wasn't the quiet, unobtrusive Astley family. George "Young" Astley VI had died unexpectedly five years ago, leaving the manor and the care of his widow in the hands of his then 20-year-old son, known to all as Hunter.

And at this very moment, Hunter was seated in one of the large rooms, reading over a report written up by the ever-present James. Hunter sighed, even witch-hunting required paperwork in this crazy modern world - but thankfully Hunter could shift all that onto

James' workload. He preferred the more active part of his job than this paperwork. And James did a tediously good and thorough job of it. James hovered over him, waiting for his response.

"Yes, that's all in order. Send a copy to the MMC." Hunter passed the thick sheaf of papers back.

The Malleus Maleficarum Council, the secret branch of witch-hunters under the pay of the crown; or MMC for short. All witch-hunters reported to them and were bound by their laws.

Hunter stood up and walked over to an old cabinet, one of those numerous antiques that filled his family's sprawling homestead. With a clink of glass he filled two whiskey tumblers and passed one to James. "Here's to the end of that, then."

James took the drink. It had been an easy one this time, a single male witch in the East Midlands causing very localised trouble. He was comparatively weak and, faced with Hunter and James, he had succumbed to be bound from his magic and be registered with the MMC, to live quietly from now on. After the necessary jail time, of course.

"Excuse me, sir. There is a young lady here to see you." The mild voice came from the doorway. The family's long-serving butler waited for Hunter's attention. "A Miss Murphy. She is waiting in the sitting room."

"Thank you, Charles." Hunter replied, quite perplexed. Murphy? It sounded familiar. He exchanged a confused glance with James, before they rose together to meet the unknown guest.

A woman sat straight-backed on the settee, her long, dark brown hair casually tied back. She turned her head at their entrance and met them with a defiant stare.

"Mr Astley, Mr Bennett. I am Sophie Murphy. You may not remember me, but you came to my aid a couple of months ago - in Venice." The young woman spoke calmly and confidently and remained seated.

"Ah, Miss Murphy, of course." But Hunter frowned. "Forgive me, why are you here? The Council provided you with a contact?"

"Yes," Sophie replied. "But I didn't want to speak to a low-level pen-pusher. This won't take long, why don't you sit down."

Hunter gaped, speechless. He couldn't believe the girl's bloody cheek; inviting to sit down in his own home. On the other hand, he was curious about what the determined-looking girl could wish to say to him. Both he and James took their seats.

"I'm sure you can understand, after what happened, after I returned home it jarred with all the - the normality of the world. I had to learn more. And what I learnt was terrible. I want to be of use to you, to the Council, I want to join the witch-hunters."

Hunter sighed. To be honest, it wasn't uncommon for those rescued from the witches to feel in debt to the witch-hunters. And there was a perfect place for these untrained post-victims...

"Well, the Malleus Maleficarum Council always needs to employ people for its offices. There's lots of ways to help," Hunter replied. Yes, lots of ways to help, stuck in four walls organising counselling for victims, processing artifacts from raids, registering bound witches... More than a little bit dull.

Sophie seemed aware of that, and she shook her head. "No. I want to join the witch-hunters. I want to do something, Mr Astley."

Hunter grew uncomfortable at this, he did not enjoy recruiting witch-hunters. "It's not that simple, Miss Murphy, are you sure you won't consider an office position?"

It wasn't something to be taken lightly, everyone with the MMC put their lives on the line just by associating with witch-hunters. But to be a witch-hunter, to enter a world of darkness and fear, to never be off duty from revenge and persecution, to gamble with your life every day until a guaranteed early death. No, Hunter did not enjoy recruiting naïve people to join this hard life. But one glance at Sophie told him that she wouldn't be easily dissuaded.

"Miss Murphy, I understand how you feel, but the best witch-hunters are born, you can't just become one by choice. No, don't interrupt. My father was a witch-hunter, and his before him and so on, over the generations I have gained a certain... protection. A protection that you don't have."

Sophie sat quietly, then rounded on James. "And what about you? Are you a predestined witch hunter?"

James looked uncomfortably towards Hunter. "Ah, no. I'm like you. New to this. What's called a first generation. Even though I've been at this for five years now and I'm fully trained - or as much as any can claim t' be, I'm dependent on Hunter here for my safety, and I'm seen as nowt more than a lowly assistant t' MMC."

"Then I have made up my mind. I'll become a witch hunter, whether it is with your Council or not." Sophie replied quickly, a clear challenge in her voice. "It's up to you now, Mr Astley, are you going to help me?"

Hunter sat back, regarding the girl. She had guts enough, but he didn't like new people, besides the guilt, they couldn't handle things as well as he could. "James, a private word, please." He said quietly, then stood up, leading the way out into the corridor, aware of Sophie's eyes following them.

James closed the door behind him and shrugged. "I know what you're thinking, Hunter, but she's got the right attitude. Why don't we get in touch wi' MMC and give her a go. After all, we always need to build our numbers..."

Build our numbers. Or in other words replace those lost.

Hunter sighed, the decision would technically lie with the Council, but both he and James knew that his opinion would weigh heavily on the outcome. "Sure, let her throw her life away. Get in touch with the MMC, James. Suggest putting her with Brian Lloyd - he doesn't currently have an assistant."

James pulled his mobile out of his pocket and wandered down the empty corridor; while Hunter turned and re-entered the sitting room.

"James is talking to the Council now. Can I get you a drink while we wait?" Hunter asked as he closed the door gently behind him.

Sophie nodded, knowing she'd won her case. "Tea, please."

Hunter pressed the intercom and shortly asked Charles to bring up some tea. Sitting back down again he stared towards Sophie. She was bloody stubborn, maybe she'd be one of the few first generations to survive this career. "You'll be joining Brian Lloyd as an assistant-"

"Not you?" Sophie broke in.

Hunter frowned, not happy to be interrupted. "No." He replied abruptly. He didn't want the trouble of taking on an untrained assistant. "Mr Lloyd is a good man, he's been hunting for years and he'll teach you a lot. He's a fifth generation and can protect you while you learn, then you'll work under him."

There was a light knock on the door and Charles walked in, carrying a large tray. "Anything else sir?"

"No, thank you." Hunter replied, lightly dismissing him as he leaned forward to serve the tea. How very British; having a nice cup of tea whilst conversing about witches.

"You keep talking about generations, what do you mean?" Sophie asked, accepting her cup.

"Exactly what I say." Hunter replied, sipping at the hot drink. "People like you, and James, are referred to as first generations, because that's what you are. If you live long enough to have children and they continue witch hunting, they're second generations. Mr Lloyd is a fifth gen, meaning that his father, grandfather, great- and great-great-grandfather all worked for the MMC. Which means that he is highly regarded at the Council."

"And what are you, then?" Sophie asked quickly.

"I'm a seventh generation."

"So, you're even more 'highly regarded'?"

Hunter paused, staring down into his hot tea. When he continued, it was more haltingly. "Yes. For two reasons. First, I mentioned protection - it turns out that when the parent fights witchcraft, the children gain a certain resistance to it. It's like evolution in fast forward. By the third generation, they can perceive magic being used, they can deflect minor curses. By the fifth generation, they are stronger, faster..."

Sophie waited, but it seemed Hunter intended to leave the sentence hanging. "And? What about when a family gets to seven generations? What about you?"

Hunter now avoided her gaze. "Obviously I'm even better equipped... You have to understand that we don't know much about the skills of sixth and seventh gens. There are so few of us. Which brings me onto my second point - there are hundreds, perhaps thousands of first gens. Only about half of these survive long enough to even have families. And those of us that become a well-known witch-hunting family become a target for all witches." He now looked up to gauge her reaction. "You didn't think this would be a nine to five, did you? So many families utterly destroyed by witches to prevent the next generation of hunters. And then you have to start from scratch."

"I am not naïve, Mr Astley, I can boast to be somewhat aware of the risk of it all." She sipped the hot tea, then gazed with that constant frosty defiance at Hunter. "Besides, your family seems to have survived these dangers - even prospered."

It was clear that she assessed Astley success with the luxurious, sprawling manor. Hunter smiled at her confidence, but was a little unnerved at how cold Sophie was. Oh well, at least she was strong, who knew, perhaps she'd be ok. "Ah, well, over the generations we've learnt how best to protect ourselves. Astley Manor, for instance, has its own protection."

He paused and looked at her carefully, gauging the girl's potential, before suddenly deciding why not. "Come, I'd like to show you something."

Hunter led the way into the back of the house. He took out a key and unlocked a heavy door. It was dark inside the room, heavy curtains drawn across every window. Hunter clicked on a light and walked in.

"This is one of the best libraries in Britain - witch related libraries, of course." Hunter gestured to the rows of shelves, the room was stuffed with books, papers, files… "It's one of the perks of 200 years of Astley family witch hunting."

He moved over to a large glass case, looking down at it with a smile. "My personal favourite."

Sophie went over, peering curiously at the large yellowed sheets, bound with what looked like leather straps. Faded ink was shaped in medieval handwriting that looked familiar, assumedly Latin. "What does it say?"

"Malleus Maleficarum, maleficas ut earum hæresim, ut phramea potentissima conterens. Which roughly translates as 'The Hammer of Witches which destroyeth Witches and their heresy like a most powerful spear'." Hunter read out the first couple of lines, his fingers tracing above the words. "It's from the-"

"Malleus Maleficarum: 'The Hammer of Witches' or 'Witch-hunter's Handbook'. Published 1487. You have an original printing, impressive." Sophie suddenly recited.

Hunter looked at her in surprise.

"As I said, I've been doing my own research." Sophie added with an off-handed shrug. "You can find out about anything on Google."

"Yes, well." Hunter walked over to a bureau and picked up another book, relatively new compared to the rest. "This is something you won't see on the net. The Malleus Maleficarum - 37th Edition. The Handbook gets updated every thirty years or so. This was brought out four years ago." He handed her the book. It was small, only A5, but thick. And when she opened it and flicked through the pages, the text was small and dense.

"These are given to witch-hunters only." Hunter said, reclaiming his copy. "The Council will give you one when you are ready. I'm sure you'll find it as interesting as reading the Bible, but it's a sorry necessity to know it well. In the meantime, there is something I'd like to give you."

Hunter turned to a little dark door and another key was taken out. It was cold on the other side and as a pale light flickered on, Sophie followed down a set of stone steps. As she reached the bottom she shivered. It was a large stone room, which had originally been designed as a wine cellar.

Now it was like a private museum for the occult. One case displayed a score of knives and daggers, all remarkably designed. A long shelf held a bizarre collection of bottles - containing what Sophie dare not guess. Everywhere there was the glitter of silver bowls, the gleam of bronze bands.

"What is this stuff?" Sophie asked, still gazing about in amazement.

"Just stuff collected over the years. Things my family have confiscated from the witchkind. Some of it is quite useful." He pulled at the chain around his neck and lifted out a soldier's dog tags. "This, for example. We think it was originally used for protection during World War Two. It's served me very well when I've gone up against witches. It deflects all sorts of spells and attacks - it must've been a very strong witch that made it."

Sophie looked disgusted. "You horde dead witches' stuff? And then use it?"

"It's not as bad as it sounds. Well, ok, maybe it is. But we're not going to turn down extra protection. Anyway, it's safe. Dangerous stuff is disposed by the Council. Everything else is analysed, then returned to the witch-hunter. Most of us have an amulet of some sort."

Hunter turned to a cabinet and took out a silver necklace with a cloudy stone hanging from it. "Look, I'd like you to take this with you."

Sophie reached out and took it, then turned it over carefully in her hand. "I don't know what to say." She replied quietly, her eyes lowered.

Hunter shrugged. He wasn't one to throw gifts at relative strangers, especially not when the gift came from his own collection, but he felt incredibly guilty about setting Sophie up for a dangerous life.

"HUNTER!" James did insist on shouting in Hunter's house, even though Astley Manor was equipped with a state-of-the-art intercom system.

Hunter traipsed up the stairs again, followed closely by Sophie.

"Hey, it's sorted." James said quickly, "Sophie's gotta go straight to Brian Lloyd. He's his usual grumbling, unhappy self about it, but he's expectin' her."

"Right! That's great." Hunter turned to Sophie and shook her hand briefly, "Nice meeting you again, Miss

Murphy. Brian will give you a good start, you'll learn a lot. James will give you directions and see you out."

And that was it; Hunter turned and left for the second time expecting not to have to see Sophie Murphy again.

## Chapter Three

Despite his promise to keep his distance, to let the girl get on with her training, business carried Hunter to Brian Lloyd's door. James was visiting family up north, and Hunter decided to use the time to go see Brian. The fact that he could discretely check on Sophie's progress had of course never occurred to him.

As he strolled up the driveway, he looked up at the familiar house. It was detached and roomy, though nothing compared to Astley Manor. Still, Hunter had spent a lot of time here. After his father had died – or more correctly, been killed – Brian had stepped in. The MMC were desperate for the 7th gen Hunter to reach his full potential, preferably while keeping him tethered to the Council. So, they had sent 5th gen Brian Lloyd, to continue his training.

There weren't many people that Hunter was scared of, but Brian was one of them. Tall, stocky, with close-shorn hair, he looked tough and was an unforgiving bastard. But he was good at what he did and in Hunter's opinion, he was always right. So, it was with some nerves that he knocked on Brian's front door.

"Don't stand there gawping, boy. You coming in or not?" Without waiting for an answer, Brian went back into the house.

Hunter sighed; things obviously hadn't changed. He stepped through into a large study where Sophie sat, deep in reading a musty old volume.

"Oi, be useful, put the kettle on." Brian barked at her.

Sophie shot Hunter a cold look and took herself out of the room.

"So, how are things going?" Hunter asked with a smile. He'd had some equally pleasant experiences of training with Brian. It was almost satisfying to see that the old man was treating his next trainee with the same courtesy.

"I don't like you throwing your weight with the Council, boy. Sending me a bloody girl. What use are girls?"

Hunter gave his old mentor a sideways glance. Ah yes, Brian was set in the old ways, and at 62 years old, he wasn't about to change.

"Brian-"

"Oh aye, I know all about your modern, pc equality crap. But if she wants to help the MMC, why didn't you stick her in an office - registering bound witches, or filing cases."

"Because no one wants to do that boring shit." Hunter replied, then grinned, "So I take it it's not going well?"

"Ah well, I wouldn't say that. She seems to be coping, picking it up well enough. Took her along to a raid, she kept her head, didn't even throw up at all the blood."

Hunter found himself gazing in the direction of the kitchen where there was the clatter of mugs. What do you know, maybe Sophie would make a witch-hunter after all, and he wouldn't have to feel guilty.

"Ugh, you do like to try me, George," Brian grumbled.

"Who's George?" Sophie appeared in the doorway, three mugs in hand.

"Ahm." Hunter shifted uncomfortably, trying to work out if he could get a cup of tea without giving an answer.

"You didn't think Hunter was his actual name, girl?" Brian guffawed, blowing everything. "George Astley the Seventh, that's him. Only he insists on adopting that daft moniker and have everyone call him it. Just egotistical, if you ask me."

Sophie turned to Hunter, her eyes glittering.

"Look, I'll have you know my friends started that nickname - and it had nothing to do with witches. Besides, do I look like a 'George'? Only my mother insists on calling me it - well, and you, Mr Lloyd."

They sat drinking tea and chatting about insignificant things for another half hour. With a meaningful look from Brian, Sophie picked up some books and excused herself.

"You didn't just come for a chit-chat?" Brian asked suspiciously.

"No," Hunter replied, then fell silent. There was something else that had been making him increasingly uneasy, especially after a recent event.

"A police contact got in touch recently. He had something he thought I might be interested in. A couple of months ago six teenage girls died in a suspected arson attack."

"And why should that concern us?" Brian asked, not sure where this was going.

"Well, it turns out they were all wiccans."

The two men sat in silence. Wiccans. Whereas witches were a whole different breed, wiccans were normal humans (normal in perspective) that treated 'magick' as a religion. They were generally harmless individuals, bored housewives and teens that wore too much black. They played with their candles and foretold wobbly futures through cards and the like and were a bit of a running joke amongst the witch-hunters. After all, who'd be scared of a cat after facing lions!

Eventually Brian shrugged. "Sometimes wiccans die. It could have been an accident; it could have been arson, but mundane normal people arson. If witches were involved, the MMC would have found the traces."

"There's more." Hunter sighed. "And I don't know what to make of it. Last week, we took on a small coven, four witches. Three were killed, one bound. But as soon as the binding was complete, she burst into tears, saying crazy things: that she didn't know what she was agreeing to. Then she committed suicide a day later. Something didn't feel right so I had James do a background check. Turns out she was a wiccan."

Ok. That was enough to get Brian's attention.

"But… wiccans cannot gain anything from witchcraft."

"I know," Hunter muttered.

"What proud witch would allow one to join them. They think wiccans are scum."

"I know."

"And the binding, a wiccan would have no powers to be bound from, so why would she agree to be bound?"

"I know."

"So… are they taking on wiccans as servants? Or using them to swell their ranks? It's unheard of."

"That's what I was thinking," Hunter agreed. It didn't seem to fit, but he was scrabbling to make sense of it.

Brian sat, idly scratching his chin as he stared into space. He was a living legend, one of the oldest, longest-running witch-hunters. He'd faced every threat out there and never backed down. If he couldn't find an answer, who could?

"Aye, leave this to me, boy. I'll look into it. Now, why don't you bugger off so I can get some work done."

Hunter smiled again and shook hands with his old mentor. Yes, time to leave, there were other sources he could get working too.

As he left he passed Sophie who was sitting in the front garden, a book on her lap. She looked up as he said goodbye and there was the briefest smile on her lips. "See you, George."

*****

His next stop was Oxford.

Possibly one of the most beautiful cities in England. The way it clung onto tradition, and the studious air that came from the abundance of intelligent young minds. Oh, the memories Hunter had of this place. The slightly dilapidated rooms at his old college, the great hall that awed all newcomers, the underground bar where he used to drink with James and Charlotte.

It had been in his first year of university that he received the news that his father had been killed. Hunter joined the witch-hunters then and there and he'd dragged his friends into his dangerous world. Now they all had their parts to play. James was a 1st gen witch-hunter and Charlotte, dear sweet Charlotte, was a very important member of the Council: she had easily switched from law student to liaison in the office of bound witches.

So, who better to ask about bound witches. Hunter rolled up to her door early the next morning. But the person that answered wasn't the black-skinned beauty, it was a tall, lanky bloke with glasses.

"Ah, morning, Steve. Is Lottie in?"

Steve King, the gormless bugger that had married the most important woman in Hunter's life. Steve King, who now looked with intense dislike towards Hunter.

"Charlotte, you've got a visitor!" Steve called, and then stepped aside so Hunter could squeeze into the hall. "She's in the kitchen."

Hunter nodded humbly and went through the familiar house, Steve close behind him. Something about that guy always made Hunter feel like he'd done something wrong. But then, Hunter always did go out of his way to antagonise him.

"Ah, my favourite lady, just how I like to see her!" Hunter greeted with a fierce hug.

Charlotte gave him a sceptical look when he let go. She was sat at the breakfast table with a half-eaten bowl of cereal in front of her. Her unbrushed black hair was tied messily back and she was still in her dressing gown.

"I wanted to catch you before you went to work."

"I'm not working today Hunter. You could have phoned ahead." Charlotte glanced at the clock. "Oh, darling, you're going to be late." Her big brown eyes fell on her husband. "Go to work, we'll be fine."

"Yes, go to work, darling. I'll look after Lottie." Hunter added, enjoying the opportunity to wind him up.

Charlotte jumped up to see Steve out the front door, hitting Hunter as she passed him.

Ignoring the loving farewell that echoed up the corridor, Hunter helped himself to the fresh coffee.

"I wish you wouldn't do that," Charlotte said as she came back, "Every time you visit, he's in a mood for a week."

"Then you shouldn't have married such a grumpy sod. Why you settled for such a boring-"

"Quiet, kind, caring and RELIABLE." Charlotte cut in, repeating what she had said a hundred times before. "Why are you here, Hunter? Apart from driving my husband mad."

Hunter repeated everything he'd told Brian. Told her everything.

"And you want me to look if we have any similar cases, and check out the backgrounds of any unusual cases?"

God, she caught on fast.

Charlotte regarded him carefully. "That's a lot of extra work, Hunter. Do you know how many cases my office has processed?"

Hunter sighed. "I know, and I hate to ask, but I have a weird feeling there's something bigger here."

"Ok. I'll do it, of course," Charlotte replied with a sorry smile. "I learnt long ago to trust your weird feelings."

"Thanks, Lottie." Hunter gazed at her with friendly affection. But then frowned. "Where's your bracelet? You know you shouldn't take it off."

He was speaking of Charlotte's amulet, a delicate gold bracelet with small rubies, a beautiful way to protect oneself.

Charlotte reached into her dressing gown pocket and pulled out the offending piece of jewellery, her fingers gently playing over the links and stones. "Steve doesn't like me wearing it too often, no matter how I explain it he still sees it purely as an expensive gift from you that he can't compete with. But don't worry, I always have it close by."

Hunter frowned at this news, disliking dear Steve even more. "What if it doesn't work like that, Charlotte? You shouldn't take the risk."

"I'm a full-grown woman, Mr Astley, it's my choice."

Ok, so Hunter felt like the petulant little boy whenever Charlotte got like this, but he couldn't help caring. "Ok, but please tell me Steve hasn't removed the protection over the house?"

"No, he sees that as a dividend of working at the MMC. If you don't believe me, you can go inspect it." Charlotte said, looking carefully at Hunter. "Can we talk about something else? How's James?"

"Reliably annoying," Hunter replied swiftly. "He's gone home for a few days, which means he will come back with that unbearable over-the-top accent again. He might as well wear a bloody badge saying: 'I'm from Yorkshire'."

Charlotte laughed, she knew that Hunter was as fond of James as she was, but that didn't stop these two southerners enjoying the peculiarities of their friend from oop north.

"And how's - what's her name - Leanne? All going well?" Charlotte asked, unconvincingly 'forgetting' the name of Hunter's girlfriend.

"Leanne?" Hunter asked vaguely. "Oh, her. She got too clingy. It's Marie now, but it's not going anywhere. Then there's Natalie of course, the girl from my mother's tennis club."

Charlotte laughed at the ever-changing women in his life. "Lord, I can't keep track of you, Hunter. What are you trying to do, work your way through the alphabet before New Year? Will it be Olivia next, then Patrice? Aren't you ever just going to settle down?"

Hunter shrugged. "What can I say? The best girl in the world is already taken, so I'm just enjoying the rest."

There was an uncomfortable silence, and Hunter wondered if he'd tripped over that invisible line of conduct they kept for their friendship. They both knew that he had been in love with her since their days at University. Charlotte was beautiful and intelligent, she had been so caring and supportive when Hunter's father had died. She had also been immune to his charms.

Charlotte had never returned his love, and their relationship had been awkwardly platonic. Some days it was more awkward than others.

Hunter was uncomfortably aware that today was going to be one of those days. He glanced at his watch, anxious for an excuse to leave. "Look, Lottie, I should be going.  I promise I'll ring before I come round next time!"

## Chapter Four

Back to work again, no matter what else was happening, the fight against witchcraft was ongoing. During James' trip to Yorkshire, he had heard of incidents that the MMC were yet unaware of. People in a small village were living in fear for their sanity. So, they had done their research and headed up. For the past few weeks, several prominent figures of the small community had been suffering from hallucinations. Constant terrifying visions of those they loved dying in gruesome manners. It all started when the village united to drive away a disturbing new resident, a middle-aged woman they suspected of carrying out sick, occult practices. And it all reached a peak when the post-office owner was found dead - verdict suicide.

It seemed like an obvious case of a witch taking revenge.

Hunter and James arrived at the village in the evening, the last of the summer sun giving it a warm, pleasant look. But the serene picture was ruined by the fact that from the moment they arrived, Hunter could taste the layers of magic and the violent, bitter tone of the spells.

James hefted their bags out of the car and slammed the boot. "So, where is she?"

They had managed to work out that the witch must be staying close to the village, but nothing more specific. That's where a trained witch-hunter came in - they could sense the use, and source of magic; and Hunter just happened to be a finely-tuned 7$^{th}$ gen.

He closed his eyes, seeing and feeling the rhythm of the last cast spell. His eyes flew open. "Hope you brought your hiking boots." He said, turning to James with a rueful smile.

Unfortunately. magic didn't follow roads, or dry paths, and the two men pushed their way through a field of corn, then a field of wet grass, avoiding cowpats in the darkening evening. The land became more untamed and a small cottage appeared in a hidden dip of the countryside.

"There. Definitely there." Hunter said, finally stopping.

James caught up, slightly out of breath. He dumped his bag and pulled out his kit: Kevlar jacket; long knife; short knife; gun; in the bag there was everything he could possibly need. He checked them over, repeatedly checking the gold ring on his right hand, even though he never removed the protective amulet.

Hunter was kitted out in similar fashion. He turned and nodded to James and they set off the short distance to the cottage in silence. Over the years they worked together perfectly and it seemed unnecessary for extraneous words.

Hunter went to the front door, then waited to give James chance to get around the back. He knew when James was in place - Hunter never challenged his senses, even he didn't know how being a 7$^{th}$ gen allowed him to do this. Then, gun in hand, he opened the old, rusty latch on the door. It made a slight creak as it opened and Hunter held his breath, but there was no response. He opened it further and slipped in, creeping towards a flickering light, carefully, carefully over the rough wooden floor.

Hunter stopped at a doorway, gently inching round so that he could see part of the room. There was movement and he snapped back, then looked again. A figure was moving about, preparing for her night's work. Candles were lit, random objects arranged on the floor - personal items such as brushes, photos, even clothing - all to help focus the magic upon her victims. Hunter knew from his research that the woman was nearly fifty, but she had the appearance of a thirty-year old. It wasn't uncommon for witches to keep a youthful appearance, they were vain and arrogant creatures.

Hunter dragged his eyes across the room, searching for further danger. Then to the only other door, where a slight shift of shadow showed James was ready.

Hunter nodded and stepped into the room, gun raised. "Stop!"

The witch jumped with surprise, she span around to see that there were two of them. But then she smiled and shook her head. She raised her arms and the shadow and firelight leapt up and formed two massive snarling beasts which rushed at the men.

Hunter didn't flinch, didn't move, as the very solid four-legged beast leapt up with teeth bared... and continued to pass straight through him.

The witch hesitated, disconcerted that her powerful illusions failed to distract these men.

"By the Malleus Maleficarum, you will surrender your-"

"Witch-hunters." The witch snarled, stepping back, her eyes sparking dangerously. "In that case..."

She kicked over the candles and before Hunter could react the fire sped with unnatural speed and threw up a wall of flame. Hunter fired once into the flames, but heard the bullet hit the wall. The fire twisted into a huge serpent and darted at James. He didn't move fast enough and his sleeve singed and ignited and he allowed himself to be distracted. The witch sent a wave of power that knocked him off his feet.

"No!" Hunter leapt to his friend's side so that he could protect them both, firing off another round as he did so.

The whole room was on fire now, the air thickening with smoke. The witch stood in the very centre, a smile on her face. But then Hunter heard the smashing of a window and the image faded - the illusion buying its master time to escape.

Coughing, Hunter dragged James to his feet and the two of them stumbled through the heat and smoke to the door. Once outside they gulped down the clean air, James dropped to the ground again, but Hunter turned and ran.

Across the dark fields, Hunter's sharp eyes could see a fleeing figure. He stopped as he reached higher ground and raised his gun, took aim and fired. In the distance the figure jerked and fell.

Still coughing, Hunter jogged along to his quarry. The witch was gasping for breath and fighting the shock of having a bullet in her shoulder.

Hunter aimed the gun at her head, just in case she had the energy for another round.

"As I was saying, surrender yourself to my authority, to be bound and charged."

The witch spat at him, then screamed. "She will be my saviour."

Hunter heard James stagger up to them as he cocked the gun. It was his experience that this attitude led to immediate execution.

But the witch seemed to claw back her wild anger and gave a grimace. "Bind me, you cowardly bastards." She dropped her head back to the ground, submitting to her disgraceful fate.

"If you will, Mr Bennett." Hunter said, without moving the gun.

James knelt down and pulled out an amulet and piece of black ribbon. He took out his small knife and cut the witch's thumb, then pressed it to the amulet and wrapped the black ribbon about her wrist.

The witch grew tense and screeched as her powers drained out of her and into the amulet.

Hunter watched dispassionately. He preferred not to kill, and now she was harmless - well, she was no more dangerous than a human now. Her power would be filed at the MMC, then disposed of; and she would be carted off to prison. A job well done, with only a few minor burns to deal with.

Only... Hunter felt uneasy. This witch had proved to be powerful, yet instead of fighting to the death, she had quickly given up on pride and been bound. It was unusual enough to make him worry. He sighed, telling himself to stop being daft, they had won.

*****

The offices of the Oxford Branch of the MMC hardly stood out. There was very little to differentiate between them and the other boring buildings that neighboured it. James had offered to take the recent deposits of files and amulets, but Hunter had insisted on doing it. After that last witch, James was still burnt and concussed. It was rather funny really, Hunter noticed that whenever good old James got concussed his Yorkshire accent got so bad that you could hardly understand the poor bloke. Besides, Hunter wanted to drop in and see Charlotte.

He knocked on the door and went in. "Hey, I brought flowers."

He handed over the bunch of yellow roses and looked at Charlotte with concern. She was always beautiful, but there was a strain in her face and she emanated tiredness.

"I - I came to see if you'd found anything?" Hunter asked, jumping straight to the point.

"Oh Hunter, they're lovely," Charlotte replied, taking them and breathing in the fresh scent. But then she shook her head. "I haven't found anything. I'm sorry, but I haven't had the time. We've had more bound witches to process this month than... well, than ever. Executions are down and bindings have shot up." She frowned and gently stroked the petals of a flower. "And we're short staffed. I don't know if you've heard, but Diane was killed, along with her family. She didn't turn up for work on Monday. They found her in the family home. Rick and little Josie, too."

Her eyes teared up, but she blinked them away. Everyone died, it was just a question of when.

"Oh, I didn't mean that the short-staffing was the worst thing. I meant... You know what I meant." Charlotte added, feeling worse the whole time.

"I'm sorry." Hunter murmured, feeling useless.

Charlotte closed her eyes and took a deep breath, settling her nerves. "We all know the dangers of working for the MMC, we know what we've signed up for. But sometimes you forget, just for a moment you forget and become attached to someone..."

Hunter watched Charlotte as she purposefully kept her eyes focused on the flowers, the timid nature of her voice only confirming how close to tears she was. Noting the redness around her eyes, Hunter wondered how many times she had cried for her colleague today.

Hunter felt a stab of guilt at how easily Charlotte acknowledged the danger they were all in. It wasn't a lie that, if she had never met him, she would be a valued lawyer somewhere. She never would have heard of witches and the Malleus Maleficarum Council.

Instead, she had joined the Oxford offices, and over the last few years Hunter had to watch her ascend to an important position. Hunter had wondered whether the quick ascension was only due to the Council realising what a bright star they had with Charlotte; or were they trying to mollify him.

"The funeral is on Friday, will you be there?" Charlotte asked, breaking his train of thought.

Hunter inwardly winced. He hated going to funerals, especially as there were so many in their line of work. They didn't help anyone, it was only one more occasion to feel awkward on.

Hunter could probably get away with not going, no one would dare openly say anything about his absence. But his absence would be noted, the famous Hunter Astley, unable to respect the passing of one of their own.

"I'll try." He finally answered, less than convincingly.

Charlotte's normally soft brown eyes were a little colder as she regarded him, a slight pout to her lips. "I'll text you and James the address."

Getting James involved was a threat. It was only one level lower than threatening to involve his mother.

Hunter grimaced, trying again. "We'll be there."

He stayed for a short while, then made his excuses and left. He could fight, kill if need be, but he couldn't face sorrow. Not even when one of his best friends needed his comfort.

## Chapter Five

The call came just past midnight. Hunter set off immediately, picking up James on the way. They roared along the empty roads at 90mph, screw speed cameras and police, they had to get there.

Less than an hour later they screeched to a halt, both breathless with fear.

Hunter had been here only a month ago, but Brian's house was unrecognisable. The garden was all torn up and half of the house had fallen down, the rest was charred and still steaming.

Someone ran up as they saw them approach. The man was white-faced. "Hunter Astley? I'm Mathew Jones, 3rd gen." His voice cracked and he held out a shaky hand.

Hunter dragged his gaze away from the ruins. He shook hands, his actions robotic. "Brian?" He barely managed to ask.

The other man shook his head.

Hunter felt as though he had suffered a physical blow to his chest. Yes, it was a dangerous life and they were all living on borrowed time, but how could Brian be gone? He was the strong one, the survivor.

"Th-there was a girl." James finally spoke up, forcing his voice to steady. "An apprentice, Sophie."

Mr Jones got a hold of his emotions again. "Yes, she's alive. The ambulance took her away an hour ago. A few minor injuries, she was very lucky."

"What happened?" Hunter asked.

"We don't know for sure. Must've been a big coven, to do this much damage. Hopefully the apprentice can tell us more. I'll take you both to the hospital with me, if you want."

Hunter nodded. Yes, they should go to the hospital, see Sophie. But first, Hunter went up to the house. A couple of MMC staff came to warn him it wasn't safe (as if he needed telling), but let him go in, lending him a torch.

The blast must have been something fierce. Its source in the study, there was nothing left of this part of the house - walls, furniture, books - they were ash alike. Hunter stood amongst the rubble; the place throbbed with magic. Who the hell had this much power?

*****

The drive to the hospital was a blur. Soon they were marching down the half-lit corridors. Sophie was in a private room, propped up with pillows, waiting for them. Her arms were a mess of shallow cuts; a thick white pad covered her right shoulder where she'd needed stitches; the right side of her face was already bruising; and dust lightened her dark hair.

Even through the effect of painkillers, and despite it being the early hours of the morning, she gazed clearly and calmly at her visitors. "I was wondering when you were going to turn up."

"Miss Murphy, we need you to tell us what happened tonight." Mr Jones asked, taking out a pad and pen.

"You should ask Brian; I won't be much help."

"Please Sophie," Hunter interrupted in a pained voice. "Just tell us what you can."

Sophie shrugged, then winced, her fingers tenderly feeling her injured shoulder. "Fine. It was late, near midnight. I was asleep up in my room when Brian came in, woke me up and told me to follow him quietly."

"Did he say why?" Mr Jones asked, scribbling away.

Sophie gave him a scathing look. "When you learn at the feet of Brian Lloyd, you do exactly what he says, you never question."

The witch-hunter looked slightly embarrassed, but Hunter, who knew this to be the blunt truth, quietly asked Sophie to continue.

"We went downstairs, to his weapons lock. He was in a hurry for us both to be kitted up. Then he just froze and said, 'No time.' Then he said, 'I'm sorry.' And... and I saw pity in his eyes - he never... But anyway, next thing he locks me in that cupboard. There was no way out. A few minutes later, the place started to shake, then there was a massive blast. The world was turned upside down and I was knocked out. That's all I remember."

"Mhmn." Mr Jones continued to write. "Do you have any idea who was attacking?"

"No, I'm only a 1st gen. It was Brian that sensed the danger."

"And can you think of any recent cases, any events that might explain this huge attack?"

"Yes, no, I don't know." Sophie answered, getting riled up now. She grunted and put her hand to her aching head. "There were so many cases. We are witch-hunters, after all."

She looked up at Hunter, a clear demand in her eyes. "Where's Brian? No one will tell me how he's doing."

Hunter dropped her gaze. "He didn't make it."

"No." She sat in shock, her eyes darting to each of them as if willing them to deny it.

Mr Jones finally put away his notebook. "We're sorry for your loss, our loss. Once you've recovered, the MMC will make arrangements."

"I'm fine." Sophie replied curtly. "And I'm not staying in some hospital bed."

"She's coming with me." Hunter said quietly.

The other witch-hunter looked at him with surprise, knowing that he'd already taken on one 1st gen, and that Hunter Astley was a famously proud man.

"I can take on another apprentice. It's what Brian would have wanted."

It took until 11am to get Sophie discharged, and the doctors still weren't happy about it. Hunter drove back, James sitting in silent sorrow next to him, Sophie asleep on the back seat. Eventually they were pulling up on the gravel driveway at the front of Astley Manor. Hunter saw an unfamiliar car parked up, but was too tired to wonder.

Charles was at the door, waiting for them. "Good morning, sir. Mrs King arrived half an hour ago and insisted on waiting for you."

"Thank you, Charles." Hunter replied wearily. "Oh, and Charles, Miss Murphy is going to be staying with us. Will you prepare her a room?"

"Yes, sir."

Silence enveloped the three of them again, and they moved together into the sitting room.

"Hunter!" Charlotte jumped up from her seat as they entered. "I came as soon as I heard. It's - I can't believe it." Her eyes were red from tears already shed and as they threatened to spill again, Hunter pulled her into a fierce hug. This time he needed her, as much as she needed him.

"The grumpy old sod had a good running." Hunter muttered, making Charlotte gulp a laugh.

There was a clink of glass as James poured four drinks. He handed them out. "To Brian, loved and hated in equal measure."

Hunter raised his glass, "To Brian, the scariest bloke ever known."

Charlotte raised her glass. "To Brian, sexist, but brilliant."

The three old friends tapped their glasses together and drank, both cheered and saddened by their memories of him.

Sophie sat in quiet exclusion, in the corner. She sipped the warming alcohol, watching the group vaguely, her eyes still glazed with shock.

"Thanks for coming today." Hunter said to Charlotte, later in the afternoon.

"I was planning to come, anyway. Oh, I almost forgot why." She said suddenly, turning to her handbag and pulling out a white envelope. "Brian and I were in contact a lot lately. Both of us were trying to solve your wiccan problem. He gave me this yesterday, before -" Charlotte broke off, then regained her composure. "He wanted me to pass it on to you."

Hunter frowned, taking the thick, unmarked envelope. He tore it open and pulled out the contents. A letter. The handwriting was ever so familiar.

> *George,*
>
> *With luck, Charlotte King has given you this. I had to get this message to you without drawing further attention to myself. I'm in danger, and I no longer have the strength to fight it. All the same, I will never forgive myself for passing this onto you. But I don't know who else to trust.*

*Things are worse than you thought. I can't go into detail in this letter. Charlotte has a key for you, it's for a locker, I've enclosed the address. In the locker is my research concerning your wiccan, and my own work I started last year.*

*Hopefully I'll still be on hand to help you with this. But I had to write. Just in case.*

*Yours,*
*Brian Lloyd*
*Beware the shadows*

Hunter's hand shook as he passed the letter to the others. In the envelope was a slip of paper, just as he said. Charlotte silently slid him a small key.

"My God, it sounds as though he knew he was going to..." James muttered as he read it.

"Beware the shadows?" Charlotte repeated fearfully. "You don't think he means...?"

Hunter shook his head; in his hand he gripped the key so tightly it dug into his palm. "We'll know soon enough." Yes, he would go, find out what his mentor was being so secretive about. There was a new threat on the horizon, they could be sure of that at least.

But a wave of fatigue from the long day and its sorrows washed over him. There was nothing they could do until tomorrow.

"Tomorrow. Tomorrow."

## Chapter Six

It was a long drive to Cumbria the next day. The fact that Brian had taken the precaution of hiding his research across the country, in such a random place, added to Hunter's fear of the enormity of what they might find.

Hunter would have gone alone, but James insisted on accompanying him, because how could he help if he wasn't there. Sophie, with some embarrassment, asked to come because she dare not be alone yet. Charlotte couldn't take such a trip - Hunter discovered with some dismay that she was suffering with morning sickness.

Hunter and James sat in the front, arguing over whether to listen to Grimshaw or Evans, and Sophie sat in the back, reading quietly.

"So, you gonna to tell us where we're going?" James eventually asked.

"Carlisle." Hunter replied shortly.

"Carlisle? Christ, we'll be driving all day!" James twisted in his seat to look back at Sophie, "Hey, Soph, did you know about Carlisle, I mean, did Brian say owt?"

Sophie glanced up from her book, frowning at the shortening of her name. "No. He never mentioned where he was going. He just used to disappear for a couple of days every fortnight. I just assumed he had a woman somewhere."

The two men shuddered at the thought of old Brian with a woman. And all settled in for a long drive.

*****

It was mid-afternoon by the time they got there. Hunter pulled up outside a plain building. "Keep the car running," He said to James. "I'll be back in a minute. Hopefully."

They waited in silence. James started to drum his fingertips on the wheel as he gazed out of the window avidly, as though expecting a witch to leap on them right there.

Sophie gritted her teeth against the annoying sound. "Can you stop that?"

"Sorry," James replied sheepishly. "Nervous."

Hunter wasn't long; he soon stepped out of the building with a large sports bag, which he dumped in the car boot before jumping back into the driver's seat and driving off without a word.

"You can't tell me we're going to drive all the way home before looking at what's in there?" Sophie asked sceptically.

64

Hunter grinned in the rear-view mirror. "You think we can wait that long?"

They drove until they were out of the town and kept going until they found a roadside picnic area. The place was empty, and it was quiet, except from the steady traffic that roared by, passengers ignorant of everything outside the car.

The three of them sat around a worn wooden bench, with the bag in front of them. Hunter glanced at the other two - this was it. He slowly unzipped the bag. Inside there were stacks of papers, some cardboard files and such. The three of them craned forward, then gingerly picked through it all.

"Well, here's some information on a period of intense persecution of wiccans by witches. It doesn't give dates on this sheet though." Hunter peered into the bag. "There should be the rest of it in there..."

"Hm, this file has records of witches and wiccans from - wow, the 1940s," Sophie voiced.

"Well, this might be important, but I'll be damned if I can read it." James said, as he leafed through some old papers with scrawled handwriting.

They continued to look through the work for another half-hour, it seemed as though Brian had a unique way of ordering things. They made no immediate discovery to how it was all linked, nor to why it was so important to Brian. It was quite the anti-climax.

James was the first to admit defeat. He pushed the papers back into the bag. "Look, we aint gonna solve this in the next five minutes, and I feel uncomfy havin' these out in the open."

"Home we go then" Hunter suggested, not relishing another five-hour drive.

"Actually," Sophie interrupted. "My mum doesn't live far away, over in the Lake District. I was going to ask if you could drop me off - I haven't seen her since I joined Brian. But I'm sure she'd put us all up for the night, and we can drive down tomorrow."

"I vote yes," James immediately piped up.

"Be careful, Sophie, that was you almost being nice to us," Hunter teased. "But yes, why not. And we get to meet your mother!"

*****

The countryside was beautiful, wild hills and deep valleys, the road twisted and rose and fell to make its way through nature. Often a wide expanse of water lay off to one side or the other, a few boats still out on the lakes on a fine evening. With Sophie's directions they came to the village of Keswick and were soon pulling up outside her mother's house. It was an old cottage on the outskirts of the village and the whole atmosphere of the place was one of rough country warmth.

Hunter lugged the big bag with him as he and James followed Sophie up to the front door.

"Mum!" Sophie called out as she opened the door.

The figure of Mrs Murphy quickly came to meet them, the poor woman getting a shock at the state of her daughter; she reached out, tenderly touching the darkly-bruised face, her eyes taking in the fresh cuts on Sophie's bare arms. "Oh my darling, my Sophie."

Mrs Murphy was just as tall as her daughter, just as graceful in figure. It was easy to see where Sophie got her looks from. Although when Mrs Murphy finally turned to her visitors, it was with a softer expression than her daughter had ever managed.

"Mum, this is Hunter and James, my colleagues," Sophie introduced.

All softness that Hunter perceived was suddenly revoked when Mrs Murphy worked out that these were the evil witch-hunters that had led her daughter astray.

"Mum, these were the ones that saved my life, when I was in Italy." Sophie stressed each word, warning her dear mother to behave herself.

"It's nice to meet you, Mrs Murphy," Hunter said, extending his hand.

"Please, call me Bev," She replied with a polite smile, still undecided on whether to like these two young men. "I'm afraid all I can offer our guests is the fold-out settee in the conservatory. I'll let you put your bags - er, bag down."

She showed them through the small cottage to the make-shift guest room. As oldy-worldy and traditional as the cottage had looked from the outside, the interior was all cool, modern lines and light colours. Hunter and James politely dawdled in the warm conservatory, giving Sophie time with her mum. But eventually they joined them back in the small living room.

The two women were sitting together on the settee, heads close as they talked, and Bev didn't look happy. "You shouldn't be travelling in your condition, only out of hospital. Oh, that you ended up in hospital!"

"Mum! It was my choice to do this, and I don't regret any of it. I've already explained how important it is." Sophie stressed, holding her mother's gaze until the older woman dropped her eyes.

"Why you have to choose such danger, I don't know. You could have left it to others." Bev said bitterly. She then looked up, noticing the two men hovering by the door. She blushed at being overheard. "Well, I suppose none of you will have eaten. You'll have to make do with my cooking."

Before anyone could say anything, or offer to help, Bev took herself off to the kitchen.

"Don't pay her any attention," Sophie said harshly. "She doesn't blame you guys - or at least, she shouldn't. She doesn't agree with my decision to join the MMC, as you probably heard."

"She's got a right to be worried," James replied with a shrug.

Sophie sighed, twisting to look towards the kitchen, clearly annoyed with her mother.

"Come on, she's not that bad for a mum, she cares for you, that's all," James continued. "Just wait til you meet Hunter's!"

Hunter gave him a scathing look. "Nobody wants to hear about her. So, was this where you grew up?"

"Yes."

"What? That's it? No childhood stories you want to share?"

Sophie looked at both of them questioningly. "No. What's to tell? I grew up, then left to work in the city. If you're wanting tales of mad, rebellious youth, I've got to disappoint you."

\*\*\*\*\*

An hour later, Bev came to tell them dinner was ready, and they followed her to the delicious smells of toad-in-the-hole.

"Brilliant." James grinned as he sat down, loving everything that remotely resembled Yorkshire Pudding.

Hunter sat down, noticing that Bev looked calmer now. It must have been the shock of seeing her daughter injured. Now the older woman was bordering on friendly.

Over dinner, they all started to chat about small things - Mrs Murphy quizzing the two men over every detail she could think of; how they'd gotten into witch-hunting? Had they gone to university? Oh, Oxford, what did they study?

She smiled down at her more reserved daughter. "I can see why you were so interested in witch-hunting, Sophie, not all professional is it? Yes, you'll have to excuse my daughter, she does have a romantic side to her."

Hunter had to stop himself choking on his food, and he looked up, seeing that James shared the joke.

Sophie, romantic?  Sure, if she wasn't such a frozen bitch.

Sophie frowned at her teasing mother's insinuations.  "Behave yourself, mother, or I'll lock you in the pantry again."

The rest of the evening passed agreeably enough, but as they were all about to retire, Bev held Hunter back.

"Look, I know you mean well, and I'm sure you're a nice boy, but I don't want you to get involved with my daughter."

Hunter was surprised at the cold look Bev gave him, "Look, Mrs Murphy-"

But Bev stopped him. "You should be going to bed, Mr Astley.  I'm assuming that you'll want to set off early tomorrow."

Then she left him.  Ugh, bloody parents.  With the exception of his own mother, it seemed they were all over-protective.

Hunter went into the conservatory, where the settee had been pulled out into a double bed, James already sitting in it - fully clothed, thank goodness.

"Hey, there's always the floor."  James laughed in response to Hunter's grimacing expression.

"No, I just hope you don't snore tonight.  Budge over."

The light was clicked off and the two mates lay there, both awake.

"So… Sophie's mum seems ok, she really warmed up after a while. I thought she was gonna kick us out when she heard we were witch-hunters."

"Yeah," Hunter grunted noncommittally. Mrs Murphy had changed from hostile to friendly in the blink of an eye, finishing things off with that motherly warning. Hunter decided that he preferred Sophie's frosty personality – at least he knew where he stood with her.

"I was thinking, about Sophie." James continued, not taking the hint. "I mean, she's a bonny lass. What do y'think, I got a chance? Or do you think the timing's inappropriate, you know with Brian and all."

Hunter sat bolt upright. "Look, just because we're sharing a bed, doesn't make this a girly sleepover."

"Ah, sorry mate."

Hunter lay down again. What did he think? That he was likelier to get any girl over James, harsh but true. But then he wasn't interested in Sophie; cold, beautiful Sophie. At least, he wasn't interested in that way. "Just do me a favour, James. Wait until we all get home."

## Chapter Seven

Home. Astley Manor was, and always had been a stuffy place to live. Growing up, Hunter associated the place with unspoken unhappiness, even before he knew about witches and his parents' unhappy marriage.

But now, it was full of life for the first time in a long while. Sophie seemed to be settling in, and it was just common sense for James to stay too - there was plenty of room after all. And since Brian's death, not a day went by without witch-hunters, Council staff, and especially Charlotte, coming for one reason or another.

Hunter enjoyed the company. His mother did not.

Hunter found it quite funny, how it riled the stuck-up old bag. Yes, of course he loved her, or at least he felt dutiful as her son, but Hunter definitely took after his father.

Sophie had a bit of a shock when meeting Mrs Astley. The first time they saw each other was in the breakfast room the morning after they came back from the Lake District. Sophie came down, still in her dressing gown and slippers, her unbrushed hair scraped back into a hair band.

Mrs Astley, in stark comparison was already dressed (in miserable black) and had done her hair and make-up before even daring to set foot outside her room. She was a very petite woman in her early fifties, but looked older, with narrow, pinched features. Her hair, which had once shone a silvery blonde, was now pale, washed of all colour and pulled into a harsh bun.

Her cold eyes fell on Sophie, immediately analytical. "Oh no, George. She won't do at all. Too fat and too common."

Sophie was taken aback by the sudden harshness from the little elegant woman. She looked about the room and saw Hunter sitting rather sheepishly in the corner, reading a newspaper.

"Mother, Sophie and I aren't... she's a witch-hunter. In training, anyway."

"I don't know, George. Taking in all these waifs and strays - it's just not nice." Mrs Astley said to her son, as though Sophie wasn't there. "Filling the Manor with all sorts. Well, I suppose your late father would have approved." Disgust entered her thin voice. "Cursed be the day I met him."

"Mother." A sharp warning came from Hunter, who immediately folded up his paper and stood up. He didn't look particularly angry, more resigned to suffering her bad manners.

"Come on, Sophie, I'll get you some breakfast," Hunter invited.

"That is what Charles is for!" The sharp voice followed as they left the room.

"Sorry about her. I think she enjoys adding more misery to the world." It was harsh, but true. Mrs Astley seemed to have no purpose in life except to criticise everyone else.

Later, once Sophie was dressed (although not to Mrs Astley's standards), Hunter offered to give her the guided tour of Astley Manor. It was a beautiful old house and they walked through the array of rooms, all stuffed with priceless antiques and portraits, Hunter keeping a running commentary as they went.

"There's George Astley II. He was the first to own the Manor," Hunter informed, pointing to a portrait cracking with age, where a suitably regal looking fellow posed in gold clothes and a white permed wig.

"I see the resemblance," Sophie retorted, almost making a joke. "Where's your portrait?"

"Ah, I don't have one. I keep putting it off," Hunter confessed. Then invited her to continue the tour. They occasionally passed more portraits of increasingly recent George Astleys, the clothes changing drastically, but the faces all familiar.

They stopped at the newest portrait, painted in the 1970s when the man in the picture was the same age as Hunter now. Hunter looked up with a sad recognition.

"And this is my father, known to one and all as Young."

Sophie gave him a questioning look that made him smile, and he hastened to explain. "It gets confusing when you're all called George Astley. I get called Hunter because that's the nickname my friends gave me. My father was always called Young, because his father was known as Old George. See, it all makes perfect sense."

"Yeah, sure," Sophie replied, unconvinced. But she continued to look up at the portrait. "He looks nice."

"He was. He was lively, always off having adventures and coming back with wild stories. He'd make friends with everyone he met. And of course, he was a great witch-hunter."

"You sound like you miss him," Sophie added in her usual cold manner. Hunter almost felt offended.

"Come on, I'll show you the gardens."

Outside the sun was shining, it was another lovely summer morning and there was the lazy buzz of bees over the well-kept flowers. Hunter and Sophie walked side by side through the perfect flowerbeds and sculpted hedges.

"When did he die?" Sophie asked, not being distracted from the topic of Hunter's father.

"Just over five years ago." Hunter replied. It wasn't that he was ashamed, or emotional talking about Young, he just never did. "I was in my first year at Oxford when the news came. The witches finally caught up with him."

"I'm sorry," Sophie said perfunctorily.

Hunter shrugged, "It happens, inevitably. But hey, how do you like the gardens? My mother keeps them. Not that she's particularly green-fingered, but she does enjoy ordering the gardeners about, telling them how to do their job and so on."

Mrs Astley was a character for endless jokes and ridicule. The old bag was probably aware that she wasn't popular with people in general, but that didn't stop her.

"Your mother, she's..." Sophie paused, wondering how best to phrase it. "Your parents were very different, weren't they?"

"Oh yes!" Hunter replied with a laugh. "They were too different, absolutely hated each other, they were always arguing when I was young. Oh, the memories."

"But they got married?"

"Yes. I suppose they were in love at one point. My father was the rich, handsome witch-hunter that saved a beautiful young lady from being sacrificed." Hunter gave the summary of their meeting. "As you heard, my mother often expresses the wish that she had been left to be killed. I can honestly say that I had an interesting childhood, growing up in that atmosphere."

On that sorry note, they continued quietly about the gardens, allowing Sophie to view the Manor from every angle. And it was a beautiful and suitably impressive place. There was just one small, niggling little detail.

"How on earth do you have a place like this and stay safe?" Sophie asked, her eyes fixed on the building.

"You said that famous families were a target for witches. Surely this Manor is a beacon to them."

Hunter looked at her, it was a smart question, and he was surprised that she remembered what he had said so long ago. "You've still got the necklace I gave you?"

Sophie's hand went to her neck. "Yes."

"And I told you that was personal protection. Well, the Manor is filled with layers of enchantments and protective amulets and wards built into the very walls and doorways. No witch is ever going to find this place, and even if they did, they couldn't do anything."

"What about sharing this protection?" she asked sharply. "I think Brian could have benefited from it."

Hunter was shocked to see fire and anger in her expression. Did she blame him for Brian's death? How could she? "Sophie-"

She cut him off by walking away. But Hunter wasn't about to let her go with this misconception. He caught up with her, grabbing an uninjured section of her arm and ignoring her fierce glare.

"Look, all witch-hunters and Council staff have the best protection the MMC can provide. But sometimes a strong group of witches can overcome these measures. We all do the best we can. And yes, I thought Brian was safe. Obviously not. I will not feel guilty about the safety of the Manor - as for sharing, I couldn't even if I wanted to because I don't understand half of it."

"Finished?" Sophie asked curtly.

Hunter felt the heat from his rant fading quickly. "Yes." He replied quietly, releasing her arm and watching Sophie walk away. He stayed where he was. He couldn't be blamed for Brian's death, no more than he could be blamed for any fallen witch-hunter, unless he invited them all to live in his Manor.

He kicked the nearest plant, sending petals flying. Now he would feel guilty about that - his mother would probably blame this imperfection on the gardeners when she saw it.

Oh well. He went back inside, making straight for his library. But Hunter stopped by the door, it was open and together at the desk, Sophie and James sat conspiratorially close.

Did Hunter feel jealous, looking at that cosy little scene? No, it must be something else. Whatever it was, Hunter felt no compulsion to join them just now. Let James have time with Sophie, so he might learn how unforgiving she was.

## Chapter Eight

Every once in a while, they all suffered to sit through the charade of a civilised dinner. Hunter, as master of the house, sat at the head of the table; his mother, styling herself as Astley Manor's own dowager empress, sat opposite him at the far end of the slightly too long table. This suited Hunter to have his mother seated as far away as possible, and he often employed the use of candelabras or a vase to block her from view completely.

James and Sophie submitted to sitting wherever Mrs Astley decided in her elaborate ideas of a perfect seating plan, even for such a small party. After all, it was easier to go along with something so harmless to keep the stubborn bag appeased.

Unfortunately, today Mrs Astley was in a talkative mood, and she raised her sharp voice so that her unimportant comments could be heard clearly down the table.

"And at least Mrs Harsmith has daughters to keep her company now Mr Harsmith is gone. All Mr Astley deigned to give me was an adventurous, cad of a son. Although I don't doubt you have half-sisters across the whole of England, George. But why I couldn't have had a daughter instead. You must get married, George, so that I might have a daughter-in-law, preferably before I die of old age."

Hunter smirked and nearly choked on his soup. In the corner of his eye he could see the slight shake of James' shoulders, as he too found Mrs Astley amusing. The newcomer, Sophie, seemed frozen in her seat, eyes wide at the open berating at the dinner table.

"Don't slurp your soup, George. Oh, you are too much like your father - I had hoped that a man from such an old family would have been well-mannered - well-moneyed was more like it. Young was as disgustingly common and ill-behaved as those football louts that always appear on the news."

"No, he wasn't mother," Hunter corrected, protective of the memory of his father.

"Don't be so sure. Going to scruffy pubs, coming back drunken on cheap beer, swearing." Mrs Astley broke off, aghast at the mere thought of it. "Oh, I wish the witch had killed me, death would have been preferable to a torturous lifetime with Young."

"Mother, please remember that we have guests." Hunter said, before she could get too depressive.

Mrs Astley looked up, as though surprised to see James and Sophie there, she frowned at her son's assumption.

"Guests? I see no guests. I see two of your witch-hunter underlings that have the cheek to live off our kindness. That you live beside your staff as equals, George! It is most unbecoming."

"They are my friends, and as I am master of this house they shall remain here as my guests for as long as they like." Hunter replied with bite.

"Friends? Oh, you keep such bad company. When I think back to the boys from school - why don't you keep in touch, invite them to stay? Better them than these two. The girl is pretty, I admit, but I doubt she has a drop of good blood in her body. As for the young man, that hideous voice resonates through the house, the indecipherable accent - and what's more he's proud of it!"

Hunter sat back in his chair, a clenched fist by his mouth and his body near shaking. He was torn between anger and amusement, his mother was irritating and offensive, but the old girl was bloody entertaining.

*****

"Bring Sophie out into the yard, James." Hunter ordered, shrugging a light jacket on.

Hunter made his way into the courtyard at the rear of the house, the smooth square open on one side to the fields beyond where high grass browned in the weak summer sun. He gently dropped the bag he was carrying and knelt down to open it, sorting through the necessary tools of training it contained.

Hunter rose at the sound of footsteps behind him as James and Sophie came obediently to meet him. It had been five days since the attack at Brian's house and although misleadingly upbeat, Sophie still showed the physical marks of the tragedy, her skin coloured with bruises and her shoulder thickly padded with bandages. But hurt or not, Hunter wanted to waste no time - he'd already waited these five days with impatience.

"All right, Sophie, I need to know what Brian managed to teach you about attack and defence." Hunter said seriously. He held out a small dull object which Sophie took gingerly.

"It may seem brutal, but guns are our main weapons," Hunter said in response to her reaction, then bit his tongue, fearing to sound too apologetic. There was nothing to be sorry about, violent witches had to be killed, and was there a more efficient method?

"I want an idea of your aim. Now," Hunter pointed out across the field, about 100 yards away a wooden board stood, targets painted in fading colours. "Aim and fire."

Sophie glanced at both men with a moment's uncertainty, then took a deep breath and did as she was bid. The gun went off with a mighty crack that reverberated about the courtyard and made Sophie jump.

Hunter ignored her, his sharp eyes watching the bullet miss the entire board. "Don't rush. Later, when a witch is charging you down with spells blazing - that is when you are permitted to rush. But here and now I want accuracy, not speed. Try again."

Sophie scowled at Hunter's little criticizing speech, but said nothing in return. She raised the gun again, and altered her aim, taking her time, focusing on a spot slightly lower, as Brian had taught her.

She fired again. This time there was a satisfying 'thuck' as the bullet embedded itself in the board, just off the target.

"Better. Again." Hunter simply said.

Sophie repeated the process, making her corrections to aim. The third bullet hit the target dead centre. She almost smiled and tilted her head in an arrogant pose. Hunter still ignored her.

"Perfect," he commented. "Again."

Sophie frowned but continued, firing until the chamber was empty and her ears were ringing.

"Not too bad, I suppose," Hunter admitted. "But I want you to practise daily. I'm sure James can give you extra tuition if you find you need it."

Hunter's comment made James redden and Sophie scowl, but he just smiled in a knowing manner.

"Right, James help Sophie into a vest," Hunter said, pulling the black stab jacket out of the bag and tossing it to James while he retrieved two tapered poles.

James caught it clumsily, hesitating. "You're - you're gonna make her fight?"

"How else am I to assess her abilities?"

James opened his mouth to say something, but thought better of it. He reluctantly took the vest and held it up for Sophie to shrug into, then fitted it snugly about her slim figure.

Sophie ignored James' lingering hands on her waist and took one of the tapered poles from Hunter, it was about a foot long and made of smooth, solid wood. She looked up at Hunter, her expression giving nothing away.

"Now, until you learn to handle yourself properly, it's safer using these. If you manage to improve, we'll move onto real knives," Hunter instructed. "So, take first position as Brian taught you, and attack me as though I were a witch."

Sophie remained still. "You're not going to put on a vest?"

"You won't hit me," Hunter replied condescendingly. "First position, if you please Miss Murphy."

Sophie bit her tongue and prepared, pole raised, her balance evenly placed over both feet and flexible.

"And attack," Hunter ordered.

Sophie lunged forward, driving the tapered point of the pole at Hunter's chest. Faster than she could follow, her pole was knocked aside with a stinging crack and Hunter was off to a side, his pole an inch from her ribs. Sophie caught her breath and stared at him in amazement.

"How…?"

"Seventh generation," Hunter replied shortly. "You were too slow, even for a first gen. Try again. First position, and attack."

Sophie threw herself into the movement with all her strength, but again her pole was knocked aside and Hunter's was hovering at her neck. This time he was frowning.

"Too erratic. You need to be fast, accurate, or you're dead." Hunter wiped his face with his hand, as though trying to rub a growing headache out of his forehead. "Great. Right, back to basics."

They spent the next hour going through every position and motion, repeating again and again, Hunter correcting every minor flaw, accepting nothing but perfection. Sometimes he pulled James in, to model and practise a succession of moves.

Eventually Hunter was happy enough to allow practise bouts again. He stood across from Sophie, whose face was already paling with the hint of exhaustion. They came to, this time Sophie moved correctly and there was the attack, parry, attack, parry, with the clacking rhythm of a violent dance. But Sophie slipped up and Hunter got past her guard, barely stopping his pole from jabbing her hip.

"Again." He demanded.

They came to again and again, each time Sophie fighting more desperately, each time she slipped up Hunter's patience shortened and he began to tap her harder with the pole, until he snapped at her incompetence and hit her harder than he meant to.

Sophie shouted in pain and shock and Hunter dropped his pole, eyes wide in self-disgust, but no apology reached his lips.

"Hunter!" James stepped in, angry with his friend, protective of Sophie. "Come on, that's enough for today, she's knackered. You 'ad no right to hit her, she's still hurt."

"She's got to learn." Hunter replied quietly, stooping to collect his pole from the ground.

"That's no reason -"

"James! I don't need your pity nor protection," Sophie interrupted sharply. She glanced at Hunter. "Again."

Hunter looked guiltily into that usually pale face that was now flushed with pain and exertion. "Look Sophie, if you're hurt, maybe…"

"I'm not in pain, I'm…" Sophie sighed, her annoyance clear and moved into first position, she spoke in a low and determined voice. "Again."

Hunter reluctantly raised his pole and nodded. Again there was the crack of wood on wood as they parried and pushed and circled. An aura of determination emanated from Sophie. She gave a great shout of rage as she attacked and her pole passed through Hunter's block and grazed his elbow.

Hunter stepped back and looked at her in surprise. He hadn't been holding back - not much anyway - it was a rare person that could land even the slightest blow on him.

"That's better," he conceded. "Let's call it a day. James can be your practise partner for the rest of the week."

Sophie pushed back her dark hair, damp with sweat, still breathing heavily she flashed a victorious smile at James who couldn't take his eyes off her.

*****

The James and Sophie 'episode' didn't last very long.

At first, James had restrained himself to being a helpful, but constant presence for Sophie. Always there to offer company, or just a cup of tea; always on hand to help with a difficult translation of foreign text, or unravelling Brian's messy handwriting.

Hunter watched his friend's progress with a detached interest. After all these years, had impulsive, coarse James finally learnt tact and charm? It was almost disappointing to see things go so smoothly between him and Sophie. The sensible part of Hunter thought that it would be best for James and Sophie to have a mature relationship that wouldn't compromise their work. Unfortunately, this sensible part was dwarfed by a hope that Sophie would get out her claws as soon as James made his move, regardless of a happy working environment. For entertainment purposes only, of course, Hunter had no other reason to not see his two companions together.

The results of James efforts came to fruition one very normal afternoon, a fortnight after Sophie had joined them in Astley Manor. Hunter had just had a long, detailed conversation on the phone with someone at the MMC. They'd wanted to know (in an indifferent manner) how Miss Murphy was settling in, whether she'd remembered anything more from the night Brian had died. Hunter had dutifully filled them in on her state of recovery and that they had taken her to visit her mother - neatly failing to mention Brian's parting gift.

The droning voice on the other end of the phone had given Hunter a headache. Oh well, nothing cured a headache like staring at a load of musty old books!

As Hunter walked down the corridor, Sophie exited the library in a hurry, slamming the door behind her, then scowling and marching purposefully in his direction.

"Did you put him up to it?" She demanded, eyes blazing.

"Did I - what?" Hunter stuttered, taken aback.

"James, did you encourage him to…" Sophie broke off, too furious for words. "And I was foolish enough to think he was being kind for kindness sake. Can no one in this bloody world see me as a witch-hunter, rather than a girl that needs to be partnered off?!"

Her question was rhetorical and she was already storming off by the time she'd finished ranting. Hunter smiled grimly as he heard the front door clanged shut as Sophie left the Manor. He had a notion why Sophie was so mad.

Curious as to the particulars, Hunter resumed his short walk to the library. True to form James had his head in a book - at least he looked busy.

"James?" Hunter asked mildly. "What have you done?"

"Nuthin'." He grunted in reply.

"Of course. So, Sophie is raging for no reason."

James looked up, his face was flushed red with either embarrassment or anger, Hunter couldn't tell which.

"It were nuthin'. I just asked Sophie out for a drink an' she said no." James replied with an overly nonchalant shrug.

Hunter watched him sceptically. "And what else did you say to upset her so badly?"

"Nuthin'." James repeated.

"Very well, if you've said nothing to offend Sophie, I'll have a word with her, get her to apologise for her temper." Hunter replied innocently.

"I-I may've been a bit rude." James finally confessed. "I mean, she had no reason to be so abrupt, not when I'd been so nice to her an' everything. So, I might've called 'er a tease - a vicious tease. And I might've said she were shallow an' arrogant."

Hunter shook his head, he wasn't sure whether he found it all too funny, or too upsetting. "You'll have to say sorry."

"Hey, she gave as good as she got," James argued.

James seemed to miss the point about being a charming gentleman, it wasn't the looks and confidence that was valuable, it was being the first to apologise, and the last to say an unkind word.

"Why did you get so wound up?" Hunter asked, thinking that this was bad even for James.

James shrugged and looked away. "Dunno. There's just something about her. I liked her, and after all that effort she didn't feel the same way. Said she weren't interested in no-one. But I figure she's lying, probably just waiting for a better offer than common ol' me."

Hunter tried to ignore the bitter, hurt tone in his best friend's voice. It was hard enough hearing this unusually open confession. But James would get over it, Hunter selfishly hoped that it wouldn't affect his work.

The final insinuation made Hunter frown, it seemed like everyone expected him to swoop down on the beautiful Sophie.

"Well, I can promise you that the ice bitch isn't going to get a better offer in this house," Hunter replied with slightly forced humour.

James smiled and relaxed, made a little happier with Hunter's promise.

*****

It had been a long day. Hunter was still wearing his suit from the memorial service held for Brian Lloyd. It had been a suitably miserable day as the black-clad crowd stood about a plinth, erected to commemorate the greatest witch-hunters.

Witch-hunters had come from all over Britain, and there were even those from foreign MMCs. Hunter had always known that Brian Lloyd was special, but his personal closeness to the man had blinded him to exactly how special and respected.

A high-standing member of the Council had stood up and spoke in a monotonous tone about Mr Lloyd's achievements and contributions. Hunter didn't hear a word of it. He stood there, hands shoved deep in his coat pockets, a sad smile as he remembered their own toasts to him.

Later, when every softly spoken conversation was exhausted, the heartfelt (and perfunctory) toasts made, Hunter and his friends escaped back to Astley Manor.

Hunter went and locked himself in his library. It seemed wrong that they still hadn't read through all of the papers Brian had left them, especially today. He was still sitting up in the early hours of the morning, matching information in Brian's work to his own collection.

"Shit." No, no, no. Hunter took a deep breath and rubbed his weary eyes, as though it could remove the revelation. Shit. Hunter jumped up, running through the sleeping house. "James!" He shouted, taking the stairs three at a time, "James!"

James came staggering out of his bedroom, just as Hunter reached the door, looking still asleep in his loose pyjamas. There was movement in the corridor as Sophie ran out, wrapping her dressing gown about her slim figure, a look of fear on her face.

Seeing her, Hunter suddenly remembered that the last time she was woken in the middle of the night had ended disastrously, and he felt a brief stab of guilt.

"Attack?" James asked, breathless.

Hunter shook his head. "Shadow." The single word managed to break out, and Hunter took a deep breath, "Brian's work, he was tracking the awakening of a Shadow."

"You're sure?" James asked, definitely awake now.

"Unfortunately, yes."

"Wait, what's a shadow?" Sophie interrupted, calmer now she knew there was no immediate danger.

"A Shadow Witch," Hunter began, fighting down his own fear. "The most powerful witch - in a class of their own. But they are rare, near unheard of, there's only been two in recorded history."

"But it's still a witch. The MMC can stop them?" Sophie asked, still not grasping the significance of the title.

Hunter shook his head. "This is magic without limits, the last Shadow Witch to gain a hold ended the Dark Ages and unleashed the chaos of the medieval witch-craze. Society crumbled through fear and witches gained positions of power, free to slaughter thousands. They turned their own hunted existence to their use, accusing and murdering innocent victims, all in the name of the good lord."

"So, this is a big deal, then." Sophie replied flatly once Hunter had finished.

Hunter checked his watch, 3am. It was definitely important enough to wake everyone up, but he'd still be hated for it.

"James, get on the phone to the Council. Hopefully the foreign delegates haven't left yet. Offer Astley Manor as a meeting place. I'm going downstairs, to see what my collection has to help." No, there'd be no sleep tonight. "Ah, Sophie, you can go back to bed, if you want."

"No, I'm awake now, I'll help."

## Chapter Nine

The Council had done a good job at dragging witch-hunters into a meeting at such short notice. By midday Astley Manor was a hub of noise as over fifty witch-hunters of various nationalities gathered. At 2pm they all piled into the long hall, where Hunter went over all the details under the sceptical gaze of his fellow witch-hunters.

Outside the closed door, two people were left out.

"This is ridiculous, we should be in there." Sophie spat, glaring at the door that separated them from the meeting.

James shrugged. "I'm a first gen too, we're not permitted to attend witch-hunter meetings, except for exceptional circumstances." Yeah, but it was still a bitch. "Besides, we know everything Hunter has to say, and he'll tell us everything they say."

"It's still not as good as hearing it for ourselves. And if this isn't an exceptional circumstance, what is?!"

They waited impatiently for a good couple of hours, hearing nothing except the odd, inarticulate shout.

"Hunter said there were two Shadow Witches." Sophie said suddenly, making James jump. "But this morning I could only find writings on one."

James grimaced. "Not many people know about the second, some don't even believe she even was a Shadow. She didn't last long and it was all hushed up. Back in the 40s. I only know 'cos Hunter-"

James broke off and eyed Sophie carefully. "Ah, I'm sure he won't mind me tellin' you. His grandfather, Old George V, brought her down. Just wish we knew how. The old man's long dead and never spoke of it to anyone."

Just then, finally, the doors opened and the witch-hunters poured out, followed in the end by Hunter. Just one look showed how disappointed he was. Several witch-hunters hung back to share a few words of encouragement, but eventually they were all gone.

"I need a drink," Hunter muttered and slunk off to the kitchen to retrieve the much needed bottle of whiskey, and quickly poured himself a healthy glass full.

James and Sophie waited impatiently.

"Well?" James finally asked with exasperation.

Hunter took his time replying. "They've decided to do nothing."

"What?!"

Again, a pause. "Oh, they believe there's a Shadow Witch at least. Took long enough to persuade them on that.  But they have decided that there is nothing more they can do - they are just going to keep on witch hunting until the Shadow Witch makes a move."

"Well," Sophie said hesitantly.  "That's not too bad."

"Hah."  Hunter grimaced, "They wouldn't change anything: putting more witch-hunters and Council staff on the case to track the Shadow down; they could increase communication between foreign MMCs; they could plan to unite all witch-hunters or at least form a plan of action in the case of the Shadow rising up.  But no, they didn't want to take priority away from normal business!"

Hunter's rant left James and Sophie silent.

"The MMC in general may not be willing, but you've got me, as much as I can do."  Sophie said with calm confidence.

"And me." James added.  "And Charlotte is gonna help too, of course."

*****

Sophie carefully carried the mugs of coffee as she descended the dimly lit stone stairs.  She hissed when the hot drink spilled onto her hand and swore under her breath.  For the past week, since the disappointing MMC meeting, Sophie felt like she'd done nothing but traipse up and down carrying drinks and sandwiches, or reading old manuscripts.  On the whole, it felt like she was achieving nothing.

Hunter and James had been researching too, but also had the more interesting duty of travelling to meet sources.  They hadn't taken Sophie, citing her inexperience, and needing to spread their resources as less than satisfactory reasons.

But today they were all in the Manor. They had found nothing more promising than Old George had killed the last Shadow Witch. Hunter reasoned that his grandfather's belongings might hold some secret, protection or a weapon perhaps? No one had looked at the Astley Collection in detail for years now, so today they were attacking it with a vengeance. And Sophie was playing the little tea lady.

"Hey, coffee." Sophie announced as she entered the library. She glanced to Hunter who was absorbed in his work, and the last mug of coffee she'd brought him sitting untouched and stone cold at the side of the desk. She sighed. "You know, I won't bother if you're not going to drink it."

Hunter looked up guiltily and took the hot, fresh coffee from her, overly alert that their fingers brushed at the exchange. Sophie seemed to notice it too, a faint rise of colour in her cheeks, and she looked swiftly away.

"Did you find anything new?" She asked casually.

Hunter shook his head, "Old George didn't believe in organisation. If he had a filing system, it wasn't one known to man. I'm struggling to find anything in his notes either."

Hunter sighed and leant back. Actually, he was discovering that he and Old George were alike in these traits. The only difference was that Old didn't have James twittering and moaning in the background, but somehow making everything miraculously work smoothly.

Sophie put her hand on his shoulder and leant forward to view the erratic notes, the papers weighted down with random objects of random interest. Her silky, dark brown hair fell forward, with a rich scent that Hunter couldn't help noticing.

"Well, we'll just have to keep at it," Sophie replied, turning to face him as she spoke.

Close to, her hazel eyes had little flecks of gold. She was as harsh as ever, but that was something Hunter had come to accept. But he couldn't help but stop with the realisation that she was beautiful. It did tend to make work awkward.

"Thank you." Perhaps he shouldn't, but he couldn't break that gaze.

Sophie frowned. Her expressions were always so slight, but they were familiar now, the way her down-turned lips were set, the delicate crease of her brow.

"Look, Hunter…"

"HUNTER!"

They both jumped. There was the sound of trainers down the stone steps.

"Intercom, James." Hunter chided.

"Yeah." James answered offhandedly. "Anyway, I just got off the phone wi' bloody Americans. Good news, they're taking this seriously and want to act. Bad news, they want to run the show."

"Ugh, I can't be dealing with them." Hunter muttered. He couldn't deny that having them on board would be a huge help, but having them in charge - America's way of running things resembled a big, bolshy kid with all brawn no brain.

"More good news," James added, waving some paper in the air. "The Germans sent this through on the fax just now. I had some friends in their Council dig up anything from the 1940s that could relate to the previous Shadow Witch. They found some letters they thought might help."

"Good, good." Hunter replied, interested now. "If you'd do the honour, James."

James grinned then read out the short letter.

"'Bericht. Wir haben schließlich befindet sich die-'"

"Wait, what?" Sophie interrupted. "In English?"

James stared at her accusingly. "You don't speak German? Shame. Things tend to lose something in meaning in translation."

"James," Hunter said in a quiet, warning tone. He'd had to put up with James being unnecessarily nasty to Sophie ever since she turned him down. Hunter had had enough.

"Fine." James grunted, then translated as he read, speaking quickly in a dull voice. "'Report. We have, in the end the items. You may report with confidence that we are ready for the first attempt - everything is very promising. Herr Braun and Herr Hartmann have proved helpful in the deciphering of the information and breaking the protection around all the items. Herr Braun demands that more witches are brought in to help with the final incantation. I suggest that

Hartmann lays immediately to go hunting more witches. We wait for your orders. Herr Richter.'"

"Richter? What do we know about him?" Hunter asked, the name completely unfamiliar to him.

James shrugged. "Not much, he was part of the group that researched occult powers for the Nazi party."

"And the others mentioned, Braun and Hartmann?"

"Braun was a witch - he got caught and killed after the war. Hartmann, well, from this it sounded like he was a witch-hunter."

Hunter frowned. "A witch-hunter working alongside a witch?"

"The Second World War was a pretty big deal, Hunter, I think the lines of what was right and wrong got skewed, especially working for the Nazi party," James responded succinctly. "But what do you think? All this magical activity and research shortly before the arrival of a Shadow Witch in Britain. Could they have found a way to raise a Shadow Witch?"

"It seems perfectly possible." Hunter took the copy of the letter and read it for himself. If the Germans found a way to raise a Shadow, the witch could have awoken anywhere in the world; in England, alone and unprepared, relatively easy prey for the local witch-hunters...

Hunter sighed, putting the letter on his cluttered desk, he didn't voice his thoughts.

**Chapter Ten**

"You really think she's up to it?" James asked.

Sophie gave an uncharacteristically inelegant snort of derision at his question.

The three of them were in the Land Rover, Hunter driving, James in the passenger seat, and lowly Sophie sitting in the back. Hunter's hands tightened on the wheel as he concentrated on the road rather than answering James' question.

"Hunter? You think she's ready?" James persisted. They were on their way to a raid, it would be Sophie's first time coming up against witches as a witch-hunter, and typically James wasn't happy about the idea.

Hunter shrugged, not the most positive gesture, he realised. "She's done her training well. Besides, would you rather she have her first time out at Hallowe'en? She needs to operate in the real world."

"Hallowe'en is nearly a month away, she has time for more preparation if you're not sure," James cautioned.

"She, she, she!" Sophie suddenly spat. "I'm sitting right here. Why don't you ask me if I think I'm ready?"

Hunter shot her a look in the rear-view mirror. "Because, my dear, we know exactly what you think. You've been champing on the bit these last few weeks, dropping increasingly obvious hints every time a job comes through from the MMC. If you had your way, this would be your fifth raid, not your first."

Sophie sat back, a rather superior smile on her lips. For once she didn't rise to the ribbing, she was getting what she wanted right now.

"This isn't my first time, anyway." Sophie suddenly said, breaking the silence. "Brian took me to a raid. Although I wasn't allowed to actually do anything, just watch him and the other witch-hunters outnumber and overpower a small coven."

"Yes, well, I'm sure Brian knew what he was doing." Hunter replied distractedly. "And I doubt you'll be doing anything this time, there are more than enough higher gen witch-hunters to deal with the threat. But you need to learn, so you are going to stand there and do exactly as instructed, even if that is to stand and watch; even if that is to return to the car and wait. Understood?"

When Sophie didn't respond, Hunter met her gaze in the rear-view mirror. "Understood?" he repeated, harder.

Sophie looked away. "Yes," She said quietly, gazing out the car window.

Hunter suddenly turned off the road onto a dirt track. The Land Rover lurched over the rubble and potholes for a few hundred metres until a big black Jeep and a blue Volvo came into view. Hunter pulled up next to the other parked cars, and as if on cue, every car door opened and seven people were clambering out.

"Hey, Hunter!"

Hunter squinted in the low afternoon sun. He smiled, matching the voice to the driver of the Volvo. "Toby! It's been a while. How's the wife?"

"Bloody chitchat. You're late, Astley." The driver of the black Jeep grumbled, interrupting the polite exchange.

Hunter grit his teeth against the insulting tone, his eyes suddenly cold. "I would say that we are right on time, Mr Halbrook. We were told to meet at 4 o'clock."

"Yeah, so good of you not to arrive a minute earlier than necessary, Mr Astley," he responded, deeply bitter.

Hunter sighed, it hadn't been his choice to have Gareth Halbrook on the team, but the MMC had assigned him, and there was no getting rid. Oh dear, best to just get the job over and done with quickly.

"Who have you brought?" Hunter asked, nodding casually to the two young men that had climbed out of the black Jeep.

"Matt and Dave Marshall, 3rd gens. I took over their training after their old da got killed a few months ago."

Gareth responded unenthusiastically. "What about your guys?"

"James Bennett and Sophie Murphy, both first gens."

The Marshall brothers looked at them all silently, their faces betraying an unprofessional interest as they glanced at Sophie. Sophie grimaced in disgust and shifted closer to James.

"Firsts? You brought a couple of firsts?" Gareth demanded, spitting slightly in his anger. "What the hell use is that?"

"They are fully-trained, Mr Halbrook. I don't have time to argue with you," Hunter said, fighting to keep his calm. "Can we please get on with the planning?"

Gareth folded his arms and glared at Hunter challengingly. "Whatever you say, sir."

Toby, the Volvo driver that had greeted Hunter, now stepped forward, shaking his head at the conflict. He laid a large sheet of paper on the bonnet of Hunter's Land Rover.

"The MMC have received reports of frequent gatherings of witches at a nearby wood. They meet and cast at sunset, I know, predictably dramatic. We estimate four to six witches, none showing extraordinary magic." Toby reeled off the information he had collected while at the MMC headquarters earlier that day. He leaned over Hunter's car, indicating the paper. "This is a map of the surrounding area. The clearing is here, about a mile into the wood. Unfortunately, there's no natural barriers, so we'll just have to surround them and hope they don't break through."

Gareth leaned over the map. "We don't know which way they'll be arriving, so we should wait until they start casting before we move into position. It is more dangerous, I know, but it's our best chance of surrounding them. We could probably park up here to wait."

He jabbed at a spot on the map, then looked up, and shrugged. "But what do I know, I'm just a 4th gen with twenty years' experience, obviously not enough to be in charge. What do you think, Astley?"

Hunter frowned. He really didn't like the fact that his 7th gen status gave him superiority over more experienced witch-hunters. And he liked it even less when odious individuals like Gareth Halbrook held it over him.

Hunter gazed at the map, uncomfortably aware of the silence and the eyes all focussed on him. Damn Gareth. "No, I agree. Let's move out." He finally admitted through gritted teeth.

Gareth turned back to his jeep, a smug smile on his face, with the two Marshall brothers in tow.

"Want a lift, Toby?" Hunter offered. "I don't think your little car is up to a cross-country jaunt."

Toby folded the map and smiled. "Sure, why not. If it isn't the witches that kill me, it'll be your driving."

The four of them piled into the Land Rover, James now demoted to the back seat with Sophie.

"Behave yourselves back there, children," Hunter teased as he started the engine.

He smiled as Sophie swore under her breath, then put the car into gear and leapt across the field, following the tracks made by Gareth, racing after the black jeep towards the dark shadow on the horizon.

"Who the hell invited Gareth Halbrook?" James demanded, holding on tight against the bumping, speeding car. "Of all the witch-hunters they could've assigned, why that git?"

Toby smiled sadly. "It's Hunter's fault."

"What?" Hunter asked sharply.

Toby spared a quick glance around the other passengers and propped himself against the door, grimacing as the car lurched over uneven ground. "The buzz at the headquarters is that Hunter is too big for the Council."

"What's that supposed to mean?" Hunter asked, not liking the sound of it.

"Ah, you know the influence you have. Enlisting Sophie here, determining where she carries out her training. Your preferential treatment of James, that he gets to see more than some higher gens, that you refused to let the Council reassign him last year. The fact that you refuse to take on 1st gens for training, and your lack of attendance at the headquarters. Christ, even Charlotte was promoted quickly beyond her years on your advice."

"That isn't fair," Hunter said, when he'd heard enough. "My influence? I will act how I see fit, but I am loyal to the MMC and they will always have the final decision in everything. This 'influence' isn't of my making - it is the Council's way of treating me."

"I know Hunter," Toby said in a pacifying tone. "But you are the miraculous 7$^{th}$ gen, no one knows what you could be capable of. The Council wants to keep you sweet, but at the same time they doubt their ability to control you. Hence, Gareth Halbrook. They're giving you your birthright to lead, yet proving that they are in charge by making you work with that arse."

Hunter sat in silent thought, staring straight ahead to the looming woods where the black jeep had already pulled up.

"You'd think," Hunter said quietly. "That the Council would have more pressing issues to deal with than these ridiculous games."

Nobody replied, it was obvious where Hunter's thoughts lay - the MMC were spending time and energy worrying about non-existent problems, when there was one very real, glaring threat of the re-emergence of the Shadow Witch about which they did nothing.

The uncomfortable silence was ended by their arrival at the edge of the woods. Everyone clambered out again, the day still too hot to stay inside the stationary vehicle. There was nothing left to do but wait for the sun to set and the witches to make their move.

Sophie was sitting against the trunk of a shady oak, wondering how best to phrase her thoughts.

"So... what have these witches done? To upset the MMC?"

Hunter stopped his pacing and looked at her. "What do you mean?"

Sophie kicked the dirt in front of her. "I was just curious as to what their crime was. The usual murder and mayhem?"

"Their crime is that they're witches, love."

Sophie looked up at the sound of the rough voice; Dave, or Matt, she couldn't remember which, was looking back with a laughing sneer.

Hunter ignored the Marshall boy. "They've done nothing that we know of, yet. This is a pre-emptive strike."

"So... they're going to be punished, possibly killed, in case one day they are guilty." Sophie frowned, trying to get her head around the concept.

Her statement stunned everyone. One of the lads guffawed; and Gareth gave a sharp 'ha', throwing Hunter a dirty look. Even Toby and James looked mildly disgusted at the insinuation.

Poor Hunter felt a flush of embarrassment at his trainee's ignorance. "You're doing it again, Sophie, you're thinking they are like humans. They are witches, it is inevitable that they'll do evil - should we wait for innocent people to get hurt before we act? And we can't punish them for things they haven't done - we'll just bind them and process them, and set them free. I doubt it will be necessary to kill them."

"More's the pity," Gareth grumbled.

Hunter's head snapped round at this. He knew that some of his colleagues harboured this opinion privately, but no one ever voiced it. Apart from this bastard.

"Oh, I know you champion the non-violent outcomes, but be serious, binding witches wastes time and resources. Honestly, the only good witch is a dead witch, and if I had my way..."

"I know what would happen if you had your way," Hunter warned. Oh, he knew. He was very much aware of Halbrook's trigger-happy reputation. "But I'm in charge here and we're doing it my way."

"Sorry, sir," Gareth responded sarcastically. "Don't worry about me, I'll take care of myself. You just watch your witch-loving first."

Hunter took a stride towards him, not sure if he was going to shout, scream, plead or punch. Maybe all four. But he stopped in his tracks. There was a faint hum of a whisper in that part of his mind that was always alert and dominant.

"It's time," Hunter said, suddenly realizing the sun had dropped below the horizon.

Nearly a minute later, Toby, the Marshalls, and Gareth cocked their heads as though hearing something faint.

On a sudden impulse, they all rose, quickly inventoried their defences and weapons, then looked to Hunter.

"Let's go," he simply said, striding into the shadow of the trees.

Sophie and James came close behind, followed by Toby. Gareth and the Marshalls left a long, defiant gap, yet followed Hunter's lead.

Hunter walked into the deepening gloom of the evening woods, his senses sharpening with every step. He was aware of the six bodies behind him, their warmth, their separate breaths and footsteps. He was aware of the building throb of magic ahead of them, drawing closer he could sense the individual rhythm of the spells that bubbled up and called to him. He couldn't read any violence from it, and repeated this observation aloud for the others.

"There are four witches actively casting, but keep alert." Hunter added in a low voice, "This should be an easy one, so let's try to keep it civil."

This last part was directed obviously at Gareth, who pretended not to hear.

"Please don't say it'll be easy," James muttered, sharply knocking the nearest tree.

The others smiled nervously at his remark, then turned in the direction of the threat. Hunter signalled them to move into position, muttering last minute instructions and warnings, before allowing them to leave.

This was the part he hated most, he reflected as the other witch-hunters disappeared into the forest, he was personally brave and would risk his life as and when required. But to send others out to risk theirs always made him nervous, and yes, a little bit guilty.

But, as the boss of this operation, he could at least put the weakest in the safest place. New girl Sophie was behind the first line, Hunter voicing that they needed someone to stop the witches breaking through their circle. The excuse fooled no one, but Sophie, excited to be on her first real raid, didn't argue and docilely fell into place behind Toby and Matt Marshall.

In formation they moved forward on silent feet, led on by the promise of firelight ahead.

It was as Toby described, a clearing only 20 metres in diameter, a fire cracking, in its light four figures moved. Physically, the witches were unremarkable and unrecognisable as something other than human. But there was the aura of something more.

There were two female and two male witches, looking, in an ordinary light, as two couples having a bonfire night.

Hunter took a deep breath and stepped into the circle of light.

"I am Hunter Astley, by the Malleus Constitution you will surrender now to my authority to be bound and registered." He called out, confidently, "If you refuse to come quietly, we are empowered to take any means necessary."

Out of the shadows, the rest of the witch-hunters stepped forward, guns raised.

The witches, who had gazed at Hunter curiously as he approached, now reacted as they were surrounded. The men instinctively moved to protect their partners.

Their breath quickened and anger and fear tainted their expressions.

"We have done nothing wrong," The nearest male witch spat.

"Nevertheless, by the Malleus Constitution, all magic must be bound," Hunter replied formally. His eyes flicked up to Gareth, who looked bored and impatient. "Please, you are outnumbered, just surrender."

The male witch exhaled, his shoulders dropping with resignation. "There are worse things than death." He muttered, then raised his hands. Everything went black.

In a blind panic, Dave Marshall fired his gun into the darkness. There was a scream as the bullet ripped through flesh and bone.

"Stop!" Hunter shouted, furious at the witch-hunter. His 7th gen eyes piercing through the magic, he could see the blurred shape of the male witch still in front of him. Hunter gritted his teeth and launched himself at the witch, moving with unnatural speed, he knocked aside the witch's sluggish reaction and dealt a blow of such strength the man fell to the floor.

Around him the darkness faltered and faded, the light of the fire and stars perceivable again. Hunter looked around quickly, the male witch lay incapacitated at his feet. Off to his right, there was the result of Dave Marshall's nerves - Toby lay on the floor, trying to stem the blood flow from his arm.

One of the female witches jumped at the opportunity and ran at this weak spot in their circle.

"Stop!" Matt Marshall stepped into her path, but a wave of magic sent him flying unceremoniously head over heels, hitting a tree with a sickening thud.

"No," gasped Hunter, as the witch faced the last witch-hunter blocking her escape.

Deadly pale, Sophie raised her gun and fired.

The female witch gave a strangled cry and stumbled, falling to the forest floor. Blood blossomed a startling red from her chest and she could be seen to be gasping erratically from pain and shock.

Hunter ignored the unconscious male witch at his feet, he ignored the two remaining witches that now surrendered to James and Dave Marshall; Hunter stepped past the bleeding female witch and straight up to Sophie.

"Are you ok? Did she hurt you?" he asked, his voice low and desperate. He quickly glanced over her, there wasn't a mark on her, but Sophie was white and shivering. Hunter slowly moved closer, reaching out and gently prying the gun from her hand. "Sophie, it's ok, it's over. You did good."

Sophie's eyes snapped onto his, wide with panic and adrenaline. She was drowning in the shock of the moment and Hunter felt a sudden urge to reach out and save her, hold her close and protect her. An urge that he fought.

Hunter stepped away from Sophie, unsettled by this sudden intimacy. He forced himself to look around and assess the situation.

Toby was sitting on the mossy ground, staunching a wound in his arm. He looked bloody and pale, but otherwise ok, with Dave Marshall kneeling next to him, babbling out incoherent apologies and excuses.

The scene re-lit the anger Hunter felt towards that arse, Gareth Halbrook, who with his trigger-happy team had ruined a smooth operation. Hunter turned to look for the offending git and was surprised to see Gareth walking calmly in his direction.

Hunter opened his mouth to shout and course his anger, when Gareth raised his gun and shot a single round at the injured female witch at his feet.

Hunter felt a shock of fury as her heartbeat and irregular breathing left the web of sounds.

"You murderous bastard. What the hell did you do that for?" he shouted.

"Put her out of her misery" Halbrook replied roughly, staring challengingly at Hunter.

"She could have survived - there was no need."

"Survived for what? The taxpayers to pay for us to keep her. No thanks. As I said, the only good witch is a dead witch." Halbrook glanced over his shoulder at the living witches, obviously picturing the same fate for them.

Hunter shook with rage, completely unable to speak after such a statement. He felt a restraining hand on his arm and turned to face a pale and worried James.

But James was looking at Gareth Halbrook. "Mr Halbrook, take the prisoners to HQ."

Gareth frowned at James' assumed authority. Damned first gen, suddenly getting bossy, just because he was the famous Hunter Astley's friend. "Look 'ere-"

"No, you look," James interrupted. "You and your boys take care of the witches, 'cos I don't want t'leave Toby in your hands. And if you know what's good for you, those witches'll arrive at HQ without a single mark on them - got it?"

Gareth ground his teeth, obviously weighing up the cost of saying what was on his mind at this point. But in the end he grumbled something inaudible and stomped off, jerking his head at the Marshall brothers. The three trouble-makers left, herding the two witches before them, Halbrook picking up and carrying the still-unconscious male witch.

James finally looked to Hunter. "Come on, let's go. I'll help Toby, if you help Sophie."

Hunter nodded, and finally dragged his attention back to his other colleagues. He watched James help Toby to his feet and support him, they set off in the direction of the Land Rover at a slow, stumbling pace.

Hunter turned to Sophie, who looked still pale, but more composed now. "Can you walk?" He asked, uncertainly.

"I'm not an invalid," Sophie snapped in a reassuringly offended manner. Her cold, sharp self

115

returning now the immediate shock was passing. "Don't treat me like a damsel in distress."

Hunter shrugged, his mind too full of other concerns to be too relieved that Sophie was okay. They walked together, slowly following James and Toby back to the car. The four travelled in near silence. When they got back to the Land Rover, they found Gareth's Jeep already gone. The four witch-hunters climbed back into Hunter's vehicle and made their way back to the road, slower this time, Hunter driving more carefully so as not to jostle Toby. Again, there was silence.

They finally turned onto a dirt track and the headlights lit up Toby's blue Volvo. Hunter pulled up next to it. Again, James took charge.

"Right, I'll drive Toby up t'hospital, then I'll head to the MMC - it's late, but I want to follow up Halbrook. Go home Hunter." After helping Toby into the back seat of the Volvo, James spoke quietly to Hunter. "Just keep an eye on Sophie. I think she's hiding her shock."

Hunter nodded, clapping his friend on the back and climbing back into the driver's seat of his Land Rover.

James said something privately to Sophie, wearing a serious expression, then got into the Volvo.

"Are you sure you're ok?" Hunter asked again, as Sophie climbed into the passenger's seat beside him.

"Yes," she replied exasperatedly. She then stared resolutely out the dark window.

Hunter nodded again. Good, silence, that was fine.

116

They were roaring down the motorways, Hunter showing a certain disregard for speed limits, when he decided to speak.

"What did James have to say?" He asked, his voice suddenly seeming loud after the silence.

Sophie finally looked at him, but only briefly. "Nothing," she muttered.

Hunter was unconvinced. He had an odd feeling that just as James had asked him to watch Sophie in case she went into shock, the annoying Yorkshireman had asked Sophie to keep an eye on Hunter's mood after the run-in with Halbrook.

They lapsed into silence again. Then Sophie shifted uncomfortably. "Does it get any easier?"

"What do you mean?"

"Killing witches, does it get easier with time?" she asked, turning to face him.

Her hazel eyes burnt with the pain of the question, she seemed shaken, yet strong. Again, Hunter felt that dragging sensation that he should hold her, that he could keep her whole.

A horn blared as he nearly collided with another car. Hunter snapped his attention back to the road, his hands tightening on the wheel. He could feel the pressure of the seat belt against his shoulder, and was bizarrely glad for such a restraint.

"No, it doesn't get easier," he replied honestly, staring resolutely ahead. "And I don't want it to, I don't want to be like him, like Gareth."

No, Hunter couldn't imagine that killing witches would ever mean nothing to him, or worse, that he'd take some sick pleasure from it.

It seemed to take forever to get back to Astley Manor. It was midnight by the time they pulled up the gravely drive to the big old house. The lights were still on, the fires lit ready for their return, and they gladly went into the warmth.

"Are you sure you're ok?" Hunter asked again, as they stood together in the hallway.

Sophie gave him a withering look. "Goodnight, Hunter."

Hunter watched Sophie walk away from him and move up the main staircase, heading straight for her room. He didn't want her to be alone; he told himself that she shouldn't be alone after such a day. But a part of him knew better. Oh god, he was in trouble.

"Sophie…" He called out, then thought better of it as she paused on the stairs. "Sophie, tell James that I don't need babysitting."

## Chapter Eleven

Hunter sat alone with Sophie in the library, books spread out down the long table. He was aware of the furtive looks she kept shooting him. Despite the dark matter of the books around him, and the oppressive environment since his discovery, Hunter found this amusing.

Out of the corner of his eye, he saw her look again. This time he smiled. "Is there something I can help you with, Sophie?"

A blush crept over her cheeks. "What's it like?" she blurted out.

"What is what like?" Hunter asked, smiling at the vague question.

Sophie closed the heavy volume in front of her, Hunter saw the faded title: 'Witches and their hunters of the Romanic region: 16th century study'. Hmm, poor girl, no wonder her mind was wandering.

"What's it like, being a further generation witch-hunter? Do you feel differently from other people?" Sophie asked, using more detail this time.

Hunter thought about this, not for the first time. "Honestly, I don't know, I've never been normal so how can I compare? Perhaps I should ask if you feel different from a 7th gen."

Hunter smiled teasingly, but closed his book, willing to be more serious. "Everything I do feels normal and natural, but sometimes I see other people's reactions when I move too quickly, or show too much strength and so on. So surely there's something abnormal enough to catch their attention. Does that answer your question well enough?"

Sophie said nothing for a minute or two, staring into space with her own thoughts. "And... what is it like when you perceive magic?"

Hunter looked at her with askance.

"What, I'm not allowed to be curious because I'll never experience it?" Sophie demanded.

"Fine," Hunter said, leaning back in his chair, his gaze fixed on his new charge. "It's... it's like a headache, or at least it used to be when I was younger. A niggling, burgeoning activity that can be mistaken for pain. But you can train yourself to concentrate on it, read it, taste it. Every strain of magic has a different taste, or rhythm. As soon as a witch casts, I can tell what the magic is for, even who cast it."

Hunter stopped, grimacing at his own description, as though he were a connoisseur of art or fine wine. Had he really gotten so expert in his dark career?

"And it improves with each generation?" Sophie encouraged. "What's the furthest you've perceived magic?"

Hunter nodded, oh yes, as the famous 7th gen he was born with unfair advantages against the witches.

"The furthest?"

Hunter broke off as James made his entrance kicking the old door open so he could carry in the coffee tray. "Couldn't find Charles, so made it meself. Hope you like strong coffee."

"James, what would you say is the furthest I've felt a casting?" Hunter asked mildly. "Ten miles?"

James slid the coffee tray onto the busy table. "Ten easy. Remember the one in Hereford last month, must've been fifteen."

Sophie just nodded, silently taking in the information.

"You know this is summat you'll never experience." James said, casually cruel. "Not jealous of our Hunter, are you?"

Sophie gave him a haughty stare in reply, flicking her brown hair back over her shoulder.

"I'm curious, surely that's allowed," she said coldly. "Besides, this all sounds a touch too close to magic."

The effect was instantaneous. James stopped laughing at her and Hunter's smile froze.

Sophie seemed to realize the severity of what she'd said, and started stuttering. "Look... it's not... I didn't mean-"

"Never say that." Hunter warned in a chilling tone, his eyes furious. "How dare you even make such a heinous association?"

Hunter stood up so quickly, Sophie flinched as though expecting him to hit her. But Hunter kept his fists by his side and turned towards the door, needing space.

"You don't seem to realize how offensive your ignorant comments are, Sophie. And showing me up in front of Gareth Halbrook and his cronies last week – no, I haven't forgotten that. I've been pretty damn lenient with your whole attitude, but one day you'll have to deal directly with the MMC, and they won't be as understanding." Hunter took a deep breath, the worst of his rant over, but his eyes still blazed. "You said you wanted to be a witch-hunter. Well, you've got to be in this a hundred percent, you've got to sort your attitude out and stop this... this sympathy for magic. Or you need to walk out that door right now."

Hunter motioned towards the open library door. The room was silent and motionless again.

Sophie was tense, her hazel eyes cast down. But the fact that she wasn't biting back showed that there was at least some truth in Hunter's outburst.

"I'm here. I'm in," she eventually muttered. She looked uncertain for a minute, then quietly turned back to her book.

Hunter felt no joy in setting Sophie straight, he felt strangely empty after letting loose, and now stood by his chair, not sure what to do.

James on the other hand felt perfectly comfortable in giving Sophie a disgusted look before turning to Hunter. "You know, this coffee isn't working. How 'bout we knock off and head down t'local instead?"

Hunter looked at his watch and sighed. "Yeah, sure. I've time for a drink before I take Rachel to dinner."

The two boys promptly left the library to get their coats, and Sophie (who was unsure whether or not the invitation extended to her) sat alone, quietly reading the dusty volume before her.

## Chapter Twelve

There's something about Hallowe'en that seemed to excite the witchkind. Perhaps it was to do with the pagan fire ritual of Samhain, their magic amped up by something earthly. Or maybe it was just the thrill of moving openly, while a world of naïve victims actually celebrated their existence.

If it was anything like last year, it would be uncontrolled chaos. Even the newspapers and the general ignorant public had suspected something after the wave of identical murders that the MMC hadn't been able to completely cover up.

So, all the witch-hunters were on high alert. Even if they looked foolish...

It was early evening, but it was already dark outside. Hunter stood close to the warm fireplace, the old house did get cold once autumn came around, and Charles worked overtime keeping it pleasant for the Astley family and their guests.

Making the effort for Hallowe'en without sacrificing style, Hunter was wearing a tasteful black suit with a long black cloak and a white mask covering half his face.

"Let me guess, 'Phantom of the Opera' meets Armani?"

Sophie stood in the doorway, looking so fantastic that Hunter was left momentarily speechless. She smiled in her own grimacing way and turned so that he could see her outfit, sultry dark red tones on black, close fitting to her slim curves, the long skirt slit to the thigh. She'd done something clever with her make-up to make her face pale, but still stunning. Oh yes, and rubber fangs sticking out over her lower lip.

"Sexy vampire?" Hunter asked needlessly.

"Well, I was going to be a witch, but I thought that would be too ironic," Sophie replied, lisping slightly over the false teeth. She shook her head and pulled them out, "Hm, I don't think I'll be wearing these all night though. I don't see why the MMC want us to dress up and go out like a group of normals, when there's going to be so much activity."

"Ah well," How embarrassing. Hunter had previously told Sophie what she needed to hear. "We have no intel on what will happen where, so the MMC likes its witch-hunters to be on the move, in the thick of it, so they can act immediately." This was repeating his earlier statement. The next bit she may not like. "But the dressing up like a prat is my idea. You know, to fit in. Come on, we've got to pick James up. Are you kitted up?"

Sophie's frown deepened, but she nodded. Hunter had provided her with a personal handgun and small dagger - where she'd managed to hide them in that figure-hugging ensemble though... Hunter snapped back to attention.

"Yes, James, let's go."

They took the Land Rover, the 4x4 equipped with protective charms and the boot stocked with the tools of their trade. Sophie jumped into the passenger seat, and they drove in familiar silence to James' modest house.

And out came a pirate. And hadn't he put the effort in: hat; dreadlocked wig; bandanna; skull shirt with homemade tearing; long shorts (again with the tears); and lord knows where he got the long boots, probably the same place he got the courage to wear them.

"Nice outfit," Sophie said carefully as James clambered into the back seat.

"Thanks," James replied, shooting a victorious look at Hunter.

Friend or not, what an idiot. "James has worn the same outfit for the past three years. He got a bit of a Johnny Depp fixation when we were at university." Hunter told Sophie, with a commendably deadpan expression.

"Hey," James shouted from the back. "I didn't have a 'fixation'. I just really enjoyed Pirates of the

Caribbean, and I dare you to say Captain Jack wasn't cool."

"I agree," Hunter conceded. "He was cool. Five years ago. Now it's only obsessives with no personal, original imagination of their own-"

And Sophie sat quietly, staring out the car window at the moonlit fields and cottages. Over the past couple of months she'd gotten used to the two boys bickering like an old married couple.

Soon, the view out her window was the stream of slow-moving cars and the bright lights of bars. The sound of music and the laughter of the revellers hit the car. Hunter parked up and they all got out and made their way into the nearest bar.

"I know the MMC like us to be out and ready for action, but this?" Sophie asked, looking around with distaste.

"Look, most activity isn't until midnight. Sure, most witch-hunters will be sitting in their cars, drinking coffee and trawling the streets. But the MMC doesn't care if we have one last party before getting on the job, as long as we stick to soft drinks," Hunter replied seriously, after just handing out the first round of beer and wine. "You never know when it's your last call. Besides, look around, we're surrounded by victims. So relax, enjoy yourself for once."

Hmm, although she didn't go wild, Sophie gave in to the party spirit and, after another glass of wine, she even deigned to smile every now and then.

James, with the odd confidence bestowed by wearing a pirate costume was enjoying the dancefloor a bit too much for his sober state. Hunter had the fun of watching his friend make an arse of himself - he'd remind James of these embarrassing intervals at later times.

Every now and then, bonny girls walked over to try and get Hunter to join in the dancing, but he declined and the girls were often chased away by a cold glare by Sophie.

"Not getting jealous, are you?" Hunter laughed, leaning in towards her. "And I thought you didn't like me!"

Sophie, stiff and frozen as ever, turned away from him. "I just don't think it is right. We're working."

Hunter smiled, she didn't change. He reached out and placed his hand on her lower back, he felt a thrill when she didn't pull away. He got the sudden image of trying to gentle a wild horse that could turn and kick you in the head at any moment.

"Come on, it's twenty to twelve. Let's get the dancing pirate and go." Hunter said to her quietly.

The trio emerged from the warm pub into the brittle, clear night. The first stop was the car, where they threw in their extraneous costume and pulled out a kit bag each. Then they meandered without any particular aim to the edge of the night scene. It was here, where drunken revellers stumbled away from their pubs and clubs, making their way home, it was here the witches were likely to hunt their prey.

All they could do was wander the streets, waiting for something to prick Hunter's senses. Hunter glanced at his watch, nearly midnight. A sigh escaped him, this time last year he was being torn apart by all the magic being used. He was pretty confident that he could sense magic within a fifteen-mile radius. But still nothing. What the hell was going on?

"Hunter."

## Chapter Thirteen

"Hunter?"

Sophie's voice came so quiet and she sounded so scared, Hunter felt fear grip his heart as he turned. Sophie stood there, looking strangely stiff.

"Sophie, you alright?" James asked, looking at her carefully.

Sophie didn't reply. Her eyes closed and slowly a smile creased her red lips. There was a bristling of energy about her.

"Oh shit." Hunter grabbed James and pulled him back from her, expecting an outburst.

But nothing flamboyant happened, yet. The energy of magic was so high that Hunter felt deafened by it.

Sophie opened her eyes, unseeingly. By the lamplight her hazel eyes were clouded over with what looked like thick white cataracts.

"Sophie, what are you doing? Can you hear me?" Hunter said loudly.

Sophie tilted her head slightly and looked at Hunter with an expression of curiosity. "Sophie can hear you, but unfortunately can't answer. You see, she has given control of this vessel to me tonight." The voice was Sophie's with something of a deeper tone, throbbing with power.

"You're a witch. She wouldn't - Sophie would not help a witch." James almost shouted back.

Sophie turned slowly to look directly at James with those clouded eyes. "Simple boy, I don't need a willing soul, she still fights my presence - quite annoying, very stubborn. But I am stronger. Shall I prove it?"

Her hand threw up and James gasped, dropping to his knees and clawing at his constricted chest, unable to breath, his heart struggling to beat.

"Stop!" Hunter screamed. "By the Malleus Maleficarum I command you to stop."

"For now." The voice replied, dropping Sophie's hand. Immediately James began to gulp down a lungful of air, his face red. "If he speaks again, he dies."

"What do you want?" Hunter asked, forcing himself to remain calm. What else could he do, a witch was attacking his two friends.

"I want to see you, you who discovered my return; you Astley, whose family seems tied to my fate."

"Shadow... The Shadow Witch." The words whispered from his lips in disbelief. Hunter had a right to be scared. "Then here I am, leave my friends out of it."

Sophie smiled. "I have not come to kill you, not tonight. But now I see your weakness, I see how close you are to these insignificant mortals. I see into this girl's thoughts and I see what pain I could inflict by killing them instead."

"No, you can't. I won't let you."

"Ah, now we come to it, *Astley*." The Shadow Witch spat his name out with such hatred, as though they had cursed his existence in their heart every day. "Can you stop me? You are a remarkable young man, I am sure. But now, I stand before you as vulnerable as you will ever find me. I am so strongly within this girl for this brief time - shoot her, kill us both."

Hunter raised his gun, pointing the barrel level at Sophie's chest. Yes, Sophie was just one person, with her death she could spare hundreds, possibly thousands of lives. His hand was steady, which was a miracle in itself.

No, he was not a murderer, not for the greater good. And he couldn't sacrifice Sophie, of all people. He slowly lowered the gun.

Sophie smiled, clouded eyes still fixed on Hunter. "I will make you regret your weakness, Astley. She will die."

"Don't you dare hurt Sophie, or I'll make it your regret. Now relinquish this girl." Hunter said fiercely.

There was one last ghost of a smile on Sophie's lips and then she crumpled. Hunter grabbed her, barely slowing her fall as Sophie hit the pavement. James, who had been hovering uselessly, now dashed to her side.

"She's still alive," James said, having checked her pulse and breathing. He glanced up at Hunter. "What on earth was that about?"

Hunter was equally confused. If that had been the Shadow Witch, what had been the point of contacting Hunter? No information given on either side, no deaths despite the threats. Surely they hadn't wished to just turn up and gloat in a big bad clichéd way.

"I don't know." Hunter responded. "But let's get Sophie back to the car."

James picked up the three heavy kit bags, and Hunter gently lifted Sophie's unconscious form. Although his senses were on high alert, Hunter felt no trace of magic remaining in the girl.

Back at the car the two men struggled to get Sophie onto the back seat.

"Shit!" Hunter jumped and swore as his mobile rang suddenly. He muttered at his own nerves and answered it sharply. It took a moment to understand the fast, panicked voice on the other end.

"Hey, slow down. Now what's happened?" Hunter asked, still not sure who he was talking to.

"They took her, the witches took her, I thought this place was protected, Hunter. But the shadows grew and wrapped around her and then Charlotte was gone."

Charlotte. Oh no. No, no, no. When the Shadow Witch had said 'she' would die, they had meant someone more important to Hunter than even Sophie.

"Look, Steve, we'll get her back, I promise you."

"If anything happens, I'll hold you responsible."

The line went dead. Hunter sat in a state of shock.

"Hunter," James' voice broke through the haze.

"Get on the phone, alert all the witch-hunters, the MMC, everyone. We need to find where she's been taken." Hunter said, suddenly spurred into action.

"Hunter." James repeated calmly. "Sophie's awake."

They both twisted in their seats to face Sophie, who was sitting straight and strong again. Looking into her eyes, although filled with panic, they were back to their cold hazel depths.

"The witch, I didn't let her, I tried to stop her but she was so strong." She looked down at her hands, flexing them, as though confirming her own control over her body again. "James, I-I'm sorry. And Hunter, it's all my fault. I could feel her, she sifted through my thoughts and memories and I was powerless to stop her. I showed her Charlotte."

"We don't blame you," Hunter said quickly, not sure if it was true. "We need to get moving, to find her before…"

His voice trailed off, so he started the engine.

"We don't even know where to start." James reasoned.

"Actually." Sophie said quietly, surprising the guys with a brief smile of pride. "The Shadow Witch was so preoccupied, she didn't notice that I could get into her thoughts. I saw a village church, it was a St Peters. It's not much to go on, but if all witch-hunters head to the nearest one, we've got more of a chance."

James was already on the phone, repeating Sophie's words to the Council. Hunter slammed the car into gear and sped off, ignoring every traffic rule. James kept his mobile glued to his ear and spewed out directions to Hunter to their nearest St Peters. But soon it was unnecessary, as the miles flew by and they drew closer, Hunter could feel the pull of magic, telling them that this was the place.

They had all fallen silent by the time they had pulled up outside the church. It was a small, stone-built with old leaded windows. It was a lonely little building in a forgotten village.

The two men got out of the car and Sophie made to follow them.

"On no, you don't, you're staying in the car." Hunter said, blocking her way.

"Hunter, I'm a witch-hunter, I'm coming." Sophie responded, trying to push the car door out of his grip.

"No. The Shadow Witch has gone after you once already - stay in the car where you're protected."

Reluctantly, Sophie agreed. James pulled the kit bags out the boot. Hunter grabbed his stab jacket, pulling it on over his shirt. He took a deep breath, well, this was it.

"Hunter." Sophie grabbed his sleeve as he moved to leave, then pulled him close, pressing her soft lips against his, the scent of her skin and perfume. She released him slowly, reluctantly. "Come back alive."

Hunter staggered back and followed a silent James up to the church door. He glanced back once, unable to see Sophie's face clearly in the dark car.

At the church door, James turned to him. "Now what?"

Oh hell. They had never faced anything this big, for someone they cared so strongly for. Was this what it felt like, to know death waited impatiently for you?

"We go in," Hunter replied, meeting James' knowing gaze. "It's been fun."

They might die here tonight, but they both knew that they would never turn back. Hunter went first, pushing his weight against the thick wooden door. Inside the church was dimly lit by candles along the aisle and eaves. It was quiet, filled with shadows, empty of life. Hunter stepped cautiously up the centre aisle; there was something at the altar.

She lay as though asleep, her beautiful face serene, her arms by her side.

"Charlotte," Hunter whispered as he forgot all his caution and rushed up to her, desperate for her to respond. He reached out, now scared to touch her, her cheek felt warm against his hand. "Charlotte."

His hand traced her chest for any heartbeat, but stopped as he felt the soaked material of her black jumper. Blood stained his fingers. "No," he growled, anger and sorrow firing up within him like never before.

"Hunter." James hissed.

Hunter turned and immediately saw what had gained James' attention. Out of the shadows, black-clad figures stepped into the candlelight until a dozen witches faced them.

Hunter welcomed them. A raw fury filled Hunter's heart and soul. He would die and be with Charlotte again, but he would take as many of these bastards with him as possible.

"Come on then!" He screamed, raised his gun and fired. There was a rumble and a crack and the world seemed to be torn apart. The twelve witches were thrown off their feet and back with a force against the stone walls and pillars. A fierce tempest whipped through the church, shaking it to its foundations. Masonry dust shook from the walls and rafters and suddenly great chunks of torn wood and stone were falling all about them.

*****

James opened his eyes, the world had not ended and he was somehow still alive. Ugh, bloody battered, but alive. The old church was nothing but rubble. He got slowly to his feet and looked around. The witches were barely visible beneath the stone, immobile limbs sticking up in awkward places.

Half fearful, James turned back to face where Hunter had been standing. The altar was still there, with Charlotte laid out serenely, Hunter standing over her. They were miraculously untouched, with only the faint layer of dust to show that they had been part of the scene. How the hell?

*****

"We need to talk about what happened," James said seriously. They were perched on the church wall and the first people from the MMC were just arriving.

Hunter remained silent, staring into the dark countryside.

"Hunter, I think the MMC will notice the church, they can count too - two of us against twelve witches that appeared out of nowhere. You're gonna have to talk to them. But first, we need to work out what happened." James paused for breath. He'd been expecting to die tonight - he should have died tonight. "That much power, it had to be the Shadow Witch, but does that mean she's playing with us, or she wants you alive for some scary reason. Did you feel her presence, her magic?"

Hunter shook his head, no he hadn't felt anything, nothing except his own anger. And now he felt dead inside. "Let's go home," he muttered.

"We've got to stay, to help the Council. We've still got work to do."

"I don't bloody care!" Hunter shouted, getting fired up again, "The Council can go f-"

He jumped down from the wall and marched off. James had to rush to catch him.

"Ok mate, we'll deal with them later. But I'll drive."

## Chapter Fourteen

It was dawn by the time they got back to Astley Manor. The trio shivered against the cold of the morning as they staggered into the entrance hall. There they stood, all unsure of what to do, how to act next.

James was the first to speak, his voice shaking with his own sorrow. "Hunter... do you want to, er, talk?"

"Will talking bring Charlotte back?" Hunter asked in a dead voice. His tired eyes looked up at James. "No, I didn't think so. I don't want to talk."

Hunter sighed and pushed past the others, disappearing into the recesses of the mansion.

Sophie went to follow him, but hesitated, every part of her uncertain. "Should I... is there anything I could do?"

"No," James snapped, then shrugged. "Sorry. But I think we should leave him for a while."

They stood in the hall for several long, silent minutes before James broke the silence again. "Perhaps you should just go to bed, you've had one hell of a night," he suggested, moving off up the staircase himself. One hell of a night for all of them. Christ.

Hunter had wandered into the sitting room, where a fire crackled in the grate. He'd been standing here only twelve hours ago, yet so much had happened.

"Oh, so you all decided to come back then?" A familiarly sharp voice came from the doorway, "I swear you use Hallowe'en as an excuse for all night frivolities, as Young did."

"Not now, mother." Hunter said through gritted teeth as he turned to face the bitter little woman.

"Oh dear, what happened?" Mrs Astley asked, somehow managing to make a possibly caring question sound harsh and spiteful.

"Charlotte. They killed Charlotte." Hunter turned away as his eyes filled with tears. Oh God, why her? He felt as though he'd lost a reason to live. The Shadow Witch was right about him, he was weak because he cared.

Mrs Astley sat down and looked at her son carefully. "Charlotte? That black girl you were infatuated with at university? Well there's no point blaming yourself, everyone dies and you know that."

"I do blame myself, it's my fault, mother. All because I loved her." Hunter felt a pang of regret, he'd never openly told Charlotte he loved her. He had stood back and watched her marry someone else and never said a thing. There was no point lying about it anymore.

"Don't start fretting over it, George. Anyway, she would never have been a suitable wife. Good heavens, could you imagine a coloured mistress of Astley Manor?"

Normally Hunter would ignore any and all comments from his ignorantly racist mother, no matter how foul, but anger still throbbed in his veins.

"Shut UP, you miserable old bag. Charlotte deserves respect, and as master of this house I will throw you out if you do not hold your tongue!"

Mrs Astley looked affronted, unused to her son being so reactive. She stood up suddenly. "I will not be spoken to in such a manner. Have Charles send tea up to my rooms. And we shall speak when you have calmed down and remembered your manners."

Hunter watched his mother leave the room. She was an irritating, narrow-minded…

He took a deep breath, his mother had never liked Charlotte, so her reaction hadn't surprised him. What was surprising was the raw energy of anger that refused to leave his otherwise numb body. Even though he'd not slept that night, he did not feel tired. He wanted to run, to fight, to do something other than give in to grief - and this anger whispered to him that he could. Yet his legs seemed not to respond.

He didn't know how long he stood there alone, leaning against the fireplace, his knuckles turned white in their fierce grip of the mantelpiece. But he couldn't feel it. He could not feel the heat from the fire burning his legs. It seemed that nothing now registered beyond the forlorn pounding of bitterness and repetitive thoughts that filled his mind.

"Hunter?" Sophie's voice broke through as she hovered by the door. But the figure by the fire made no comment, nor even recognised her presence. "George, please."

Sophie moved quietly towards him.

"She's dead," Hunter said in a harsh burst, finally turning to face Sophie. "Charlotte's dead. I couldn't save her. Never, never has my job - if I can't protect those I love... And I'm up against a Shadow."

"You should have killed her when she was in me. You could have ended it right there."

When Hunter looked at her he was surprised to see guilt and sadness in that normally cold face and icy hazel eyes. "I could never have killed you, though."

He stepped forward and took her in his arms, his lips pressing against hers, driven not by lust but utter despair.

Sophie pushed him away immediately, and when she spoke there was a warning plea in her voice. "Hunter, don't."

Hunter paused, his thoughts catching up with his actions. But his heart was beating and his breath coursed his lungs. This he could feel. He stepped towards her again.

"Then tell me you don't want me." He said softly, wrapping his arms about her elegant frame. His lips found hers again, and this time he felt Sophie yield to his embrace.

*****

It was the morning after the night before. That's how they described it, wasn't it? That period of time when rash, passionate actions were shown by the harsh light of day, provoking regret, guilt, and possibly embarrassment.

Hunter awoke early to a still-darkened room. He felt oddly calm, as though the stress, grief and rage of the last two days had, if not dulled, been pushed back to a more manageable perspective.

Hunter shifted his body slowly to sit up. In bed next to him Sophie was still sleeping soundly. He watched her for several long minutes, even in the half-light before dawn she was beautiful, and there was something softer, more serene about her face while she slept. He supposed it had to do with her chill and sharp intellect being reserved for dreams and out of his reach.

He moved slowly so as not to wake her, slipping out of bed and pulling on any old clothes before going downstairs. The rest of the house was still sleeping and as Charles hadn't lit the morning fires yet, the Manor was cold.

Hunter made his way to the kitchen for his first cup of coffee. He sat at the counter, nursing the steaming mug. He waited for the regret to kick in. In general Hunter enjoyed women and never worried about hurt feelings, he never hung around long enough. But Sophie was, well, a friend - and in a moment when he'd been mad with loss he had used her.

Although ashamed about the circumstances, he didn't regret it, nor did he want to scarper. He hated to admit it, but everyone had been right: he wanted her, cold, unyielding, frustrating Sophie.

Strangely he did feel guilt. That after professing to love Charlotte for so long, he suddenly dared to have a new focus in his life when he should be concerned with mourning.

It was over an hour later when Hunter gained company. Sophie hovered in the doorway.

"Morning," she said quietly, for once looking completely uncertain.

"Morning." Hunter echoed.

Sophie made herself a drink then sat opposite Hunter, her gaze averted. They sat in an increasingly uncomfortable silence.

"Look," Hunter finally started. "I wanted to apologise. My behaviour yesterday was unforgivable; I should never have taken advantage of you like that. I'm sorry."

"Oh." The single sound was the only reply Sophie could muster. She stared down at her hands, frowning as per usual.

'Oh'? Hunter was used to much wittier and informative responses from Sophie. He didn't like not knowing where he stood with her, he'd rather face her anger than try to be sufficed with a little 'Oh'.

The silence grew and Sophie offered nothing more, her face dark with her private thoughts. Oh dear, this was uncomfortable, bordering on embarrassing.

Hunter didn't deal with that sort of thing, especially when work was likely to be involved. If Sophie didn't want him, Hunter would have to rethink this living and working arrangement.

Sophie stared into her steaming coffee, her fingers gripping the mug so tightly that they were turning white.

"That's fine. I understand that you just needed a distraction. So glad to prove useful," she finally answered bitterly, her eyes snapped up to him, cold and furious.

Hunter was a little shocked by her response and sat quietly, his early morning brain trying to catch up. And poor Sophie took his silence as agreement. She sighed, muttering something beneath her breath and sliding off the stool, only thinking of taking her coffee to the privacy of her own room.

"Is that really what you think?" Hunter asked, standing up to block her way out of the kitchen. "That you were just convenient and distracting?"

Sophie reluctantly met his gaze, her anger fading and replaced by what had caused it - fear of the unknown.

Hunter reached out, gently catching her by the arm to stop her from bolting. "I'd never dare think so low of you, Sophie. In fact, the truth is that I think about you more than I should, and I am only sorry that it took the shock of Hallowe'en to make me act."

Sophie just continued to stare up at him, her breath increasing in rate, as her eyes dilated as her agitation grew.  Obviously, Hunter's new answer was no more welcome than his previous one.  But then it was suddenly as if she made a decision, to take the risk and the consequences.  Sophie leant in closer towards Hunter and kissed him hesitantly.

Sensing that she was no longer about to hit him or storm out, Hunter kissed her back, pulling her in til he could feel the warmth of her body and -

And then he pulled back sharply, swearing and shaking his hand where he'd spilt the hot coffee she'd been nursing so protectively.  Hunter shook his head at how smoothly that had gone, then chuckled at an afterthought.

"James is not going to like this," he said guiltily, not wanting to think how uncomfortable his best friend would be feeling.  Hunter smiled at Sophie, taking her hot drink from her and setting it firmly on the side before trying that kiss again.

## Chapter Fifteen

The next few days were a blur. There were the inevitable visits by the MMC. They questioned Hunter and James over and over about Hallowe'en. Poor Sophie had been grilled by several 'experts', trying to understand the Shadow Witch; whether Sophie was in danger; even whether Sophie was dangerous.

The Council had finally been scared into action, pulling people off mundane tasks and setting them to research and defence. When they came to Astley Manor with a long list of work for the resident witch-hunters, Hunter set his mother on them; they got the hint and didn't come back.

Hunter wasn't ready to face the world and didn't have the energy to survive it. He would happily have disappeared into nothingness. Only his new closeness to Sophie made him want to live.

Then one morning Hunter, Sophie and James finally left the Manor, all three dressed in black. It was a cold

November day, with the first proper frosts of the year. Hunter felt Sophie shiver and he held her closer as they all stood in the graveyard, a silent crowd gathered, their breath fogging over the prayers.

It wasn't that long ago that they'd all been standing over another funeral, when Brian's death had seemed the worst thing to ever happen.

The crowd slowly departed, people stopping to say their own goodbyes, and to console the inconsolable widower. Hunter looked up. Steve stood by the graveside, his tall, thin figure swamped by the heavy black coat, his eyes so red from crying.

"Steve, I'm so sorry." Hunter said, finding himself walking up to Charlotte's husband.

Whack! Hunter recoiled in shock as timid Steve punched him squarely in the face. Through watering eyes, Hunter saw Steve rub his sore knuckles.

"You have no right to be here Hunter!" Steve shouted, ignorant of the other mourners that turned and stared. "It's all your fault - you got her into witch-hunting, you were supposed to protect her. Leave. If I ever see you again, I swear I'll kill you."

Hunter was dragged away by both Sophie and James. He shouldn't have expected anything else from Steve. But now that Charlotte was laid to rest, Hunter was ready to get back in the action. Everything would work out, it had to, especially when he had James and Sophie still with him.

*****

That night, Hunter found the concept of sleep impossible, even with the comforting warmth of Sophie beside him. He watched her sleep with a quiet fascination. She seemed so peaceful, until the early hours of the morning, when the rhythm of sleep became disturbed. A pained expression crumpled her face and she struggled against the bedclothes.

Suddenly, Sophie jolted awake with a strangled cry, sitting up in bed now, her body tense and trembling.

"Sophie, Sophie, it's alright." Hunter murmured gently to her, his hand placed against her flushed cheek. "Did you have a nightmare?"

Sophie, eyes wide with panic, her gaze roving over him in slow understanding as she tried to shake off the images. "Just a dream," she muttered, forcing herself to be calm. "Just a dream."

"Do you want to talk about it?" Hunter asked.

"No," Sophie replied shortly, lying back down.

Hunter sighed. "It might help," he insisted. Yes, it might help him pass the hours until dawn, when he no longer had to pretend to need rest and bed.

Sophie looked at him in assessment. "It was nothing, it..." She broke off, unable to shake the possessing dream. "Fine, the truth. We were at the graveyard, like today, and the Shadow Witch was waiting at the gate. She was wearing Death's garb and called to you. I begged you not to go, but you walked through the gate with your head high and your stupid pride. Then, knowing that you were dead, and I alive - in the dream I was distraught, I... I..."

149

Sophie stopped, struggling to find words to express her feelings. "It was a physical, inescapable pain. And I hated you for making me grieve your death."

Hunter remained quiet for a while, taking in this open answer. "It was just a dream. Probably set off by the funeral today."

Sophie frowned, forever fighting with herself, and building up the courage to say what was on her mind. "I don't want you to fight the Shadow Witch."

"What?" Hunter laughed, surprised by this sudden, ludicrous request.

"You don't have to go up against her. There are a hundred other witch-hunters that can face her," Sophie argued, in a quiet voice that was already defeated.

"Sophie, don't be ridiculous. How can I turn my back on the biggest threat of our time? I'm one of the best witch-hunters out there, if I don't stop her, who will?" Hunter argued back, logically.

"But if you face her you will be killed."

Hunter hesitated in his response, feeling a faint wave of foreboding. He shrugged it off. "That was nothing but your dream, Sophie. I may actually survive this thing, trust me."

Sophie propped herself up on her elbow in a sharp movement, her whole body emanating anger. "No, it's not just my dream, Hunter. Why don't you listen to me? I've seen inside the mind of the Shadow Witch, I've seen how she wants your death above all others, how she's imagined it a hundred different ways. She is your Death and you march proudly and stubbornly towards it."

Hunter was temporarily silenced by this revelation. "You never said -"

"It never seemed important." Sophie bit back. "But does it make you reconsider?"

"No," Hunter replied quickly.

Sophie hissed in disgust and rolled away from him. She lay still for so long that Hunter began to think that she'd fallen back to sleep.

"You awake, Sophie?" He eventually whispered.

"Yes," she snapped, remaining stubbornly turned away from him.

"Sophie, this is who I am. I cannot turn away from this fight, it's against my nature," Hunter said seriously. He reached out and stroked her back gently, frowning as she flinched away from him. "You wouldn't love me if I were any different."

The scene seemed to freeze. Neither of them had mentioned the 'L' word, nor even allowed themselves to think it in their most private thoughts.

"You're right," Sophie replied, finally turning to face him. "How I wish you were any other man right now, one not cursed by the Shadow Witch. If you should die, it would cut me down also."

Sophie reached out, her hand tracing his face, committing his features to memory. "Promise me you won't die."

Hunter smiled, then pulled her close to him, lips brushing her hair. "How I wish I could promise that."

Held close in Hunter's arms, Sophie slowly fell back to sleep, gentle and dreamless. Hunter sighed, the same foreboding reawakening in him, that all this was a temporary happiness.

"I am afeard. Being in night, all this is but a dream, too flattering-sweet to be substantial." He muttered to himself, unable to smile at the fitting words. Ah, was all this a premonition of the end, rushing up to greet them.

*****

Sophie dragged her bag down the wide main staircase, she hated getting Charles to carry her stuff when she could do it herself.

Hunter glanced out the window, checking for her taxi. "You're sure about this? The MMC can send someone."

Sophie dropped her bag by the front door. They'd already been over this. "I know, but I need to do this. If the Shadow Witch goes after our families, I want to be the one to protect my mum."

They had no idea where the witches would hit next, and it was logical that anyone connected to Hunter and Sophie were in danger and should be protected.

"I could come up with you." Hunter said, pulling her close.

"You have enough to do here." Sophie argued, pushing him away.

Hunter turned to pick up a small wooden case, about the size of a shoebox. He pressed it into Sophie's hands. "Now, the protective amulets will work best in the furthest four-"

"Corners of the house, and as many doorways and windows as they'll cover," Sophie finished impatiently, taking the heavy box. "James has already drilled me on this."

"I know, I'm sorry," Hunter apologised. Suddenly interrupted by the sharp blast of a car horn outside. Well, here was her taxi, come to take her to the station. "I'll miss you," he said seriously.

"Good," Sophie replied, finally deigning to smile and kiss him lightly before lugging her stuff to the waiting car. She opened the door then stopped, turning to look at Hunter with those fierce eyes. She hesitated, as though she wanted to say something, but in the end just frowned and got into the car.

Hunter watched as the taxi pulled away down the gravelled courtyard and then off down the long drive. Sophie was right, there was work to do, and she had been trained well over the past six months, she'd be ok.

James was waiting in the library, and it was easy to see he was annoyed. Hunter couldn't blame him, it must have been awkward working around Hunter and Sophie lately.

"She gone?" James asked gruffly.

"Yes. Anything to report?"

"Nothing new." James sighed, "All authoritative figures in Britain are under MMC security, America and Europe are following suit. Russia's still not on board."

James handed Hunter some papers. "As for our own work, a name popped up. Sara Murray, she was the 1940s Shadow Witch. Born 1916 in North England, died 1945. No known descendants. Sorry it's nothing useful."

Hunter flicked through the papers, taking in only a few words. What was the point? So far, being better informed had not helped them against the witches. What was the Shadow Witch waiting for?

"Never mind," Hunter muttered. "When are we next on duty?"

"Thursday. We're on rota along with John Ward for seven days on Downing Street," James replied.

"Right." That was better, being out there, even if they weren't prepared. "But, James, this time no swearing at every politician you meet."

## Chapter Sixteen

It was nine o'clock in the evening, outside it was dark and miserable. Inside the building, the empty corridors were dimly lit by the glowing exit signs. The Council staff that were on night-shift were tucked away in little rooms, with no idea anything out of the ordinary would occur.

The light flickered and the shadows began to move, sliding across the plastic floors and twisting up into a physical being. The female figure was dressed entirely in black, a heavy hood pulled up, completely shadowing the face from view. The witch walked through every defence and protection as though they did not exist, and the guards were not alerted to her presence. She let herself into an empty office with a gloved hand. On the glass door, bold letters spelt out 'Bound Witch Office'. The witch swept past the empty desks to a door at the back of the room. It was locked, but the witch had taken the pains of procuring the key, there was a faint click as it unlocked.

Beyond the doorway, a short series of steps led to the floor of a long dark room, with the faint gleam of metal shelves that stretched into the darkness. The witch knelt down and pressed her hand to the concrete floor, a crack of pale light appeared, then ran the distance of the room, criss-crossing and lighting the bottom rows of a hundred shelves.

Everywhere there were amulets and stones, each containing the essence of power from every bound witch of the past 150 years. All irretrievable, irreversible - unless you had the key.

The witch-hunters had been greedy and naïve in keeping these amulets - did they think they could use the stolen magic of witches somehow? Or had they never found a way to truly destroy them? It didn't matter either way.

The witch took out a bronze dagger. The security of this place was pathetic. The MMC had thought themselves safe, they had thought themselves very clever indeed. There was only one key in the world and they'd given its secret location to one trusted member of the Council.

Did they really think this was protection enough against the Shadow Witch and her followers? It had taken a while to track down, but the key, the bronze dagger, was hers.

The witch knelt down again and drove the dagger on the throbbing light of the crack with all her strength.

For a moment nothing happened, then the light flashed red and flared up from the floor, sparking and spitting. The light touched one amulet, then another, they all cracked with a piercing scream until the room vibrated with the sound of a thousand broken vessels.

Beneath the shadow of her hood, the witch smiled. All of her bound kin were free - let's see how the MMC would handle the mass uprising of all the quiet little witches locked up together in prisons in their hundreds.

The witch retrieved the dagger, her trophy, and turned to leave, her job was done. The only thing left was to leave her signature.

The Shadow Witch held her arms out, and felt a familiar rumble as her magic built up. With an almighty blast it was released, throwing aside concrete, brick and metal. The entire wing of the building was rubble, and the Shadow Witch was nowhere to be found.

## Chapter Seventeen

The world was turned upside down. There were worldwide reports of mass breakouts from high security prisons. There were attacks on MMC headquarters and strongholds. The general public were driven into fear at the orchestrated and sudden violence, they struggled to explain it, grasping wildly at terrorism, or even more wildly, witchcraft as inexplicable occurrences happened in every town and city in the British Isles.

Hunter and James were dragged from sleep by an emergency phone call. The witch-hunter on the other end could hardly remain calm enough to pass on the message - the impossible had happened, a witch had managed to get into and destroy the MMC headquarters and now all bound witches in the UK were re-empowered. They acted in an organised manner, which meant they must have been planning this for a while.

Hunter and James raced to reinforce the nearest prison for witchkind. James drove, as Hunter's senses violently sparked with the strength of magic that almost deafened him. Both were nervously aware of the enormity of what lay ahead.

The big grey compound was alight with fires and the glow of spells and illusions. The injured witch-hunters were being pulled back to relative safety, while the survivors fought desperately to keep the witches contained.

Hunter and James ran into the fray without a second thought. All about them, witch-hunters were firing into a half-illusion crowd of witches. Magic was flying erratically in every direction, spells to distract, spells to burn, spells to kill.

A burning block of stone suddenly flew into a dense area of witch-hunters, and there was screaming mixed with the thunder of collision. Hunter pulled James out of the way of flying debris.

"Get the injured to safety," Hunter shouted over the noise.

James nodded and headed into the bloody and broken mess. He wasn't a coward, but all 1st gens had their uses away from the actual battle.

Hunter turned back to the front. A black shadow was rippling and spreading over the ground towards them with an incredible speed. Hunter's sharp eyes broke through the haze to see hundreds of oversized spiders scuttling towards them.

"Spiders. Knives." Hunter shouted down the line.

The other witch-hunters didn't hesitate but pulled out long knives (and one or two swords). The wave of arachnids hit. Hunter slashed through the first wave with quick and deadly accuracy, no time to feel fear of the dog-sized spiders.

To his right he could see a witch-hunter fall to the powerful venom, and the spiders broke through to the second line. But he didn't have time to think about it, as more and more of the creatures scuttled on and Hunter fought to keep cutting them down.

More gun-shots rang out from the far wing of the witch-hunters, and the plague of spiders began to abate as their creators were killed. They had a brief chance to catch their breath, but Hunter noticed the thinning of the witch-hunter lines as casualties were pulled back.

They needed a miracle.

Everything got quieter, stifled and slowed. The world got darker, a darkness that even Hunter's eyes couldn't pierce. Hunter's heart pounded with fear as he felt a familiar rhythm to the blanket of magic. The Shadow Witch, it had to be.

There was a voice, muffled and just beyond hearing. Then everything switched back to normal.

The noise and the cold returned. Hunter looked about, trying to find an answer for what just happened, but the other witch-hunters appeared not to have noticed, or even been affected by the odd period.

A drop of cold water hit Hunter's face and he looked up. The previously clear night sky now rolled with thick, ominous clouds, tinged with colour. A storm was coming unnaturally fast.

Shouts rose up from the witch-hunters, bringing Hunter's attention back to the fight. Like an organised force, the witches threw out a thousand vicious illusions that swooped towards the witch-hunters.

There was a crack of thunder across the sky just as the wave of illusions hit. The line of tired witch-hunters wavered, and lesser gens attempted to fight the incorporeal monsters. With his highly trained senses, Hunter saw through the mass of illusion and saw the witches run away into a growing black shadow. His heart pounded again as they just vanished. That was impossible, witches couldn't physically disappear or transport themselves. The Shadow Witch. It was the only explanation.

Hunter snapped to as screams and shouts rose again from the ranks. He went to move but suddenly felt a stinging pain across his shoulder. He saw blood start to trickle from a shallow cut. Hunter looked up briefly. The storm clouds seethed and boiled and suddenly thousands of shards of ice were pelting down into the witch-hunters, cutting, slicing, blinding. The wind picked up, driving the sharp pieces harder against them as they started to run in every direction, slipping on the ground as it turned white beneath their feet, chased by the ice.

## Chapter Eighteen

It was a sad dawn. Half of the witch-hunters had been killed, the rest were sporting various degrees of injury. No one had escaped unscathed. Word filtered through of similar results across the country. The MMC was in tatters.

Astley Manor had been converted into a makeshift headquarters for the MMC. After all, it was famous for housing and protecting seven generations of witch-hunters. No one wanted to face the fact that no protection had yet stopped the Shadow Witch.

Hunter limped through the busy rooms, noting that everyone was bruised, and sporting cuts and bloody bandages. But they were alive. That's what counted. They'd given some of the rooms over to casualties and the doctors and nurses they'd dragged in. Others had been designated as control and communication for the remaining rabble of MMC staff and witch-hunters.

Hunter was looking for someone in particular. James had come into his own over the past few hours, fielding calls, making arrangements for medical care, and keeping track of everyone.

Hunter found him as soon as he got chance to. "James, I still haven't been able to get in touch with Sophie."

It was true, since returning to Astley Manor that morning they had been trying to locate every witch-hunter - even 1st gens. Hunter had been trying Sophie's mobile and her mum's number all morning, both without success. In the present climate, and with Sophie's recent run-in with the Shadow Witch, this was very worrying.

James checked his watch. "You're right, there should've been contact by now. I'll have a couple o' witch-hunters up there swing by her mum's, check it out."

A witch-hunter came up, interrupting them. "Mr Astley, we've managed to track the Shadow Witch's movements."

Oh yes, even when James was the most competent person in the room, because it was his house and he was famously a 7th gen, everyone turned to Hunter as their general in this time of war.

"Go on then, give us the summary."

The witch-hunter shuffled his papers nervously, obviously too dependent on coffee. "The Shadow Witch struck us, er, the UK headquarters first. Then every European and the two African divisions within the next three hours. They report similar outbreaks.

"Then when night hit America, the Shadow Witch attacked their MMC, then Canada, Mexico, each South American division.

"We've warned the eastern MMCs, and Australia. But what they'll be able to do..." The witch-hunter finished, then stood there somewhat awkwardly.

"It seems impossible - one witch hitting every country in the world in 24 hours, and still being able to attack us back at the prison." James muttered. "How though?"

"Did you never wonder how Father Christmas did it?" Hunter asked bitterly, taking out his frustration on those around him. "It's a Shadow Witch, remember, magic without limits. I think she is very much capable of disappearing from one place and reappearing in another. And I think she can move others too - back at the prison I saw the witches retreating into a shadow and vanishing. And remember what Steve said - that the shadows grew and wrapped around when they took..." Hunter broke off, but after a deep breath continued. "That's how she was able to get into Steve's house, the MMC, how she took over Sophie - all those amulets, wards, protections are nothing to her. Because she can become nothing."

When Hunter finished, his pulse raced with the excitement of the revelation. Wait, excitement, shouldn't it be fear? But, whatever, he knew he was right, he had to be.

"But, if nowt can stop her, she could attack here." James voiced, trying to sound calm.

"No, I don't think so." Hunter replied, then hesitated, glancing at the witch-hunter that still hovered with them. "At any rate, they'll have to find us first. Can you check on the PM and royal family?"

The witch-hunter jumped with caffeine-heightened nerves. "We managed to relocate them before the witches hit London."

Hunter frowned, the man really didn't get the hint. "Then go help organising our forces."

They watched the man slink off. "Well?" James asked quietly.

Hunter led off to a rare quiet spot in the house, James fell into step beside him.

"I think Astley Manor is safe." Hunter confided in a quiet voice. "After all, Old George was linked with the last Shadow, and the Manor was never attacked, even after he eliminated her. I think the house has had more protections built in than anywhere else - the stones for instance. The fact that no witch has ever attacked the Manor."

"And you couldn't say this in front of t'other bloke?" James asked, completely unsure of why his friend was being so secretive.

Hunter shrugged. "There's something going on around us that I don't understand, and I have a feeling it's something that's no good. Something the MMC won't like, even if it aids us." Hunter shook his head, he didn't know how to describe it. "Besides, I don't want to raise false hope, I don't want the witch-hunters thinking they are safe, now that they are here."

*****

The next few hours passed in a haze of activity and breaking news - none of it good.  Australia fell, despite the positioning of a small army at their MMC headquarters.  Japan fell; China; Russia; India - with the witch-hunters nearly completely destroyed.

Reports came in from the battles that were still going on, with varying degrees of failure.  But one thing was becoming clear, for some unknown reason, even when the witches were winning against the witch-hunters, they all pulled back like obedient troops and disappeared.

Which meant that this was only a brief calm and something worse was in store.

*****

"Astley!"  A 5th gen witch-hunter called out.  Hunter struggled to remember the man's name as he walked over.

Short bloke, looked about fifty, had the same stubborn air about him as old Brian had.  Anthony Marks, that was it.

"I've just had the Americans on the phone.  They're blaming us for the worldwide uprising of bound witches."

"What?"

Marks grimaced.  "They claim that we failed in our duty to protect the Key."

"That's ridiculous." Hunter replied, angry now at their American cousins. "The key could have been anywhere in the world, in the deepest jungle, or buried in Antarctica for all we know. How can they blame us?"

"Because somehow their Council knew where it was. It was placed under heavy protection with an English member of the MMC - Mrs Charlotte King."

"What?" Hunter's voice came out louder than he'd meant, several people looked up at the shout. But Charlotte, his Charlotte? He couldn't believe that she had never told him. But then, if she'd confided in him, Hunter would never have allowed her to take on the role of Key Keeper, it would make her a target for every witch - it had made her a target. The Shadow Witch, had she known and planned all this.

"Hunter."

Hunter looked up at the witch-hunter, but it wasn't he that had spoken. James came up behind him.

"Hunter, Sophie's missing. I've just had a call from a couple of our guys. They went to her mum's house in the Lake District, neither Sophie or Bev were there. They said there was no sign of a struggle or foul play."

Hunter had feared that this would happen, he'd been expecting it, he realised. He was tied to the Shadow Witch, and on top of all the violence and chaos, she was systematically attacking him where it hurt most.

"Where are you going?" James demanded as Hunter marched off.

"Where do you think? I'm going up there," Hunter replied, pulling on a coat and checking for car keys.

"Hunter, you can't. They might be waiting for you," James reasoned, then stopped, realising that particular argument wouldn't stop him. "Let some other witch-hunters go up and trace them."

Hunter looked at James ruefully. "I'm not sending anyone anywhere that I wouldn't go first. Besides, no one can feel the traces of magic better than me."

James grabbed his arm to stop him leaving, Hunter tried to shrug him off and got the surprise of mild James throwing him with some force back down the hall.

"Look, I know you're a bloody hero, we all do," James said angrily. "But it's tough shit, because right now you're the only man that can lead us. Sending people into difficult situations and trusting them is part of leadership. Get used to it."

The two best friends stood facing one another in silence.

"Don't try to compare this James," Hunter eventually spoke. "Because I'm not going to let the Shadow take Sophie, and I'm the only one that can bring her back."

As he said it Hunter knew that it was the truth, it wasn't just his ego, he actually believed that he could bring her back alive.

"Nothing you can do or say will stop me, James. I'm going, and I'd prefer not to have to break your nose to get there."

At first it seemed as though James wasn't going to move, but then he stepped aside, grabbing his own coat.

"No, you're not coming. It's too dangerous, and I need someone in charge of this place," Hunter argued immediately.

"Shut up, or we will fight. Someone's gotta keep you out of trouble. Besides, next to the rest of the witch-hunters here, I'm a useless 1st gen. Let's go."

## Chapter Nineteen

It took them less than ten minutes to hand over control to the trustworthy 5$^{th}$ gen Marks; and to be in the Land Rover for a long drive north.

The roads were almost empty. The world had been shook by fear, a state of emergency had been announced and everyone stayed at home while official-types tried to recreate normality.

The two men drove non-stop to the Lake District in silence. Once or twice James attempted to engage Hunter in conversation, having the opinion that Hunter knew more than he'd let on. But Hunter remained in stony silence, paying full attention to the roads as they hurtled down them.

It was an early winter's evening and they were driving in near darkness now, the headlights cutting through the black countryside. Eventually they were driving down the familiar winding roads that led to the edge of Keswick. They were almost holding their breath as they turned the final bend to look on Bev Murphy's cottage.

Everything looked quiet and untouched. They kitted up and made their way down the path to the front door. It was unlocked, and when Hunter opened it, inside it was dark and silent. Hunter paused, but he couldn't feel any magic in the area.

He clicked the hall light on and the two men went into the familiar, modern interior of Bev's cottage. They did a quick sweep of the rooms. They were all empty, with no indication of where Mrs Murphy and her daughter were. The last witch-hunters to stop by had been right, there was no sign of anything happening.

Perhaps, perhaps Sophie and her mum had been out, and had either been taken or caught up in the fights. But Hunter fought back the fear of these mental images, he needed to stay focussed.

James was on the house phone to Astley Manor, clocking in and picking up any new reports. Hunter busied himself by going over the house again. By the front and back door he saw the amulets that he had given Sophie only a few days ago.

Hunter hesitated. Something pricked his senses. It was so faint that he could hardly feel it. He turned on the spot, then began to move slowly in different directions, even pressing up against the walls to try and find the source of the magic. But wherever he went, the magic got neither stronger nor weaker.

"James," Hunter called out uncertainly.

Suddenly he staggered, unbalanced, and the lights flickered and then snapped off.

Hunter waited, but couldn't sense anything else. He stumbled about the hallway, trying to find the light switch. Finally he felt it, he flicked the switch several times, but nothing happened.

"Hunter!" There was a crash and some strong swearing from James as he tripped over lord knows what in the dark. "Hunter, the phone's dead."

Hunter frowned, felt in his pocket for his mobile and pulled it out. The screen still glowed, but there was no signal.

By this time James had pulled out his torch and made his way to Hunter. "What do you think it is? Ambush? I knew we were walking into a trap."

"Shut up a minute," Hunter replied. In the silence, nothing disturbed his senses. "I can't sense anything."

"You mean there's no witches in waiting?" Asked James hopefully.

"No, I mean I can't sense anything. At all. There's no trace or residue. That wasn't magic." Hunter replied, knowing it sounded ridiculous. He didn't know how to explain it. He somehow knew that the earlier hint of magic was responsible, but the spell hadn't been performed here.

"The street lights are out." James mentioned, looking out the window onto an unlit world. "Why would witches knock out the power grid for the Lake District?"

"My honest opinion?" Hunter asked as James turned back to him. "I think it is part of something bigger. We need to get back to the Manor." He paused, pulling out his own torch, adding a little more light to the dark house. "Sweep the house for any clues Sophie might have left, then we go."

They kept together this time, twin beams of light flickering over every surface in a quick assessment of the cottage. It helped fight the fear of the incomprehensible happenings, to think, to move, to concentrate.

They'd just come out of Sophie's room after a thorough search, but finding nothing. Hunter stopped in the hall, he thought he heard, or sensed, a third person breathing. It was such a small sound, only half-heard that he wondered if it were his desperate imagination.

He flashed his torch down the corridor, but it was empty. About to confirm it as a trick of his nerves, Hunter felt his heart contract as the torchlight that touched the walls dimmed and became indistinct. It was as though a black fog was inside the house. As though the shadows were growing.

"James." His voice was strangled.

"What is it?" James asked in a returning whisper, coming back to him. But stared at the darkness with a sudden understanding.

"This is Hunter Astley of the Malleus Maleficarum Council," Hunter called out steadily. "We are here to demand the safe return of Sophie and Beverley Murphy."

Hunter drew his gun, holding it low. James kept close behind and silently followed suit.

There was an echo of humourless laughter within the confines of his own mind. Hunter frowned, not overly disconcerted, witches seemed to enjoy whispering directly into the mind as a means of terrorising victims and witch-hunters alike.

"You have no authority over me, Astley." The words cut into his mind, eerily with the effect of his own voice. "But I am glad to have found a way to gain your undivided attention."

Hunter glanced over to James, wondering if he too heard voices. But it was impossible to read his expression in the dimmed torchlight.

"If you want to see them again, come."

Hunter wondered at the command. He stared into the shadows that suddenly expanded, then stopped just in front of them. It was so persuasively solid, that Hunter had to stop himself from reaching out to touch the darkness.

"The Shadow Witch wants me," he said simply to James, and stepped.

If he'd been asked how he knew what to do, he couldn't have answered, in fact, the little voice of sense in Hunter's head was screaming at him as he stepped into the all-consuming darkness. It was warmer than he'd expected, and the shadows clamped onto him with a certain softness, muffling sound and blocking light, with all the effect of being wrapped in a huge black duvet.

The darkness faded to grey, and Hunter felt solid ground beneath his feet and cold air in his lungs again. He looked about, he quickly figured he was in an empty room. There was a dark window, a wooden door and a bare wooden floor, all lit by a single yellow bulb.

"Well, that was an experience."

Hunter span round, in utter shock to find James standing behind him. "No James, you shouldn't be here. Go back now."

"I go where you go, remember." James answered with a sorry shake of his head. "Besides, I think it was a one-way trip."

Hunter paused, suddenly paying more attention to their predicament. Hunter no longer had his torch in his hand - wait, hell, he no longer had his gun, knives, kit bag. His hands patted down his body, feeling the unnatural absence of weapons. Then his hand flew to his throat. Yes, there was still the metal chain and the old dog tags. Not that that was much comfort at the moment.

Another look around the bare room and Hunter noticed the lack of shadows. Whatever path had been opened was now well and truly closed.

James seemed oddly calm, accepting whatever nightmare he'd entered with courage. "Well, we've confirmed that the Shadow Witch can transport herself and others. Although I think I managed to gatecrash this one."

"Yeah, well, let's hope it's to our advantage," Hunter replied, pacing the room. He walked up to the window, it was large enough to admit a person if they could just open it. He pressed his hand against the cold pane - he could feel the rhythm of magic expertly woven over the glass and its frame. Even if they could break through the spell and smash the window, several iron bars prevented escape.

Not out the window then.

Hunter went to the door. Here there were no spells to keep them in, instead there was a heavy oak door with lock, and probably bolted from the other side.

"We stuck here?" James asked mildly.

"Looks like," Hunter replied, equally calmed by the knowledge that they couldn't actively do anything.

"Jolly good. How long do you think it'll be before-"

James broke off as there was the sound of a key in the lock. "Ah, perfect timing," he grumbled.

The thick wooden door opened and a woman stepped in. She took one (rather shocked) look at James and went out again, the door locked behind her.

"Short but sweet. Do you think they'll send us home now?" joked James.

They didn't have long to wait before she returned, this time with company. Half a dozen male and female witches came into the room. They took their cue from the original woman and surrounded the two witch-hunters.

"Which of you is George Astley VII?" The woman asked.

"I am." James piped up before Hunter had a chance to speak.

"Shut up with your Spartacus routine. I am George Astley, and I shall prove it if you doubt me," Hunter responded, defiance in his voice and steel in his gaze. "I want to see Sophie Murphy. Now."

The woman-witch smiled, almost bristling with the joy of having power over these defenceless witch-hunters. "You are in no position to be making demands, Astley. You will do precisely what the Shadow Witch commands, and see only those she allows."

The witch nodded to her companions who stepped forward and roughly seized the men's arms, yanking them back. Hunter felt the cold touch of metal against his skin and the soft click as his wrists were handcuffed behind his back. He forced himself not to struggle or fight back, as much as his nerves screamed for action.

"Are the cuffs really necessary?" he asked, for the sake of asking.

"Let's just say we can't take too many precautions, where you are concerned," the witch replied curtly, then turned to lead the way out of the door.

Hunter and James were pushed into step, the witches always holding them, surrounding them.

"Hmm, I remember the last time I wore handcuffs - you remember Dervla?" James started prattling.

"James, I don't think this is the time for that particular story."

## Chapter Twenty

They walked silently along a well-lit corridor. With the thick carpet beneath their feet and passing expensive cabinets and paintings it looked like they'd been brought to a very posh house, maybe even a manor. Hunter didn't know what to make of it, but he could hardly blame the Shadow Witch for wanting a luxurious set-up.

The lead witch opened a set of double doors, looking back at the prisoners with a poisonous smile.

They were taken into a large room. Black curtains were pulled across the large windows, the room lit with an ostentatious chandelier. There were long tables arranged in a horseshoe. Sitting around the table were at least twenty witches, looking very much like a civilised council - which was probably down to the suits that the majority were wearing, although the burn marks were not common in most boardrooms. All heads turned at the entrance of the witch-hunters.

Hunter could almost see the magical aura that bristled threateningly, at the same time he read the victorious feeling in their shining faces and quickened breath.

"Ladies and gentlemen. George Astley VII, as promised." A quiet female voice spoke, barely above a whisper.

Hunter looked at the speaker, sitting in a position of authority at the top table. She was the only one to wear a cloak, the dark material oddly mobile about her tall figure, the heavy hood filled with impenetrable shadow. Finally, they were face to face with the infamous Shadow Witch.

Hunter gritted his teeth against the whole irritating stereotype of the situation.

"But you are not supposed to be here." The Shadow Witch said softly, raising a pale hand to indicate James.

"Yeah, sorry 'bout that," replied James daringly.

The whole room scowled at him, but let him be. They waited to follow the lead of the Shadow Witch.

"You wanted me, you got me," Hunter spoke up, "Now, I will only ask once. Give Sophie back to me."

The Shadow Witch stood up suddenly, and every eye was on her. "She is already here."

The Shadow reached up, and slowly slid the hood back, the dark shadow thinning to reveal the haughty beauty of Sophie Murphy.

Hunter felt a physical blow at this revelation and he heard James gasp behind him.

"Release her," Hunter breathed, his voice barely audible.

The Shadow Witch gently shook her head, "Not this time, Astley."

Hunter dared to look her directly in the eye. Her eyes... they were not clouded like the last time, instead they shone with familiar gold-flecked hazel depths.

The Shadow Witch smiled. "It's all over. The witchkind have won, the hunters are destroyed. There is no longer a need for disguise. So look, Astley, on the face that brought your downfall and curse your every mistake."

"No, you're lying." Hunter stood, heart pounding. It was all a trick, the Shadow Witch must have something yet to gain by possessing Sophie again.

There was a titter of laughter and scornful muttering broke out amongst the present witches. They were silenced with a single motion from the Shadow Witch.

"Why do I need to lie, Astley?" she asked innocently, "I have achieved my every desire. I have returned my fellow witches to their former glory. In fact, you join us on the night of our greatest achievement yet, perhaps you noticed a little power loss."

Neither witch-hunter responded, but the Shadow Witch didn't seem to expect an answer and continued.

"Yes, you can thank the Americans. Their MMC has been experimenting - unwisely, I might add - with magic stolen from witches. They managed to create a weapon that we would never have dreamt of. Used in a specific way, it could be directed to permanently disrupt every piece of technology, and with a little magical aid from me, it worked on a global scale."

Hunter thought back to the blackout, how he'd perceived something magical, yet distant and untouchable.

"Er, you expect us to believe that? 'Cos unless I'm mistaken this place is blazing with electric lights." James said suddenly, looking up at the gaudy chandelier.

The surrounding witches bristled at this, but the Shadow Witch just looked at him curiously.

A wave of power swept the room, blasting James off his feet and dashing him against the wall. He hit it with a sickening thud and slid to the floor. Hunter went to move, but strong hands held him in place.

"He doesn't learn, does he?" The Shadow Witch said coldly. "Tell him when he regains consciousness that there are more than enough witches here to light a few bulbs."

"Why - why destroy technology?" Hunter asked, struggling not to react.

"Because the Witches Council wished it so." The Shadow Witch replied willingly, looking at the faces of her associates. "The witches of today possess as much magic as they ever did. So why do we no longer inspire fear and worship, why are we ridiculed and cast aside as myth and fantasy? Because of the 'general ignorant public' as you so perfectly put it once. They are all so clever, so all-knowing, swallowing every story the MMC gives them.

181

"We have tried for generations to gain power politically, by mortal means. Yet witch-hunters persecuted all witchkind. So our new aim was to take the world all in one go.

"Imagine the fear and chaos when suddenly the world was plunged into darkness. There was no communication, suddenly no answers. It is in this chasm of disorder that those blessed with magic can step into their rightful roles above the ignorant and powerless masses."

There was a general cheer and a spatter of applause as the Shadow Witch finished speaking, the group of witches high on their recent victory.

"You're mad," Hunter muttered.

The Shadow Witch looked at him with an achingly familiar coldness. "Mad or not, we have won Astley."

"So what, you brought me here to do the clichéd gloat before killing me? Or do I get the option of watching you destroy everything first."

"I destroy only to create the world how it was meant to be. God Himself would do the same, if he existed." The Shadow Witch replied with cool logic, then half-smiled. "You have no idea how good it is to say all this openly after months of pretence and hiding around you."

She broke off, suddenly seeming to notice the rest of the room, hanging on her every word. "Take them away, I shall see them tomorrow."

She sat down and the two witch-hunters' audience was over. Hunter was shoved out of the room, while the unconscious James was carried by two male witches.

And it was back to the dull, empty room.

Hunter had been pacing the room for a while, when James finally groaned and opened his eyes.

"Wha' 'appened?" he asked groggily.

"The Shadow Witch threw you against a wall. How many fingers do you see?" Hunter peered at him carefully.

"Three."

"Close enough." Hunter helped him sit up, his back against the wall.

"Next time, remind me to stay quiet around her," James said, gingerly rubbing the back of his head. "Oh, they took off the handcuffs, that's nice."

Hunter sighed and sat down next to him.

"How bad is it?" James asked.

"Bad," Hunter admitted, thinking it an understatement.

"What are the witches planning to do?"

"Take over the world."

"Oh, that is bad. Did the Shadow Witch give a bad guy speech?"

"Oh yes, very impressive and clichéd - shame you missed it."

The two friends fell silent. It was James that spoke first, and this time he was much more serious.

"What about Sophie? You don't really think that she is the Shadow Witch - surely she's just possessing her again."

Hunter sat, looking quietly into space. The Shadow Witch was an evil entity. He wanted so much to believe that she was tricking them, that perhaps she needed to possess someone as the only way of taking physical form. That would mean that Sophie, his Sophie, was innocent and had loved him.

But there had been something about the witch, the clarity of her eyes and something else that made cold dread stab deep into his soul.

"I don't know, I honestly don't know," Hunter finally replied.

## Chapter Twenty-one

The black window lightened to the cold grey of predawn. Hunter shifted, feeling stiff from his uncomfortable sitting position on the wooden floor. His eyes were gritty and he was tired - he and James had taken turns to keep watch while the other slept.

Hunter got up with a groan and looked out the window. It was still too dark to see anything. He traced the window again, reading the magic - it had a skill and a sense of logic that he'd not seen before. He knew that it was the Shadow Witch's handiwork. And that only she could break it.

"Is it tomorrow?" James asked with a yawn.

"I guess so." Hunter replied, looking at his watch out of habit. He frowned, the bloody expensive thing had stopped. It was stuck on a minute after 8pm.

They heard the bolt being drawn on the door and James jumped to his feet. The door opened and the same witch from last night came in with two male witches, standing with her like a pair of heavies.

"The Shadow Witch wants to see you," she said.

They both stepped forward, sharing the opinion that they might as well get it over with.

"No. Just you," she said, pointing at Hunter.

Her companions walked up to Hunter and, in a repeat of last night, he was abruptly handcuffed behind his back.

"Handcuffs again? You never told me Sophie was the kinky sort."

"James, I've already told you, not now," Hunter said, before being roughly pushed out of the room.

As the door was closed and locked behind him, he heard James call out, "What, no brekkie?"

As inappropriate as the situation was, Hunter couldn't help but smile. He'd never appreciated more, James' determination to have one last joke before death claimed them. He shouldn't be here, Hunter shouldn't have let him, he should have stayed in the relative safety of Astley Manor.

But Hunter never did have any control over James. It was maddening, how Hunter could walk into a room of the best witch-hunters and wave his 7th gen status, and they would usually respect, follow, obey etc.

But James? From the day he'd met him, James seemed to purposefully ignore and wind Hunter up, yet he always did the right thing.

Down the fancy corridor again, he was taken further this time. The lead witch finally stopped and knocked on a door.

A few moments passed, and then the door was opened from the inside. Hunter recoiled in shock at the sight of the woman who held it open for them. Tall, graceful with dark brown hair and an ageless beauty. Beverley Murphy.

"Bev?" He gasped.

Bev turned her eyes to the floor, looking so meek compared to the fierce, but friendly mum they'd visited. The older woman muttered her excuses and left, sparing Hunter a single glance. Hunter was left with the idea that she was somehow angry, or perhaps just disappointed with him.

The door closed, shutting Bev from sight as she hurried down the corridor. Back in the room, Hunter noticed the soft-looking chairs, a roaring fire and a table with breakfast on. Three things that hypnotised him after a cold, uncomfortable night.

"I have brought Astley, ma'am." The lead witch said with a note of pride, and Hunter had the impression that it was all she could do not to bow or curtsy to the Shadow Witch.

Sophie was sitting close to the fire and turned her head to look at the group. "Bring him here."

Hunter was (unnecessarily) shoved towards Sophie. Sophie looked him over with those cold, analytical eyes of hers.

"You may go," she said, dismissing the others.

The witches hesitated, and again it was the female witch that spoke, but hesitantly, as though she feared offending Sophie, or revealing some ignorance.

"Please, ma'am - he - surely it is safer for us to stay."

Sophie glared at the witch, an aura of power rising threateningly. "I can manage Astley. Now go."

The witch frowned, unconvinced, but obediently left the room, with her heavies in tow.

The Shadow Witch, or Sophie, which should she now be known by? She waited for the other witches to leave then set her eyes solidly on Hunter, her expression lightening with a familiarity that seemed sinful now.

"You look terrible," she said with a frown, looking at the bruises and half-healed cuts that decorated any skin on show.

"I ran into a few of your new friends at the prison," Hunter answered irritably.

"I'd hardly call them friends. As for new - I have known them a lot longer than I've known you."

"Saw your mother outside. Is she part of your little army too?" Hunter spat bitterly.

"My mother is here of her own free will. She had every right to be a part of this. And before you ask, yes, she is a witch, although her powers were bound before she was born. Now, will you join me for breakfast - a cup of coffee at least?" Sophie asked, as though everything were normal.

"It's kind of difficult to hold a cup behind my back," Hunter replied pointedly.

"Oh, of course." She rose from her seat in a graceful movement, stepping next to him at once.

Tired as he was, Hunter forced himself to remember that this was the Shadow Witch as he breathed in that familiar, enticing scent. There was a faint click and the cuffs fell away from his wrists.

"I'm sorry, but I'm sure you understand, it's for my colleagues' safety," Sophie said gently, then returned to her seat with a smile.

"One question," Hunter said, his voice rough.

"Just one?"

"For now."

Sophie watched him carefully. "Ok then. Why don't you sit down?"

Hunter sat slowly, hating the soft, comfy seat and having an odd déjà vu of when Sophie had first come to Astley Manor seeking his help. "Answer me truthfully, is Sophie, my Sophie, the Shadow Witch?"

She sighed. "Your Sophie is, and always has been, the Shadow Witch."

Hunter took a deep breath, and sat silently.

Sophie watched him with cool curiosity. "Help yourself to coffee and toast - if you're in the mood for something else, I'm sure I can magic it up."

Hunter ignored her dry humour. He looked suspiciously at the pot of coffee, but didn't take any, wary of poison and potions. He turned his gaze back to Sophie, she was still cold, beautiful, intelligent - but everything had changed. She was now the enemy. The Shadow Witch, against whom they all fought. The woman responsible for plunging the world into chaos and darkness.

"Come now, Hunter," Sophie said bitterly. "You're not going to sulk, are you?"

"Why?"

"Why what?"

Hunter gazed unflinchingly at the young woman. "Everything. Why did you pretend to be a hunter? Why am I here? Why haven't you killed me yet?"

And more, unspoken questions hung tangibly in the air, why did you get so close, was it all a pretence?

"Everything is a lot to tell, Hunter, you've already accused me of gloating, why should I indulge you?" Sophie sat, quite unperturbed, casually continuing with her breakfast.

"Back in Italy, I saved you from witches. Was that planned?" Hunter persevered.

Sophie seemed to be measuring him up, then suddenly smiled more openly than Hunter had ever seen. "You really want to know, to hear every devious detail?"

"Tell me."

"Ok. I wanted to learn from my natural enemies, the best way I possibly could. So I planned a little sacrifice with me as the innocent victim, then I would use my ample negotiating skills to become a witch-hunter - what better way to learn about the MMC than to be part of it.

"I chose to stage it in Venice, back in the 'old country' one could say, it would all be safer and easier to pull in an Italian witch-hunter, away from my roots. Which is where you messed things up." Her eyes flicked up on him, she looked half-amused, half-angry. "You, of all witch-hunters, Astley, so closely tied to my family. You turned up and were my hero, slaying the evil witches and rescuing me from certain death. I was so angry that I could have killed you there and then, and blown everything we'd worked towards."

"So what, you allowed other witches to get killed to make the scene more believable?" Hunter asked, disgusted.

"You really think me that cruel, that ambitious as to sacrifice my own kin?" Sophie asked with a soft shake of her head. "No. Although we were not short of volunteers. The male you killed was a bewitched wiccan, there for you to get your blood quota. The two females were witches, under orders to make sure it all ran smoothly and then to surrender. After all, they knew they'd be free to fight again."

Hunter was suddenly hit with an array of memory - his own research into a wiccan found with witches, the arson attack, Charlotte commenting on the increase in bound witches... they all knew they would get released and restored.

"What, should I applaud you for your ingenuity?" Hunter asked bitterly, feeling a wave of nausea and shame. He'd fallen for it, every part. He'd killed a human - a wiccan albeit, but human all the same. He felt sick.

"No," Sophie mused. "But I would like to thank you, for pulling strings with the Council and getting me a place as a 1st gen."

"Brian. You killed him." It wasn't a question, the truth was hovering there in front of Hunter.

Sophie shrugged, "It was very frustrating. For one exciting moment I thought you'd take me on - I would have the chance to fool the best there was, it was thrilling. But perhaps it was best that I went to Brian first, his senses were so unevolved compared to yours, I didn't have to worry about slipping up as much.

"He taught me a lot, even though he was a condescending sexist bastard. I often struggled to stay calm when he treated me as less than nothing - I, the greatest witch for almost a century. But I was willing to put up with it.

"Then I found out that Brian was doing work and research on the side, he'd made links with the unusual events that we had not completely covered. He was getting too close and needed removing, along with all his work. I have a certain skill for pure destruction, as you saw at his house. I had to make sure that everything was eradicated, I didn't want the MMC knowing that a Shadow had risen. Not until I was ready."

Hunter couldn't help but smile ruefully, good old Brian, the grumpy old sod would've been pleased to be so inconvenient. "You slipped up, we got the info and discovered the return of the Shadow Witch."

She nodded in fair agreement, but her smile didn't fade. "Yes, and thank you again, this time for taking me in. I admit that at first I wanted to destroy all the information, but that would draw unnecessary attention. So instead I spent the next week, on your orders, searching for anything important in the notes and reports, then secretly removing anything that was too obvious. It was rather interesting to learn about what I was from a witch-hunter's perspective."

"We still found out though." Hunter argued, remembering vividly the night after Brian's memorial service.

"I underestimated you," Sophie admitted. "But it didn't matter in the end, you learnt nothing that would endanger me and your MMC refused to act. In fact, it worked out better than I could have ever dreamt - I got to see what protection and weapons you had to use against me. It was pitiful."

"Then let me guess, you left as soon as possible and struck and now you've won," Hunter said bitterly, not wanting to hear more of her gloating confessions, yet desperate for answers.

"As soon as possible," Sophie repeated under her breath with a hint of regret that surprised Hunter.

"So, now you've revealed all your evil doings, are you going to cackle madly and kill me?"

"Evil?" Sophie asked, almost sadly. "Do you really think me evil? You think I've done this to hurt you? I have done what is right for my kind - freeing them from persecution by you and your bloodthirsty Council.

You - you demand that we witches do not live by our nature, that we should be vilified because we are something more than you. What gives you and the MMC the right to impose morals and judgement on what you don't understand?"

Hunter didn't meet her eye, he didn't want to get into a moral debate, especially with someone that presented their facts so civilly.

"You didn't answer my question," he reminded her.

Sophie hesitated. "They want you dead. The others, the witches' council. They fear that I grew too close to you and they want proof that I can kill the best the witch-hunters have. They argue that your death will be the ultimate blow for the remnants of the MMC and will further boost our morale and power."

She paused, and when she spoke again it was with carefully restrained anger, her hazel eyes blazing. "And how I long to kill you Astley. How I have cursed you every day of my life for what your family took from the witchkind, from me."

Again, hesitation. Sophie shrugged, the anger fading quickly as she fell back into her cushioned chair. "But I'm not going to kill you. Instead I'm going to offer you something. To join the witches, instead of fighting them. Together we can create a greatness that will eclipse everything that has gone before. We will build the world to our standard. You would be a ruler, answering to no one - except me of course."

Hunter sat in a state of shock. He definitely hadn't been expecting that. To never have to await MMC approval again, to switch to the winning side, to have Sophie with him. It was incredibly tempting. His mouth was dry as he responded.

"Ah, no, I'm going to turn you down because I don't want to sell my soul. Besides, I don't think your witchy pals would agree to a witch-hunter in their ranks, especially when you say they're all so keen to see me dead."

Sophie smiled at his goading reply, which was a rather disconcerting reaction.

"Have you ever heard of the Benandanti?" She suddenly asked.

Hunter scowled, but finally agreed to reply. "No."

"Let me tell you a little story."

"Another one?" Hunter snorted.

Sophie ignored him and started to speak again. "In Friuli, Italy, there was a small peasant group called the Benandanti. They lived simply enough, with one special feature, they protected themselves and those around them from witches, and had been doing so for centuries. This was a very elite group, one couldn't just join the Benandanti, one had to be born into the clan. They were special, bred to repel witches; they were stronger, faster, could even detect magic being used. They could travel far distances in a blink, they could change the world around them to chase off, or even destroy witches.

"They lived peaceful little lives with surrounding villages. But they were discovered by witch-hunters and, in self-reflection saw that they had become what they most feared. Witches."

Hunter frowned, an uneasy feeling about where this was heading.

"Don't you see? Did you never wonder what the witch-hunter generations were leading to? What you are, as a 7th gen?" Sophie asked, excited now, leaning forward with her eyes glittering. "Just think of the possibilities."

Hunter let the flickering fire in the grate distract him, watching the sparks from the logs. Stronger, faster. He knew that he was gifted - an unheard of 7th gen. No one knew what he was capable of. But having magic?

"Nice theory. But I think you're a couple of generations early. I'm no witch."

"Have you ever tried?" Sophie questioned. "It didn't come easily to me when my powers were first awoken. It took months to gain control. And I know it is you, I have seen you use magic with my own eyes."

This made Hunter pay attention. "What? I've never-"

"Hallowe'en." Sophie interrupted. "At the church. I had the key from Charlotte and every piece of information I needed, so pulled in our best witches to finish off you and James - you had both outlived your uses. Then I felt something I didn't understand, a huge build-up of magic that I didn't recognise. And such a release to rival even my own. Then I saw amongst the rubble and bodies you, standing alone and untouched with an aura of magic that outclassed so many."

Hallowe'en. Hunter had tried not to think about it, it was too painful. But it all came rushing back with amazing clarity. Charlotte lying there as though asleep, then out of the silence James alerting him to the witches. There had been so many, by all logic he should have been killed that night. But Hunter had been so distraught that at the time he had acted without thinking. Afterwards he had not thought about it, the eerie lack of magic as the church blew apart. He and James had assumed that it was the work of the Shadow Witch.

"You're lying."

"No Hunter, I'm not," Sophie replied softly.

"Do the others know this?"

"No." Sophie admitted. "They think you're just a normal witch-hunter that I like to toy with. Please, Hunter, this is the only way – it's either live like a god with me, or be killed by the others."

Hunter watched her carefully, she wasn't threatening him, it was more of a warning. But what did she care if he lived or died, after all he was just a plaything.

"And what about James?"

"What about him?" Sophie said impatiently, not wanting to get off topic. "His fate was sealed when he came here, I couldn't save him if I wanted to. Besides, he's not important, you are."

Hunter looked at her with disbelief. How could he ever have thought he could love her. This amoral women that had murdered Brian, Charlotte, and would throw away James' life so easily.

"Promise you'll think on it. Just remember that I can only keep you safe for a day at the most."

Sophie looked away to the door and Hunter felt a ripple of magic in the air, he tensed, but nothing happened.

"Relax, I've just called the others. They'll take you back to your room unharmed," Sophie said, standing up.

Hunter heard the click of the door handle and he sprang from his seat. Unarmed and outnumbered, this was still his best chance.

As though reading his desperate thoughts Sophie rushed forward and grabbed him, with a surprising force she turned him towards her and suddenly kissed him.

Along with her familiar lips and warm breath, something passed to Hunter. He staggered away, his limbs suddenly leaden and shaking. He looked up to Sophie, her face swimming.

"For your own good, Astley." She said quietly.

And then he blacked out.

## Chapter Twenty-two

When Hunter came to, he was lying on a hard, wooden floor. He felt very odd, the aching pain from his last injuries felt distant, like they didn't belong to him. He groaned slightly from a pounding headache - he could feel that.

"Hunter? You awake?"

Hunter opened his eyes a fraction to see the blurry image of James hovering over him.

"Yeah," he grunted.

"Thank god. When they brought you in, I thought - but it doesn't matter now."

Hunter fully opened his eyes and his gaze returned to its usual sharpness. Daylight poured in through the one sealed window. "How long have I been out?"

"A few hours." James replied, helping him to sit up.

Hunter recoiled. "Jesus, what happened?"

James winced. His eyes were dark and puffy, promising some stunning bruises, dry blood spotted beneath a newly broken nose, and from the way he held himself it looked like a cracked rib or two.

"The witches. They've been forbidden from using any magic on us, so they delighted in practising more mortal forms of violence. Don't worry, it looks worse than it is." James tried to take a deep breath, but grunted with pain. "Actually, scratch that."

He stood, collecting himself for a few minutes. Hunter could only imagine how the witches had taken it all out on poor James while he was away being breakfasted by their boss.

"Come on then, tell us everything. It'll help distract from the pain," James said, half hopeful.

Hunter repeated everything Sophie had revealed, interrupted frequently by James' questions which he did his best to answer.

James gave a low whistle after he'd finished. "You know, if we get out of this alive, we'll never live this down. The Shadow Witch living under our noses the whole time."

Hunter could only give a twisted smile in agreement, he was feeling guilty over the whole affair.

"Did Sophie say why we're here? I mean, they haven't killed us yet."

Oh dear. Hunter didn't want to mention this to anyone, if it was true, the MMC would have to treat him as a witch; or he'd have to do the decent thing and end his own life - neither were appealing. But telling James was different, surely. He could trust years of friendship.

"Have you heard of the Benandanti?"

"Sure, an Italian pagan group of anti-witches that developed powers of their own and were ultimately prosecuted for it. Why?" James reeled off, making Hunter just a little jealous of his infinite knowledge.

"Sophie thinks I might be one. Or something similar." Hunter confessed.

That silenced James. Hunter didn't underestimate James' intelligence he'd probably figured out everything Hunter hadn't said.

*****

The witches brought food and drink for them that evening, and although wary, they were too hungry and thirsty to care about poison.

That night they took shifts again keeping watch. The first few hours passed by without incidence, and Hunter nudged James awake, stifling a yawn as he did so. He waited for his friend to be entirely conscious before allowing himself to drift off. Before he had a chance to sleep though, James grabbed his arm painfully tight.

Reopening his eyes, Hunter saw across the room the light from the bulb was fading, darkness and shadow forming.

"Sophie?" Hunter tried to call, but his voice came out a whisper.

A figure stepped out of the shadows, tall and gracefully slender with long brown hair and a beautiful but older face than they were expecting.

"Bev?"

The two guys sat stunned, and more than a tad confused.

She motioned for them to be quiet, while pulling a large bag off her back.

"I've come to get you out of here," she whispered.

"But... how? Sophie sealed this place, only she can undo it." Hunter whispered back.

Bev frowned in a familiar way. "I am her mother and I know a few tricks. I've borrowed her powers, Sophie is drugged and none the wiser."

So a loving, caring mother, Hunter thought, but had the wisdom to say none of it aloud.

"But how?" He repeated. "And why should we trust you?"

"Why should you trust me? How many other witches are here offering to help you escape?" Bev asked hurriedly. "As for how, Sara Murray was my grandmother. I could have been the next Shadow Witch, but I didn't want it. Yet I can siphon off a little of my daughter's powers now. I may only be able to do this once, though."

Sara Murray, the previous Shadow Witch that Old George had killed in the 1940s.

"Sara Murray didn't have kids," James whispered.

"She did," Bev replied. "But when she became the Shadow Witch she knew her daughter, my mother, wouldn't be safe. So she bound her powers, and had her adopted, then destroyed all evidence of her existence. Please understand Sara was a good woman who didn't deserve to be a tool of evil. Who knows what good could have come from her. But Astley killed her and planted a seed of hatred and revenge in the heart of every witch. I tried to protect Sophie from it all, but she took it to heart, carried the promise of revenge as her own burden."

"Why are you telling us all this now?" Hunter asked.

Bev looked away from them and sighed. "I want you to understand why Sophie seems - she has her reasons. But we must be quick."

"We're unarmed and locked up," James hissed.

Bev knelt down and opened the bag. She pulled out two hunting shotguns and two kitchen knives. "The best I could do, I'm sorry. Now, I think I can manage to get you into the grounds."

With an intense look of concentration, the thick shadow rippled along the wall to head height. Without notice, she grabbed them both by the arm and stepped into the darkness.

Again, Hunter felt surrounded by warm nothingness. But it didn't last long. The cold night air hit him hard, he couldn't help but shiver. The night sky was cloudy, and it was hard to see anything. He turned around and only a couple of hundred yards behind him was the shadow of a huge house, with light pouring out of windows.

"I have done what I can," Bev suddenly said. "I have to go back."

"Wait, come with us." Hunter argued, surprising himself with the offer. "There's so much more you could tell us. And to be honest we could do with the help."

Bev didn't reply immediately, but stared back at the house with shining eyes. "Sophie is my daughter. Whatever happens, I have to stand by her. She needs me, or at least she soon will."

If either of the men understood this, they didn't say anything.

"Well, thank you." James finally said awkwardly. "We owe you our lives."

"You owe me nothing." Bev replied. "I didn't do it for you, I did it for Sophie."

Bev turned to a frowning Hunter. "If you were killed, it would destroy her. And she could never kill you herself, for two reasons. Mainly because - as much as she denies it - she loves you, irrevocably. Ah, I must go before they miss me."

"Wait," Hunter said, reaching out. "You said two reasons. What's the second?"

Bev's eyes met his in the dark. "She is pregnant with your child."

And she was gone.

## Chapter Twenty-three

The two men ran into the night, Hunter leading with his sharper sight. They had no idea where they were or where they were heading, only running to get away from that house of witches.

Ahead of them lay only darkness. It was eerie to see the English countryside without the punctuation of lights from roads or villages. But they just kept going, hoping to stumble on some form of civilisation.

Eventually they hit tarmac and followed the road to a sleeping town. The houses sat in absolute shadow, and as they walked past, a couple of dogs stirred and barked, but no one came out to see two men armed with guns and knives walking down the night-time street.

Hunter looked at the cars parked along the roadside. "Can you get one of these running?"

James got closer so his weaker eyes could see the shiny new BMW. "No. But... trust me on this. Come on."

Without explaining himself, James set off down the street, stopping to look at each car. Then, as though making his mind up, he raised his gun and used is to bash in the driver's window. There was a loud shatter of glass.

Hunter frowned at James' choice. An M-reg rustbucket of a Fiesta. A worrying option, because it was essential for them to make it all the way home, however far that might be. "Do you think this one ever worked?"

James used his sleeve to get the worst of the glass off the driver's seat. "Look, I had a lot of time to think when they treated me as a punchbag, at least, thinking helped distract me. I have a theory about their little power cut."

He broke off, pulling out his knife and busying himself under the steering wheel. He suddenly swore and pulled back, sucking his freshly bleeding hand.

"Not the best tool for the job," he admitted. "Anyway, as I was sayin'. The lights and the phone went dead. But not all technology was knocked out - our torches worked, your mobile phone battery still worked, you just didn't have any signal. Hey - you still got your phone?"

Hunter frowned, but rather than try to make sense of James he reached into his pocket. Miraculously his phone was still there.

"Cool, flick up the screen so I can get some light an' see what I'm doing."

Hunter did as directed and held his glowing phone near the dangling wires. James tinkered for a minute and was rewarded by guttural choking, followed by the small engine rumbling to life.

"Well done, now shift over." Hunter said, pushing James over to the passenger seat. He frowned at the wheel, never having driven such a wreck. "But James, you didn't give your theory."

James clipped on his seat belt as Hunter pulled away, the old engine roaring and lights showing up an empty country road.

"Theory? Oh yeah, well they knocked out all the big and complex stuff - even down to your watch. So anything that requires power or radio signal. But very simple technology with its own power source wasn't affected."

"Which is why you wanted the old car?" Hunter said slowly, catching on.

"Yes, less electronics that could go wrong." James replied with a yawn.

*****

As they rattled along empty roads the wind whipped in through the broken window, freezing Hunter to his seat, but keeping him bloody awake. Next to him, James snored lightly. Hunter felt so guilty about what he'd gone through, that he barely felt jealous of him getting some sleep.

He wouldn't have been able to sleep anyway. His body clock told him it was around five or six o'clock in the morning, the world was still dark and silent.

In his mind he lived and relived everything from the moment he'd met Sophie, seeing it all in a new light. She'd played them all perfectly, made Hunter believe that he...

He didn't know when he fell in love with her, it had happened so quickly, yet the realisation had taken weeks to crawl up to him. He remembered her mother, Bev, warning him off - he had assumed she was being an overly protective mum, not trying to save him from - from this. But she had already been too late, he had already been falling under Sophie's spell.

He grimaced at his private thought's choice of word.

Had Sophie cast a spell he hadn't felt? Or slipped a love potion in the many coffees she had brought him? All to blind him from what she was really up to.

'As much as she denies it - she loves you irrevocably.' Bev's words rang again in his ears. He could only hope it was true, that she would never kill him because she loved him.

But... what about her, would he be able to kill her?

Of course, the voice of reason screamed, she was the Shadow Witch and needed to be destroyed. But when Hunter imagined himself standing in front of Sophie and pulling the trigger-

He leant forward, trying to let the road drive out the image. It was only an enchantment, it would wear off. He'd be able to stop thinking about her, get back to normal.

It wasn't long before his spinning thoughts came inevitably to the very disturbing idea that he could be

a witch. Here, alone in the dark (a snoring James didn't count), it seemed scarily possible. Each generation of witch-hunter took them further away from their human roots. Why shouldn't the next step be magic.

Hunter sighed, he hadn't asked for it and didn't want it. But if he was entirely honest with himself, if it turned out that he was strong enough to oppose the Shadow Witch it could only help. Like the anti-witch Benandanti. Only one problem, really, he'd never intentionally used magic and he'd seen how skilled Sophie was.

Hunter leant closer to the windscreen, concentrating on keeping up a decent speed in the old Fiesta as he navigated amongst the cars that had been abandoned by their owners. They must have been travelling at the time of the hit, there were signs of collisions as drivers lost control as their trusty vehicles gave up. Hunter wondered how many had been hurt, and his fears were raised as something caught his eye. He squinted into the dark, not sure what he was seeing. The car's headlights picked up increasingly large chunks of debris across the abandoned motorway.

Hunter pulled up on the side of the road and nudged James awake, before climbing out of the car. In front of them the tarmac was ripped up and the grass bank was a churned mess of mud and metal. Hunter clambered up the short bank with James stumbling behind him. The remnants of an aeroplane crash landed.

"Hunter..." James caught up with him. "Hunter come on, there's nothing we can do."

Hunter ignored him and ran over to the fallen craft, he paused at one of the gaping holes, then ducked inside. He called out, but there was no response. As his eyes adapted to the near-pitch darkness inside, Hunter saw that the plane was empty.

"Is there anyone there?" James asked, standing in the broken gap.

Hunter made his way back out of the plane, taking a deep breath. "No. Whether they survived or not, they've already been moved. But then it has been 34 hours since the hit."

Hunter shuddered and walked slowly back to the car, the little old Fiesta was still running with lights on and doors thrown wide at the bottom of the small slope.

The two friends got back in and set off once more, both silenced by what they'd seen. Both of them could only guess at the extent of the damage done.

*****

There was the thin grey light of a late winter's dawn as they finally turned out of the village of Little Hanting and onto the Astley estate. Right on cue, James groaned and woke up.

"Home?" He muttered.

"Yes, two minutes," Hunter replied shortly, starting to feel tired again as the familiar ground flicked by.

They were driving straight up towards the Manor when a man stepped into their headlights, blocking the way. He waved at them to stop. More commanding was the gun he aimed at the windscreen.

210

"Who goes there?" The man shouted as the car stopped.

Hunter leaned out, "Hunter Astley, 7th gen; and James Bennett, 1st gen."

The witch-hunter didn't move or lower his weapon. "Do you have proof of identity?"

"Proof?" Hunter gasped, not in the mood for this. "Look, this is my bloody house, so if you don't mind shifting."

The witch-hunter looked uncertain, but a second armed figure moved in the darkness to their right. He began to walk warily towards them, then stopped. "Mr Astley? You're back. Let him pass, Dan."

The first man moved aside and Hunter got the rattling vehicle down the remaining short length of drive to the front of the Manor. The Fiesta stuttered to a rolling stop as the engine packed in with perfect timing.

Hunter and James went into the wonderfully familiar Manor, and were immediately surrounded by witch-hunters.

"Mr Astley, thank god. We feared the worst when we lost contact." Anthony Marks, the 5th gen that had been in charge in their absence now stepped forward.

The worst? Yes, the worst had happened, Hunter thought sleepily. His bed was upstairs, warm and comfortable.

"Communications have been down for two days, we've been struggling to track down other witch-hunters, trying to re-establish links with police and army forces."

"Yes, the Shadow Witch knocked out everything technological. James'll explain later," Hunter said, struggling to pay attention. "Right now, we have to prepare for an attack. The Shadow Witch is coming. As soon as she finds out that we've escaped she'll know where to find us. She could be here at any moment, so we don't have time to lose."

"But the Manor is safe against her."

Hunter nodded. "Even if it is, it won't stop her coming as close as possible and forcing us to fight - I think we may have managed to piss her off. Little Hanting. The village, it needs evacuating. Get the villagers as far away as possible, or get them in here if there's room, I don't care."

The surrounding witch-hunters stood there looking far too gormless for Hunter's liking. "Well, go!"

Hunter turned to James who, although still looking a bruised mess, was keen and wide-awake. "I'm going to lie down. Wake me when - when it's time."

## Chapter Twenty-four

Hunter felt like he'd only closed his eyes for ten minutes when he was suddenly shaken awake. His eyes snapped open and he bolted upright. Sitting on his bed was a familiar figure.

"James?" How long have I slept?"

"Um, dunno, 'bout ten minutes." He replied distractedly.

Hunter groaned, but pulled back his covers and started looking for his shoes. "Sophie's here already? I had hoped we'd have more time to prepare."

"What? No, she's not here yet." James replied.

"Then what...?" Hunter frowned at his friend, tempted to push him off the bed, roll over and go back to sleep. "James, you are a pain in the arse. What is this about then?"

James looked down at a book he held in his hands. When he spoke it was in a conspiring whisper. "The

Benandanti. I knew I'd seen info on them in the library, so I went t'find it."

Hunter sighed, but paid attention, his nerves sparking inside him. "Anything useful?"

"Depends," James answered. "I've only flicked through, but it does describe some of their, ah, abilities. Eye witness accounts of Benandanti standing in front of witches: a feeling of a cushioning atmosphere that blocked all use of magic, forcing witches to fight by mortal means."

Now that did sound promising, but Hunter still frowned. "If, if I'm capable of that, would it apply against a Shadow Witch - magic without limits? And does it say how it's done?"

James paused, scanning through the marked pages. Eventually he shrugged. "No, no mention on how. You'll have to work that out alone. As for bein' up against a Shadow, I doubt the Benandanti ever met one."

Hunter stared at the book unseeingly. "Do you think this is how Sophie worked it out?"

"Probably. She had open access to the Astley collection and library," James replied honestly, sharing a portion of the guilt and shame.

"I think we can assume that, even with my questionable abilities, Sophie will be prepared. She'll bring a small army of witches."

James didn't interrupt, but did wonder how Hunter could sound so sure.

"An army of witches." Hunter repeated quietly. "And we have what, fifty witch-hunters?"

"Forty-three," James corrected.

A pitiful number, sure to be crushed. They had personally seen thirty witches just in that house. Hunter didn't doubt that Sophie could double or triple that within hours. Hopefully she'll be impatient and come with only a handful of witches, rather than patiently mustering more.

"Why don't we build our own army?" James suddenly asked.

"What, with forty-three witch-hunters? Or are you suggesting that the villagers of Little Hanting join in?"

James ignored his sarcasm. "No, I mean the actual army. They've gotta be on alert after the comms went down. If we get some troops here, we'll be winning on numbers."

"James!" Hunter cut into his enthusiasm. "First of all, they aren't witch-hunters."

"But they are trained," James argued.

"And numbers might not help against a Shadow," Hunter persevered.

"But they'll help, 'specially if you knock out the magic."

"And the closest base is nearly two hours away. Even if someone set off now, by the time the troops were kitted and mobilised, they couldn't get back here for what, five hours. It could be too late."

James shook his head, opening his book again. "Look, the Benandanti could travel in the blink of an eye. You could go tell them. Even if you can't transport them with you, it'll cut two hours off the time."

"James, I am not Benandanti!" Hunter argued. Yes, things would all work out if he did have all these powers, but all he felt was bloody useless at this point.

"Just try, what's the harm?"

The harm? He could be accused of witchcraft and cast out by the witch-hunters when they needed him most.

"Even if I can, it might not be soon enough. What if she attacks while I'm away?"

"Then you will survive to fight again and find a way to destroy the Shadow Witch," James answered seriously. "Hunter, try, you're our only hope."

"I don't know how," Hunter continued to argue.

"Concentrate, I guess," James said encouragingly. "Ah, if it works, I'll keep an eye on the others. I think its best that they don't know 'bout this til necessary."

Hunter stood up and instinctively closed his eyes. Feeling rather stupid he twisted his mind, trying to feel something, tingly, or warm and smothered like the Shadow.

"This is never going to work." He muttered, opening his eyes.

"Just keep concentrating." James suggested. "Picture yourself on base."

Hunter took a deep breath and closed his eyes again. He remembered visiting the base when he'd first joined the MMC, he'd been to see the general, an open-minded, trustworthy man who'd been made aware of the witch threat and occasionally passed on witch-sightings and helped with some of the cover-ups.

Hunter could see clearly the general's office, with the desk and walls decorated with photos and certificates. It all seemed out of reach.

"I feel stupid." He muttered.

There was a faint click and a man's voice came from behind him.

"Raise your hands and turn slowly to face me."

Hunter's eyes flew open, instead of his navy bedroom there were cream walls. He lifted his hands and span quickly to see the familiar office.

There was the crack of a pistol as the man fired at his hasty movements. Hunter's eyes widened with fear and his heart leapt... but nothing hit him. He looked down, confused. A shining bullet hovered just inches from his chest. Stopped dead.

"Huh. That's useful." Hunter reached out to touch it. His finger brushed the metal, before he swore and snapped his hand back from the heat. Hunter frowned and stared at the little thing, then it dropped onto the floor.

Hunter looked up. There was a shocked middle-aged man standing behind a desk, holding a gun with impressive steadiness. It had been a few years, but he was still recognisable.

"General Hayworth." Hunter stepped towards him, hesitating as he realised that he was barefoot. Bother, next time he'd have to remember to be fully dressed before attempting transporting himself.

"Sir, my name's Hunter Astley, from the Malleus Maleficarum Council. We met a few years ago."

"Astley? Astley, yes I remember." The general glanced down at his bare feet with a frown. "We thought only witches appeared out of nowhere."

The general half-shrugged and lowered his gun, obviously thinking he'd given enough explanation for having fired at the sudden appearance of a person in his office.

"It's a long story," Hunter admitted. "But I don't have time to explain everything. We need your help. We know where the Shadow Witch will strike next, we just need an army to face her."

The door of the office suddenly opened and a younger man burst in. He stopped, staring at the General and witch-hunter. "General, I, ah, heard a gunshot."

"It's nothing, Dawkins, return to your post," General Hayworth replied calmly.

The young man, obedient but confused, backed out of the office, closing the door behind him.

"Sit down, Astley." The general said, motioning to a chair in front of his desk. "As I was saying to Marks before the phones went down, the army doesn't take orders from your MMC. In times of chaos we have to follow the proper channels, but-"

"But we don't have time to follow the proper channels," Hunter interrupted with frustration. "The Shadow Witch could attack at any time."

"Will you let me finish, Mr Astley?" The General said patiently. "But, I understand that things have changed. Those that wrote the rules could not have predicted this. I also understand that the MMC may well know best. Yet my men are not trained to fight witches."

"You can't choose your enemies," Hunter reasoned.

"No, but we are better defending than fighting," The general mused. "Your Council does know best, I suppose. We will rally to your aid."

General Hayworth walked over to the door and opened it. "Sergeant!"

Dawkins reappeared obediently. "Yes, General?"

"I want the men armed and ready to leave in thirty minutes. Then return here."

Dawkins blinked with surprise. "Yes General."

The sergeant disappeared down the corridor to pass on the order.

"Thank you, General," Hunter said as the general closed the door and returned to his seat.

"Don't thank me yet," he replied. "You have half an hour to explain this to me."

## Chapter Twenty-five

Hunter decided that relaying his story was the least he could do for this good man. Hunter went over a lot, but not everything, he left out most of his mistakes, aware as he did so that he was leaving gaping holes in his story.

The General just sat there, building up a better understanding of their enemy. He raised a brow whenever he felt that Hunter was being evasive or less than honest, but said nothing until he'd finished.

"I agree that we need to get to Little Hanting as soon as possible. That travel 'in a blink' thing you did, can you take others?"

"I - I don't know." Hunter replied truthfully. "I haven't really had time to work it out."

The General nodded and stood up, going to his office door once more. "Dawkins!"

The mild young man popped in for the third time.

"Yes General?"

"I'm going to inspect the troops, Dawkins. You are going to help Mr Astley with a little experiment." He turned to Hunter. "Astley, I want a definite answer in fifteen minutes."

General Hayworth exited the office, leaving Hunter with a now very pale Dawkins.

"Experiment?" The sergeant asked weakly.

Hunter hesitated. He could try explaining it to the fellow, but he'd be likelier to scare him rather than reassure him. The idea of taking another person along brought up a lot of questions for Hunter. What if it didn't work? Or worse, what if it only partially worked and half of poor Dawkins got left behind?

"Just... stand still and bear with me." Hunter suggested, shutting out his worries.

Hunter reached out and held the sergeant's arm tightly. He shut his eyes and pictured home. He took a deep breath and opened his eyes.

Damn, still the office. Dawkins stood tense and still beside him.

Hunter frowned, concentrate, concentrate. Home, his room with the oak panelling, the cream and navy sheets and curtains, the table with the-

Hunter felt Dawkins snatch away from him and feared the worst. His eyes snapped open. The first thing he saw was his bedroom; the second was a very whole and very pale Dawkins.

"Yes!" Hunter shouted. Finally, something had gone right.

"How do you feel? All in one piece? Dizzy?" Hunter asked the sergeant rapidly.

Dawkins gazed about him open-mouthed and wide-eyed. "What was...? Ah, yes sir, fine sir. A little dizzy I guess."

"Great." Hunter replied. "Ok, I've got to get back to General Hayworth, you might as well stay here. Go downstairs, find someone called James Bennett. Tell him Hunter is going to bring the army."

Hunter broke off. He didn't know how many men would be coming, but no part of his Manor would hold even a hundred, he'd struggle to get even fifty into any room.

"Tell James they'll be in Little Hanting's church hall within the hour."

Hunter was getting excited now. Death and war beckoned to them, but now they had a chance. He stood tall and closed his eyes to go back to the General's office, then broke off.

"Shoes, shoes..." He pulled them out from under his bed and hopped about as he pulled them on. He grabbed his coat and closed his eyes.

When he opened them he was in General Hayworth's office. This blinking thing was getting easier. Hunter felt hope burn bright in his chest as he left the office to find the General.

Outside, a hundred soldiers stood, kitted and ready, silent and waiting. Hunter could see a single figure moving up and down the ranks, the general inspecting the troops.

Hunter ran up, aware of the many eyes that followed him.

General Hayworth took one look at him. "So you were successful?"

Hunter nodded, then couldn't help but smile. He was bristling with the excitement and opportunity of this new ability.

"Well, let's get this over with." The general said. "How do you suggest we go about this? It'll take a while to go one at a time. Can you take several?"

Hunter, buoyed up by recent success was thinking of something a little more effective. "I have an idea. Can we use a wall?"

Without explaining himself, Hunter turned to the nearest building and went up to the side wall that stretched about 10 metres wide. The Shadow Witch had done it with shadows, why shouldn't he be able to do it with what was on hand.

"I figure that if I create and maintain a link you should all be able to, well, to march on through." Hunter tried to sound convincing.

General Hayworth frowned, but sighed. The General was out of his depth where magic was concerned, he'd go along with almost anything at this point. After all, what did they have to lose?

"Very well." He turned to his troops. "Fall in, four abreast. Forward march."

There was the co-ordinated movement of well-trained men. The General halted them in front of the building.

"When you're ready, Astley."

Hunter tried to ignore how very pale and dubious the first four men at the front of the column looked, and placed his hand on the cold brick. Closing his eyes, he did his best to picture the old church hall, without going there himself. Ready, he nodded.

On command the first four stepped and - slammed into the wall. Hunter opened his eyes as about him soldiers laughed with a note of panic.

"Wait, wait, I've got it now, I promise," Hunter said, concentrating so hard it was difficult to get the words out.

The General ordered his men to go again, which they did gingerly, reaching out and finding their hands passing through the solid wall. This caused as much subdued panic as before, but soon the men marched through under the stern eye of their General.

Gradually the court cleared as the troops disappeared. Hunter was sweating with the exertion of keeping the link, he had no idea it would be so hard to concentrate for so long. As the last soldier stepped through, Hunter broke off from the wall and bent over at the knee, his heart pounding and breath panting, a wave of exhaustion came over him as though he'd just ran a bloody marathon. He vaguely thought that he should have made them all drive instead.

"Buck up, Astley," came the general's voice. "You're not done just yet."

Hunter took a deep breath and stood up straight. He dutifully took hold of General Hayworth's arm. One more trip, he'd manage it, he'd have to.

When he opened his eyes, Hunter was surrounded by soldiers beneath the dusty roof of the old village hall. Next to him, General Hayworth looked about business-like, apparently unfazed by the magical journey.

They'd only been there a minute when Sergeant Dawkins and Anthony Marks pushed their way towards them. Hunter didn't like the look on Marks' face, and guessed what was coming. But any unpleasantness was put off by the necessary introductions and briefings.

"… squads are placed beyond Astley Manor, we were just dividing the rest to place about the village," Dawkins reeled off, obviously recovered from his earlier shock.

"We can't thank you enough, General," Marks said.

"We're all on the same side, Mr Marks," General Hayworth replied, brushing aside his thanks. They could be grateful when, and if, they won.

Marks nodded, then finally turned to Hunter. "A word please, Mr Astley."

Oh no, Hunter definitely didn't like the sound of his voice, and followed Marks out of the hall like a naughty schoolboy. He'd just brought them an army, surely that proved he was still one of the good guys, surely they wouldn't damn him as a witch and therefore evil.

Outside it was bitterly cold with a bright sun. Little Hanting had never looked so idyllic on this sharp, clear day. The villagers were gone and the only movement was that of uniformed soldiers and their witch-hunter guides.

Anthony Marks stopped abruptly and turned to Hunter, his eyes blazing. When he spoke, his voice struggled to remain calm. "Well? Are you going to explain what the hell is going on? We're under serious threat from the Shadow Witch - a threat you've seemed to exacerbate, I might add - you disappear and your assistant refuses to say anything. A sergeant from the British Army materialises in the Manor and the Army is in the church hall. This all smacks of magic, Astley."

Hunter couldn't meet Marks' gaze, instead he looked vaguely over his shoulder.

"It's... complicated. Do you know what happens when a 7th gen witch-hunter is created? It turns out that we have evolved to be something more... gifted. Similar to the Benandanti, they were-"

"The Italian anti-witches, yes I know, get on with it," Marks interrupted harshly.

Hunter frowned. Christ, was he the only person not to have heard of them?

"I have some of their abilities, which I've used to bring in the army. We couldn't hope to win without their help. I know this sounds dodgy, but I'm not a witch and I'm still a witch-hunter, still the same guy. When this is all over, we can debate the issue, but right now we don't have time. You just have to trust me."

Hunter watched Marks carefully, but the older witch-hunter gave nothing away with his stern expression.

"You were wrong to hide this from us, Astley." Marks eventually spoke, "How can we wage a war when you are going off on private jaunts with your own aims… What's left of the MMC could prosecute you on that alone. I knew your father, Young, he was a good man, and I'm sure you are too. Just promise me, no more secrets, no hidden agendas."

Hunter nodded. "I promise."

Marks took a deep breath and looked about the empty village. "Well I suppose we best form a council and go over the battle plan."

Without another word, Marks headed off. After a moment or two, Hunter followed, not sure whether or not he should be relieved.

## Chapter Twenty-six

Everyone was on edge as they waited for the attack. But the short winter's day rolled on with no sign of activity. The soldiers and witch-hunters alike grumbled in the cold, and even Hunter began to doubt his assumption that Sophie would come for revenge, for him.

About 4 o' clock that afternoon, the sun dropped to the misty horizon and the world was half-lit in a grey light. Twilight.

"They're coming." Hunter breathed, his hand tightening about the cold handle of his gun

There was a suffocating silence, and a gentle breeze that was oddly warm. In the open space outside the village, figures began to appear, black and solid against the insubstantial evening. There was a throbbing pulse of magic that raised the head of every witch-hunter.

The witches were more than fifty in number, and they bristled with excitement as they marched behind their leader, the Shadow Witch. They came to the edge of the Astley estate and stopped, the magic of the Manor doing its work. None could cross the invisible line without rendering themselves mortal.

In the privacy of every man and woman's mind, a voice echoed an ultimatum.

"Surrender and your lives shall be spared. All we demand is that you turn over Astley. Resist and you die."

Those inside the Manor exchanged grim looks. They did not sacrifice one of their own, nor did they compromise with witches. And upon feeling the hateful magic that brewed, none would trust their lives to the gathered witchkind.

Hunter gazed about the other witch-hunters that stood waiting in the hall for his signal. Their anxious faces lit by flickering firelight - at least they were warmer than those on patrol outside. James, Marks and twenty others, all silently relying on his questionable ability to protect them.

They might all die tonight. But there was no backing down.

Hunter took a deep breath and nodded, no point delaying the inevitable. The twenty fellow witch-hunters scrambled to their feet and followed him out of the warm Manor and into the cold, darkening evening. They marched over the flat ground, directed by that inner sense that detected magic.

There was a crowd of witches awaiting them, all charged with magic and excitement. They shifted so two opposing lines were formed, witches facing witch-hunters, just twenty feet apart, the Astley Estate border between them. The witches outnumbered the witch-hunters three times over.

The Shadow Witch stepped forward closer to the border. Her eyes immediately settled on Hunter. "You have come to give yourself up?"

Her question was answered by the tensing of the line and the metallic click of several guns readying.

"No, I didn't think you'd make it easy," the Shadow Witch said bitterly, a familiar frown creasing her beautiful features. "You can't win. Have your men lay down their weapons and they may live."

"Why don't you come over here and we'll discuss it," Hunter responded, stalling for time while others moved silently into position.

"I don't think so," Sophie replied. "Shall we see how the Astley protection stands up against the destructive power of the Shadow Witch?"

She raised her arms and there was the crackle of immense energy building up. Hunter suddenly saw in a flash the ruins and rubble of Brian Lloyd's house.

A gun discharged as one of the witch-hunters lost his nerve.

"NO!" Hunter barked, snapping back to the present.

The witches stood unfazed, apparently protected from something as insignificant as bullets.

"You can't win," Sophie repeated, her eyes unfocussed as she prepared to release her most destructive magic.

"You won't hurt anyone," Hunter whispered.

With those around him in danger, he let his desire to protect grow. It spread like a blanket over the witches and witch-hunters, regardless of borders. The Shadow Witch either couldn't feel it, or was too absorbed in her own spell to notice. She smiled and released her magic...

Nothing happened.

Sophie frowned, thinking it had been the power of the enchantments of the Manor that had stopped her. But it shouldn't be, she had lived there for months, she knew every defence and how to overcome it. Her eyes found Hunter again and her confusion turned to rage.

"ASTLEY! You utter bastard. How dare you... You weren't..." Sophie spat, her anger boiling over. "I warn you not to do this."

"Too late," Hunter replied quietly.

From the darkness, lines of soldiers and witch-hunters ran forward, aimed and fired.

The gathered witches laughed scornfully as the first shots rang out - for what could harm them in the presence of the Shadow Witch? But the laughter turned to screams of shock and fury and pain as the bullets ripped through, killing and maiming.

As one body, the witches turned to face their attackers, preparing to raise their reliable magic to destroy them. But again nothing happened, they were defenceless against the slaughter.

Sophie span, turned from one scene of tragedy to another as her loyal witches were shot down. They were surrounded, no escape on foot. Sophie tried, and failed, to raise her shadows to get the survivors out. Hunter, this was his doing. No bullet could penetrate her seething aura as she sought him.

Hunter stood firmly on Astley ground, using his Manor's enchantments for protection. Everyone else had gone forward to engage the enemy.

Hunter's eyes were open, but unseeing. He trembled in his stance as he struggled to maintain the block. He was starting to weaken, to slip, magic started to seep through the defences, he had to hold on.

He was vaguely aware of someone approaching. He was unsurprised that it should be Sophie.

"You shouldn't have told me... what I was," he gasped. "Your fault. It's your fault."

"Your magic shall die with you, Astley." Sophie spat, drawing closer, crossing the border that made her powerless.

Hunter shook his head with some difficulty. "You can't kill me."

Sophie hesitated. "Don't be so sure."

There was a flash of metal and movement. Hunter couldn't move fast enough to block the knife that drove into his torso. It felt cold, he realised, before the pain came.

He looked into Sophie's eyes, so close to his, and saw that her anger was gone, replaced by shock that drained the blood from her face.

Hunter felt the protective magic slip and fade, and he crumpled to the ground.

There was more gunfire, closer now.    People continued to scream, but now others were calling his name.

It all grew fainter.

'What do you know, I was wrong,' he thought.

Then the world disappeared.

## Chapter Twenty-seven

Hunter was lying somewhere warm, soft, and familiar. He was comfortable, so he stayed as he was while his mind caught up. Images of an army and a battle flashed behind his eyes, and somewhere the knowledge that he should be dead. Was he?

He was breathing, he could feel his heavy limbs, but not much more. He finally opened his eyes, squinting against the daylight. It looked like his bedroom in the Manor. He sighed, that wasn't his idea of heaven.

There was the sound of someone else in the room, alerted to his consciousness by the sigh.

"Hunter, you're awake. Thank god." The familiar voice was accompanied by a familiar figure hovering over him.

"James, you look terrible." Hunter said, his voice rough.

James grimaced, his face still bore the signs of torture at the hands of the witches. "Thanks mate, nice to see you too. Thought you were never gonna wake up."

"How long have I been out?"

"A couple of days," James replied.

Hunter frowned, then struggled to sit up, noticing the thick bandaging around his midriff and the odd, pain-free, sensation-free feeling. Which he guessed had plenty to do with copious amounts of morphine. Sitting up probably wasn't a good idea.

"What happened?" Hunter asked.

"Sophie stabbed you. You're lucky to be alive."

"I know that." Hunter grimaced. "But what happened in the fight? Sophie, was she..." killed? He couldn't bring himself to say the word.

"Sophie's gone. Not dead, as much as we tried. She ran and vanished. As for the rest, we'd eradicated most of the witches by the time you were attacked. Then there was nowhere for them to go, they were all eliminated, with surprisingly few casualties on our side," James filled in dutifully, still buoyed up on success.

Hunter sat quietly, taking it all in. They'd won, they had slaughtered their enemies. Never had Hunter been upset by the death of witches. So what had changed; was it because he was one? No matter how you phrased it he possessed magic. Or was it because... because he had loved one.

James, sensing that Hunter had a lot on his mind, made a weak excuse and left. Hunter hardly noticed him go, his thoughts were now on Sophie.

With no proof or reason, he had believed Bev when she said that Sophie could not kill him. Yet she had tried, she had meant to, it was only luck that had kept him alive.

Hunter remembered how pale Sophie had looked in that last moment, as if she were sharing his pain. Then she'd fled.

What came next was anyone's guess. Hunter could predict that he and Sophie would be the most hunted people by opposing parties. And neither could exist without seeking to destroy the other.

The future was dark and definitely interesting, and wholly full of possibilities.

And then the truth niggled away in a quiet corner of Hunter's thoughts and heart. He was in love with the woman that would kill him, and she was carrying his child.

Mind the Threefold Law you should, three times bad and three times good.

When misfortune is enow, wear the blue star on thy brow.

True in love ever be, lest thy lover's false to thee.

Eight words the Wiccan Rede fulfill: An ye harm none, do what ye will.

# The Shadow Reigns

## Witch-Hunter 2

### K. S. Marsden

## An insight from our villain

For hundreds of years witches have been persecuted; forced to keep their heads down and conform to laws that we never agreed to. To be a witch is to live a hunted life; to suffer the stupidity and ignorance of those around you, even though you could outclass them with the simplest spell.

I was born to free the witches from oppression. I am the Shadow Witch. I have freed my kin from the so-called justice of the witch-hunters and their Malleus Maleficarum Council. In one night, the world was thrown into chaos, and for once it was the witch-hunters that were forced back.

We followed our victory with a second. We pitched the world into darkness and removed the advantage technology gave our enemies. The new world has already begun, and in this spiralling darkness, those with magic will finally be able to rise above all others.

Then why do I feel guilty? Why do I feel doubt?

Ever since the witches told me of my destiny, when I was thirteen and powerless, I have never felt any doubt in my path. When my powers were awakened seven years later – the witches conducting sacrifices on Hallowe'en to break the ancient spell holding them back – I was even more sure of what lay ahead.

But it is shallow of me to even pretend I do not know the reason that I finally question everything. Him. For years I hated the very name Astley, knowing that they were the witch-hunters that killed Sara Murray, the last Shadow Witch; and all its consequences. I would not be the same if she lived; I would not have to take up this brutal destiny.

I had not planned to fall in love with the current bearer of the name: George "Hunter" Astley. I ignored the attraction at first; whenever he was around, I told myself it was the excitement of playing him for a fool that thrilled me so, not his presence itself. But after months of secretly savouring each glance, each touch, I wanted more. I knew from the beginning that our relationship was doomed; I could not stay with him and soon we would be on the opposite sides of a war. Is it wrong I tried to find a way to keep him with me? If not for my sake, then for our child's?

Not that it mattered. In the end he chose his side, and I chose mine.

I knew that I was expected to kill him when we met again, and I was prepared to do so. I came so close and failed. As my knife got past his guard and cut deep into him, I felt a shock of pain stab through me. It was all I could do to evade his witch-hunters and return home, where I collapsed at my mother's feet.

I have been recovering slowly for a month now. I cannot explain it, there is no physical wound; I can only guess that what was inflicted on him rebounded to me. None of the witches can explain why, but some theorise that the child links us – we can only guess what powers he or she shall inherit.  In which case, if this is true; I shall withdraw as much as possible until it is born and hope the spell breaks.

## Chapter One

Little Hanting was a picturesque village in the English countryside. Quaint bungalows and farmhouses fanned out from the church hall, with its perfectly manicured green in front of it. Not that the grass could be seen; fresh snow had again fallen the previous night, coating everything with a perfect whiteness. All it needed was children with mittens having a snowball fight, and the scene would be idyllic.

But Little Hanting silently suffered. The inhabitants had all been evacuated when the village had been the setting for a decisive battle. Now all the homes lay eerily quiet, save for the ones that had been temporarily taken over by soldiers. They sheltered from the cold and waited – waited for answers and for their next move. They would huddle around the fireplaces, casting glances in the direction of the local manor house.

Hunter drifted in a haze of painkillers and nightmares. He saw the flash of the knife a hundred times, Sophie's hazel eyes, and the pain that tore through them both.

The scene would change, and it was Hunter's first day at University, and Brian was coming to tell him that his father was dead. Charlotte should be here to comfort him. Where was Charlotte?

When Hunter was awake... lucid was hardly applicable. He lay in his bed, staring at the high ceiling, with all its familiar cracks. Or he would turn his head to observe the dark drapes that someone opened and closed with the passing of day and night. Huh, probably the same someone that fed the fire in his bedroom to stop it being too cold.

Not that Hunter cared, the cold was numbing, and combined with the morphine, opium – whatever drug they managed to dredge up, it was a good haze. It stopped him having to think as much. Or at least, it kept his thoughts strangely disconnected from himself.

So, this was what it was like to wallow. Hunter had never been much of a wallower: not when the witches had killed his father; Brian; Charlotte... Hunter was a witch-hunter, as they all had been. It was accepted as fact that you would lose friends and family, that you yourself would be a target. To be a part of the Malleus Maleficarum Council, to protect the people from the violence of witches was to invite that violence onto oneself.

But the pain of the past was nothing compared to what he was putting off feeling now. It wasn't as if Sophie had died – although Hunter wished she had. No, it had been worse. The woman he loved had turned out to be the Shadow Witch. It sickened him to think of the nights spent together, the caresses, the half-asleep conversations. And the days when he had never doubted his trust in her as a colleague and a friend. How could she have acted so innocently and seemed so honest when she had just killed his old mentor and closest friend?

Before, grief had only driven him harder to fight back against witches. Now Hunter felt confusion over his life's work in eradicating witches. He had fallen in love with one, and now she carried his child; and Hunter had recently discovered his own magic-like abilities.

Hunter had thought Sophie mad, and looking for a loophole when she had sworn that he was different from his fellow witch-hunters.

It was something that Hunter, and every MMC worldwide took for granted that, in a family of witch-hunters, each generation would become more adept. By the 3rd gen they could perceive spells being cast, and were immune to some magic; as well as being stronger and faster. As an unheard of 7th gen, Hunter Astley had been revered by the MMC. How little everyone (including himself) knew that he would evolve into a magic-wielder.

Which left him with the question: should he use his new talents in this war; or should he copy the fabled Benandanti and kill himself for being a witch?

He had no answers, and the thoughts just swirled incessantly in his head while he tried to numb them.

The only thing that broke the cycle of monotonous thought was mealtimes. Usually someone left a coffee on his bedside table in a morning, although chances were that it would still be sitting there, stone-cold, by midday. And then someone would bring him some lunch.

This irritating someone came in the form of Hunter's best friend, James Bennett. He was a pretty average guy – average height, average brown hair and eyes. He was a little more intelligent than most. But this 1st gen witch-hunter was the truest and bravest person that Hunter knew. Oh, and James also had an invaluable knack for putting up with Hunter on a daily basis. Hunter couldn't remember a time when James hadn't been there for him.

Which included bringing him meals while Hunter was injured, it seemed. Hunter was never very hungry and would have left the unappetising food if James hadn't stayed. Not that James was watching and making sure his friend actually ate something. No, it just so happened that mealtimes coincided with James having found something interesting in the Astley library, and brought up one old book or another to get Hunter's opinion.

Twice a day. Every day.

Today was a little different. James sat with the typical book on his lap, and the non-typical red pointy hat on his head.

Hunter shot him a few looks, but today James was staying quiet. Hunter dutifully finished his soup and the last of the bread, pointedly putting the bowl aside to state it was empty.

"Why?" Hunter asked simply.

"Why what?" James returned innocently, looking up from his book.

Hunter sighed. "The hat?"

"Oh, that. I thought it'd annoy your mum." James replied with a shrug. "And it's my birthday. One of the soldiers found this and thought it wa' funny."

That made Hunter sit up and pay attention. "What? It's the end of January already? Oh shit, I'm sorry James, I forgot. It's just... it's been a blur, I lost track."

James shrugged again, but Hunter noticed the mischievous glint in his eye. "Hey, it's fine. We've all been preoccupied with somethin' a bit bigger than my birthday. Besides, I distinctly remember you saying that if you forgot my birthday, I could have that bottle of '82 Chateau Gruard Larose that's in your cellar."

"Oh, I said that, did I?" Hunter tried to keep a straight face.

"Yep, absolutely." James replied sincerely, pushing the reading glasses back up his nose.

"Ok, so I get the hat. What's with the glasses?"

James looked a little surprised at the question. "Dunno, I just find it easier reading with them. Maybe the witches did some damage when they beat the crap out of me. Or maybe I should just admit I'm getting old."

Hunter snorted. "Twenty-five is not old. Oh, sorry, twenty-six now. Happy Birthday."

"I thought they made me look more intelligent." James continued.

"Well you couldn't look any less so." Hunter returned quickly.

James looked ready to throw his book at him, but seemed to think better of it. Instead, he got to his feet.

"Well, you seem back on form, Hunter. So perhaps you'll think about getting your arse out of bed. We've a war to plan. And we could do with your help in keeping Mrs Astley in check."

Hunter groaned, more at the mention of his mother than impending war.

"And you might want to shave." James added, eyeing the scruffy attempt of a beard his face was sporting. "Or not. I could be the handsome one, as well as the smart one."

With a chuckle, James turned and finally left.

## Chapter Two

Hunter finally made it downstairs that afternoon, cleaned up, dressed, and looking much more his old self. The beard was gone, and his black hair combed into something resembling control. He'd managed to find a clean jumper and jeans, and looked presentable.

He was greeted by a warm chorus from a crowd of people in what used to be the dining room. Astley Manor had been in his family for nearly two hundred years; the image of extravagant Georgian architecture, it was comfort and luxury for the line of Astley witch-hunters. And the house had its own secrets, no witch could enter the Manor without their powers being stripped; no magic could be used in the extensive estate. The only exception being Hunter's anti-magic talents.

Which made it the perfect emergency home for the Malleus Maleficarum Council after the witches had destroyed their base. After their initial defeat, witch-hunters had trickled into Astley Manor, seeking safety, and planning their next attack.

Hunter was more than happy to open his home to his allies, but even the vast Astley Manor was not big enough to house them all, especially after the additional influx of soldiers for the last battle. Those that could not be made comfortable in the Manor stayed in the village and travelled in every day to learn of any progress made.

The over-crowding of the Manor was not universally welcomed. One in particular loathed it - Mrs Astley. Hunter's mother had always had very strict rules over protocol and etiquette, and this flooding of the Manor with all sorts insulted her deeply. The last straw was the dining room. After the witch-hunter hooligans converted that into a war room, Mrs Astley resigned to her rooms and refused to come out unless absolutely necessary.

At this very moment, about a dozen people sat around the large table, most of them nursing a fresh mug of tea. The two most senior stood up at Hunter's appearance.

"Mr Astley, it's good to see you up and about." General Hayworth smiled as he looked over Hunter, a touch of concern in his blue eyes.

"Thank you, General." Hunter replied, trying to hide how breathless he was from just coming downstairs. "My nurse has cleared me for duty again."

"Huh. Well, sit down before you fall down, Astley." 5th gen Anthony Marks said with a shake of his head.

Hunter smiled bitterly, embarrassed at how weak his body had become. He obediently took an empty seat and looked expectantly towards the two older men. "So, can you bring me up-to-date?"

General Hayworth returned to his chair and started first. "It's been three weeks since the battle, the witches must know about it by now and are giving us a wide berth. Communications are still down, so it's hard to get any real idea of what they're doing at this time. They are probably doing the same as us – assessing the situation and strengthening their forces."

"And how are our forces?"

Anthony Marks sighed. "Again, with no way of getting in touch quickly, we can only guess. Aside from the forty-seven witch-hunters that were in the battle, we've had others making their way here over the weeks. There's nearly a hundred now. We've housed them in Little Hanting alongside the soldiers. We have been sending out patrols to try and find more, but it's a slow process."

"This lack of technology is a pain in the arse." Hayworth interjected.

"That would be why they did it." Hunter muttered. He remembered Sophie gloating over the blanket of magic that disrupted most technology. Hunter and his colleagues had been thrown back into the dark ages, while Sophie and her witches had their magic to get by and make faster progress.

Marks frowned at Hunter's comment, but brushed over it. "We've started sourcing generators, most of them are in working condition, we've just got to keep an eye on fuel usage. Luckily the Manor was built before our dependency on technology, so no problems here. As for the MMC... the Council is destroyed. As the most senior member, I have officially assumed control. Until someone more senior steps up, of course."

Hunter grew uncomfortable under Marks' steady gaze. It was crazy – Anthony Marks was twice Hunter's age; Hunter had grown up hearing nothing but positive accounts of this witch-hunter from both his father and his trainer, Brian Lloyd. But because Hunter had been born an unheard of 7th gen, that automatically gave him superiority. All he had to do was claim it.

"I'm not going to do that, Mr Marks. I never wanted to lead."

General Hayworth chuckled at his comment. "Who the hell does want to take responsibility and lead? Especially now the world's screwed up." He looked over at Marks. "Looks like you're stuck with the gig, Anthony. Now, pay up."

Sighing, Anthony shifted in his seat and pulled a crumpled note out of his pocket, handing it reluctantly to Hayworth. Around the table there were a few more subtle exchanges.

"We had a little wager going on. Had to amuse ourselves somehow, waiting for you to pop up again." Hayworth grinned as he explained to Hunter.

Hunter wasn't sure how he felt about this amusement at his expense, but he let it slide. "I

255

wouldn't trust myself to make the right decisions. I'm too close to this."

The room fell silent, and Hunter wondered how much these men knew. James knew everything, having gone right through it all with Hunter. The General knew an edited version that Hunter had shared with him before the battle, but how much more had he learnt? And how much did the others know, or guess?

"Fine." Marks finally said. "Well as your Head of Council, I need to know how soon you can start that travelling in a blink again. It would be a monumental advantage to have you cover so much ground. It'd also mean we can save our fuel rations for something more important."

Hunter stared down at the table, his 'blinking' still felt like a dirty secret. But at least these guys weren't preparing to burn him at the stake. Yet. "I need to build my strength again. I will keep you informed on my progress, sir."

"Good. You go do that. And, ah…" Marks pulled a face, which told Hunter exactly what he was going to bring up next. "Perhaps you should go see if you can placate your mother. She doesn't seem too chuffed to have us here."

Hunter nodded and, finding no reasonable excuse for putting it off until later, he promptly made his way to his mother's rooms.

Mrs Astley had a whole wing to herself, with a bedroom, office, drawing room and a large bathroom all for her private use. She liked having the space to herself, especially when her son insisted on bringing all sorts of waifs and strays to stay. Her space was even more important to her now that her home had been invaded and militarised.

Hunter rarely came to this part of the house. His mother was not his favourite person, he'd had very few reasons over the years to seek out her company. Especially as Mrs Astley would often pop up and interfere, whether she was welcome, or not.

Hunter turned the handle to her main room, pushing the door open and giving it a couple of sharp knocks to announce his presence. He walked into the expensively furnished drawing room, looking for his mad ol- dear, loving mother.

"Mother?" He called out.

"George, how many times must I tell you that it is common decency to wait for permission to enter." The familiar sharp tones snapped.

Hunter turned to see his mother, and their butler Charles, sitting by the window, playing chess.

"One of these days you will walk in while I am indisposed, and I daresay the embarrassment will be punishment enough." Mrs Astley added, her fingers hovering over a black rook, then finally making her move.

"I'm sorry, mother. I won't do it again." Hunter replied, wincing slightly at the image she provided.

"Of course, you'll do it again, you never learn from your mistakes – just like your father."

Ah yes, there it was. Hunter wondered if they could make it through a single conversation without his mother bringing up George "Young" Astley. Hunter worshipped the memory of his late father. His mother still blamed Young for ruining her life. She often wished he had left her to be sacrificed by witches, rather than give her this life. How many times had Hunter heard that over the years?

"I haven't seen you for a month, why have you been avoiding me this time?" Mrs Astley cut through her son's train of thought.

Hunter stared at her, wondering if she was really so ignorant to everything going on around her. "Mother, I've been an invalid. Laid up in bed for three weeks, recovering after Sophie tried to kill me."

"Oh." Mrs Astley finally looked away from her chess game to see her son. Her eyes ran quickly from head to toe, but seeing no real problem, she finally met his gaze. "Sophie, that common girl you were dating? Well, I did tell you not to bother with her."

Hunter clenched his fists and tried not to show how much his mother was winding him up right now. She told him not to bother with Sophie? Oh, so somehow Mrs Astley could tell that Sophie was evil, and the biggest threat this century? No, more likely the stuck-up Mrs Astley was offended by her son's interest in a "common" girl.

Mrs Astley sighed, reading her son's reaction. One that did not need an audience. "Charles, more tea."

The ever-dutiful Charles nodded, and stood up from the chess game, more than happy to leave the Astleys to yet another family interlude.

Once the butler had gone, Hunter drifted over to the table and chessboard that were set by the window, to get the most of the winter sun. He could see that Charles' white pieces could checkmate his mother in three moves. It wouldn't happen of course, Charles always let Mrs Astley win.

"Don't look at the board pretending you know how to play chess, George." Mrs Astley snapped.

"I do know how to play chess, mother. James taught me years ago." Hunter replied calmly.

"Oh, don't mention that odious boy!" Mrs Astley fumed, something about the Yorkshireman always seemed to rile her up. "He is still staying here, I presume? You should start charging him rent."

"Mother... things have changed. Witch-hunters need somewhere safe to stay." Hunter said, trying to change her way of looking at it.

"And that Marks fellow – running around like he owns this place! I imagine he always had his beady eye on the Manor, when he used to come visit Young. Now he goes and fills it with all sorts!"

Hunter waited impatiently for his mother's rant to end. "No mother, I own this place. And as lord of Astley Manor, I turned it into a centre of control for the MMC, I have encouraged witch-hunters to use it as a sanctuary. And I pushed Anthony Marks to take command."

Mrs Astley sat thin-lipped, considering this. "I am not sharing my rooms." She eventually announced.

"No one is asking you to, mother." Hunter replied with a touch of exasperation. "They are being housed in the village too, there's space enough."

"What?" Mrs Astley looked up at her son with surprise. "The villagers will not take kindly to you pushing house guests on them."

Hunter narrowed his eyes at his mother. "The villagers were evacuated three weeks ago to save them from the witches."

"Oh." Mrs Astley took this bit of news in. "So that must be why Mrs Harsmith has not been to visit. I assumed she had the flu again."

Hunter was caught at that familiar place between wanting to laugh at her and being thoroughly annoyed by her. He decided to take the safest path.

"I will leave you to your tea and chess, mother."

## Chapter Three

"Oi Hunter, wake up!"

Hunter groaned and rolled over, tucking the warm sheets tighter about himself.

"Any time today mate."

Hunter cracked open one eye to see James hovering by his bedside, holding a candlestick for light. Funny how his family's stash of old-fashioned items were finding use again.

"What's this about, James?" Hunter croaked.

"We're going running this mornin'. Get up."

"What? What time is it?" Hunter asked, pushing himself to sit up in his bed.

"Nearly six am."

Hunter groaned. "Come back at a more reasonable time."

"Get your arse out of bed Hunter, before I send your mother in." Threatened James. "We need to get you back to your old self. Which means back to our old training routine."

Sensing he wasn't going to win this one, Hunter finally got up and dug out some running gear.

"Meet you downstairs in five." James stated, ducking back out.

The sun wouldn't be seen for another hour, but the world was bright with the lightness of the snow. It wasn't too deep, only an inch or two in most places, and it had a thick frost on the surface that was childishly satisfying to crunch through.

It was bloody cold, and Hunter jogged on the spot to try and keep warmth and sensation in his body. James stretched next to him, then stood straight and gave a nod.

The two men set off at a jog – their routine was to keep it steady for a quarter lap of the estate, then kick it up a gear. This morning though, when Hunter would usually be the first to run, he was lagging behind, his breath burning his lungs and an unfamiliar dizziness threatening to take over.

James looked back and slowed a little. "You know, I'm liking being the fastest for once. Makes up for all those times you left me in the dust."

Despite the cheeriness of his voice, it was obvious that James was worried about Hunter. Not just the here and now, but what would happen if the witches attacked while he was like this? James had never gone into a situation without knowing the strong, fast Hunter was beside him.

"Quick break?" Hunter suggested, embarrassed that he needed one already.

James nodded over to the old gatehouse that wasn't far away. The door was unlocked, and soon they were inside the single, simple room. It wasn't warmer inside this old building, but at least they weren't standing in snow for five minutes.

James kept moving with some stretching exercises, waiting for Hunter to carry on the run; to talk; anything.

"This is embarrassing. I've never been this weak." Hunter eventually muttered.

"Yes you have. It's been a year since you were recovering from that coven attack in Wiltshire, remember?"

Hunter paused, he'd been so wrapped up in this near-death experience, he had forgotten about that one. "Oh yes. And then you persuaded me to take a holiday. So, I did, and ended up meeting the Shadow Witch."

"So, I won't recommend a holiday this time." James shrugged.

Hunter flexed his knees, feeling his muscles protest. "I can't believe how unfit I am."

"I can." James replied. "Oh, come on, when was the last time we went running? Ever since you've been shacked up with Sophie, I haven't seen you on a single mornin' run!"

Hunter was surprised at James' outburst and was immediately defensive. He'd had a lot to think about these last few months. Charlotte's murder; the destruction of the MMC; the woman he loved wanting to kill him. But Hunter had to confess that James was right, he'd been too distracted by Sophie, neglecting his friend... but she had been too tempting to tear away from. Not that it mattered now.

"She fooled me too." James said quietly, reading Hunter's thoughts. "Oh, I thought she was a cold bitch at times, but I trusted her too."

Hunter looked over to his friend. Any response that sprung to mind was pathetically incapable of expressing how foolish he felt. Not that he wanted to get into this right now, or anytime soon.

"Let's get moving." Hunter said, heading back towards the door. "We'll take the shortcut back to the house and do the full lap tomorrow."

James shrugged. "Fine. Then after breakfast we'll practise combat. I'm looking forward to knocking you on your arse for once!"

## Chapter Four

Hunter was pleasantly surprised at his rate of recovery. After a week of training, he was as strong as James, and then he started to win some of the spars and was soon running ahead of him once more. The Yorkshireman pretended to be sour over his new losing streak, but he was (not so-) secretly relieved that Hunter was getting back to his old self.

Not only that, but slowly others began to join them in the pre-dawn run, and even more joined the sparring sessions. Witch-hunters and soldiers that were restlessly waiting for this war to progress first came to watch out of curiosity, most of them never having seen Hunter in action. Hunter suspected Marks and Hayworth had encouraged them to participate, and after being initially annoyed at the invasion of his privacy, Hunter welcomed them. They moved the session from the indoor hall to the courtyard as numbers grew.

It quickly became habit that Hunter would drift through the men and women that fought barehanded, or with short poles. He would offer correction and advice where necessary, but on the whole, it was uplifting to see the level of skill.

A couple in particular impressed him. A sergeant from the army, Ian Grimshaw proved unbeatable in hand-to-hand combat, grappling and flooring every opponent. When Hunter spoke to him, Sergeant Grimshaw was a very quiet man in his late thirties, who just happened to turn his hand to martial arts from a young age.

The other was a 3rd gen witch-hunter, Alannah Winton, a petite brunette Welsh girl who was scarily accurate and fast with the poles. When asked about her background, she just grinned mischievously and told them that they should see what she could do with real knives!

Hunter quickly promoted them to step in and help the others, he watched as Ian and Alannah moved through the others with purpose.

Near the end of each session, everyone began to wind down, and stayed to watch Hunter. It had been annoying at first, to have the audience, but Hunter quickly shut them out.

Normally he fought James, but today both Ian and Alannah faced him. All three held the short poles and stood as the three points of a triangle. Ian and Alannah were kitted out with padded vests and gloves, but Hunter shunned the safety equipment. He knew that he was too strong and fast to allow anyone to actually land a hit, he allowed himself to be more than a little arrogant in that respect.

Hunter took a deep breath, letting his shoulders drop down and relax. He felt his usual wave of calm and confidence wash over him; he raised his eyes to look at his opponents, waiting for them to attack.

Alannah was the first to move, and she didn't hold back. For someone so young and standing half a foot shorter than Hunter; she was strong and fast – faster than he expected a 3rd gen to be. She swung her pole at his right side, which Hunter deflected with a resounding crack; then brought her knee up to his exposed left side. Surprised at her dirty move, Hunter barely got his arm in place to stop her. He went to grab her leg, but Alannah read his intention, and pulled back before he could unbalance her.

Before Hunter could recover, there was a blow to his right shoulder. For a man so big and looming, Ian could move bloody quietly – Hunter hadn't even noticed him! Ignoring the spike of pain, Hunter spun round, raising his pole just in time to deflect his second strike. He threw his weight behind the move, pushing Ian back.

Hunter rolled his injured shoulder, and smirked at his own over-confidence. It was going to get him killed one day.

This time they both came at him, Alannah forcing him to block high, while Ian tried to slip past his guard.

Hunter grunted as Ian's hastily deflected blow caught a rib. 'Move faster,' Hunter scolded himself.

He twisted away, causing Ian to unbalance, and catching Alannah with a bruising crack on her outstretched arm. Alannah was the first to reach him again, she moved quickly and rattled out a few sharp attacks that Hunter had to focus to parry. The Welsh girl was more than impressive, despite her youth.

Partially distracted by having to stop Alannah knocking his head off, Hunter had momentarily forgotten Ian and was shocked to feel a pair of arms pin around his chest. He struggled against the iron grip – he had seen others unable to break out, but it surprised him that neither could he. He took a deep breath and prepared to throw Ian over his shoulder; he felt Ian's muscles tighten and lock down in anticipation for the move.

Hunter closed his eyes and… and no longer felt the constricting arms around his torso. There were gasps all around, and Hunter opened his eyes to see that he was standing behind Ian…

Hunter glanced around and saw only shock on the faces of the audience. Ian span round, his expression one of confusion, as he looked from his hands to where Hunter now stood.

It finally dawned on Hunter that he had instinctively blinked the short distance to escape the grip. That was useful, but-

"That's cheating, Astley." Anthony Marks stood in front of the crowd, his arms crossed over his chest, as

he assessed the other witch-hunter. "But it looks like you're ready for duty. Report to myself and Hayworth when you're finished up here."

Hunter nodded, and watched the older witch-hunter retreat. He turned back to his opponents, who stood a little dazed, and looking a little cheated.

"Ah, no hard feelings guys?" Hunter asked.

Alannah shrugged, pushing her sweaty fringe out of her eyes. Ian stared towards Hunter, but then gave a rare, crooked smile.

"Hey, we're on the same team. Can't wait to see you pull that shit out on the witches."


As Hunter approached the dining room, he thought about knocking, but it seemed ridiculous to knock in his own house, so he walked straight in.

General Hayworth was standing in the room with another man that Hunter found familiar.

The General looked up to see Hunter, then turned to speak to the other man. "Sergeant Dawkins, can you send for Marks. And bring the list."

Hunter watched Dawkins leave, suddenly remembering the sergeant that had played the guinea pig when Hunter had been experimenting with transporting himself and others in a blink. The man appeared different now he wasn't looking pale and nauseated.

"Anthony told me you're ready to go?" General Hayworth took a seat at the dining table and motioned for Hunter to join him.

"As ready as I'll ever be, sir." Hunter replied. He found it odd that he should be invited to sit in his own house, but everyone was quickly signing up to the attitude that this was just another base for the MMC, in which Hunter was just another witch-hunter.

The far door opened, and Anthony Marks and Dawkins walked through. Dawkins carried a thick folder, which he promptly set on the table.

"Dawkins, this is your project, so if you wouldn't mind." The General said, opening the floor to his second-in-command.

Dawkins nodded, his hand resting importantly on the folder. "After the fall of your MMC, we've been trying to recover as much data as possible. I've been heading the team in charge of listing MMC employees. This is the most current list of witch-hunters and last known locations."

Dawkins opened the folder and lifted the first few sheets, setting them aside. "These are confirmed fatalities."

Hunter looked at the papers covered in dense writing with morbid curiosity. He didn't really want to concentrate on those they'd lost.

Dawkins took a slightly thicker wedge of papers from the folder. "These are witch-hunters relatively local to Little Hanting. We've already sent teams to attempt contact, with varying success."

The Sergeant tapped the still-considerable stack. "And these are the ones further afield."

"Now that you're up for travelling again, we need to make use of your… talent." The General broke in. "We need real time communication and answers, not wasting fuel on days of travel with no promise of result. You will co-ordinate with Sergeant Dawkins, who will prioritise the most likely locations. You will establish communication protocols with any groups, and bring individuals here. Plus, I want reports on any updates about the witches and their leader."

Hunter sat a little perplexed by his orders. He was a witch-hunter, the MMC sent him targets and he took the necessary actions. He wasn't a soldier, but Hayworth was treating him as one. Maybe that would be a good thing, making the MMC a more controlled, and militarised establishment.

Marks cleared his throat. "We've assigned you a team. Alannah Winton, 3rd gen; Sergeant Grimshaw; and Lieutenant Coulson. You leave tomorrow on your first assignment."

Hunter looked up at Marks. "With permission, sirs, I'd like to include James Bennett in my team."

Marks looked over to Dawkins, questioningly.

The Sergeant stayed quiet for a moment, then shrugged. "I suppose I can spare him from my team. If the famous Hunter Astley insists."

Hunter didn't know how to take Dawkin's comment, but hoped it was misunderstood humour. He was surprised that someone else valued James, when he had only ever been a lowly 1st gen to the MMC. But then Hunter felt guilty for his surprise.

"Is there anything else, gentlemen?" Hunter asked.

After a chorus of 'no', Hunter stood and excused himself.

## Chapter Five

The following morning, Hunter met the rest of his team at breakfast. The five of them were quiet and awkward. How did one act when suddenly expected to work with, and put their life in the hands of four strangers?

Hunter glanced over towards Ian. The sergeant was the calmest in the group. But as he was also the oldest, in his late-thirties, Hunter wondered if that had anything to do with it.

Lieutenant Maria Coulson leant against the kitchen top near Ian. Her blonde hair was scraped back into a hasty bun, and her blue eyes were half-closed over her coffee. Hunter hadn't personally met Maria before, but had heard good reviews about her. She was supposed to be one of the best gunmen in General Hayworth's regiment.

James yawned, looking outwardly relaxed as he slumped over the breakfast bar. But Hunter could see his nervous tells as James irritatingly tapped his mug.

Next to James, Alannah was wide-eyed and positively bouncing. When she noticed Hunter looking her way, she grinned.

"It's my first big assignment." She spurted out in her lovely Welsh tones. "I'd just finished training when all this kicked off."

"Who did you train with?" Hunter asked.

"Timothy Jones, near Cardiff." Alannah replied. Tucking loose hair behind her ear. "He's on the missing list, so I'm hoping we get to find him."

"Well, I can talk to Colin Dawkins for ya." James piped up, beside her. "Get him to bump up the priority of Jones."

Alannah turned to James, smiling at his help; just as Hunter rolled his eyes at his friend's chumminess with the sergeant.

"Sorry to interrupt, but when are we going?" Ian suddenly asked, looking over at the three witch-hunters.

Oh yes, the business of the day. Hunter glanced round his team. "Get kitted up and meet me back here in ten minutes."

Hunter checked and re-checked his gear. The black stab-vest was comfortable and familiar, his hands traced over the guns and knives that were MMC issue; finally his hand rested on the ever-present dog tags at his neck. This tarnished accessory wasn't just a memento from the last World War, it had come from the Astley collection and was charmed to protect the wearer from certain spells.

Hunter tucked the dog tags into his shirt and made a detour to the vault that lay beyond the library. Taking a lamp with him into that windowless room, he quickly picked out a few suitable pieces. Hunter made his way to the kitchen where everyone was already waiting for him.

"Here, take these." Hunter handed out a necklace to Alannah; a brooch to Maria; and a bracelet to Ian.

Alannah looked excited, understanding the gift immediately, but the two soldiers looked a little confused.

"Uh, thanks?" Maria replied, turning the bronze brooch with amber stone in her hands.

"They're charmed items for extra protection against witches." James explained with a chuckle. He raised his right hand, showing the thick gold ring that he never went without. "You're part of a select group now. Hunter doesn't openly share his treasures."

Hunter stood quietly by the kitchen door. Since he'd taken charge of Astley Manor and its contents six years ago, he'd only given out a very few of these items. James Bennett and Charlotte King had been the first. Sophie Murphy had been the most recent, Hunter wondered whether she still wore the silver and opal necklace.

"Come on, if everyone is ready, we should go." Hunter closed the topic.

Maria pinned her new brooch onto her shirt, then looked up at Hunter, nervous for the first time. "So… what do we have to do? Set candles? I can't promise to be any good at chanting."

Hunter ignored James who immediately burst into laughter at Maria's naivety.

"No, it's not magic. And not that type of magic – that's casting you're thinking of."

Maria blushed, but remained defensive.

"Well I didn't know. Two months ago, I didn't know witches existed, so give us a break while we catch up." Her eyes narrowed in the direction of James, who was gaining control of his mirth.

"All you have to do is hold onto me, I'll do the rest." Hunter explained calmly. "Close your eyes if you want. It can be a, ah- disorientating experience the first time."

"Tell me about it." Ian muttered. He was pale from the mere memory of it, having been part of the regiment Hunter had brought to Little Hanting to face the Shadow Witch.

Hunter sighed and held out his arms. Once he felt four hands gripping him tightly, he closed his eyes and let his mind refocus.

The next moment they were gone.

They reappeared in the middle of a field, the rain pouring relentlessly down and soaking each man and woman to the bone within minutes.

"Right, we're five miles outside of Newcastle, there's a small MMC branch a mile to the East of our location." Hunter stated, looking up to see the Angel of the North to confirm his bearings, but only seeing grey cloud. He hoped he wasn't too far out.

Hunter looked at his team, and was hardly surprised to see the youngest, Alannah, on her knees in the mud trying not to throw up. James hovered next to her, trying to be supportive.

The two soldiers had a little more control, although they looked very pale – but that could just have to do with the rain rather than Hunter's method of travel.

"And we've gotta do that every mission?" Maria gasped, half regretting her promotion to this team.

"There and back." Hunter confirmed. "But don't worry, I'm sure you'll get used to it."

Maria groaned at his lack of helpfulness.

"Well, what are we waiting for?" Ian asked. "Winton, you good?"

Alannah nodded and with James grabbing her hand for support, she got back to her feet.

"Lead the way, sir." Ian turned to Hunter.

Hunter recognised the expression that flickered across the usually cool sergeant's face. It was the same expression that so many wore when first working with Hunter. Doubt. So many people were sceptical of the supposed skill of the 7th gen and questioned his right to lead. Especially when that person was older or more experienced.

Hunter felt his pride flare up. Well, he'd just have to prove to Ian, and anyone else that might question him just why he deserved to lead.

But for now, they had to get out of this rain. It was no fun, trudging across the muddy field, slipping in the harrows and their boots getting heavier with mud and rain. Eventually they hit a road and followed it until it led to the A1. The motorway was eerily quiet, and Hunter and his team jumped across the barriers and walked across the tarmac, the only noise the consistent rain.

On the other side of the main road was their destination. It looked like any other trading estate, with industrial offices standing blandly side by side, and the token car depot. But amongst the boringly normal enterprises here, the MMC had held an office for years.

Hunter led the way to a red-brick building. There was an electronic keypad by the main door, which had been rendered useless along with most other things, when the witches had overturned technology with magic.

But there was a keyhole. Unfortunately, Hunter didn't have the key. He wondered… Hunter focused on the lock, tried to mentally feel out the latch and give it an invisible shove… It felt like it was about to move, but always slipped at the last moment.

From the back of the group, James huffed and pushed to the front.

"Get out the way." He muttered to his friend. Hunter might want to experiment, but James was bored with getting soaked and was impatient to get inside.

James took out his tools for the job and knelt by the door. Less than a minute later there was the rewarding sound of a click, and the door drifted open. James stood back and allowed Hunter to lead the way into a dark corridor.

"Stop there. Identify yourself." A voice came from the far end of the corridor.

Hunter's sharp eyes made out the shape of a person kneeling, a gun in hand. He had no doubt that this person could see them, silhouetted in the doorway.

"We're from the MMC. I'm Hunter Astley, 7th gen."

"Really?" The voice remained wary. "Come to the control room, and we'll see."

A door opened, letting daylight in the far end of the corridor.

Hunter spared his team a quick glance, then led the way down to the door. He stepped into the 'control room', which looked like it had once been the main meeting room for this MMC branch. Now tables had been pushed together and were piled with papers. On the wall were two maps – one local and one national – both had marks and notes covering them.

But more importantly, half a dozen men stood aiming guns at the trespassers.

"Hunter?" One of the men lowered his gun and moved to the front. "James? Christ, I'm glad to see you two!"

"Toby?  What on earth are you doing here?"  James piped up.

Hunter quickly placed the face.  Toby Robson, a 4th gen witch-hunter that had been listed as missing.  But they had been searching for him near his home of Oxford, not Newcastle.

"Oh, long story.  I was on my way back from a family excursion to Scotland when everything happened.  I got stuck here, and well, we've been busy ever since.  We had no idea if there were other survivors."  Toby replied, his eyes locked on his old friends, savouring the sight of them again.  "What about you?  I mean, what's the state of the MMC?  What happened after the blackout?  Hell – what was the blackout?"

"Sir?"  Maria piped up from behind Hunter, the soldier looking amused at the flood of questions.  "Perhaps we should check the others off our list while you fill your friend in."

Hunter nodded, glad that someone had suggested something sensible.  He coughed, wondering where to start for Toby.  "So… what do you know?"

An hour later, Alannah was still quizzing the other witch-hunters over what they knew of their colleagues and witches; and the other three members of Hunter's team sifted through the stacked data.

Hunter was sat with Toby, who looked a little dazed at all he had just been told.  He'd been sitting like that for nearly ten minutes, and Hunter wondered whether he should speak, or wait patiently for his friend to snap out of it.

Hunter coughed, and less-than-subtly drummed his fingers on the table-top.

Finally, Toby looked up at him. "Sophie, you're sure?"

Hunter nodded. "I hoped it was some spell, a charm or possession of some sort. But no, it was her all along. She took great pleasure in ridiculing the trust I put in her."

"But... weren't you-"

"Can we change the topic?" Hunter cut through, before Toby could go any more in-depth. "So, tell me, how did you end up here?"

Toby shrugged, not finding his own story half as interesting. "We took the baby up to see the in-laws. Little Molly is a few months old now; it was her first trip to Scotland to see Claire's side of the family. We were still up there when the mass-breakout occurred. I made sure Claire and Molly were safe, then went to fight at the Glasgow prison.

"It took a few days to help with the casualties and a few sporadic witch attacks. After that, I was determined to get back and report to our MMC, but only got as far as Newcastle when everything blacked out. I came straight here to get answers, but everything was chaos. They'd lost all contact with the head office, and of the witch-hunters that hadn't been killed, many were missing. I stayed to help – I've been here a month now."

"Are you in charge?" Hunter asked. "What have the primary aims been?"

Toby nodded in answer to his first question. "Yes, I'm the highest gen here, and even though I'm not a Geordie, they seem to trust me; and need me. As for what we've been up to – re-establishing links; trying to find lost hunters; trying to get in touch with other survivors and sounding out what the witches are up to."

"Sounds much the same as us." Hunter murmured.

"Do you need me to come back with you?" Toby asked.

Hunter shook his head. "I think you're more useful to the MMC here, doing what you are already doing. As long as you don't mind?"

Toby sighed and leant back in his chair. "I want to go home, but at the same time it's a relief not to. I don't know how I'd cope to see everything in ruins."

Hunter could understand Toby's logic. Didn't they all want to hide from seeing the worst.

*****

Hunter and his team returned to Astley Manor in the early afternoon. They held gingerly onto their leader and allowed him to rip them from one place to another.

They suddenly appeared in the kitchen, startling Sergeant Dawkins so that he dropped his tea. Not that he seemed to care; he smiled openly when he realised who it was, and what it meant.

"Back already? Amazing!" Dawkins glanced over the team, noting their pale faces with a knowing smile.

282

He wouldn't voluntarily travel with Hunter again. "What did you find?"

"The Newcastle branch is still going strong. We managed to check off eighteen names that reported to their commanding officer, Toby Robson. And, ah, twenty-six confirmed dead." Hunter reeled off.

"Very well. Deliver your notes to my team, and I think a successful first mission deserves the rest of the day off. I'll have your next packet ready in the morning." Dawkins replied. "Ah, James. While you're here, could I steal you? I want your opinion on your replacement."

## Chapter Six

After their debrief, Hunter left his team and wandered down to the library. The Astley library was famous in witch-hunter circles. It was the most extensive known collection of books, grimoires, and witch-hunter chronicles. All collected over the last two-hundred years by the Astley family.

He picked up the book that he'd left on the desk yesterday: 'Witches and their Hunters of the Romanic Region: 16th Century study'. The cover was old, brown leather; the lettering dull and cracked. It was just one more book amidst a room full of older, and much more interesting books. But this was the one that contained the reference to the mysterious Benandanti.

There was only a little information, barely a page's worth; giving a brief account of their history as defenders of the Friuli region of Italy and their abilities. Oh, and of course, their ultimate prosecution as witches by the MMC.

Hunter had read it enough times to know the words by heart, and now he stared at the cover, as though willing it to divulge more. Hunter sighed and put the book back down. He wondered how Sophie had made such a questionable connection between himself and these Benandanti, from such a small piece of information. Had she found more details somewhere in this library? Or had she been so desperate to find a way to keep Hunter with her, she'd made the mental leap?

Hunter couldn't say which answer made him more hopeful. To know that the information was somewhere within reach was what brought him here so often. But it would also be a relief to know that Sophie had loved him… Oh, logically he could say that the strength of her affections could make her less likely to be able to kill him; but if he was being honest, he just wanted some evidence that she had loved him back.

Hunter shook his head. He had to stop thinking about her. Sophie Murphy was just the human façade of the Shadow Witch, designed to mislead him. That woman was gone, and she was not coming back.

He stalked over to the bookshelves, where James had left a marker for the next in the 'to-read' pile. Researching both his new-found abilities, and an answer to defeating the Shadow Witch would be distraction enough.

Hunter picked up a book by an American scholar, Eliade. Being from only the 1970's it was positively new compared to some of the others in this room. But

Hunter was tired of reading and translating the varying spellings of Olde English, at least this would give his brain a break.

Half an hour later he was engrossed in an account of the history of the interaction between the Inquisition and the Benandanti when a shadow crossed into the room.

"Still reading?"

Hunter glanced up to see General Hayworth with his arms crossed in the doorway.

Hunter shrugged, putting a bookmark in place. "I… I need to find out more about what I am."

Hayworth looked down steadily at the younger man. "Hunter… may I make a suggestion? The books will still be here tomorrow. Spend some time with your team, that's just as important."

The General sighed at the stubbornness of this younger generation, then turned and duly left Hunter to his own devices.

Hunter ran his fingers across the spine of the book, not completely convinced. He knew he couldn't settle to read that stodgy material once more – damn Hayworth for breaking his concentration!

Muttering to himself, Hunter extinguished the lights in the library and sloped towards the living room, drawn by the sound of voices and laughter. He opened the door to see his team sitting around the coffee table, fully entertained by a simple pack of cards. And a few bottles of wine.

"What's the celebration?"

Four heads turned in his direction.

"Well, you know, surviving our first mission seemed a good enough excuse." Maria replied with an innocent air.

"Yeah, just to let you know Hunter, you kindly donated the booze." James informed him.

Hunter shrugged. "Fine. I just hope you guys are fit for duty in the morning."

Three of them looked suitably abashed, but James just snorted. "Ignore him – he'll be as rat-arsed as the rest of us by the end of the evening. Ian, deal him in!"

Hunter's smile finally broke through the stern façade. He stopped to grab a spare glass from the sideboard, then joined his team at the table.

"What are we playing?"

"Blackjack." Ian replied, dealing seven cards in Hunter's direction.

Hunter sighed. "Really? Was this James' idea? You won't beat him."

"I might have suggested it." James replied, smirking as he reordered his cards.

Hunter shook his head, but joined the game. He hadn't played this particular card game since university – where James Bennett had taught him all of the rules, and none of the cheats.

The group continued to play, each of them occasionally winning, but James coming out on top most rounds. They steadily drank through the wine that he had raided from the Astley cellar, and chatted away.

Hayworth had been right, in Hunter's opinion, he was learning more about the people he was expected to work with and trust in this one tipsy evening, than he had with weeks of training.

But occasionally a serious question popped up that made Hunter shrink back.

"Why does the Shadow Witch hate you so much?" Alannah asked Hunter, her cheeks flaring red as she dared ask.

Hunter felt a cold soberness stab through the haze. "It's complicated. My grandfather killed her great-grandmother. She blames my family for setting a witchkind revolution back seventy years."

"That the truth?" Ian grunted, as he leant forward to refill his glass.

"What's that supposed to mean?" James snapped, suddenly defensive on his friend's behalf.

Ian shrugged. "Seems a weak reason for that attack the other month."

James grew redder, and Hunter could see the warning signs. He turned to Ian before James could embarrass them. "Yes, it's the truth. The Shadow used my family name as a focus for her anger and revenge. I imagine that has intensified. Not to boast, but being the only 7th gen witch-hunter, she sees me as a major adversary."

Talking about why the Shadow Witch hated him was easy. Hunter was glad that his team was ignorant enough of certain facts, that they did not quiz him over why the same woman loved him. That was a twisted story.

"I'm sorry, I didn't mean to cause upset." Alannah gushed, her cheeks burning red with embarrassment.

Maria chuckled at her side and put down a card on the pile. "Last card."

"Don't worry Ian." James said, throwing three cards down. "We've all joined Hunter on the top of the witches' hitlist, just by associating with him. Pick up five, Hunter."

Hunter groaned at how the game was going. "You are taking the proverbial piss, Mr Bennett. Why can't we play poker instead?"

Alannah put down a single card, pouting at the collection she had amassed. "Only if it's strip poker."

Maria laughed, while Ian groaned. "Nah, if you guys are starting that game, that is my cue to leave."

Maria looked over at her superior, a spark of challenge in her eyes. "Afraid you'll lose, sir?"

"Never! But someone has to maintain decorum and control." Ian replied, in equal jest. "Plus, I don't think my partner would approve of me playing strip anything with you youngsters."

James threw his cards on the table. "I'll start with a handicap, as I'm not gonna lose a round." He said, and before anyone could stop him, he dragged his jumper over his head.

Alannah watched his bare torso with a certain admiration, but Maria only snorted at his actions.

"Hey, I was going to win that last game! You did that on purpose."

James very maturely, retaliated by throwing his jumper at her.

## Chapter Seven

Over the following week, Hunter and his team fell into a steady pattern. They would run before dawn, then have breakfast together. Then James would bring the latest assignment from Sergeant Dawkins, and off they would go.

One morning, James audibly groaned as he opened the manila containing their assignment.

"Shit, I thought I'd pushed this off onto another team." James muttered, looking warily towards Hunter.

"Who is it?" Maria asked, grinning at his discomfort. James remained silent, passing the document to his team leader.

Hunter took one look at the sheet and swore. "They want us to enlist this git? We are better off without him."

"Ok, you're just teasing now." Alannah chided, trying her best to look disinterested. "Who is it?"

Already bored with the morning banter, Ian moved across the room and snatched the sheets from Hunter. "Gareth Halbrook. Never heard of him."

Maria shrugged, none the wiser. But Alannah sat trying to remember what she knew on the man.

"He's supposed to be good, isn't he? Like, really good. He's a high gen too; 3rd or 4th?"

"4th." Hunter confirmed. "But he's an arse."

"Why?" Maria asked, her blue eyes narrowing in James' direction.

"You'll see." He sighed. "Come on, the sooner we go, the sooner we get this over with."

Maria and Alannah shared a look, curious who could get their witch-hunters so riled up. In contrast, Ian got quietly to his feet, ready for whatever came his way.

Once they all had a firm hold on Hunter's arms, they were pulled into the temporary darkness, before opening their eyes to an empty car park.

Hunter noted how his team looked a little pale, but steady. That was good news, to know that people could get used to his method of transport. He felt the need again, to explore what he was capable of. But this was not the time, nor place.

The place, according to James, was the South side of Leicester. They had blinked into a small car park that was a few streets from Halbrook's house.

Finding no reason to put this off, Hunter sighed. "Let's go."

Ten minutes later, James stuffed the AA roadmap back into his bag, as they traipsed down the street where Halbrook lived. It was deserted, like everywhere else. They had caught a sight of a couple of youths, but they had run away, out of fear no doubt.

Hunter wondered how long it would take for everyone to go back to normal. Or what form would the new normal take?

Hunter was spared having to think about it by their arrival at Halbrook's house. Hunter hammered on the door and waited.

"Sod off!" A yell came from inside.

Hunter threw James a weary look, then knocked again. "Halbrook, open the bloody door!"

There was silence on the other side of the door, followed by the shuffle of feet and the click of a key in the lock. The door opened, and Halbrook showed his face. He didn't look like Hunter remembered; neat enough in appearance, with an over-whelming arrogance. No, now his face was sunken and ashen behind the patchy growth of beard. Even more over-whelming was the stench of stale alcohol, and stale unwashed bodies.

But Halbrook looked at Hunter with an almost reassuring expression of contempt.

"What the hell do you want, Astley?"

"We're here to discuss the Council. Can we come in?" Hunter asked, not keen on entering the house, but aware of the protection it would have.

Halbrook looked over the group that crowded onto his porch, then shrugged. Leaving the door open as a reluctant invitation, he walked back along the hall and into the sitting room. Halbrook opened the curtains to allow a little light into the room; which was helpful because there was all manner of clutter obstructing the path of his visitors.

"Thought the MMC had fallen." Halbrook muttered.

"Yes, and no." Hunter replied. "The headquarters were destroyed, and our forces scattered. But we are re-grouping."

"So, who's in charge, you? You grasping, little-"

"Marks!" Hunter barked, cutting him off. "Anthony Marks is in charge now."

Halbrook guffawed at that. "Should'a guessed. You'd never step up and take responsibility boy, you're too busy acting the hero."

Hunter took a deep breath and tried not to rise to Halbrook's tormenting.

Seeing his friend about to lose it, James stepped in. "Mr Halbrook, we need to make a record of-"

"You're still keepin' this pen-pushing 1st gen around?" Halbrook barely spared James a glance. "And what other useless groupies have you brought with you?"

"Sergeant Grimshaw; Lieutenant Coulson; and Alannah Winton, 3rd gen." Hunter reeled off, going down the line.

Halbrook snorted, not impressed. "A measly 3$^{rd}$ gen that looks like she should still be in school, and a couple of grunts from the army – their ranks only distract from the fact they're as incompetent and unprepared as your pet 1$^{st}$ gen."

Hunter felt his anger boiling over, when a quiet voice spoke at his shoulder.

"With your permission, sir?"

Hunter turned to see Ian looking challengingly in Halbrook's direction. He had the sudden flashback of when Ian had fairly bettered him on the training grounds, and he had only gotten away by cheating. The idea of Halbrook getting floored was enough to make Hunter smile, and fight back his mood.

"Maybe another time." Hunter replied calmly.

James coughed, trying to break the atmosphere. "Mr Halbrook, can you tell us about any other witch-hunters? Colleagues? Apprentices?"

"Dead. All dead." Halbrook nearly shouted, then continued in a much quieter and more bitter voice. "I watched my apprentices killed by witches after the black-out. They had us marked, see. Hunted, by orders of the Shadow Witch."

"What?" Alannah gasped.

"Yeah, anyone who met her while she was pretending to be human has been marked. Guess I'm top of her list." Halbrook looked across to Hunter. "Well, maybe second."

"How did you survive?" Hunter asked, trying to bring the conversation back to point. He didn't know how much Halbrook knew or suspected, and he didn't want to find out.

Halbrook shrugged. "The bastards underestimated me. I got away, and stayed holed up here since. Couldn't leave – there was always a witch or two around on watch. But they disappeared a week ago and I haven't seen them since. Makes me wonder what else is important enough to call them away."

"I don't understand, they just let you stay here?" Maria asked. "Why not break in?"

Halbrook looked at the soldier; she had confirmed that she was an idiot. Wasn't the answer obvious? "Witch-hunter houses are kitted out with protective amulets, as MMC standard. No witch can hurt me here. You'd know that if you had done any research into this organisation you've joined."

Maria's pale skin flushed red, but she did her best to remain calm to his taunts. "Actually, I have done the required reading. Less than a year ago, a better witch-hunter than you was killed, his home destroyed. The initial verdict was an attack from a large coven, though it was later confirmed as the work of the Shadow Witch. But perhaps you didn't find the report on Brian Lloyd important."

"Ho! This one's got teeth! And maybe a brain in that pretty little head of yours." Halbrook spat, his lip curling back. "You're still damn useless, as far as I'm concerned. Won't have no 1st gens next to me in a fight."

"Ok, enough!" Hunter snapped, defending his team. "I thought the Shadow Witch was injured in the last battle; her lack of involvement in getting rid of you, Mr Halbrook, may well be evidence to support that theory. We must assume that she will recover, though."

"Yeah, which is why we need you to come with us." James added.

Hunter turned to face James, aghast. "I'm not taking him to the Manor."

"We have our orders, Hunter. Lone witch-hunters are to be taken back to base."

Halbrook snorted. "Orders? Astley is flamin' infamous for ignoring orders. Why should he listen to them now?"

"Actually, I agree with Halbrook, for once." Hunter replied, feeling slightly queasy at the very idea of agreeing with an arse like Halbrook.

Ian stepped forward, and clapped Hunter on the shoulder. "Get over yourself Hunter. Let's get back, out of this shit-tip. No offence." He shot the last couple of words to Halbrook.

The older man just grunted.

"Please hold onto Hunter." James directed, as he grabbed his friend's arm. The two women took their cue and held on.

Halbrook stared at them all. "I don't know what sort of namby-pamby New Age crap you're into, but I am not doing a group hug."

Everyone looked at him, and Alannah ducked into James' shoulder to stifle a giggle.

"Just… hold on." Hunter said, holding out his hand.

Gingerly, Halbrook reached out and held Hunter's wrist as loosely as possible.

Before Halbrook had a chance to back away, Hunter blinked them all into the entrance hall of Astley Manor. His team, now fully habituated to the process, remained standing and unfazed.

Halbrook dropped to his knees, his head on the rug as he groaned.

"What… what the hell…" He broke off as he started to retch.

"Oh, not on the rug." Hunter moaned, gritting his teeth as he watched the bastard defile his house. "Ugh, you are cleaning that up."

Maria tilted her head sweetly as she looked at him. "Don't worry, Mr Halbrook. You're only a measly 4th gen. It's not like you can handle this."

Halbrook wiped his mouth with his sleeve. "You-"

"You are in my house now." Hunter broke in. "Which means you will watch your tongue."

At that moment, Sergeant Dawkins emerged from the dining room, drawn by the sound of voices. "Ah, back already?"

"Colin – this is Halbrook, you can deal with him now." James replied, keen to get rid of the responsibility.

The sergeant looked down at the mess of a man at his feet. "Of course, come through to our control room, and we'll get you some water."

Halbrook pushed himself up so that he was standing, albeit unsteadily. "I might need summat stronger than that."

Sergeant Dawkins glanced over at James, but gathered from the Yorkshireman's calm expression that this was ordinary behaviour from their newest recruit.

They made their way into the dining room and Hunter followed – not out of any desire to support Halbrook, but rather to know first-hand what Halbrook had to say. It seemed that he was not the only one that was worried, Hunter noticed the concerned looks that passed between Anthony Marks and General Hayworth.

"Dawkins, can you lead the debriefing of Hunter's team, please. Anthony and I will handle this one." The General stated.

If Dawkins had any objection to this, he remained quiet, and dutifully left.

"Mr Halbrook, it's good to see you again." Anthony Marks said coldly. He was well aware of Gareth Halbrook – not only his absolute lack of manners, but his reputation for leading 'shoot first, ask later' operations. He hadn't wanted the difficult witch-hunter in their ranks, but when General Hayworth insisted they enlist the 4th gen, he had to concede that it was probably best they kept Halbrook in line. He could only imagine what trouble he might cause if he were left alone.

"Marks, heard you're the man in charge now." Halbrook replied, dragging out a chair and making himself comfortable.

"I am. Along with General Hayworth." Marks confirmed, giving a small nod in the General's direction.

Halbrook took a brazen look around the grand dining room, his piggy little eyes taking in everything. "Well, I can guess where we are. Not that I was ever invited to the great Astley Manor. Me and ye dad weren't what you'd call friendly." Halbrook looked towards Hunter, explaining the obvious to the stuck-up, entitled little shit. "But is someone gonna explain how I got here?"

Anthony glanced over at Hunter before replying. "It turns out that Hunter has developed certain powers like the Benandanti."

"What's that?" Halbrook huffed.

"Who's that." Marks corrected. "They were a pagan anti-witch cult from Friuli, Italy. In the 16th century they devoted their lives to repelling witches, and became stronger, faster; they could shield from magic and travel in a blink. Who knows what else they could do?"

"And what happened to them?"

Marks looked at little uncomfortable at this question. "They were, ah, discovered by the MMC and punished as witches."

"So, we're going to follow their example?" Halbrook pressed. Hunter couldn't help but wonder if the older guy sounded too cheerful at the prospect.

"No." Marks replied calmly. "Can't you see what an advantage Hunter gives us? Besides, I'd like to think we are a little more educated than the 16th century MMC."

"Perhaps. Or maybe just a little more desperate."

Hunter narrowed his eyes at the odious bastard. "You know, there is a chance I'm a good guy."

Halbrook shrugged, not won over by Hunter's argument, the witch-hunter revelling in the news that the famed and respected Hunter Astley had received a more perfect punishment than Halbrook could have dreamt up.

Then the General finally spoke up. "I don't give a crap about your antiquated MMC prejudices or politics. Hunter has proven himself time and again. In fact, he's the reason we're all here and all still alive and fighting. If you insist on being difficult, I will ask Mr Astley to drop you off to the witches – let them deal with you."

Halbrook tried to maintain his disinterested air, but the General's threat had at least silenced him.

"Mr Halbrook, is there anything you can tell us about the Shadow Witch?" Marks asked, trying to get this interrogation back on track.

"Nowt that you don't already know. Deadly, unstoppable, magic without limits. If you want other details, ask your boy over there."

"And what is that supposed to mean?" Hunter asked coldly.

"Oh, come on, the Shadow Witch – Sophie Murphy." Halbrook guffawed. "The signs were all there, it was bloody obvious. Maybe you were too busy to notice, Astley. Had she blinded you with her charms?"

Hunter stood suddenly, his chair scraping back across the wooden floor.

"Hunter, sit back down." The General ordered. "And Halbrook, we have decided to keep Hunter's past friendship with Sophie Murphy classified. There is nothing to benefit from it going public, but a lot of damage to morale could occur."

"Friendship – my arse!" Halbrook muttered. "And by damage to morale, you mean damage to your golden boy's image."

The General just smiled in response to Halbrook's taunting. "Well, if you can't follow these rules, we're straight back to the 'hand-you-over-to-the-witches' option."

Halbrook crossed his arms and hunched down into his seat, looking a lot more petulant than a man of his age and reputation had a right to. "Fine. Where am I staying?"

"Ah, not here." Hunter was quick to clarify.

"We'll speak to Wardell – she's in charge of accommodating allies. She'll find space for you." Marks replied. Finding space might be easy – finding other lodgers that could put up with Halbrook might prove tricky.

## Chapter Eight

"You used to work with Halbrook?"

Hunter was snapped out of his private reverie, and back to the dull, unused warehouse situated in one of Manchester's boroughs. The rain thrummed down on the distant roof. James and Alannah stood staring out of a grey window, and Hunter stood with Maria and Ian beside some silent machinery.

Hunter saw the incredulous look on Maria's face as she voiced her question.

"Not if I could help it." Hunter said with a shrug.

Beside him, Ian grunted, although Hunter could not tell if it was from amusement or disbelief.

"Regardless of the fact that he is a prick, with no social graces; Gareth Halbrook was always too rash, too gun happy." Hunter explained. "He always believed that all witches were evil and must be killed. There were others that thought similarly – but he was the most vocal about it. The MMC is – sorry, was – moving away from considering it all so black and white. Personally, I always strived to capture witches alive."

"Perhaps Halbrook was right." Ian muttered.

Maria shushed him. "You don't mean that!"

"Maybe not." Ian replied. "Look Hunter, I don't blame you for hoping witches can be redeemed, or whatever. I mean, you're one of them now."

There was the thud of Maria's punch to Ian's side, although it came too late to stop her comrade's heresy.

"Don't take this the wrong way, Hunter, it's just that up until a few months ago, witches didn't exist outside storybooks for us. Even with what we've scrabbled to learn about the MMC... it's hard to tell the difference between what you do and magic." Maria kept a steady eye contact with Hunter, she wasn't embarrassed about her ignorance, she was just stating the facts. It was a relief for Hunter to have someone so matter-of-fact.

"It's not magic. It's sort of the opposite. Having seven generations of fighting against magic and witches, I guess I've evolved to oppose them."

"You know that's a weak-arsed argument." Ian replied, looking very unimpressed.

"So, you're basically an anti-witch?" Maria asked, trying to keep a straight face after Ian's interjection.

"Something like that." Hunter replied. "But that's no reason not to trust me."

"Who doesn't trust Hunter?" Alannah piped up defensively. She and James had wandered back to hear the tail end of the conversation.

Maria rolled her eyes, proving that you never outgrew that little expression.

"No one."

"If you want the proof – look at that blinking thing of yours." Ian argued. "We basically put our lives in your hands every time we travel."

Hunter stood silently, suddenly touched by the mutual respect in his team after such a short time. He didn't know why these good people trusted him; but he was grateful.

"Sorry to break up this love-in. But they're here." James announced, nodding towards movement in the west side of the open warehouse.

Hunter and the rest of his team turned to face the newcomers, automatically defensive. A small party made their way towards them, six figures in all, each looking alert and wary.

"Astley?" A woman's voice called out.

Hunter moved forward; his hand reflexively touched the dog tags at his throat, but managing to stay away from his gun.

"It's good to finally meet you." A woman stepped forward, holding out her hand. She looked very young, but the creases around her eyes, and the threads of grey in her otherwise black hair made Hunter guess that she was in her forties.

"Nadira Shah, 4th gen."

Hunter shook her hand, feeling slightly embarrassed that he should finally meet Nadira Shah properly. Oh, he'd seen her years ago, when she'd had occasion to visit his father, but this was different.

"Nadira, a pleasure. How are things going in Manchester?"

Nadira paused, considering how to phrase her answer. "We are winning, for now. The interim mayor has accepted our help. The people are starting to build their lives again. We have neighbourhood watches that sweep designated areas and report anything suspicious. Some sort of communication has been established."

Hunter listened, impressed with their progress. "And the witches?"

"We've had a few individual confrontations. Nothing that felt orchestrated. But it's only a matter of time before the Shadow looks this way."

Something about the way Nadira said it made her statement very foreboding.

"You know this?" Hunter asked.

"Manchester is the capital of the North. Logic tells me that – after London – Manchester will be her next target." Nadira stated, then glanced uneasily over her shoulder. "But there's also whispers, ones that we would be foolish to ignore."

"What do you mean?" Hunter frowned, worried that they were missing something.

Nadira motioned one of her men forward. "This is Jonathan. He is here to represent his kin."

"His kin?" Hunter felt foolish for echoing Nadira and looked to the man instead. He looked like an ordinary person, but then so did witches and witch-hunters on the surface. Hunter looked a little more closely, then understood.

Over the years, Hunter had noticed that there was a faint residue of magic everywhere. Witch-hunters naturally repelled it; and witches acted as both a source and magnet of it – which they could increase, or hide completely with practise.

Normal people were not aware of these residues, and the magic ignored them. But this man, Jonathan, fell into a different category. The flecks of magic moulded playful to his fingertips and followed each breath in and out. It did not belong to him, but was there to be borrowed.

"You're a wiccan!" Hunter stated, trying to keep the note of accusation out of his voice.

"Very astute, Mr Astley." Jonathan returned, mildly amused at the witch-hunter's reaction. "They told me you would be."

"A wiccan?" Ian's deep voice rang out. Hunter did not have to look to know that his friend was tense with the idea of the unknown.

"Relax." James answered. "It's like a witch without powers… or a human with magic. Something like that."

Jonathan looked as confused by James' description as the rest of those present.

"I am just a normal man. Wicca has been my religion and education, which allows me to access the world around me."

"What I want to know is why you're here?" Hunter asked, surprised that Nadira would bother with a wiccan. Historically, witch-hunters didn't bother about them – they were relatively powerless, not worth seeking as an ally. And if they turned bad, that was a job for the good old police force, not enough of a threat for the MMC to bother stepping in.

Jonathan smiled bitterly, as though reading Hunter's mind. "Let's forego the traditional prejudice, and you and I might just get on."

"I'll reserve judgement for now." Hunter replied, crossing his arms. "It's the best you're going to get."

Nadira tutted in the background. "You are as arrogant as your father, Hunter. Men are such bothersome creatures. Jonathan is here because his coven, and other cousin covens wish to form an alliance with the witch-hunters against the witches."

"Wait." Maria spoke up. "I would have thought that wiccans would be on the witches' side. What with it all being magic."

Jonathan shrugged, and shoved his hands into his jeans pockets, looking very normal and non-magical indeed. "It's true that some wiccans have been seduced by the promise of power, they have broken their Rede with us and joined the witches."

"Rede?" Maria interrupted.

Jonathan took a deep breath, and began to recite. "' An Ye Harm None, Do What Ye Will.' It's basically the codes and rules that bind us. Including binding us from doing harm. We are the servants of nature – and

309

nature is very much out of balance. It is our duty to rectify that."

Hunter sighed. "I appreciate your good intentions, but what good does that do us? We're in the middle of a war, and you've already explained that your code binds you from helping."

"There are more ways to help than fighting and killing!" Jonathan returned sharply. "We have methods of communication for simple messages, and spies that have infiltrated witch ranks as wiccan absconders. Both of which you need, I would imagine."

"Oh." Hunter couldn't think how to reply to that.

There was a snicker from James, the Yorkshireman amused and impressed that the wiccan could silence his friend.

Nadira looked similarly amused. "You honestly thought I would waste your time with someone of no use, Hunter?"

"Fine, what do-"

Hunter was interrupted by a sudden and familiar sound. A single gunshot echoed through the warehouse. Jonathan grunted as the bullet hit and knocked him to the ground.

Hunter shifted closer to the others, throwing up his shield – it was designed to defend against magic, but he had been known to stop a bullet. Once.

There was another resounding shot... this time the bullet hit Hunter's defences in front of his chest. Hunter glanced down at the small lump of metal, but after learning his lesson last time, didn't touch it. He let it fall to the ground.

Movement on the gangway on the far side of the warehouse caught Hunter's eye.

Luckily, it caught Maria's too. Without hesitation, she raised her gun and shot two rounds.

There was a human cry of pain, and the figure slumped.

Hunter nodded to the lieutenant, and they both set off, running in the direction of the attack. The gangway was twenty feet in the air, but Hunter found the metal ladder, going up first. As he drew up to the level, Hunter could hear laboured breathing. He took slow, measured paces, with his gun steady before him. Hunter noticed a spatter of blood by his feet and followed the red trail.

Hunter spotted the gunman, collapsed in a corner, his breathing shallow, and his face already pale and sweating profusely. The man's black jacket and trousers were wet with blood at the shoulder, and thigh. The man's eyes widened with fear as he spotted Hunter, and he made a weak attempt to raise his gun. Hunter knocked his slow movement aside with his usual speed and dexterity. The gun clattered across the metal gangway.

Hunter heard Maria's light tread behind him. "Let's get him down to the others."

"Yes sir." Maria replied automatically. Then frowned. "How are we going to get him down? I mean, I'm not averse to throwing him over the edge..."

Hunter snorted without humour. Not wasting words, he knelt down and touched the man's shoulder.

A moment later they were back in the midst of the group. The gunman was ash white, but Hunter could only guess whether it was the travelling, or the blood loss that was the cause.

Across the warehouse, Hunter could faintly hear Maria swearing, and clanging back down the metal staircase as she was left to take the slow route.

"I thought you guys could detect witches." Jonathan muttered as soon as he got over his shock at seeing two people materialise in front of him. The wiccan sat on the floor, his shoulder being strapped with a makeshift bandage, by the ever-practical Ian.

"We detect magic, not witches." Hunter clarified. "We can't feel anything out of the ordinary, unless they start casting."

"Oh fantastic!" Jonathan groaned. "I'll remember that excuse later."

Hunter frowned but looked down at the bleeding gunman at his feet. "Anyone you recognise, Nadira? Jonathan?"

"No." Jonathan replied with a sharp hiss as Ian tied off the bandage.

"Well someone has given our position away." Hunter said, looking down at the gunman.

"What do we do with him, boss?" Ian stood, having finished his first aid, and nodded to the now-unconscious man on the floor. "Cos if we continue this chit-chat, he's gonna be dead anyway."

"Kill him." James said, uncharacteristically cold.

"James!" Alannah snapped, grasping his arm.

"Think about it: a single witch gunman was sent to take out a wiccan. If they had known Hunter was involved, it would have been a dozen at least. But all we've gotta do is let him live and get word back to his boss that a witch-hunter could stop his bullets and travel in a blink – how long do you think it will take them to work out Hunter was here? Then what – they come in force to Manchester, and Nadira and her followers suffer."

"Ok, you've been spending too much time with Halbrook." Alannah accused, her green eyes narrowing at James. "What you need to do is take him back to base for questioning."

Ian coughed to get their attention. "Too late. He's gone."

They all stopped, and looked at the gunman, pale and lifeless at their feet.

## Chapter Nine

Nadira escorted Hunter and his team back to their base. Two of her men helped Jonathan, who was pale, but insisted on walking back.

Soon they were all settled in a grey and dull office.

"Jonathan will be back after the doctors have seen him." Nadira stood by the door, her arms folded. "Today did not go how I expected."

Hunter pulled out a chair and got comfortable for a possibly long wait. "I doubt it's your fault, Nadira. But we should look into who might have betrayed you."

Nadira stared straight into one of the grey walls, her lips down-turned. She took a minute to process the particulars, then shook her head. "It would have been someone with only partial information. As your man pointed out, they did not know it was you we were meeting."

Nadira sighed. "I almost wish it were someone in my immediate circle of advisors, they are limited in number. But to search for a possible mole in the hundreds of allies here… this war may be over before they are discovered."

"With any luck, this will be over quickly." Hunter replied.

Nadira bit back a smile. "You are too optimistic, Hunter. You remind me of Young, he was the same. Now, I shall see about getting tea."

The woman left Hunter and his team, but was back before they could cause much mischief. This time Nadira brought company into the office.

Jonathan came in, his bloody clothes changed and a fresh white bandage acting as a sling for his left arm. Another witch-hunter followed behind him, carrying a box, which he set on the table.

"How is your arm, Jonathan?" Ian asked.

"It's fine, thank you, Sergeant. No major damage." The wiccan replied. He looked very pale still, but determined to finish this meeting. He nodded to the box. "If one of you could do the honours, please."

Alannah, who was closest to the box, opened the lid. Inside there were at least a dozen smaller boxes about four inches wide. Glancing up to Jonathan, to make sure she had permission, she picked up one of the small boxes and opened it. Inside, on a bed of paper, were two rose coloured stones.

Hunter leant across the table, trying to see what it was. "Is that-?"

"Quartz." Jonathan answered. "Those ones are rose quartz, to be precise."

"What are they for?" Maria asked, looking down at the unimpressive stones.

"We use them for basic communication." Jonathan explained. "These two stones have been cut from the same piece, and have been charmed to interact with each other. If you would pass me one, please, Miss...?"

"Alannah Winton." The Welsh girl offered her name readily, and passed one of the small pinkish stones to Jonathan.

"Thank you, Alannah." Jonathan smiled. "If you would hold the other one."

Alannah grinned as she took up the second stone, it was cool and smooth in her palm.

Jonathan smiled at her cooperation. "So far we have been using these to warn of emergencies. The stones stay connected, no matter the distance. And if I run into trouble and need back-up, I simply focus on the stone..."

Jonathan shut his eyes, and closed his fist over the small stone. After a minute of concentration, Alannah yelped, dropping her stone on the table with a clatter. "It got hot!" She exclaimed, looking at the wiccan for an explanation.

"Not enough to burn, or do damage, but enough to get attention." Jonathan turned the cool rose quartz over in his hand.

Hunter looked on, wondering if he was supposed to be impressed.

"When you mentioned basic communication, I did not realise you meant this basic."

Jonathan did not look fazed by the witch-hunter's apathy. "You are letting yourself be blinded to its usefulness, Mr Astley. If I sent a distress signal, how quickly could you get to me? Opposed to how long it would take for a message of trouble to come via mundane means – providing there's someone able to get that message out, of course."

Jonathan handed his stone back to Alannah, and indicated that she should put them back in the box. The Wiccan waved his good hand at the collection. "Quartz is a powerful magical amplifier, long used for communication. We've just adapted it to suit our needs. There's rose quartz, citrine and amethyst in there, they won't fail you. The stones are reservoirs for magic, once charged they won't run out."

"Isn't quartz the stuff they use in crystal balls?" James asked, reserving some scepticism still.

Jonathan sighed. "That's a different type of magic. But yes. Not that I hold with that type of thing."

"You mean, there are prejudices within Wicca to different types of magic?" James was positively intrigued by the idea.

Jonathan shrugged. "It tends to change with each generation. Whereas clairvoyance was all the rage ten years ago, a lot of us now are taking a more traditional route. Although I hear there's a Boston movement-"

"As interesting as this is, can we please focus?" Hunter interrupted. He got the feeling that Jonathan would prattle on about his religion for as long as James wanted to listen. And Hunter recognised that light of interest in his friend's eyes. They could be there all day. "Let us say that the stones work, and prove useful, there are only a dozen or so here. We would need a lot more if we intended to make it part of every team's essential kit."

Jonathan nodded. "They will work. These are all we can spare, at the moment. My coven needs to wait until the next full moon before we can charm any more. You can pick up the next batch in a few weeks' time."

## Chapter Ten

Summer was starting to break out over the English countryside in its usual sporadic fashion. The rain grew warmer, and the grass would grow. The sun would shine promisingly for a day or too, before the grey clouds would roll in again.

The situation was relatively stable, with steady reports finding their way to Astley Manor. Jonathan's communication stones had been implemented with reasonable success, although they hadn't yet been put into practise in an emergency.

Because of the quietness, Hunter had secured home-leave for his team for a week. Using his talents actually felt good when he was blinking to Brecon to reunite Alannah with the rest of her family and taking Ian back to his home in Bristol. When Hunter and James blinked to Doncaster, Hunter had to stay for dinner with his aunt and uncle, and had to suffer the incessant chatter of James' younger cousins.

Back at Astley Manor, there was only one team member left.

Maria was just finishing washing the pots from her lonely dinner, when Hunter walked into the kitchen.

"How were James and the family?" She asked, grabbing a tea towel from the rail.

"Loud." Hunter replied, grabbing a warm beer from the pantry. "Were you alright, eating alone?"

Maria paused with her drying, then shrugged. "It was kinda nice to have some time to myself. I half expected one of Dawkin's team to come in and cadge a meal – it's what usually happens."

Hunter nodded, he understood that the Manor had turned into a hive of activity. He enjoyed it for the most part, filling this big old house with noise and movement. But occasionally it was necessary to find a quiet corner to oneself.

"Are you sure you don't want to go home this week?" Hunter asked.

"Home. It doesn't mean much to me." Maria replied with a sigh. "No mum. Dad died when I was nineteen – just after I joined the army. I married young, then the git left me when I was promoted before him."

Hunter inwardly winced at her casualness. "I'm sorry." He murmured, knowing that it was a largely ineffective comment.

Maria shook her head. "It's fine, it's life."

"Well, I could take you to visit friends instead." Hunter offered.

Maria chuckled at his obvious attempt at cheering her up. She didn't need it; she was content with her life now. "The only friends I have are in the unit stationed here. Thanks for the concern, but I'll spend my free time catching up with them in Little Hanting."

Maria tossed down the tea towel and copied her boss, by grabbing a bottle of beer.

"So, I've shared, now it's your turn." Maria locked her blue eyes on Hunter.

Hunter returned her gaze, feeling a little uneasy. "Ok…"

"Why is the Shadow Witch obsessed with you?"

Hunter frowned and shook his head. "We've been over that already. I'm-"

"Yeah, yeah, you're a major threat and your families have history." Maria interrupted. "I don't buy it, and neither do the others."

Hunter leant back against the hard kitchen work top and took his time to drink his beer.

"Oh, come on, Hunter!" Maria snapped. "We have a right to know – haven't we proven that you can trust us?"

Hunter sighed and idly picked at the label on his bottle. "I do trust you, it's just that Sophie… When I met the Shadow Witch, she was pretending to be human. I saved her from a fake sacrifice, then I helped her join the Malleus Maleficarum Council. So, it's my fault she learned so much inside information."

Maria listened quietly, a little frown forming between her brows as she took in what Hunter shared. "But that doesn't explain why she's focused on you."

Hunter shrugged, thinking back to last summer. "Sophie came to train with me, she came to live here. I thought she was someone I could trust. She was smart, beautiful… a little cold, I'll admit."

Maria's eyes widened as she realised where Hunter was going. "You and the witch?" She asked breathlessly.

Hunter twisted the bottle in his hands, unable to say anything. He knew if he confessed this to another witch-hunter he would be met with disgust. But Maria was new to this fight, she didn't have years of prejudice behind her – or so he hoped.

"Does anyone else know?" Maria asked.

"James – he knew Sophie too. But General Hayworth and Anthony Marks know some details, and I think they have filled in the rest."

Maria chewed over this, then finally looked at Hunter. "Thanks for confiding in me. But Hunter, you should really think about telling Ian and Alannah."

With a sorry smile, Maria ducked into the pantry to grab another beer, then took the bottle and headed to the room she had been allocated.

## Chapter Eleven

One pleasant summer's evening, Hunter walked in the gardens of the estate. The flowerbeds of Astley Manor had once been strictly cultivated to Mrs Astley's design. But the two ground-staff and full-time gardener that the family employed had been evacuated with the rest of the village six months ago and had not yet returned.

In those six months, nature had taken control of the garden, and personally, Hunter thought it looked better for it. There was one small corner where his mother actually got her hands dirty and tried to maintain a few flower beds. It was amusing to watch her narrow and focused attempt.

Spoiling the peace, Hunter felt suddenly alert, a flash of pain as he recognised magic in use. It was close, a few miles at the most. Hunter closed his eyes and focused on it – there were two different rhythms - two witches casting, and from his experience, the magic seemed weak.

Hunter sighed, why would such weak witches cast anywhere near the famous Astley Manor – they were asking to be destroyed. Unless it was a trap; and they the bait to the bloody thirsty witch-hunters.

Hunter cursed to himself that his quiet evening was ruined. He glanced about the beautiful grounds, taking a last deep breath of the scented breeze, he turned back to the house.

Hunter had only just opened the front door and stepped into the entrance hall, when he looked up to see his team already mobilising, thanks to Alannah. Her senses might not be as developed as his, but it was useful having another higher gen witch-hunter around.

"Ian, can you get us some back-up?" Hunter requested.

The sergeant nodded and left.

"Big threat?" James asked.

Hunter shrugged as he pulled on his stab vest. "Minor. Too minor, it might be an ambush."

Hunter gave directions to the soldier that would follow on foot, and when Ian returned, they took the quicker route.

The five of them appeared near the lake on the south side of the Manor. The setting sun cast the beauty spot in reds and purples, glinting off the rippling surface of the lake; the manmade dock and benches softened by shadows.

Hunter felt the unsteady throb of magic, and silently motioned for the other four to follow him. Guns ready, they made their way along the shoreline until they reached a copse of trees. Voices came out, too quick and quiet to decipher.

Hunter stepped forward with care and precision, not making a sound in his advance. When he pushed through the last barrier of foliage, what he saw made him halt.

There were six young people – the oldest could not have been older than seventeen, and the youngest looked barely fourteen.

"What the-?" Ian said, stepping up beside him.

The teenagers turned at his voice, and those that had been casting threw spells in their direction.

Hunter drew his shield up, the magic breaking uselessly against it – it was hardly worth the effort, Hunter was convinced their magic was so weak, the talismans his people wore would protect them fully. The shield dropped, but Hunter remained alert for any witches waiting in the shadows to ambush them. But he found it hard to believe that any person could use children as bait – even the witchkind.

"What are you guys doing here?" Hunter demanded.

One rather cocky-looking lad stepped forward as self-appointed spokesperson. "Aren't you meant to give that Malleus speech when addressing witches?"

Hunter paused. This was a new situation. "I save it for the adult witches. Why, do you want me to say it?"

"No." The youth replied immediately, a blush creeping up his neck that he was speaking with the Astley; and because he would never admit that he wanted to hear it.

Hunter sighed. "Fine. By the Malleus Constitution you will surrender now to my authority to be bound and registered. If you refuse to come quietly, I am empowered to take any means necessary."

The youths' reaction was easy to see, they all stood straighter, defiance in their eyes.

"So, go home." Hunter ordered.

The leader looked dismayed. "But-"

"No." Hunter interrupted. "This isn't your fight, so go home to your families."

A girl pushed forward, raising her rather spotty face to look up at the big bad hunter. "We don't have no family. You killed them."

"What?"

The boy put his hand out protectively towards the girl. "Yeah, last winter – you killed Jodie, Missy and Mark's parents at the Midlands prison. Then me, Lucretia and Tommy – you killed ours in that little village place."

"Little Hanting." One of the kids backed him up.

"Yeah, there."

Hunter had to stop himself from stepping back. He'd killed people, of course he had, but he never liked associating those people with a life and loved ones. Even if the people were witches, and their loved ones were obnoxious children.

James read his friend's hesitation and stepped in before anyone else noticed. "Ok, so are you gonna explain how that brings you 'ere? Because you have two options – you can surrender and be bound; or you can piss off."

"Or we can kill you!" The leader shouted, riled up by their dismissal. "We out-number you!"

"Not going to happen, kid." Ian stated calmly, crossing his arms and staring the youth down.

The boy tried to keep eye contact, but quickly dropped it.

"Last chance, go home, or we'll be forced to subdue and bind you." Hunter warned, silently wondering if any of his team had brought the necessary items to carry out a binding. Personally, he might have one amulet and silk in one of his many pockets, but since the rebellion, things had turned violent. Hunter's first instinct was no longer to bind a witch – a worrying acknowledgement.

"We ain't afraid of you." The spotty girl snapped.

"You should be." Alannah answered. "Maybe not of Hunter, he's the good guy. But definitely the rest of us."

She pulled out one of her knives, turning it in clear view of the group. "Ian's been known to wrench the odd limb from its socket; Maria will shoot you between the eyes before you can even begin to cast; and James – you don't want to know what he's been accused of."

Her lovey Welsh voice grew colder as she spoke, and as she carried on the teenagers' resolution began to waver. They exchanged worried glances.

Noticing his friends' loss in confidence, the leader turned back to the witch-hunters, furiously pulling a spell together.

Hunter felt the build-up – raw emotion giving it more strength but less stability. He threw up his shield just in time to block the magic as the youth released it. The magic exploded against his shield and bounced back, knocking the boy and his friends flat on their backs.

They scrambled up quickly enough, nothing hurt save their egos.

"Go home and learn what you're doing before you challenge us." Hunter insisted.

The leader stepped forward again, but the spotty girl and another gangly lad grabbed his arms and pulled him back. With an awful lot of noise and pushing, the group made a hasty retreat.

"You've got to admire their courage." Alannah remarked, returning her knife to her belt.

"I can't believe how scary you are for a short person." James remarked. "But what on earth were you about to accuse me of?"

Alannah flashed him a smile. "Best you don't know." She purred.

Hunter ignored their banter and the laughter that followed, he turned to lead his group back out into the open. It troubled him that –

"Stop it right there, Hunter." Maria warned as she hurried to walk beside him.

"Stop what?" Hunter hesitated in his stride, wondering what was wrong.

"You – worrying about those kids." Maria explained.

"But how…?"

"You were looking all pensive." Maria said with a shrug. "We don't need you moping again."

Her dry statement made Hunter smile. "It's just… they are so young. Too young to be in this fight."

Maria glanced over her shoulder at the other three members of the team; Ian walked along silently, while James and Alannah still joked at the back. It was a good team, they were all in their prime, and the best at what they did.

"How old were you when you started being a witch-hunter?" Maria suddenly asked him.

Hunter paused, knowing where this was going. "I was twenty."

Maria rolled her eyes. "Sure, you just turned twenty and suddenly you're a witch-hunter. When did you start training?"

"Actually, physically training – probably about thirteen."

"And I bet you were just itching to start earlier than that." Maria pressed her advantage. "I mean, my dad always told me how I was playing soldiers with the local boys when I was five years old."

Much to Hunter's relief, their conversation was drawn to a close by the arrival of twenty soldiers on the scene.

Hunter greeted the lieutenant in charge. "False alarm. Just a few weak witches that didn't realise where they were – when they did, they scarpered."

The lieutenant looked ill-at-ease. "Shall we track them down, sir?"

Hunter shook his head. "No, they are not worth our effort."

"But sir, our orders are to capture or kill any witches found." The lieutenant stated boldly. "Even 'weak' ones may have information."

"I said no, lieutenant." Hunter snapped. "I will report this incident directly to the General, he will agree with my decision."

Hunter wasn't entirely convinced of his argument. General Hayworth was a decent man, and there was a good level of mutual respect between them, but what if he disapproved of letting the youths go…

Oh well, what was the worst that could happen – they could hardly kick him out of the headquarters and his own house. And putting any kind of restraint on him was impossible, he could blink out of any attempt of confinement. Not that he thought it would resort to such things.

His team shifted closer to him, anticipating that they would travel with Hunter now that business was finished. But Hunter gave a minute shake of his head, and they stopped in place. His team might prefer the quick route home, but Hunter thought it advisable to walk back with the extra soldiers, in case any of them disobeyed, or if any of the kids were foolish enough to come back.

Falling into an unhurried march, Hunter found Alannah next to him.

"Well done for, you know…" Hunter trailed off.

"Dim prob." Alannah replied. "I'm always happy to scare and intimidate."

Hunter smiled as he looked down at the youngest and least intimidating member of the team.

"I can understand why they wanted to fight." Alannah continued. "A few years ago, I was that foolhardy, though I knew it all and that I was invincible. I got into a few scrapes, but I was lucky – Timothy Jones pulled me out of the worst of it and trained me properly. That desire to fight doesn't leave you, though."

"I blame Harry Potter." James piped up as he jogged on to catch up with them. At their disapproving glares, he pressed his point. "No, really, a bunch of pubescent witches and wizards defy and destroy the bad guy."

Hunter marched along; he supposed the comparison made some sense. "So, does that make me Voldemort?"

"Sure." Alannah replied, warming to the theme.

"You've got the looks for it." James added.

Hunter raised his hand to his thick black hair, which honestly needed a cut. "I assume you mean the Tom Riddle phase?"

"Nah."

"Does that make us your Death Eaters?" Ian asked, breaking his usual silence.

"And what does that make Sophie?" Maria added.

"Dumbledore?" James ventured, making everyone laugh.

"Ew, no." Alannah squirmed. "Because that means they, you know…"

"Well, Dumbledore was gay." Ian answered.

There was a pause, before everybody laughed together. A few of the soldiers marching ahead turned to look back and see what the noise was about. Hunter coughed and looked to his team.

## Chapter Twelve

One night in the middle of August, Hunter found himself unable to sleep. It could have just been the summer heat that made it uncomfortable, but he felt something foreboding nagging at his senses.

Finally, he dragged himself out of bed, and padded barefoot downstairs to the library. It quickly became a habit now, that when he did not know what to do, he headed to the library in the hope that the next book would yield answers to his problems.

There had been a few hints from his research, but nothing solid. That the Benandanti could walk through dreams, that they could control the elements and manipulate the world around them. But no one mentioned how. He supposed only a desperate and heretical witch-hunter like himself would wish to know the dynamics.

As he entered the library, he tried for the umpteenth time to spark a little life and light in the now defunct light bulb. It wasn't much, to heat the tungsten by exciting the atoms. But no matter how logically he broke it down, Hunter couldn't make the slightest difference.

He thought back to the first time he had transported himself, the first time he had used his shield. It had all happened so easily then, so why was it so hard now? Did he honestly have to wait for his life to be endangered before he unlocked more powers? Or was this it?

Hunter moved to settle down to do more reading but froze. It was so faint, that at first, he thought it was his sleep-deprived imagination. But no, there was the familiar pain that radiated through his brain. Someone was using magic. Hunter got to his feet and focused on it. The source was fifteen miles to the North, only just within range for him to detect.

Before he could even think of getting a team together and investigating, Hunter worked out why this felt so odd. Fifteen miles. He remembered talking to Sophie in this very library, about how a witch-hunter perceives magic. About how he could detect further than the lesser generations. And how far had they agreed he could sense magic?

This was for him. Someone wanted him alone to know that they were there. Before common sense got the better of him, Hunter took a deep breath and focused on the site of the source.

One moment he was in the library. The next he was in the woods that stretched most of the way between Little Hanting and the nearest town.

"Sophie?" He called out, stepping forward. Hunter stopped abruptly, feeling the dewy grass beneath his feet. Barefoot again, damn it. He glanced down to confirm that he was still in his scruffy grey pyjamas.

"Sophie's not here." A familiar voice called back, as a figure stepped forward.

Tall and willowy like her daughter, with the same dark brown hair. Beverley Murphy.

"Bev? What are you doing here? Is Sophie alright?" Hunter rattled off before he could help himself.

In the darkness Bev smiled, her assumptions correct on how this man still felt about her daughter.

"She's fine, Hunter." Bev replied. "I'm here to pass on a message: yesterday she gave birth to a healthy baby boy."

Hunter was struck silent, and after a minute he reminded himself to breathe. He had known that Sophie was pregnant, had known that this day would come. But it was still a shock. He was a father.

"A boy?" He repeated, unable to bring together a more coherent sentence.

"Yes." Bev smiled at the thought of her first grandchild. "Sophie named him Adam."

"Adam?"

"You didn't expect her to call him George, did you?" Bev gave him a shrewd look. "Sophie has had trouble enough hiding the fact that you're the father."

Hunter frowned at this information. "The witches don't know?"

Bev glanced away into the dark woods. "The few that do know decided that it was best the truth was hidden. They don't want the masses to know that their heroic Shadow Witch might have formed an emotional bond with their enemy."

"Sounds familiar." Hunter muttered. Then his eyes narrowed in Bev's direction. "Sophie took a risk sending you, I could have killed you. Why didn't she come herself?"

Bev crossed her arms defensively. "Sophie gave birth yesterday, she's at home recuperating with her new-born son. I was the obvious choice of messenger – you know me, and I, well…"

"You helped me and James escape." Hunter finished, knowing that Bev was telling the truth. She was the one witch he would be willing to listen to. "Thank you, by the way."

Bev shrugged off his thanks. "And Sophie wanted me to… renew her offer."

"The offer where I switch to the side that was willing to kill my best friend?" Hunter returned.

"If you joined us, what is left of the witch-hunters would crumble and yield. You could end this war; you could save so many lives." Bev near begged.

"Do you really believe that I am that important?" Hunter demanded. "Each and every witch-hunter is driven by their own desire to do what is right and good.

I could disappear tomorrow, and they would still fight on."

Bev remained silent, as though she had expected this reaction, even as she hoped for better.

Hunter took a deep, calming breath. "If Sophie's so desperate to join forces, tell her to bring a white flag and re-join the MMC."

Bev tutted at the younger man's suggestion. "As if they would accept her. You have more in common with witches than she has with the witch-hunters."

The scene fell silent, Hunter and Bev stood facing each other without speaking as another long minute dragged on.

Eventually, Bev was the one to break the silence. "If there is nothing else, I should be getting home."

Hunter realised that if he had any true conviction, he should stop her, apprehend her for witch-craft, kill if necessary. But instead he just nodded.

"Is there any message you would like me to pass on to my daughter?" Bev asked.

"Tell her... tell her that I..." Hunter grimaced as he broke off. "Never mind. Goodbye Bev."

Before he could break and show emotion, Hunter blinked back to the Manor.

Leaving Bev in the woods. The sound of a sob broke through the night air. Beverley turned to the sound, to find her daughter behind one of the trees.

"I told you not to stay, my darling." Bev said in a hushed voice.

Sophie tilted her head back, taking deep breaths to restore her calm. She brushed the tears from her cheeks, then held her hand out to her mother. Her hazel eyes burnt all the brighter, and they too were gone.

## Chapter Thirteen

Hunter blinked back to the library, hoping that way no one would notice his absence. But as he made his way upstairs, the house was quiet and his caution unnecessary.

Instead of heading for his own room, Hunter stopped at James' and knocked on the door. Hunter leant against the doorframe, waiting for James to get his arse out of bed, and was surprised to hear muffled voices from the room.

A minute later, the door cracked open and James' head popped round. He squinted in the bad light until he recognised his friend.

"Oh Hunter, it's you. What's up?"

"I was hoping we could talk."

"What, now? It must be two in the mornin'." James grumbled, then sighed resignedly. "Fine, what is it?"

"Let's go downstairs, I think I need a drink. Plus, it's kind of private." Hunter said, pointedly looking at the door and whoever James was trying to hide behind it.

"Alright, let me just... let me put summat on." James replied, then shut the door in Hunter's face.

Hunter could hear voices and movement, and then the door opened, and James was back.

Despite being plagued by thoughts of tonight, Hunter smirked as James tightened the tie on his robe.

"What?" The Yorkshireman demanded.

Then the door opened behind him and a familiar figure shuffled out, half asleep, and with a white guest robe about her.

"Maria?" Hunter started.

"Ugh, now you've woke me up, I need the loo." Maria muttered. "Don't keep James all night."

Hunter watched in silence as the blonde woman padded barefoot down the corridor to the nearest bathroom.

"I'm surprised, that's not who I expected to come out." Hunter admitted.

"What?" James repeated.

"Well, you and Alannah always seemed so chummy, I thought..."

James frowned. "Alannah? Nah, we're just friends. Come on, I thought you wanted a drink?"

Before Hunter could interrogate him on his love life and further, James led the way downstairs to the drawing room. Once inside, Hunter made a beeline for the drink's cabinet.

"Whisky?" James warily watched Hunter pour healthy measures into two glasses. "This must be serious."

Hunter handed his friend a glass, then jumped straight in before he could lose his nerve. "I have a son. Sophie gave birth yesterday."

James stood there, holding his drink half-way to his lips. A minute dragged by until he was able to speak.

"Con…gratulations?" The single word rose in pitch. James coughed and tried again. "Are you alright, Hunter?"

Hunter shrugged and tilted the golden liquid in his glass. "I don't know. I mean, I knew the day would come."

"What will you do about it?" James asked, sitting on one of the armchairs.

Hunter let out a groan. "What should I do? I can't reconcile things with Sophie. I can't take a new-born baby from its mother. So where does that leave me?"

James shrugged helpfully. "Carrying on as before? It might be a terrible thing to suggest, but Sophie isn't going to hurt him. Maybe… let's finish this thing, then we can concentrate on getting your son."

Hunter drummed his fingers against the glass. "You know what else this means – Sophie is going to step back into the fray, and things are going to get worse."

"You know this?" James asked sceptically.

"It's an educated guess." Hunter countered. "It has been my suspicion that the absence of the Shadow

Witch has been due to her pregnancy, rather than any injury gained from the last battle."

James exhaled. "You're gonna have to tell Hayworth and Marks. Even if you don't share all the facts, they need to know to expect a backlash."

*****

After speaking with James, Hunter returned to bed, but tossed and turned and didn't sleep. Eventually when he felt dawn arriving, he could stop pretending and get up.

Pulling on his trainers, he headed out running alone – no one else was mad enough to be up and running before six in the morning. He ran harder and faster than normal, pushing his muscles to the limit, and feeling the sweet distraction of his breathing becoming more rugged and his heart pounding in his chest. Hunter lapped the estate twice, then put in a third at a more leisurely pace to bring his vitals back to normal. But he was still filled with an electric energy. He wasted some more time with a cold bath, then made his way to the kitchen, hoping to catch his boss.

Eventually General Hayworth padded in, looking half-asleep and in the search for caffeine.

"Sir, could I have a word, please."

Taking the General's silence as permission, Hunter took a deep breath and began to explain his theory that the Shadow Witch had only been delayed by pregnancy, and that her return was imminent.

Hayworth stood silently listening to him, giving the odd grunt when he thought Hunter was being less than honest in his account.

"And who told you this?" He barked. "The Shadow's flying monkey?"

"No, her mother." Hunter replied quickly.

"Why would..." Hayworth trailed off as he quickly put the pieces together. "You know what, I don't want to know. So, have you got any theories on where and how, she will strike?"

Hunter sighed, glad that he had gotten the General on side. Or at least as much as Hayworth could be. "Nadira Shah's intelligence points to an attack on the capital. This is backed up with the suspicions of other allies."

The General took this in, then finally nodded. "Right, we'll deploy extra men to London. Dawkins can lead this op."

"Sir, I really think that I-" Hunter started to protest.

"You are too valuable to be stuck in one place, organising troops." Hayworth countered, guessing where Hunter was heading. "You will continue your duties here. Then, if Dawkins sends a distress signal, you will join the fight. Understood?"

Hunter's shoulders dropped, feeling very much like a castigated child. "Yes sir."

## Chapter Fourteen

Little Hanting seemed very quiet indeed after the upheaval of its military residents. They left one gloomy autumn morning, packed into the vehicles they had spent the last few months salvaging, and coaxing into life.

Hunter saw them off, then returned to the Manor.

The next few days felt strange, as Hunter went about his daily routine. When he went running in the morning, only his own team accompanied him; and when he trained after breakfast, less than a dozen joined him in the courtyard. Any less, and they could move the training sessions back inside, like they had at the beginning of the year.

Another week went past, and no news came from London or Manchester. Hunter knew that he was not alone in wishing that the witches would get their attack over with. Wherever they hit, he would take the remaining forces to bolster numbers. Staying at home waiting was getting tedious.

Then one evening, dusk was settling over Astley Manor, the beauty of the sunset lost behind thick clouds. When there was a crescendo of magic that nearly deafened Hunter. Before stopping to think, he jumped out of his seat and sprinted to the control room.

"Attack!" He shouted, barging into his former dining room.

The control room was already a hive of activity, as people boxed files, and hurried about.

"Yes, Marks felt it too." Hayworth snapped. "Get outside, scout numbers and location. You are not permitted to engage the enemy."

Hunter nodded, and pausing only to arm himself, he left through the front door.

Rain was just beginning to fall, and the heavy cloud and low light would help him to remain invisible. Hunter only hoped his eyes were sharp enough to spot any stray witches, before they noticed him.

He kept off the crunchy gravel of the drive, and padded silently along the lawn, moving as quickly as he could. Up ahead, he could feel more than hear the presence of many. Magic hummed in the air.

Hunter was surprised that Sophie and her minions hadn't just tried blasting down the front door of the Manor. Instead, they were hovering on the border of the estate, as though they were still wary of the protection the Manor offered its occupants – and still wary of Hunter.

They were near the location of the last battle of Little Hanting. In fact… they were exactly at that location.

Hunter felt uneasy as he moved close enough to see the milling crowd. He tried to count them and estimated two hundred or more.

Suddenly in the centre of the masses, Hunter saw her. Sophie. Her dark brown hair tumbled down her shoulders, her face tanned from the summer sun. Hunter had forgotten how beautiful she was. Obviously motherhood suited her.

Sophie stood with her arms open, her lips moving. Hunter was too far away to hear her chant, but a chill crept up his spine.

Hunter silently swore. He had heard rumours of this ritual, but had never witnessed it. Less than a year ago, more than fifty witches had died violently on this spot. Today Sophie was channelling it.

Having seen enough, Hunter wasted no time and blinked straight back to the Manor.

"Hunter, what news?" Marks asked.

Hunter turned to see Anthony Marks and General Hayworth standing by the window, both armed.

"Not good, sirs." Hunter reported. "At least two hundred individuals, plus the Shadow Witch is tapping into the power left by the last battle."

Marks swore violently enough to make even General Hayworth look surprised.

"We're heavily outnumbered. I doubt we'll be able to call back the troops in time." Hayworth assessed aptly. "We have to retreat."

Hunter blanched at the idea of abandoning his family home, the famous Astley Manor. But there were more important things to protect than a pile of bricks, surely?

Without warning, Hunter's chest constricted, and a voice rang through his head.

"Astley, give yourself to me, or I shall destroy everything in my path to find you. You have two minutes."

"Sophie." Hunter gasped as air flooded his lungs again. He looked up at Hayworth and Marks, and in that moment he could tell that both men had heard the voice too.

"Don't you bloody dare." Hayworth growled.

Hunter scowled at them curtailing his sudden urge to be a martyr.

"Right, that's sorted then." Marks announced. "Hayworth, get everyone to the back of the house, have Hunter take them to join Nadira Shah. Hunter, go fetch your mother."

Hunter was about to leave, when Marks grabbed his arm. The older man watched the retreating back of General Hayworth, then turned to Hunter.

"Make sure Hayworth escorts your mother first. He must secure the other side. Then send the others, and go. Promise me you'll go."

"What?" Hunter looked at Marks with a heavy suspicion. "And what do you plan on doing while all this takes place?"

"Stall them." Marks replied. "The Shadow is already building up to end this – you can feel it too, don't deny it."

"But-"

"No time, Hunter. Get everyone out, including yourself – that's an order. Then promise me you'll do everything you can to get a handle on this power of yours. It may prove to be the decisive weapon."

Lost for words, Hunter nodded numbly.

Before any further argument came up, Marks stepped back. He looked on the verge of saying something more, but just shook his head and walked away.

Hunter caught his breath. Now was not the time for emotion! He turned and ran up the main staircase, rounding the corner to his mother's wing of the house.

"Mother!" He yelled as he flung the door open.

"What now, George?" Mrs Astley's voice came from the dining area she'd had Charles set up for her.

"We need to go. Now." Hunter replied. "The witches have us surrounded."

Mrs Astley blinked, taking this in. "How very inconvenient, I've just made a pot of tea."

Mrs Astley sat there, looking at her pale blue teapot for a regretful moment. Then with a sigh she got to her feet. "Is there time to pack?"

"No mother." Hunter answered firmly.

"Well, let us go then." Mrs Astley commanded. "If things are so dire, I cannot understand why you are dallying, George!"

Hunter looked at his mother with surprise, but Mrs Astley just huffed and grabbed a coat on the way out. Hunter followed his mother downstairs, the amount of magic in the air was suffocating, his overwhelmed senses made him jumpy. But Mrs Astley led the way calmly.

The dozen people that had remained at Astley Manor were huddled near the library in the recesses of the house. Hunter was relieved to see his team amongst them and took a moment to do a head count.

"Everyone's here, Hunter." Halbrook snapped. "Except Marks."

"He's rear guard." Hunter replied shortly, pushing his way through. He noticed that a section of the wall had been cleared of all pictures and clutter in anticipation of use.

"You're front guard." Hunter added, placing his hand on the wall. "Escort Mrs Astley though, and secure the other side."

General Hayworth looked affronted at being ordered around by the younger man, and there was the gut-wrenching realisation dawning on his face at what Marks was really up to.

But before he could collect his thoughts and argue, a very determined blonde battle-ax linked her arm through his. Despite the fact of the difference in height and build, the petite Mrs Astley led the General to the wall.

Whether it was in compliance through shock, or the sense of duty awakening, Hayworth stepped forward.

Hunter concentrated on opening a link and watched as Hayworth and his mother vanished through the solid wall. With a curt nod, the rest of the men and women filed through, until only his team was left. Sweat was breaking out at the strain of holding it open, but the four remained, in a protective circle around him.

"Go." Hunter ordered.

"Hunter…" James started.

"Go." He repeated. "I'll follow. I promise."

James sighed at his friend's stubbornness but signalled to the others. Without another word, they left.

Hunter dropped his hand from the wall and let the link go. He stood panting for a moment, then turned in the direction of the front hallway. He had spent less than five minutes here. Was he too late to stop Marks? Probably.

Was he too late to save him? Possibly, but he was going to take that chance anyway.

Not wasting a moment, Hunter focused on the location of the witches, then closed his eyes. Hunter felt the familiar pressure close around him, increasing as he attempted to move closer to the source of his distress, until it was suffocating.

Hunter tried to push through again but found a blockade of magic. Even though he wasn't convinced he was physically anywhere, Hunter could feel the burning in his lungs from the prolonged lack of oxygen. He had never felt anything like this and started to panic over his inability to set down. A debilitating pain began sharp spikes in his mind, as he found his struggle for control slipping. And fading.

"Hunter!" The female shriek pierced faintly through his conscious.

Then Hunter felt a wedge of energy knock the last of the breath out of him.

Hunter landed with a heavy thud and coughed, gasping at the cool air that was a relief to his lungs. He opened his eyes and spots danced before them, but he could see, of a sort. It was night, but he could make out the long grass that surrounded him.

The next sense to reawaken was his hearing, he could just hear the hurrying of feet, and several people calling his name.

"Here." He choked, then cleared his voice. He raised his arm sluggishly to make his point. "Here!"

The feet came closer, and Hunter felt a pair of hands run over him in assessment.

"He's ok." James' familiar voice came through. "What happened?"

Hunter sat up, which seemed a good idea at first, but quickly made his head throb again.

"Hunter, where's Marks?" General Hayworth insisted.

Hunter sighed and hung his head. "I tried. I tried to save him." His voice came out as weak as his argument.

There was an abrupt roar, which took Hunter by surprise, as Hayworth turned and swore at the night sky. Anthony Marks had been an ally, and had become a close friend.

Ian moved into Hunter's eye line and pulled a small stone out of his pocket. "A distress signal was sent to Nadira. Hopefully her witch-hunters will be on the look-out." Ian turned the stone in his palm, before re-pocketing it.

## Chapter Fifteen

Nadira's patrols found them within a couple of hours and that same night, Hunter and the other survivors were housed in cramped, but welcome accommodation.

It was nearly midday by the time Hunter dragged himself out of bed by the following day. His limbs felt like lead after the previous night, and his head pounded as though he'd downed a bottle of whisky.

As soon as he left his sleeping quarters, he bumped into Alannah, who recognised his need for coffee and steered him to the nearest source. Once he had his second cup, Ian arrived and let Hunter know that he had been requested for a meeting.

Hunter allowed himself to feel relief that his team was alive and well, before he succumbed to the dread of the meeting ahead. He hated meetings; he had often made James go as his representative when the old Council at Oxford expected his presence. But Hunter guessed that he couldn't get out of this one. If anything, he respected Anthony Marks too much to miss it.

The meeting came and went; it was exactly how Hunter imagined it would be. With frayed tempers and 'what ifs'. It didn't matter, a great man was still dead. After they had lost George "Young" Astley and Brian Lloyd; Anthony Marks was one of the last of that generation.

Oh no, wait, there was Gareth Halbrook too. Hunter thought that fate had a cruel sense of humour that he was still alive, when they had lost so many good guys. At least Halbrook was posted down in London with Sergeant Dawkins and was well out of the way.

During the meeting they had quickly discussed Mark's successor, all eyes turning expectantly towards Hunter.

"I nominate Nadira Shah." He had immediately voiced, surprising them all – none more than Nadira herself.

There were no objections to the promotion, and Nadira was named the first female leader of the Malleus Maleficarum Council. The congratulations on such a momentous occasion were diluted by the mourning for a good man.

*****

Hunter took a couple of days to recover from his suspended time in nothingness. Outwardly he was very subdued. Inward, he was scared. It was a wake-up call that he knew next to nothing about his powers.

354

Had he been foolish in using them so frequently when he was unaware of his limits? The threat of the witches' rebellion had made him desperate enough to rush in, head on.

And he'd almost died. Oh, Hunter had come close to death on countless occasions, but it was different when an enemy was going to kill you, rather than his own ignorance.

If it hadn't been for that final push... Hunter thought back to the moment when he'd been catapulted away. He didn't recall doing something, at that point he was close to incapable of planning anything. But he had instances in his past when he'd acted subconsciously. The image of a church brought to rubble flashed into his thoughts.

Yes, it had to be that. Because the only other explanation... that was too hard to take in, and Hunter purposefully refused to think of her.

James drifted in and out while Hunter recovered, much like he had done at the beginning of the year. He was concerned for his friend again, not wanting Hunter to lapse into depression once more.

General Hayworth had drilled Hunter over every detail of what had occurred at the Manor, and Hunter had replied honestly, but perfunctorily. It was only when he repeated it to James one afternoon that Hunter felt the reality of it stab him afresh.

James chewed his lip, worried. "Truth is, we don't know shit about what you can do. With the most extensive library in the UK, we've found nowt substantial for months."

Hunter shifted, trying to get comfortable on the awful camp bed he'd been given. "A library we no longer have." He muttered, feeling a spark of anger, knowing that Sophie and her minions might have destroyed it all by now. Or at the very least, would have pawed through all the contents.

James shrugged, he loved Astley Manor, but that wasn't the point he was trying to make. "We was getting nowhere, mate. Maybe you need another trip to Italy."

Hunter narrowed his eyes, remembering his last holiday to Italy, when he had first met Sophie.

James could tell where his friend's thoughts were going, and he was quick to clarify. "Look, it's the home of the Benandanti. If you're gonna find anything, it'll be there."

Hunter groaned and rested his head back against the wall. "The Benandanti were killed hundreds of years ago, I think that's the definition of a cold trail. Besides, I'm needed here. I am not going to leave you guys facing the witches alone, while I'm off on a wild goose chase."

"But it could answer everything!" James argued. "It'd be worth the risk."

"James, things are only going to get worse here, I can't leave." Hunter replied calmly. "Be honest, if you were in my position, you would do the same."

James sighed and muttered something beneath his breath, then stood up to leave.

"Just… don't leave it too late."

## Chapter Sixteen

A few weeks after they had relocated to Manchester, they had company.

Sergeant Dawkins arrived in an old jeep, accompanied by three other soldiers. He was ushered straight into a room with the General and was introduced to Nadira.

"Must have been a long journey. Why did you drive? Hunter could have brought you." The General mused while he put the kettle over a portable stove and dug out the rations of coffee.

Dawkins looked over at Hunter. "No offence, General, but nothing short of a life or death emergency will entice me to travel with Mr Astley again."

Hunter looked up, a little surprised at Dawkins' boldness. "Colin, I'm hurt. You know I'm just looking for another opportunity to make you faint."

The sergeant tried to keep a serious face, but a smile flashed over his lips.

"Ok, down to business." Dawkins pushed on. "We've got a good handle on London. It's too big to know we've covered everything, but it turns out the witch-hunter running things, Tyler, knows what he's doing."

"Tyler who?" Nadira asked.

Dawkins looked a little sheepish. "I've been down there a month, and I still can't pronounce his surname. Begins with an M. But yeah, Tyler – tall, imposing guy, used to part-time as a lawyer..." Dawkins looked about, hoping something would sound familiar. "2nd gen, used to report to the London Bridge branch."

"A 2nd gen?" Hunter echoed, surprised that such an important role would go to such a new family.

"Not every higher generation witch-hunter is made for leadership." Dawkins replied drily, with more than a tad of insinuation. "Tyler has a good network of allies down there. And then there's the wiccans. There's a lot of wiccans."

"London has the densest population of them." Hunter suddenly reeled out. "It's a very... accepting city."

Dawkins looked over at the unnecessary interruption. "Well, they've been very helpful."

The sergeant looked over to his General. "Sir, I know your intel points to an attack on the capital, but we need to be prepared for elsewhere. We are strong there, possibly too strong for the witch army. I can't imagine they'd throw their lives away on uncertain victory with high prices."

Hayworth nodded, as he listened to his sergeant's opinion. "I will take this into consideration, Dawkins. But until we have firm proof, let us proceed as though London will be their target."

## Chapter Seventeen

"Hunter!"

The cry rang through the makeshift barracks. It was nearly 10pm, and Hunter was trying to get some sleep before his turn on watch duty in the early hours. It was Hallowe'en, and they were taking their watch duties seriously.

"Hunter!" General Hayworth's familiar voice blasted through the silence.

Hunter cracked open an eye and groaned. "Yes sir."

"Emergency signal from Dawkins. Get your team and get to London. Now."

"What?" Hunter asked, now fully awake. He threw back the bed sheets and grabbed his trousers from the pile of clothes on the floor.

"Dawkins sent an emergency signal through the wiccan stones. I need you to go assess the situation. We'll be mobilizing here if he needs back-up."

Hunter nodded, as he pulled on his shirt and hunted for his stab vest. He was still checking his gun when the door opened again. This time James walked in, followed by Ian, Maria and Alannah. They were all kitted up and looked ready to go.

"We got the message, let's go." James announced.

Hunter felt a wave of respect at how quickly his team responded, followed by a wavering doubt on his ability to get them from Manchester to London safely. He'd done a few practise runs with James, but that didn't completely eradicate his worries.

But he didn't say a word and waited for his team to take their positions. Hunter counted to three, then closed his eyes and let his focus shift.

There was the familiar, suffocating darkness, followed by the cool air of their destination. Hunter opened his eyes to the sight of the MMC's London Bridge base.

"You took long enough."

Hunter spun round to see Dawkins standing by a black window. He ignored the sergeant's snarky comment. "What's happened?"

Dawkins didn't reply immediately, something outside at ground level was occupying his attention.

"The witches have gathered to burn us alive. You've got to appreciate the irony."

Hunter frowned and moved to join him. They must have been ten floors up, which made the angle incredibly awkward, but Hunter could make out the orange glow at the base of the building.

"We're about to burn to death? Great." Ian stated in his usual dry manner.

"Care to explain, Colin?" James asked.

Dawkins looked over at him. "I was wrong over how secure we were. The new mayor and his team switched sides. They must have been planning it for a while, maybe they never really believed that we could permanently take London back from the witches. The wiccans split, the majority staying with us, but still a sizeable group joined the witches."

"Casualties?" Hunter asked.

"We're not sure yet, sir." Dawkins reported formally. "Tyler went down in the first attack, along with a dozen others. After I sent the alert, I saw we were outnumbered and ordered a retreat. The rest of our forces have scattered, with orders to meet at the MMC branch in Oxford asap."

"And you stayed behind, Colin?" James frowned at his friend's bravado. He only hoped the sergeant didn't have ideas of martyrdom. They were still reeling from the loss of Anthony Marks.

"I'd already sent the emergency call to you, I had to await your arrival and fill you in. I didn't trust leaving a note to be adequate."

"Um, sorry to break this up guys." Ian interrupted, the tall sergeant standing by the next window. "But I think they've set the building on fire."

The rest of the group pushed closer to the window and it seemed true, the orange glow had grown fiercer, and smoke began to cloud visibility of the stars.

"Do we engage them?" Maria asked, as she checked her gun.

"We'll get revenge for Anthony Marks." Alannah concurred, her green eyes sparking.

"No." Hunter commanded. "We'll leave and reconvene with the others at Oxford."

There was a moment of silence when everyone looked to Hunter, their disappointment evident.

"Y'know, I thought being part of this team would include a little action. Not acting as glorified messengers." Ian growled, perfectly expressing the thoughts of the group.

Hunter stood, not sure what to say. To be truthful, he wanted nothing more than to lead them down to the witches baying for their blood, and solve a few problems with violence. But someone here had to be logical and sensible. Bloody hell, why did it have to be him.

"Look, we can go down there and repel a few witches before we die. Or let's not be cocky, we might toast in the inferno on the way." Hunter snapped, feeling his own frustration at the prolonged passive nature he'd adopted. "There is no guarantee that the Shadow is with them, and I won't waste your lives despatching a few of her servants. I promise, the time will come when we face her – soon."

Hunter looked from face to determined face, when eventually his team conceded.

There was a cough from the side of the room. "Well, if you're all done team motivating, do you think we could get out of here?" Dawkins asked, hardly able to keep the sarcasm out of his voice.

Hunter shot the sergeant a suitably dirty look, but held out his arms in what was becoming the usual manner. Without a word, his team stepped in and held onto him. Only Dawkins hung back, the nerves finally beginning to show as he looked down at Hunter's outstretched arm.

"Any time, Colin." James snapped, ready to get this over with.

Dawkins swallowed nervously, then gingerly held onto Hunter's forearm.

Hunter didn't give him the chance to change his mind, and immediately blinked from the burning building at London Bridge, to the grounds of the old MMC headquarters in Oxford.

As he felt the cold, fresh breeze on his face, and the light spattering of rain, Hunter looked about him. This had been his MMC office, where he had been registered when young, and where he had made constant trips for reports and meetings since he had become a fully-fledged witch-hunter six years ago.

It was as familiar and frustrating a building as any workplace.

Or it had been.

Hunter looked at it now and saw only rubble. A couple of walls still stood, useless monuments to what had once been. Oxford was the oldest MMC headquarters, and as such was the historical seat of the

Council, as well as storing most processed amulets from the binding process.

The Shadow Witch had hit this place first, after she had procured the Key from Hunter's dear friend, Charlotte King. The Key had released all the bound power the MMC had been storing away for generations – not a good system, in hindsight.

It was painful for Hunter to look on to his old, ruined offices. A reminder that, despite the wheels set irreversibly in motion in Venice, here the war really started.

A heavy pat on the shoulder brought him back to the present, and Hunter turned to see James looking back at him with a similar pain in his usually light brown eyes.

"It's really quiet. Where is everyone?" Alannah asked, looking around uneasily.

"We blinked…" Dawkins gasped out, trying not to retch. "They'll arrive… in a few… hours."

Ian smirked at the sight of General Hayworth's right-hand man so disabled. "Maria and I will make a perimeter check. We'll be back in half an hour." Ian stated, volunteering for the walk. Well, it was better than huddling in the rubble of some building while they waited.


The survivors came slowly, in dribs and drabs. Many had emergency vehicles and used precious fuel to escape the city, and they brought as many as they could with them.

Ian and Maria had found a disused theatre that might be big enough to house them for the night. With the help of James and Alannah, and the locals who awoke to all the noise, food and spare blankets were acquired; and a section of the theatre was cordoned off for first aid.

Hunter had managed to round up Oxford's promising medical students. Despite the witch revolution, they were all here to learn, and still socialised in the same places they had when Hunter had gone to university here. The young meds had come willingly to the theatre, that was now full of people; soldiers, witch-hunters, and helpful locals.

Once the first mad rush of caring for the wounded, and organising the able-bodied had passed, Hunter stepped back to observe the place. Despite the injured, it was warming to see how his old town of Oxford rallied to help them. That was something the witches would never understand, would never overcome in their drive to control all – the average person could step up and do things they would never account for.

*****

Hunter tried to get a few hours' sleep, then the next day he worked alongside Sergeant Dawkins to organise the troops. They would send those willing back to London, to be their eyes and ears, to make sure the people they left behind were not treated too harshly.

To the rest, they offered a chance to leave, to go home to safety. Or to go on with them to Manchester, to face the next fight with the witches. Hunter was

367

heartened that nearly every man and woman immediately signed up to travel North.

Leaving Dawkins with the wiccan stones in case of emergency, Hunter took his team back to Manchester that very afternoon, to report to the General all that had occurred.

## Chapter Eighteen

The notion that Manchester was the next target of the witches became a firm fact. For the past couple of weeks, ever since London had been hit on Hallowe'en, their wiccan spies had been running back with information. It was the first time all details pointed in one direction.

But this time, they were ready for them.

Nadira and General Hayworth had divided their forces into groups, bolstered by the volunteers from the city. Hunter looked over his group, noting how soldiers now outnumbered witch-hunters, after they had been targeted so fiercely by the witches. Both were outnumbered by the citizens of Manchester and the surrounding area – it was cheering to see so many step up to defend their city, their home.

Hunter was glad to see the familiar faces of his team in the sea of strangers. They sat together, outwardly looking calm and ready, a highly skilled team that was comforting to the rest that were new to battle. But Hunter knew them well enough now to see the nervous tells. James was twisting the gold ring on his right hand that blocked minor spells; Alannah sat polishing an already gleaming knife; Maria fiddled with the zips on her stab vest and jacket; and Ian – well, Hunter had yet to work out what nervous tick that man had, he was constantly calm and in control.

Hunter drifted back to his friends, causing them to look up.

"You sure about…" Alannah started. She coughed and lowered her voice. "You sure about your plan?"

"Course he is." James interrupted, then glanced at Hunter. "Aren't you?"

"Already told you James, if you don't feel confident, you can stay here and keep charge of the others." Hunter replied, repeating an earlier suggestion. "The four of us can handle it."

James snorted. "Yeah right, as if I've ever hesitated in following you into madness."

Hunter just smiled in response, not sure James should be describing his leadership skills and plans as 'madness'. At least, not in public.

Hunter was saved from trying to come up with a suitably intelligent reply by the sudden headache that accompanied magic and spells being cast. It was immense, almost over-whelming, and Hunter took a moment to tune it out enough to concentrate. He could see Alannah making the same mental struggle, as the other three just looked on expectantly.

"They're here." Hunter murmured. The witches had come. They were about a mile to the south, if his senses were correct.

Hunter was distracted by a sharp pain in his side. He pulled the wiccan stone out of his pocket, watching as the lump of quartz flashed hot, then faded back to its normal smoky colour. He held it up for the others to see, as proof that their allies were engaging.

"It's time."

Hunter turned to the masses and shouted for attention. The chatter and general noise immediately died down, and everyone looked to him.

He took a deep breath, realising they were expecting some sort of glorious, heroic speech – because wasn't that what he was to these people, a hero they had heard could do miracles and lead them to victory?

But Hunter's throat closed up at the very thought.

"Let's move out." He shouted in a strangled voice.

There was a snicker besides him.

"Oh aye, very inspiring, Hunter." James didn't even try to hide his amusement as he watched his friend struggle over something so simple. "I hope that speech doesn't go down in history – really shite final words."

Hunter was tempted to retaliate, but he remembered his audience. They probably wouldn't like to see the man they were trusting with their lives, beating a friend.

So, Hunter turned and nodded to the rest of his team.

The hundred or so men and women picked up their arms and followed Hunter to the south, where magic was bristling so strongly, Hunter was surprised the 1st gens couldn't feel it.

There was a blast of light to one side as they approached, followed by the screams of the spell's victims. The ground shook with the strength of magic that ran across it, and the wind picked up, whipping through the forms and fields that had become the site of battle.

As they approached within sight of the witches, Hunter saw the illusions of monsters that were hastily thrown up to gain the witches time to bring out harder spells. Fire burst out on their left flank, as salamanders and fire-wrought creatures moved into existence.

Hunter threw up his shield, the illusions of monsters faded to nothing. The fire wavered, but having enough dry fuel to sustain it, it spread on.

The witches hesitated, seeing their spells falter, and knowing that the infamous Hunter Astley must be behind it. Hunter took advantage of the moment and led his fighters on, forcing the witches in close combat that served knives and guns better than magic.

Hunter cut a swathe through his opponents. His anger spurred him on, with each thrust of his knife, broken neck, or shot to the heart, he was avenging Anthony Marks, and countless other witch-hunters and innocents that had been caught in this rebellion. He did not spare a thought for the blood that coated his hands and arms, he ignored the cuts and wounds he gained as adrenaline surged through his body. But he was aware that he had pushed further than anyone else, and started to back up, enemies on all sides able to pick him out.

There was a gunshot, close enough that Hunter could hear it over the fray, and one of the witches before him crumpled to the ground.

A pat on his shoulder made Hunter start, but he turned to see James and Maria moving up to join him, Maria turning her gun to her next victim.

There was a wave of magic so strong, Hunter was nearly knocked over. By the time he regained his balance, he recognised the swirling clouds overhead, and felt the now-familiar rhythm of Sophie's magic. The wind picked up, and Hunter swore.

"Maria!" James' voice cut through the noise.

Hunter turned to see Maria unmoving on the ground, and James dispatching the witch that had managed to take down their best gunman.

Hunter felt a renewed strike of magic against his shield, but he pushed it back with a mental shove, then knelt by Maria.

James was already searching for signs of life with shaking hands. He then gave a sigh, his shoulders drooping. "She's got a pulse."

James closed his eyes and muttered something to himself. If Hunter didn't know him better, he would have sworn it was a prayer of thanks.

Hunter was distracted by something sharp cutting into the back of his exposed neck. He looked up to see wind-driven ice starting weakly but gaining momentum. Cries of pain went up around him as his allies were forced to stagger back. The witches seemed immune from the sharp fragments, or at least were not the intended victims.

"Hunter, we need to move." Ian barked as he ran up, Alannah on his heels.

"Maria?" Alannah's green eyes were filled with fresh worry above a blood-stained cheek.

"She's alive, she'll be fine." Hunter replied quickly, determined to keep positive.

James huddled over Maria, protecting her from the cutting ice. "Hunter, I can't... I need to..."

Hunter put a hand on his friend's shoulder. "I understand. Get her to safety. We'll go ahead."

James nodded and swallowed hard. He scooped up Maria, who stayed lifeless in his arms. "Good luck." He said to the others, then began to jog in the direction of their back line.

## Chapter Nineteen

Hunter stayed just long enough to watch James get to a safe distance. He was surprised to feel let down; this had been the first time that James had chosen not to be at his side to face life-threatening danger. Hunter grimaced at his own thoughts – James was not a coward, far from it. But personally insisting that he take care of Maria... he must care for her more than Hunter had guessed.

"So, what now?" Alannah asked.

Hunter glanced from Alannah to Ian, they both awaited his next orders.

"We carry on as planned." He answered with a shrug.

There was a flicker of fear from Alannah, but Ian just nodded.

"Right, let's go." The sergeant simply said, then started in the opposite direction James had taken – further into danger, instead of away from it.

Hunter hurried after him, then moved into the lead. Despite the fact that Hunter's senses were nearly over-whelmed by the volume of magic and casting witches, Sophie's magic rang out as a clear chord of power. With an unsettling ease, Hunter followed it towards the source.

He didn't trust himself to blink them safely to her location, so they had to take the mundane route. As they fought their way through loose groups of witches, they came more heavily under attack. Hunter doubled the shield around the three of them, reluctantly letting his shield fade from the other fighters. He couldn't possibly maintain both.

In a thick bubble of anti-magic, the trio pushed forward. Hunter was glad to have his two best fighters with his, as Ian floored a witch, and Alannah made sure he didn't get up again.

Hunter could feel Sophie's presence getting closer, and finally spotted her. Her witches had pulled back, as though even they could not stand to get close to her magic. Her long brown hair was half-falling out of a plait and she was dressed for combat, with the stab vest that Hunter had given her on top of a short, dark jacket and jeans.

Everything was muted, and everyone seemed to clear the space between Hunter and the Shadow Witch. A hundred yards apart, Hunter's pulse raced with anticipation – it would all be over now.

Sophie stopped mid-spell and faced the witch-hunter. Without her support, the clouds and the wind settled, and the ice eased off.

Taking a deep breath, Hunter started to move cautiously forward, Ian and Alannah flanking him. He was aware of the eyes that turned their way.

Hunter felt Sophie's magic curling and preparing for release. Within a heartbeat, his own power reacted with it. A visible dome of energy crackled over them, and Hunter could only stare at it in wonder. Was this him?

"Astley!" Sophie snarled. "Don't do this."

Ah, she was pissed off, so it had to be his doing.

"I can't stop it. Even if I wanted to, I would not." Hunter replied. "Your witches are on their own, now."

Her witches were powerful, but without the aid of their Shadow, Hunter hoped they could be overcome.

Sophie's lip curled as she wildly looked around her for a point of weakness. Finding none, she suddenly became calm. She took a few steps forward, her movements achingly familiar.

"So… what's the plan now, Hunter? Kill the big bad witch while she's defenceless?" Sophie asked with a sigh, knowing how her lover saw her now.

"It has to happen, Sophie." Hunter replied. "It's the only way to stop them."

Sophie gave a bitter laugh. "Oh, that you believe that! I miss your optimism, Hunter. So… will you kill me?"

Hunter fought to keep his expression neutral. "Me, or others."

There was a flash of metal, as one of Alannah's throwing knives whipped across the distance. Ian pulled out his gun and fired off half a dozen rounds.

Sophie raised both hands, and the bullets slowed and stopped in an invisible barrier. She looked surprised at the block, but her expression turned to pain, as the knife sank into her upper chest. Alannah, by mistake or design, hitting the weak point of her armour, near the neck.

Hunter steeled himself, as Sophie's scream rent the air, and she dropped to her knees.

Sophie flicked her long brown hair out of the way, as it sought to escape, and her furious eyes focused on Alannah. "You little bitch!"

Sophie took a deep breath and grabbed the knife, wrenching it out with another scream. She gasped, and wiped a hand over the wound, where the blood flow was already ceasing and healing.

"Do you really think you can kill me?" Sophie spat, then turned the knife in her hand and threw it with all her strength at the shell-shocked Alannah.

Alannah's eyes widened as she witnessed her own knife being used against her. There was the sudden movement of a huge bulk, who stepped in the way, and grunted as the knife embedded itself in his back.

Ian gripped Alannah tightly by the arms, and gave a reassuring smile, before he slumped.

Hunter's breathing increased, his pulse speeding. His window of opportunity was closing up and everything was going wrong.

Sophie smiled, and waved a blood-stained hand. "Bye."

Without thinking, Hunter charged towards her. Already her image was fading to the grey of shadows, but Hunter reached out desperately. He felt that familiar soft, warm nothingness, followed by the cold wind and hard ground beneath his feet.

Gasping, Hunter got his bearings. There was light and noise, and deafening magic a mile or so to his right. And directly in front of him was Sophie.

"You shouldn't have come." She said softly, pity in her usually cold eyes.

Hunter shrugged. "You didn't give me much choice."

He slowly removed a long knife from his belt and watched as Sophie silently did the same. With an unspoken signal, they started to circle, each watching for weak spots in the other. Then they attacked.

Hunter was surprised at Sophie's speed, but didn't have time to marvel, as he followed up his attack with deflections and taking a step back that only intensified Sophie's attack.

But Hunter wasn't the best in the MMC for nothing, and caught a lapse in her guard and forced her to retreat in turn.

They both backed off to catch their breath, and Sophie took a moment to wipe blood from a new cut on her arm.

"You've remembered all your training." Hunter remarked.

Sophie bit back a smile. "I had a good teacher."

They came to again, the strike and parry patterns getting longer and more intricate.

"You were holding back on me before." Hunter gasped.

"So were you." Sophie countered, her hazel eyes flashing.

Sophie fainted to the left, then tackled him from the right, so that they both lost balance and fell to the floor.

Hunter felt the breath knocked out of him, and suddenly found himself on his back, Sophie straddling his legs to pin them down.

"Well now." She murmured, looking down at Hunter, her gaze warming. "Join me, please Hunter. Together we can set this world straight."

"After you destroyed it?" Hunter snapped back, bringing up his knife in a half-hearted effort.

Sophie easily caught his wrist, and pressed it to his chest. "No, after I destroyed the only reality you knew. Don't mistake comfort and familiarity for something right. Please Hunter, don't you want to be in a world free from all the wrongs you knew were in your Council? Don't you want a world where you could be with me? With your son?"

Hunter stilled at the mention of his son. Where was he now? At home with his grandmother, while his mother went on her killing spree?

"Not at this price." Hunter replied quietly.

Hunter gathered himself, and threw Sophie from him, he scrambled to his feet and glared at her. Hunter pulled out his gun and pointed it at Sophie's chest for a moment, before reluctantly letting it drop.

"You saved me at Astley Manor, didn't you?" Hunter asked. When Sophie made no effort to reply, he sighed. "Consider this a life for a life. Get out of here, Sophie. Take Adam and get away from this fight. If our paths cross again, I will kill you."

Sophie stood, the colour draining from her face. She took a moment to weigh her options, then turned away from Hunter. The shadows thickened about her, and tendril-like wrapped around her form and claimed her. Then she was gone.

Hunter let loose a shaky breath. He really hoped he'd done the right thing. With a quick glance at his surroundings, he blinked back to his friends.

## Chapter Twenty

"Are you sure I can't get you anything else?" Alannah crooned, leaning over the hospital bed.

Ian grinned, it was only natural that she'd want to make it up to him – he had taken a knife in the back for her, after all. "No, I'm fine Alannah. Now settle down – I'm getting tired just watching you."

"I can bring you a book, or a change of clothes from camp." Alannah persisted.

"I'm not much of a reader." Ian sighed, relenting a little. "Clothes would be good though. These are a bit…"

"Blood-stained?" Hunter offered, as he leant back in an uncomfortable plastic chair he'd dragged over.

"Tatty." Ian corrected.

It was nearly midday, and it was hard to believe that the battle had only been over for ten hours or so. They had had an obvious victory, decimating the witch army, and driving back the survivors. The mood was incredibly up-beat, the winter suddenly holding the promise of a hard-won peace, there was no way the witches could mount a retaliation any time soon. Now there was only the slow recovery of their own forces to concern themselves with.

Ian was recovering well. He was already bored of staying in his hospital bed, and wasn't about to let a knife wound turn him into an invalid.

Further down the ward, James leant over the bed where Maria lay. The lieutenant had awoken a few hours before, still feeling weak from whatever had hit her. Of course, James had never left her bedside.

Hunter glanced towards them every now and then, but stayed with Ian to give them a bit of privacy. It occurred to him that even the invulnerable Sergeant Ian Grimshaw might need the comfort of a loved one.

"I could bring your partner, if you want company." Hunter offered.

Ian thought about it for a moment, then grinned. "Nah, not just yet. It'd scare him to see me in this state. Wait until I'm looking a little less…"

"Tatty?" Hunter ventured.

Ian chuckled, then winced in pain. He glanced over at James and Maria for the umpteenth time.

"So… how long has that been going on?"

Hunter shrugged. "Four months." He guessed.

"Six." Alannah corrected.

The two guys looked at her, making her blush.

"What?" She challenged. "We may be in the middle of a war with witches, but me and Maria are still allowed girl talk."

"Girl talk?" Hunter echoed. "Why does that phrase fill me with fear?"

Ian chuckled. "I think you're referring to the ability of women to intimately discuss everything and everyone. I'm exempt, right? Too old for that nonsense."

Alannah just grinned in response and winked. "Forty is not old. Well, I think they're good together."

Ian coughed. "They're coming over."

Hunter looked up to see James pushing a wheelchair, with a tired-looking Maria in it.

James glanced around the guilty faces. "What?" He demanded.

"Nothing." Alannah squeaked.

Hunter shrugged. "We were just talking about you, that's all. Maria, how are you feeling?"

"Like I've been hit by a bus." Maria croaked. "S'fine. I don't need the chair, but Mr Protective here…"

"The doctors said rest." James interrupted. "You shouldn't really be out of bed."

"I wanted to hear what happened firsthand." Maria replied with a sigh, then turned expectantly to Hunter.

Hunter looked at the waiting faces of his team, then began to recount what happened last night, starting with Alannah and Ian's part in it. He finished with a less than faithful account, leaving out the fact that he had let Sophie go, making it sound more like she had escaped.

When he finished, there was silence.

"Guns didn't work, knives didn't work, our miracle 7th gen didn't work." Alannah huffed. "I'd like to know what can kill her."

"She's just another witch." James offered, unconvincingly. "She got lucky this time, that's all. Right, Hunter?"

Hunter looked up at the sound of his name but didn't reply. She'd gotten very lucky. But what if they met again, could Hunter kill her?

"What's she like?" Maria croaked. "The Shadow Witch?"

"Suitably scary." Ian answered.

"Beautiful. No one mentioned she was beautiful." Alannah added, gazing at the boys accusingly. "Well Hunter, I can see why you'd not be interested in… anyone, after her."

"Beautiful, huh?" Maria repeated, twisting to look up at James.

"I never noticed." James added, flashing a warning look at Hunter. "She wasn't my type."

Hunter turned to Alannah again. "We've just fought our biggest battle to date, and you want to go over my dating history?"

Alannah grinned, pleased that he'd caught up. "Yup."

Hunter chuckled. "Uh-huh. Well I wasn't interested in her because she was beautiful."

The silence was immediate, and the look of disbelief was shared by all.

"Ok, it might have had a little to do with it." Hunter conceded. "But it wasn't everything."

"Oh aye, there was her sparkling personality." James added, rolling his eyes. "Cold-hearted bitch was the term we used most often, weren't it?"

As the rest of the team laughed, Hunter crossed his arms.

"If you lot are going to take the piss, I'm going."

"Getting back to the main point." Ian said sombrely, as he re-adjusted the pillow behind him. "I refuse to believe that she's impossible to take down."

"You said there were other Shadows." Maria asked, her voice rough. "How did they die?"

"There were two." James confirmed. "One was a thousand years ago. The second was in the forties – the one that Hunter's grandfather killed."

"And how did he do that?" Alannah asked, her big eyes turning to Hunter.

"No one knows. Old George never made an official report of it."

"Did you never ask him?" Ian asked.

"He died when I was very young." Hunter replied quietly. People in his profession didn't have the longest lifespans. The fact that his grandfather had survived into his sixties was impressive. "I don't remember much about him, only that he was a very private and miserable old man. From my father's stories of Old George, that impression was only intensified."

"So, he never shared?" Alannah sounded very disappointed.

"No." James answered. "And we've exhausted every line of research into that area."

"Well, we'll find something." Alannah said, getting to her feet and stretching. "I'm off to get some sleep."

She leant over the bedside and kissed Ian's cheek, then kissed Maria. "I'm glad you two are ok."

Hunter pushed himself out of the uncomfortable chair. "I'll walk you back to your quarters."

He pulled on his coat and scarf, ready to brave the winter weather.

## Chapter Twenty-one

Christmas was a suitably joyful time. Despite the fact that the world had not recovered, people were making the most of it and gathered with friends and family. Hard-earned meals were cooked, presents had been rustled together, everything was feeling festive.

It was only five in the afternoon, but already it was dark, as Hunter wandered the streets of Manchester, his hands shoved deep into his pockets, and his shoulders hunched against the cold rain. He saw the firelight, bright in the windows of each home, people casting shadows against the curtains. They were all safe and warm, there had been no witch attack since the post-Hallowe'en battle. Hunter felt a little pride at that. But mostly he felt lonely.

Alannah had gone to her parents; Ian had gone to stay with his partner's family; and James had taken Maria, to introduce her to his aunt and uncle.

James had of course invited Hunter to his family's Christmas, like he did every year. But this year Hunter felt like he would be imposing.

Hunter sighed, his breath fogging before him on this wonderfully miserable, grey Christmas. He reluctantly turned on his heel and headed back towards the MMC camp.

It was quiet. Most of the witch-hunters and soldiers had gone home for the festive occasion, just like Hunter's team. But there were a few that were still milling around like lost souls.

Hunter drifted about until he found who he was looking for – he admitted that only severe loneliness would force him to look for her.

"George, you missed the first course." His mother snapped.

Her beady grey eyes followed the tray of sliced turkey that the ever-faithful Charles was carrying. "I hope this is not more of that regurgitated swill – the processed food."

Hunter made an apologetic face in the direction of the people that had joined his mother's table.

"It is fresh, mother. Charles and I went to the Whitaker farm yesterday to pick up our order." Hunter explained, watching as Charles placed the turkey down and came back with equally farm-fresh, steaming vegetables.

"Hm, very well." Mrs Astley conceded. "Although you know I prefer goose."

Hunter sighed and helped Charles bring in the rest of the food, before he could say anything he could regret. Then he sat down and began what truly resembled a Christmas dinner. Roughly a dozen people sat around the table with them, and after a few awkward introductions and clumsy passes of the sprouts, everyone was cheery and content.

"Room for one more?"

Hunter looked up to see Gareth Halbrook, of all people, hovering at the end of the table. Hunter nearly choked on his potatoes.

"Not for you, no." He said, the words leaving his lips before he could stop them.

"George, cover your mouth." Mrs Astley ordered. "And don't be rude to Mr...?"

She gazed up questioningly with her cool, grey eyes.

"Halbrook. Gareth Halbrook." He answered.

"Halbrook..." Mrs Astley pursed her lips. "Any relation to Derrick Halbrook, from the London Tennis Club?"

Halbrook paused, not expecting that. "No."

Mrs Astley exhaled and relaxed her shoulders a little. "Oh, then I suppose you are the Halbrook that has been a thorn in the side of both my son, and my late husband."

Hunter bit his cheek to stop himself from laughing, as Halbrook looked well and truly on the back foot.

"Now look 'ere, just 'cos I don't worship the famous Astley family, don't mean-"

"You truly have the most atrocious way of speaking." Mrs Astley interrupted, her eyes narrowing in Halbrook's direction, before flicking to Hunter. "I thought your friend James was bad, he's positively eloquent next to this, this…"

"Hey, now!" Halbrook cut in. "I didn't ask for your opinion. I thought I was being proper polite asking to join you lot – it's not as though we're at Astley Manor where you're queen of bloody court."

Mrs Astley considered him for a moment longer. "Hm, I like him. Sit down and help yourself, Mr Halbrook. Shall I ask Charles to send for a bib, or are you quite educated with a fork?"

Halbrook looked dazed and a little speechless, but gathering that the result of this interaction was that he was allowed to sit and eat, he parked himself in a spare chair.

He leant across to grab an empty plate from the stack and muttered to Hunter. "Why don't you send her off against the witches? We'd have won by New Year."

Mrs Astley accepted another glass of wine from the very nervous-looking young woman sat next to her.

"Speaking of the New Year, George, I intend to go home. You can do your little magic trick and take me."

"Mother." Hunter started carefully. "The Manor is deemed unsafe. I cannot let you go there."

Mrs Astley looked at her son, her sharp grey eyes not understanding. "While I respect your concern for my safety, it is not for you to allow me anything. Astley Manor must have an Astley in it, it is not up for discussion. Besides, Mrs Harsmith wrote to me lately, to inform me that more of the villagers have returned to Little Hanting. She tells me that no witch nor human has been near the Manor for a month."

"Mother-"

Mrs Astley held up a hand to silence him. "That is quite enough of that, George. I have made up my mind. Now go, help Charles bring in the next course."

Hunter cursed beneath his breath, getting to his feet to help the long-suffering Charles.

Halbrook smirked at the mother and son interaction, but was quick to hide it before the formidable Mrs Astley noticed.

## Chapter Twenty-two

The next few months passed by in a haze of peace. A year since the witch rebellion ruined so many lives, people were beginning to make the most of their new world. The communities were well on their way to rebuilding what was destroyed, and despite the lack of technology and slow communication, the people fell into a new routine. A new normal.

Which included maintaining the great British tradition of going to the pub. On evenings when his whole team were free from duty, Hunter and the others frequented a nice place that was quite close to the MMC base.

The building was old-fashioned, with stone walls, and dark timbers that were well-suited to the atmosphere created by lamps and candles. It was quite a large establishment, but still managed to always feel cosy. It was popular with the locals and the witch-hunters alike, with good ale. Occasionally it was extra-popular, when a band would come in to play live, and the tables would be pushed to the sides to make room for a dance floor.

Hunter enjoyed the live music; it always made an evening that little bit more special. The band that was on tonight was good, although it made Hunter smile to watch the singer trying to fight to be heard without a microphone.

"What are you smirking at?" Alannah shouted over the noise.

Hunter shook his head, not about to explain himself. Instead he offered to get in another round. He made his way to the bar and looked over his shoulder. Alannah and Ian sat on the table he'd recently vacated. James and Maria were on the dance floor – Hunter grimaced at James' lack of co-ordination. Poor Maria.

He quickly got served and carried the three pints and a bottle of white wine on a tray back to their table.

"You know, on a night like this, I can almost forget that the war is happening." Alannah's sentiment lost a little by her need to shout over the music.

Hunter passed her the bottle of wine. "Make sure Maria gets at least some of that."

Alannah grinned. "I don't think she'd notice."

Her green eyes turned in the direction of the dance floor, where despite the upbeat song, Maria and James danced in each other's arms, circling slowly amidst the more energetic dancers. Hunter watched them for a minute, they always acted so professionally around the others, this sort of down-time was the only time he ever witnessed them act as a couple.

Hunter looked away, surprised to feel a little jealous that his best friend was so happy. He picked up his pint and engaged Ian in a conversation about the vehicles the MMC had managed to collect; which moved on to the different techniques of hot-wiring, in which Ian was almost as proficient as James.

Alannah sat quietly at the table, a third-wheel to the conversation. When she finished her wine, she set the glass purposefully down on the table. "I'm bored. You guys want to dance?"

Both Hunter and Ian looked at her, their matching expressions telling how very little they wanted to dance. Ian was the first to crack, seeing how determined Alannah was. The sergeant stood up and took one of her hands.

"Come on, Hunter. If I'm dancing, you are too." Ian ordered.

Hunter sighed, but dutifully pushed himself to his feet. He took Alannah's other hand, the little Welsh girl almost bouncing over the fact that she'd bullied them both.

The band had just moved into another fast track, the song a popular one with the crowd, who filed to the floor. Luckily, Hunter could get away with the minimum amount of movement from side to side. He kept his eyes fixed towards the stage, rather than allow himself to notice that people were watching him in his embarrassment.

James and Maria had broken from their close contact dance, and came to join the rest of them. Maria was shaking her hips next to Alannah, and James was... well, James was jumping around and making a fool out of himself. Hunter saw that even Ian was chuckling at him.

They stayed together for another song, then Ian put his hands up in defeat, and left the youngsters on the dance floor, in favour of his beer.

The band played the final chord of one song and moved seamlessly into the next. The tempo had suddenly slowed. Hunter noticed the active dancing being replaced by couples gently dancing together, including James and Maria, who drifted away from him.

Alannah stood awkwardly beside Hunter, and when he looked in her direction, she gave a hopeful little shrug.

Sighing, and feeling that he might regret this, Hunter slipped his right arm about Alannah's slim waist, and took her right hand in his left, holding it close to his chest. He led in an informal pattern, Alannah was stiff at first, but soon relaxed, and softened to lean against him, her cheek against his chest.

"I thought you couldn't dance." Alannah remarked.

"I can dance, I just choose not to." Hunter corrected.

He twirled her out elegantly, then pulled her back a little less so. They both laughed as they collided.

"I need a drink." Hunter admitted. "Dancing is dangerous."

He dropped his contact with Alannah and without waiting for her, made his way back to the table. Ian gave him an odd look as he re-joined him but didn't say anything.

Alannah pushed her hair away from her sweaty forehead, as she looked down at the table with greatly reduced drinks. "My round?" She said breathlessly, then turned and practically skipped in the direction of the bar.

With Alannah gone, Ian leant forward. "I hope you know what you're doing."

Hunter sat in confusion at his statement, but before he had chance to answer, they gained extra company at their table.

"Hey, do you mind if we sit here? Everywhere else is full."

Hunter looked up, to see who the voice belonged to. The first thing he noticed was the legs in skin-tight jeans, and the long black hair, followed by the pretty face.

"Sure." He said, waving to the spare seats. "I'm Hunter, this is Ian."

The black-haired girl flashed him a smile and sat next to him. "I'm Kayleigh, this is Tegan." She responded, motioning to her blonde friend that sat shyly on the other side of her.

"Nice to meet you both."

"You don't sound like you're from round here, Hunter." Kayleigh remarked.

"Guilty, I'm from a village near Oxford." Hunter answered, leaning closer to be heard over the music.

"Really, what brings you to Manc, then?"

Hunter grinned; how many times had he gotten into conversation with a normal person, and had to come up with some fake job that dictated where he went. He could never tell the truth, because no one had known about his organisation. Now, though... "I'm with the witch-hunters."

Across the table, Ian gave him a disappointed look. Disappointed, but as he glanced at Kayleigh, unsurprised.

The black-haired girl grinned. "You're kidding me! Really?"

"Not interrupting, am I?" Alannah called out, as she slid a tray of drinks onto the table, her green eyes narrowing in the direction of the newcomers.

"No, hi! Girls, this is Alannah, she's a witch-hunter too. And Alannah, this is..." Hunter broke off, struggling to remember their names.

"Kayleigh and Tegan." Kayleigh repeated, looking amused, rather than offended at his memory loss.

"Nice to meet you." Alannah said stonily. "You know, I think I might head home, I didn't realise how late it was."

Hunter looked up, realising that she did look a little pale. Probably too much wine and dancing.

Noticing that Hunter wasn't playing the part Alannah had hoped, Ian stood up. "I'll walk you home."

Alannah snatched up her coat and left without another word.

"What was that about?" Kayleigh asked.

"Dunno." Hunter muttered.

*****

The following morning Jonathan moved through the witch-hunter's compound towards the sleeping quarters but stopped when he saw Hunter.

"Hey, I was just coming to find you. Were you on duty?" Jonathan asked, frowning. He wasn't sure Hunter's attire was suitable for night duty.

"What? No, it was my evening off." Hunter replied distractedly.

Jonathan paused, then filled in the blanks. His confusion changed to amusement. "You've only just got back in? You'll get a reputation."

"Already got one." Hunter huffed, as he shoved his cold hands into his pockets. "Was there something you wanted? Other than discussing my promiscuity."

"Promiscuity? Is that your snobbish way of admitting you're a manwhore?"

Hunter narrowed his eyes in the direction of the wiccan. "Have you been talking to James?"

Jonathan finally broke into a grin. "That obvious, huh? On top of other things discussed, James wanted me to chat with you – about magic."

Hunter cringed at the very thought. He might be a little more open-minded than the old him that saw witches and magic in black and white, and sneered at wiccans as a pesky shade of grey – but he wasn't ready to fully embrace magic.

"Fine." He relented. "But let's go inside, it's freezing."

"You're just nesh." Jonathan chuckled at the soft southerner, but obediently followed Hunter indoors.

It didn't take long for the two men to acquire vital coffee and head for an unused office.

"Ok, what did you have to say?" Hunter asked as they sat down.

Jonathan wrapped his hands about his steaming mug, looking up at the witch-hunter. "James came to me for advice. He filled me in on the whole Benandanti thing, including the fact that your research has dried up. As you're not willing to seek them out in Italy-"

"I did not say *never*." Hunter stressed. "It's just a very inappropriate time to leave."

Jonathan held his hands up defensively, and pressed on. "So... short of finding an amiable witch to chat magic with, James and I thought that I might prove helpful."

Hunter frowned, he had not thought of asking magic-users about his own skills, mainly because he was too proud to share his private problems. Which he was equally unlikely to admit.

"Technically it's not magic." Hunter argued.

"No, it's the opposite." Jonathan agreed. "But from what I've heard, and what I've seen for myself, it acts a lot like it."

A sleep-deprived Hunter failed to come up with any logical counter of this point, so instead he leant back in his chair and crossed his arms.

Jonathan tried to hide his smile as he noted the small win. "So first, what can you do?" He asked, blowing on his hot coffee.

Hunter sighed. "Not much. I can travel in a blink, taking others with me. There's a shield I can project, temporarily blocking magic, and bullets on the rare occasion. Oh, and I destroyed a church, once."

"You destroyed a church..." Jonathan echoed, not sure whether to be amused or appalled.

"Mmm, it was quite the scene." Hunter confirmed, thinking back to the night Charlotte had died. "Although I did not know it was my doing until later."

Jonathan took in the mental image, but then shook his head. "Ok, let's focus on the shield. How do you do it?"

Hunter paused, he had never really taken time to dissect and explain it. "I honestly don't know. It seems to happen almost reflexively when spells are being cast. But once it's up, I can move it, expand or contract it..."

Jonathan nodded, looking very serious. "What does it *feel* like?"

"Like... a weight, barely noticeable at first, but tiring the longer I hold it. It's like an extension of me, I can feel everything that hits it." Hunter answered. It felt weird discussing his skills so logically with someone that wasn't James.

"And have you tried to do anything else with your magic?"

"A few things, nothing successful." Hunter replied; the warmth of a blush tickled his neck as he thought back on his foolish attempts. "Lighting candles and light bulbs, picking locks, healing grazes... from what I've read, these are the simplest spells even weak witches can manage."

"From what you've told me, what you possess is not magic, you cannot expect to do the same things." Jonathan reasoned. "Can I suggest something, Hunter? Allow me to train you in the basics of wiccan practices."

Hunter scowled, but Jonathan pressed on. "No, listen to me, I may be able to help you. A wiccan's manipulation of magic might have similarities to how you use your anti-magic – we might unlock something new. It can't hurt, can it?"

Although he was far from happy at the prospect, Hunter had to admit that Jonathan's reasoning was sound. Shit. Which meant he had no valid excuse.

"Fine. We'll give it a go."

## Chapter Twenty-three

The Malleus Maleficarum Council in Manchester had become the biggest gathering of witch-hunters in the North. New protocols and duties were devised as they went. For the most part, daily life went on in an almost mundane routine; but that was not to say that everything went smoothly. There were still constant threats from smaller covens that tried to stake their ground too near the towns and cities. The MMC were regularly called upon to deal with such threats. It was almost like the old days.

One day in the middle of May, a similar message was brought through to the Council that almost had James bouncing. The Mayor of Doncaster had sent out a request for back-up, after the witches had attempted to blackmail her to aid them. General Hayworth delegated the job to Hunter, who quickly called his team, plus another fifty soldiers and witch-hunters. It seemed an excessive number, but Hunter would rather be over-prepared than caught out-numbered.

They set out that very evening, Hunter transporting them all in a blink, rather than wasting precious fuel. They arrived in Campsall Woods and set up camp. The information the Mayor had given them was that the witches were stationed in the nearby Brodsworth Hall.

James moved about the camp, making sure that no one was feeling too faint after blinking over here. He then made his way over to where Hunter and the rest of his team waited. They were poring over a map with a Sergeant O'Hara.

"I remember camping up here as a kid." James said, nodding at their map. "The trees will offer plenty of coverage, and we have the advantage of higher ground."

Hunter nodded, knowing that here was as good as anywhere. "We'll stay here tonight. It seems the safest option. O'Hara – send scouts on a five-mile radius. No one should know we're here, but I want to be sure. My team will take first watch."

"Yes sir." O'Hara moved away from the meeting, to find his second-in-charge.

"Trust the witches to get the first-class accommodation, while we're in tents." Alannah muttered.

"Well, at least we're not doing this in winter." Maria replied. "We'd freeze our arses off."

Alannah elbowed her in the ribs. "You wouldn't freeze. You've got someone to cuddle into."

James smirked at the comment. "Come on, Alannah. If you were desperate for a cuddle, I'm sure Hunter or Ian would oblige."

Hunter folded up the map and tucked it away. "Of course. If the alternative was hypothermia, I would definitely share body heat."

Alannah's cheeks flushed red as the rest of the team laughed. "That's the most romantic thing you've ever said to me, Hunter."

Hunter walked past her towards the tents, pausing to ruffle her hair in a very brotherly way. "I try my best."

Alannah squeaked, and ducked away from him, then flattened her hair again. She looked to the other three that were looking very amused. She shook her head. "No comment."


It was nearly the end of the first watch and Hunter sat nursing a hot drink as he stared down the hill. His mind was running over the smooth running of his team. They'd been working together for nearly a year and a half, and Hunter had to confess that he depended on them now. He didn't want anything complicating their unity. James and Maria were strong, and they seemed stronger together. Hunter marvelled that James had not done anything yet to cock things up. Or perhaps Maria was just very forgiving.

It had not passed Hunter by, that Alannah was becoming a little more insistent in her hints. Did the little Welsh girl expect him to sweep her up in his arms?

Hunter didn't want to give thought to where Alannah's fantasies led, he was not going to indulge them. Perhaps he should get Maria to have a quiet word and persuade the girl to look elsewhere.

Hunter drummed his fingers on the tin cup of now lukewarm tea. When did this happen? A few years ago, he would have enjoyed the attention. She was a pretty girl - they could have flirted, possibly slept together, and entertained some short-lived relationship. Hunter blamed Sophie, it had to be her fault. Or was it because he was a father – did that automatically make you mature and responsible?

Adam was going to be a year old at the end of summer. A year old, and Hunter still wouldn't have seen his son. He wondered if he looked like him, or did he take after his mother?

Hunter thought back to the conversation he'd had with James, the night he had learnt of Adam's birth, that they would wrap all this up and then claim his son. It had seemed an easy promise to make then, but nearly a year on, and they were no closer to their aim.

Hunter's thoughts stopped mid-track. Something didn't feel right. He checked his shields, finding them all intact, then sent his senses further down the wooded slope. Nothing, there was no- Hunter froze. There was movement in the woods, but camouflaged in such a way that Hunter could barely perceive it. He stood up, barely breathing as he tracked the faint whisper of life that moved up the hill, still hidden to his normal senses.

Hunter swore and ran back to the tents. It was only ten in the evening, and most were still at least half-awake.

"Ambush." He warned in a stony voice, quickly getting the attention of those in the campsite. "I don't know how many, coming up the hill. Get everyone ready for my signal."

The witch-hunters and soldiers moved without question, to follow his orders.

Hunter moved to the edge of camp and crouched in the darkness. He felt a pang of unease, that this was going to go terribly wrong. He closed his eyes and tried to sense the magic that was being used to cloak the witches. It was very subtle, by a very adept witch, but it didn't have the same feel as Sophie's magic. Hunter guessed that she had no part in this, but for some reason that did little to comfort him.

The witches were near impossible to perceive, and as Hunter waited to call for the counter-ambush, he heard the sudden cry of one of his men, taken out by an invisible enemy that had moved up the hill faster than Hunter had anticipated.

Hunter ignored the following outburst of cursing and gunshots, knowing that his men were fighting blind, he concentrated instead on breaking through the magic that disguised the witches. He grimaced at the skill of the caster; their spell seemed infallible. But then Hunter found a crack the breadth of a spider's web. He pushed the weak link until the spell faltered and broke. Suddenly the enemy was clear before their eyes again.

There was a rallying shout from the witch-hunters and soldiers as they pressed their new advantage.

Hunter heard a stuttered moan and heavy breathing beside him. James lay slumped on the ground by his feet, a trickle of blood starting to roll down from his mouth. Hunter swore, and knelt down beside him, throwing up a shield about them.

"James... what...?"

"Couldn't see... I couldn't see them. B-but had to defend you." James mumbled, then winced.

Hunter took in his surroundings and noticed two inert bodies lying nearby. He hadn't even noticed them approach, he'd been so focused on breaking the spell. He didn't know whether the two witches were dead yet, but that was the least of his worries right now.

"Come on, I'll get you to the first-aid tent." Hunter muttered, frustrated at his friend's heroism.

He moved to pick James up, but James just cried in pain, and pushed him away.

"Don't. It hurts, you bastard." James spat, then closed his eyes. "T-tell my family they should be proud of me. And Maria, tell Maria..."

Hunter felt the distracting attack along the lines of his shield and mentally shoved it away as though it were a mild irritant.

"Why are you talking like this? You're going to be fine. We'll finish up here, then get you patched up." Hunter said firmly.

"Need a bloody big patch." James laughed, his eyes straining at the effort, and his teeth stained red. He lifted his hand from his torso – his dark jumper looked damp, but deceptive – only on the pale flesh of his hand did the true extent of his blood loss show. "They hit me hard mate. Too hard even… even for you to fix."

James spoke calmly enough, only a groan of pain puncturing his control. James reached out and suddenly grabbed Hunter's arm with a bloodied hand. "I - I need to tell you…"

Hunter pushed him back down, desperate that he should rest and conserve his energy. "You can tell me after the battle."

"No… now." James growled weakly, as his skin paled, and sweat mingled with the blood on his brow.

"I don't blame you for any of this – I don't regret any of this. Except dying maybe." James smiled and laughed at his own useless joke. "I trusted Sophie too."

Hunter shook his head. He again felt magic attack his shield, and again he repulsed it. He was not listening to his best friend's final words, because James was not going to die, he could not die.

Hunter closed his eyes, trying to find something, that spark that made him different, that magic. He had done things people considered miracles, was it so hard to believe that he might be able to heal a simple wound? His powers always showed themselves when Hunter was at his greatest need – this time definitely counted.

"Please." Hunter whispered.

James' grip loosened on his arm and fell limply to his side. Hunter opened his eyes in time to witness the last breath leave his body. Hunter stared, frozen. He felt that if he even breathed, the world would shatter. But his emotions were beyond his control. He felt the anger and grief roil inside him, making his limbs quiver with excess energy, a demand that needed to be sated.

Hunter blacked out.

When he came to, Sergeant O'Hara had gently placed a hand on his shoulder, making Hunter jump. Hunter was still kneeling over James' body. Obviously only his mind had blacked out, his body was still working fine. He looked up at the soldier, who in turn looked warily back.

"What happened?" The man asked.

Hunter blinked, his mind slow and uncomprehending. "What do you mean?"

O'Hara pulled back his hand, looking quite scared. "Well sir, one minute we're being attacked by an enemy we can't see. Then we see them, but they couldn't touch us, and then – well just look at it, sir."

Hunter frowned, looking past the soldier. Even in the dark, Hunter's eyes were sharp, he could see the rest of his team moving cautiously across the open towards him – the open! The moon shone down onto a ravaged scene, the trees torn up by their roots, or blasted where they stood.

"Casualties?" Hunter asked weakly.

"Five on our side from when the battle began." The soldier reported. "We're still checking, but so far we haven't found any surviving witches."

Hunter took a deep breath. No surviving witches. The scene echoed back to the only other time Hunter had felt such a release of rage. But that had been in a church, the night Charlotte was killed.

"James? James!" Alannah's voice pierced his thoughts.

There was the added noise of footsteps now hurrying in his direction. Hunter didn't even bother looking up, as the rest of his team descended on them.

## Chapter Twenty-four

Hunter did not sleep that night. His limbs were still filled with the restless energy of his grief. Which meant that he had dug a grave in the early hours of the morning, and by dawn, his team held a tearful burial.

Sergeant O'Hara stood with them to pay his respects.

Hunter stood there, unable to process any thought or feeling. Alannah clung to Maria's arm, her face streaked with tears, whereas Maria seemed to be experiencing the same numbness that was affecting Hunter. Ian stood next to Maria, his hand on her shoulder; he looked over to Hunter, the older man uncertain for once, of what to do.

Hunter let out a rattling breath and eventually moved away from the graveside, his legs just about working, though they felt like lead. He motioned for O'Hara to join him.

"We need to get moving. Send the men and women back to Manchester the mundane way. Also, can you organise an investigation into this – no one knew that we were here, save the Mayor. I want to know if she is implicated, or someone in her office has betrayed us. If it is possible, take our fallen back to their families."

"Yes sir." O'Hara answered automatically, then hesitated. "Sir, this does not have to be done now, if you need-"

"Sergeant. I-" Hunter interrupted, but stopped, looking back to his team that still huddled by the grave. It was impossible to think that James simply wouldn't be there anymore. It didn't make sense. But at least he was buried in his hometown. It's what he would have wanted. Now there was the monumental task of telling his family. Hunter's insides froze at the mere thought of the emotions and distress that he would be causing good people. People that had always welcomed him and treated Hunter as an extended part of the family.

"Sergeant, can you please inform James' uncle and aunt – I can provide you with an address, they don't live far from here."

Sergeant O'Hara frowned, obviously not comfortable being the bearer of bad news, and probably wondering why the best friend did not take the message.

Hunter saw the look and winced. "I cannot go, I cannot be the one to tell them. You have to understand; I am the one that dragged James into this world.

Without me, he would have lived a normal, boringly safe life. It- it's my fault."

Hunter took a deep breath and moved away from O'Hara. He drifted closer to his team again. He had to get them back to Manchester, get them out of his charge and custody, so he could be selfish and grieve.

*****

"Where are we?" Alannah asked, confusion in her weary voice.

It was dark, the weak sunlight blocked by drapes.

Hunter took a deep breath; the very air was familiar and comforting. He easily navigated the chairs and low table and pulled back the heavy curtains.

"Astley Manor." He murmured, then shook his head. "Sorry, I wasn't concentrating."

Alannah moved closer to him, slipping her delicate hand into his. "It's ok."

Hunter wanted to express some gratefulness, but he couldn't even squeeze her hand, or raise the corner of his mouth in a grim smile. He just stared across the room, unfocussed, waiting to feel normal.

Ian coughed. "I'll let Mrs Astley and Charles know we're here."

He shot a concerned look at Maria, who hadn't said a word since last night, then left to find the other occupants of this house.

"I should…" Hunter broke off, not sure what he was going to say. He felt that he needed to do something, unused energy still burnt through his muscles, even as they felt like lead. But what could he do, he had already

414

killed the witches and had his revenge. Should he go after their leader, should he face the Shadow Witch and take his anger out on her?

A life for a life. He had spared her, now James was dead.

There was a tug on his hand.

"Come to the kitchen." Alannah insisted. "You too, Maria. I'll make tea, then find something for us to eat."

Hunter glanced down at Alannah, the green of her eyes even brighter against the redness from crying. He nodded and allowed the girl to lead him to the kitchen.

Maria wrapped her arms protectively about her own chest, and silently followed.


It must have been the very early hours of the following morning, yet Hunter lay wide awake. He turned over again, sleep eluding him.

He didn't even have to close his eyes for the battle to play over and over, the pictures bright and bloody.

Hunter told himself that he knew – they all knew – that fighting meant the chance they might die. Hunter accepted that. But to lose someone else?

Hunter shuddered at the memory of the shattered forest, the energy that had boiled within himself. He had only ever experienced it once before, when the witches had killed Charlotte, his closest friend, save James.

Was that why the witches had done it? Had they wanted to – to defuse him? Sophie would have known that after Charlotte, only James could evoke such a reaction. Hunter thought bitterly that, once upon a time, the same could have been said for Sophie, herself.

Had she targeted him?

Hunter threw the cover away and got out of bed. Hardly thinking about what he was doing, he grabbed his dressing gown to cover the bare chest and boxers he had slept in – or tried to sleep in.

Hunter made his way down the silent corridor, until he got to a certain room. He took a deep breath and pushed open the door, stepping inside.

He wasn't sure what he was hoping to see. Perhaps a pair of glasses on the side-table, or an open book on the desk. But it was disappointingly tidy. Charles must have cleaned the room since the last time they came to stay – there was no hint of James left.

Hunter let out a breath he didn't know he was holding, when he heard a sob in the dark room. Hunter shuffled further into the room, to see Maria huddled in the shadow of the foot of the bed.

"Maria?" He said, but even his soft voice was startlingly loud.

Maria snapped her head in his direction. "Hunter." She hiccupped, fiercely wiping tears from her cheeks.

Hunter stood, uncertain as ever in the face of emotion. "You ok?" He asked, inwardly wincing at the pointless words.

"Yeah…" Maria coughed to kick the waver out of her voice. "I… I know I shouldn't be in here, but I – I-"

As she broke off, Hunter heard her breath hitch as she tried to control herself.

"Shh, it's fine." Hunter replied, stepping closer, then sliding down to sit next to her.

Maria groaned, and wiped her eyes again. "You know, this is the first time I've cried since my dad died, twelve years ago. I don't do crying; I don't do emotion."

Hunter guessed this was one of those times it was best to stay quiet and let Maria vent. He leant his shoulder against hers, but otherwise said nothing.

"Not when I lost friends in Afghanistan. Not when my husband left me." Maria sighed. "You know, you get in the habit of not feeling, not connecting."

Maria drew her knees up, hugging them to her chest. "But James was… unexpected. I don't even know when I fell for him. And I never got a chance to – to tell him…"

Maria broke off in a sob. Hunter put his arm reassuringly about her shoulders. "It's ok. He knew, he-" Hunter paused to steady his voice. "He knew, and he loved you too."

Maria huffed, and shoved him with her elbow. "You're lying, you're just saying that to make me feel better." She said, but couldn't hide her smile through her tears.

Hunter shrugged. "I've known James for years; I've never seen him look at anyone the way he looked at you. Plus, you're the only woman he's ever taken home to meet his family."

Maria leant her head against Hunter's shoulder. "I hardly knew him. I was foolish enough to think that we'd have forever. I'd give anything to have just one more day with him."

Hunter closed his eyes, tears leaking out the corners of them. "Me too."

Maria sighed, wiping her eyes on her pyjama sleeve. "I don't suppose time travel is one of your tricks."

Hunter grunted. "No. At least, I don't think it is." Hunter gazed at the dark ceiling, he hated to admit that he honestly could not say for sure. He felt anew the gaping hole in his knowledge. Should he have done what James once requested – sought the traces of the Benandanti instead of fighting the witches?

They sat like that for what must have been an hour. Maria had grown so still that Hunter thought she must have drifted to sleep.

"So, what now?" She suddenly asked.

"What now, what?" Hunter repeated groggily.

"I mean, what's going to happen next? We can't stay at this stalemate."

Hunter sighed. "Next, we force the witches into battle, and we kill them."

There was a pause, before Maria dared to ask a burning question. "Including Sophie?"

Hunter grimaced. "Sophie Murphy has ceased to exist. The Shadow Witch has killed James, and countless others. There can be no forgiveness."

## Chapter Twenty-five

The next morning, after Charles had force fed them all a hearty breakfast, Hunter assembled with his diminished team to return to headquarters.

When they blinked into the secure compound, a few of the newer recruits jumped at their sudden appearance, but the rest seemed to accept that four people had appeared out of thin air. It was amazing how 'normal' they considered Hunter's new-found skill, and if Hunter had been in the mood for it, he would have felt relief. It had not been long ago he had feared being outcast – or worse, killed – for his magic-like abilities.

Hunter led the way to the Council's makeshift meeting room, where his team settled in. They waited in gloomy silence, nothing to be said.

Eventually the door opened, and General Hayworth marched in, a look of relief crossing his face when he saw them.

"Sergeant O'Hara explained what happened. I had hoped only grief delayed you, but I was worried the rest of you had another run in…" The General paused for breath. "You couldn't have bloody sent word that you were fine, and took a detour, could you?!"

A delicate hand reached out, cautioning him, as Nadira Shah came in beside him. "Now General, there's little point berating them over what has already happened. They are back, that's what matters."

As she turned to face the others, her beautiful brown eyes were filled with sincerity and sadness. "I am sorry for your loss. I have never heard anything but high praise for James Bennett."

Hunter looked down at the table before him. He knew that Nadira meant well, but every time he lost someone, he knew the words wouldn't help

"Thank you, ma'am." Ian's voice rang out, speaking for the first time today.

"Alright." Hayworth started gruffly. "On with business. I daresay we all need the distraction."

Nadira drifted to the meeting table and sat down, indicating that the others should join her. "While you were gone, the Council has been discussing our next step."

"I hope it involves killing a lot of witches." Alannah bitterly interjected.

Nadira smiled compassionately in the young girl's direction. "We cannot go on as we are, allowing them to pick us off one by one. We need to face them in a place of our choosing, for once. We need to bring them to battle."

"So, they can pick us off en masse." Ian added darkly.

General Hayworth shot him a warning look. "Not so. Our intelligence tells us that we have the greater numbers now. With Hunter to block their magic, our numbers will overwhelm theirs, just like Little Hanting."

Hunter felt uneasiness knot in his stomach, but he pushed it aside. This was what he wanted, what he needed. An end to it all, and revenge for James, for Anthony Marks, Charlotte King, Brian Lloyd...

"When and where?" He asked.

"Three weeks should be enough time to rally the troops, everyone is keen to make this stand."

"Three weeks."

"We need to hit them before the summer solstice." Nadira confirmed. "We don't want to risk them channelling its power for their next offensive."

"The 'where' is Salisbury Plains. I've had men down there for months, salvaging equipment. They've even got a tank working."

"Will a tank be enough to kill the Shadow?" Alannah asked warily, remembering their last encounter with her.

Hayworth made a noncommittal gesture. "I really hope so; we've got nothing stronger."

"Magic isn't about strength." Hunter muttered. Magic often manifested in the physical, but that didn't mean brawn alone could defeat it. On the other hand, Hunter couldn't imagine anything surviving a few mortar rounds.

"Fine. So, what are our orders, General?" Hunter eventually asked, doing his best to appear contrite.

Hayworth exchanged a look with Nadira. "We appreciate everything you've done, but in view of your loss, we think you should all take leave until the battle."

Hayworth was met with four very disbelieving faces.

"You want your best team to sit and twiddle their thumbs?" Maria snapped, finally breaking out of her miserable silence.

"You all need time to recover and come to terms with James' death. We cannot trust your judgement in the field at this time." Nadira said firmly.

Hunter leant back in his chair, observing the two leaders. So, they were worried that he and his team would crack, or act rashly. Huh, they might have a point.

Hunter pushed back his chair, the legs scraping across the wooden floor. Without a word, he stood up and walked out of the meeting room.

*****

Half an hour later, Ian came to find him. Hunter was working out his frustration in the gym, with a punch bag. His feet moved half-heartedly, but he threw his whole weight behind each punch.

"Hey, want to spar?" Ian called, breaking Hunter's rhythm.

422

Hunter stopped, glancing up at the intruder. "Not really, Ian, no."

"I'll go easy on you." Ian offered.

Hunter sighed and backed away, the punch bag having lost its appeal, with Ian providing distraction. Hunter sat down on the closest bench.

"You ok?" Ian asked.

Hunter rolled his shoulders to loosen them up. "I'm fine." He snapped.

"Uh-huh." Ian sat down on the bench beside him. "And truthfully?"

"I'm... I'm good enough, I don't need the Council thinking I need mollycoddling." Hunter threw his arm out in the vague direction of the Council's offices.

"They're just worried about you." Ian replied.

Hunter snorted. "They're worried what I might do, I am the freak of nature and breeding, after all."

Ian crossed his arms, his patience for the snarky comments from the younger man running lower than normal today. "No, they care for you, and they're worried because you lost your best friend."

Hunter stood up again, feeling restless energy through his limbs again. He paced to the punch bag and back. "Don't pretend that you know how I'm feeling right now, Ian."

Ian stood up so quickly, that Hunter froze mid-step. "Don't presume you have monopoly on grief right now Hunter. I may not have known James as long as you, but you will not trivialise my friendship with him."

Hunter backed off a little, he'd never seen Ian show emotion, nor speak so strongly. It just added to his guilt that waited impatiently to kick in.

"I'm sorry." Hunter mumbled, sitting down again.

They sat in silence for a minute, before Ian finally spoke. "So, are you going to follow orders this time, or did you have some plan concocted?"

Hunter shrugged. "I hadn't actually gotten that far yet."

Hunter ran over his initial desire to kill as many witches as possible. Was it best to take out their leader, instead? Once they had lost their Shadow Witch, would the rest crumble.

"It did occur to me that a small team could slip through their defences and overcome the Shadow Witch." Hunter admitted.

Ian nodded. "Ok, but what then? We couldn't kill her last time, what makes you think we could be any more successful this time."

Unfortunately, the sergeant had a point. But what if they didn't kill her, or not immediately so. "We could bind her."

"You might want to clarify what you mean by that." Ian replied with a chuckle.

"We used to bind witches that surrendered. Using an amulet, you can bind their power from them, rendering them harmless – or at least, as harmless as any human." Hunter explained. "If we could get to Sophie, distract her and bind her, she'd be powerless."

Ian nodded again. "Ok, sounds plausible. We've only got to subdue her; that should be... interesting. You know, the best distraction will be an army with tanks."

Hunter's shoulders dropped. "You want me to wait, too."

"Whatever you decide, I'll be there with you. So will Alannah and Maria. But it's just three more weeks to wait, and we can go in with the army at our backs."

"Waiting three weeks is as impossible a task as overcoming the Shadow Witch." Hunter muttered.

Ian clapped him on the shoulder. "Good, I knew that you'd see things my way. Now, do you think you can find one of those binding amulet thingies?"

Hunter was about to remark that that was James' job. But he settled for a silent nod.

## Chapter Twenty-six

A fortnight before the summer solstice, Hunter began to transport the troops that had been gathering at Manchester, taking them down to the abandoned village of Imber, which served as a temporary place to regroup.

Witch-hunters from all over the UK made their own way there, having gotten the message that the MMC was finally making a stand. Hunter watched as the numbers on Salisbury Plain swelled. Most of them were military, the number of surviving witch-hunters was depressingly low – a few hundred, no more.

Hunter greeted those he knew, seeing the same determination in each face that they would finally put this world right, they would finally get revenge for their lost friends and colleagues. There were a few missing faces that Hunter had yet to see, he hoped they had just been delayed, but there was no one from the Newcastle branch here. But his concern for Toby and the others had to be put aside as the chaos of their army had to be organised.

Hunter pushed through the crowd to one of the houses that had been set aside for those in command. Recognising him, the soldiers guarding the door let him through.

Hunter saw the familiar faces of General Hayworth, Nadira Shah and Sergeant Dawkins. There were also the less familiar faces of the regional leaders. They gave Hunter a curious look when he entered, obviously intrigued by the famous 7th gen that had been flitting about the country.

"Any sign of Jonathan and the wiccans?" Nadira asked.

"No, ma'am. But it's still early." Hunter answered.

Nadira looked troubled. "They promised they would come."

Hunter frowned, he had gradually begun to trust Jonathan, and had started to take him seriously; it would be shame if he let them down now.

"They're only wiccans." One of the other witch-hunters voiced. "Are they really so important, if they cannot fight?"

Nadira turned her brown eyes in the direction of the one that spoke, until he dropped his gaze, ashamedly. "They have been an important ally to us all. They cannot fight, nor do harm, but they have been trying to emulate the shield Hunter creates, with some success. They might just save your skin tomorrow."

Hunter tried to look as though this was not news to him, but he was as shocked as the rest of the room. Was that why Jonathan had quizzed him about his powers, whenever he got chance? Hunter had thought it mere curiosity.

"That's ah, very good news." The witch-hunter replied, sounding much more contrite. "Why did you not share it sooner?"

"We have kept their attempts secret; we did not want the witches to target the wiccans." Nadira met the eye of each and every person. "It is still early days and in the experimental stages. But our needs are at their greatest, now."

"So, does everyone know their role tomorrow?" General Hayworth asked.

There was a chorus of confirmation. This would all be over tomorrow, the main body would await the witches in the centre of the Plains; two groups would keep hidden to the east and west, attempting to catch the witches from as many angles as possible. A select group was in charge of the military vehicles and heavy artillery.

And Hunter? No one had given him an outright order; it was assumed that he would go where he was most needed. Hunter had the feeling that the General knew that he intended to tackle the Shadow Witch and was simply turning a blind eye.

"Well then, tomorrow at 0600 we will move into position." General Hayworth said. "Our spies will

428

make sure the message gets to the witches – we can expect them tomorrow, the day after at the latest."

****

The witch-hunters and their allies amassed on the Plains, making a defiant stand. Hunter had walked amongst them and had been comforted by their numbers. But when he blinked away to the copse that hid another portion of their fighters, he looked back and saw their army dwarfed by the expanse of the rolling Plains. A knot of anxiety tightened in his stomach, knowing that others were watching and judging his confidence in this endeavour.

Were they brave, or just mad, to pit themselves against the greatest magical threat in centuries?

Hunter thought over the event ahead. He would need all of his team when tackling the Shadow Witch. The potentially impossible task of killing her might be easier than distracting her and subduing her long enough for Hunter to use the amulet to bind her.

He put his hand in his pocket, wrapping his fingers about the black silk ribbon, and smooth opal stone. Hunter had had to rummage through some dusty boxes in Manchester to find an item he thought would be strong enough. The smooth curves of the stone were supposed to make it a strong reservoir of power, and this type had never failed him before.

It was a pretty commonly used tool for binding witches. Or at least it had been – as far as Hunter was aware, no witch had been bound since the rebellion. Now, it was kill or be killed.

Quickly bored of waiting for the witches to arrive, Hunter flitted between the groups, checking for news and acting as messenger for those in charge. He watched as the men and women slowly lost the look of anxiety and determination, and as the day wore on, they set up casual groups to share food.

Those in charge kept a positive and controlled look, but to Hunter they all grumbled over the same thing.

"Hayworth said today."

As evening drew in, Hunter went to find General Hayworth for the fifth time that day.

"Anything new to report?" The General asked.

Hunter shook his head. "No sir. Only that everyone is wondering where our enemy is, and why they're taking so damned long."

The General sighed, gazing out across his troops, intuitively knowing they were all thinking likewise. "It has been the witches' habit, to date, to run in when provoked and to be ruled by haste and passion. We will give them another twenty-four hours, and then question whether they are up to something more devious."

There were many remarks that Hunter wanted to give, but he just bowed his head and retired to where his friends were setting up camp.

*****

The following morning, dawn rose on the impatiently waiting army. It had been a restless night, with those not on watch hardly daring to sleep, for fear of a night-time attack.

Hunter didn't think he'd slept at all, and as soon as it was a socially acceptable time, he began to repeat his rounds of the different camps. The summer night had been mild, and most people were in a positive mood.

Time slowly ticked by, and after midday, Hunter sought the General. For once, even he looked disappointed.

"I wish I knew what devilry they're up to." General Hayworth muttered as Hunter approached. They stood side by side, looking out to the hazy, summer horizon.

"There's still no sign of the wiccans." Hunter commented.

Hayworth sighed. "That doesn't make me feel any better. I never pegged Jonathan as a coward."

"Toby Robson and the rest of the Newcastle branch haven't arrived, either." Hunter added.

The General looked towards Hunter; his expression troubled.

"I could go, search for foul play." Hunter offered, it did not cross his mind for a moment that Toby or Jonathan were playing the coward. The rest of the groups of witch-hunters and wiccans were questionable.

Hayworth thought about it, but eventually shook his head. "No, I need you here. I can't risk you getting delayed or caught up when the witches hit here."

Hunter bit his tongue, knowing that any comment he made about this long wait had already been said.

## Chapter Twenty-seven

It had gone 9pm and the long summer evening was finally starting to darken. The gathered witch-hunters and soldiers settled in for another night out on the Plains. It had been deemed illogical to move them before morning. They would go back to their designated bases, ready to re-group when a new plan of action had been determined.

Hunter sat in silence with Maria, watching the sun set. There was no need to speak, just sitting there was enough. As the sun dropped below the horizon, leaving the darkening sky streaked with red, Hunter felt a familiar warmth burn through his jacket pocket. He pulled the wiccan stone out, to see it glowing bright with warning. It had become such habit to carry it, Hunter had not thought twice by pocketing it.

Not understanding the message behind this basic rock, he looked up to see that several others had gotten to their feet, holding out stones and looking as bemused as he.

"They're coming!" A distant cry rang out. "They're coming!"

The shout was taken up across the army, and there was a hive of activity to kit up.

Hunter scanned the dim horizon, until he found a patch of darkness that was so thick that even his eyes could not make sense of it.

Out of that darkness came the movement of figures. They came out in ones and twos, then tens and hundreds.

Hunter quickly pushed through the gathered witch-hunters and soldiers, to get to the forefront. He was vaguely aware of Maria following him, and the familiar, broad-shouldered figure of Ian joining them.

The witches amassed on the grey horizon, their numbers spreading out and standing ready.

Hunter's sharp eyes picked out one stepping forward with achingly familiar movements. The Shadow Witch turned her gaze across her enemies, trying to pick out the leaders.

"I give you this chance to surrender." Sophie's voice rang out across the expectant quiet. "The witchkind have won, your allies are destroyed, and you are all that remains of the resistance to the new world."

The army stood as one, silent and unmoving to this offer.

"So stubborn." Sophie continued, when it was clear that none would respond. "A demonstration then."

With a wave of her hand, two male witches dragged a man forward. Hunter gritted his teeth as he recognised their prisoner. Jonathan.

The usually calm and collected wiccan looked panicked as he was thrown at the Shadow Witch's feet. His hands were bound, and his face was bloody, eyes black and swollen from his treatment.

Hunter's gut twisted at the thought of what the man had suffered.

"You fight against magic." The Shadow Witch shouted. "But are hypocrites that use it as and when you need. Not only is one among your number as guilty of magic as I…"

Hunter felt more than one set of eyes turn in his direction, but he held back the need to wince as his enemy continued.

"…but you ally yourselves with wiccans – parasites who cling to magic." Sophie looked down at Jonathan with clear distaste. "I don't know whether to be disgusted or insulted, that you would plan to overcome us with these – these…"

Sophie's lip curled as she failed to find the words to express herself adequately. Oh well, actions always spoke louder than words. She took a step back, and with an idle flick of her hand, the two male witches cast the spell they were forming.

There was a flash of light and a piercing scream, as flames engulfed Jonathan. The sound of his pain rolled over the Plains and made the assembled army stir. Hunter felt bile rising in his throat, but before he could do anything, Jonathan's screams were cut off by a single gunshot. The wiccan slumped, lifeless to the ground.

Hunter glanced to his side and saw Maria slowly lowering her gun, pale but calm. Unable to speak, he simply nodded. They couldn't save their friend, but they could cut short his suffering.

On some unspoken signal, the two armies charged.

Hunter felt the swell of magic, and his own power respond, throwing up a shield that was soon hammered under the weight of hundreds of witches. His movements were slow, as he focused on maintaining it, while keeping his gun steady on the next witch in his eye line. Things were quickly dissolving into chaos.

Hunter shouted for Alannah; his voice lost in the melee. His eyes tore from one struggling fighter to the next, his heart pounding with exertion and fear.

Ian grabbed his shoulder. "There!" He pointed.

Hunter allowed himself to feel relief as he spotted the fourth member of his team making her way towards them. The young Welsh girl held her side and limped slightly, blood stained her cheek and arm, but otherwise she was fine.

She looked around the group, her green eyes bright. "Well, what are we waiting for?"

"Come on then." Ian stated. "Let's make this bitch mortal."

Ian turned and led the way, his bulky form pushing a path through the battleground. Maria followed him.

Hunter made to follow them, but Alannah caught his arm.

"What's wrong?"

Alannah looked up at him with determination. For an answer, she moved onto her toes. Her hands locked behind Hunter's neck and she pulled him down to her.

Hunter was more than a little surprised at the kiss but didn't pull back as her lips caught his gently. When Alannah let him go, Hunter straightened again.

"Alannah..."

Alannah shook her head. "I didn't want to go into this with any regrets."

Hunter glanced about, checking for immediate danger; now was not the time for this. "Alannah, we'll talk after the battle."

Hunter grabbed her hand and dragged her with him before she could oppose. He was glad there was an important battle to deal with before he had to have that talk with Alannah. She was a friend, and a little sister to him now.

When they caught up with the others, Ian gave them an odd, concerned look; at which Hunter realised he was still holding Alannah's hand, and guiltily dropped it.

The four of them fought their way through another line of witches, leaving their opponents dead or incapacitated as they pushed on to the next clearing.

Hunter had a feeling of déjà vu as he saw Sophie standing alone, her power rolling off her. With a single breath, he felt his own anti-magic stir and react with hers. A dome of energy spread out in a shimmer of colour against the dark night. Sophie immediately detected the source, and her furious hazel eyes snapped onto Hunter.

"So, you've brought an extra friend this time?" Her eyes flicked across the rest of his team.

Hunter's jaw tensed, there was nothing to be said to this woman that had played him for a fool, while killing those closest to him. Alannah noticed his mood, and supportively squeezed his arm.

Sophie noticed the gesture, and her eyes snapped to the Welsh girl. "You again."

Alannah flashed Hunter a smile, then turned to the witch. "Yes, me." She confirmed. Then attacked.

## Chapter Twenty-eight

Alannah's knife glanced off the Shadow Witch's arm, the cut healing as soon as it was inflicted.

Sophie snarled in pain and her hand shot out, taking the opportunity to grab Alannah by the neck. Her fingers closed tighter.

"He'll never be yours." She hissed at the little Welsh girl, jealous eyes flicking to Hunter.

Alannah scratched at Sophie's iron hold, starting to choke. "Wanna bet?" She gasped.

Sophie leant in closer, her expression of fury suddenly changing to shock as she felt two arms encircle her and pin her in place. She instinctively struggled, but the arms just tightened.

Alannah broke free, and fell to her knees, gulping in precious air. Hunter rushed to her side.

"You said distract her." She croaked.

"Not by using yourself as bait." He growled, furious at her crazy move.

"Hunter!"

Hunter looked up at Maria's shout, to see the lieutenant aiming her gun steadily at Sophie's head. Oh yes, there was something to do. He pulled the opal stone amulet and black silk from his pocket and stepped closer to Sophie. Her hazel eyes locked on the items and immediately grew wide, she began to struggle in earnest against Ian's hold, but with little effect.

Hunter hurried to press the amulet against her hand and bound it with the black ribbon. Sophie shrieked as she felt her power sapped by the ritual, the opal glowing with the strength of the power it absorbed.

Hunter stepped back, nodding to Ian, who released his prisoner from his grip. Maria's aim followed the witch as she dropped to the ground, shivering. Hunter felt the magic in the air suddenly lessen and he looked at his enemy, so weak upon her knees.

"What have you done?" Sophie demanded.

"What needed to be done." Hunter replied. "Surrender now, and you will be charged for your crimes. Or, by the Malleus Maleficarum, I am empowered to take the necessary measures."

Sophie narrowed her eyes in his direction – that he should give her the formal spiel!

Before she could reply, another wave of pain shot through her, knocking her flat on her back.

"What's happening?" Alannah asked, as she pulled herself to her feet. Even though she was a young witch-hunter, she could see this wasn't going normally. The

440

Shadow Witch writhed in pain, and the amulet still glowed – in fact it was getting brighter than when Hunter had performed the ritual.

Alannah stepped forward to inspect the amulet more closely.

Without warning, the world was dissolved in a bright flash, as the amulet exploded.

Hunter came to, aware of movement around him, but the sound sluggish. The next thing he was aware of was that he was flat on his back, and there was an immense pain resonating from his right shoulder and back.

Movement caught his eye, a figure stepped into his eye line, from the lack of military gear he guessed it to be a witch.

Hunter forced a painful breath into his lungs and let his eyes scout his surroundings. The night was lit by fire and spells, but he could tell little else.

Bracing himself for the shock of pain, Hunter pushed himself onto his side. His head throbbed with a migraine, as well as from the overwhelming magic in the area.

His ears began to hear again, starting with the curses of witches, their footsteps as they hurried back as they realised he was alive. He heard his name hissed by several voices but ignored them all.

Hunter focused on seeing the inert bodies nearby. He hoped that they had just been knocked out like him, but seeing Alannah's open, unseeing eyes, dropped a weight in his stomach.

Not wanting to think or feel, Hunter staggered to his feet. His eyes snapped onto Sophie, she became the only thing in focus, and he threw himself in her direction.

Sophie's hazel eyes widened at his approach and she threw up thick shadows about herself in defence.

Hunter ran forward, ignoring the spike of pain in his ribs and shoulder. He charged into the darkness. He felt a delicate hand touch his, followed by the familiar, disorientating warmth and nothingness that accompanied being transported by the Shadow Witch.

Hunter landed on cold, hard ground with a thud. He rolled onto his side and retched. He couldn't remember ever feeling so dizzy with pain. He cracked open his eyes to get his bearings. All he saw were a pair of feet in front of him.

His eyes travelled up, to see Sophie standing over him. She looked blood-stained and exhausted, much like how he felt. She sighed, seeing him regaining consciousness, and knelt beside him. Her lip curled at his weak struggles.

"You just can't admit defeat, can you?"

Sophie looked up, beyond him, to where Hunter could detect weak flashes of light.

"It's over." Sophie stated, gazing firmly back down at him.

Hunter felt the blackness at the edge of his senses sweep up and overwhelm him.

## Chapter Twenty-nine

Hunter awoke – which in itself seemed like a major achievement. Sophie had not killed him, even when she had the perfect chance to. Hunter's head hurt to process any reason behind it, instead he focused on the simpler things.

It was light. With the low-hanging sun and cool air, Hunter sluggishly surmised that it was early morning.

He raised his head just enough to confirm that he was still on the Salisbury Plains. He could make out the deserted village that they had used, and the copse of trees their reinforcements had hidden within.

Hunter felt a stab of uneasiness. It was far too quiet.

He steeled himself to get to his feet. Hunter did not trust his ability to blink to the battleground, so made the slow and steady march to cover the distance.

There was no sign of life, only bodies laid strewn across the Plains. Hunter choked down the bile that threatened to rise.

Hunter gave the fleetest glances to each noting those he recognised. With each familiar face, his heart hardened. Now was not the time for grief. Instead he had to... to...

Hunter stopped in his tracks as he saw General Hayworth, such a steady source of leadership over the past couple of years. Now he lay with vicious burns on one side. But he had not gone down alone, the bodies of half a dozen witches were testament to his fight.

Hunter waited for the overwhelming power and blackout that had accompanied James' death, but he only felt numb.

Eventually he moved on again, further into the battlefield. There were less witch-hunters and soldiers here – proof of how far his team had successfully pushed through the witch ranks.

He saw three bodies ahead, and despite his nausea that begged for attention, his feet carried him mercilessly forward.

Hunter dropped to his knees as he struggled to breathe. The blast from the broken amulet had lifted them all off their feet. His friends had been killed in that moment. Sweet young Alannah; the dependable Ian; and Maria, who had never recovered from losing James. He had failed them all. They could never have guessed that trying to bind Sophie's powers could have such a result, in fact he remembered Sophie's look of surprise at the glowing, burning amulet. But Hunter could not forget that he had been the one to suggest this plan.

Hunter had no idea how he had survived the blast, he wished he had not.

Hunter lost track of how long he knelt there, the hot sun burning the back of his neck. His thoughts were struggling to connect, and his emotions had completely abandoned him.

They had been defeated.

Had anyone else survived? Surrounded by the dead, Hunter found it impossible to be optimistic.

What did he do now? What allies did he have left? He couldn't stay here; he was an easy target if the witches returned.

Hunter closed his eyes, letting his subconscious direct him as he blinked away from the battleground.

Despite it being the middle of summer, the air in the Manor was still cool.

Hunter looked down about the sitting room in which he had appeared, there were little signs everywhere of Mrs Astley and Charles' occupation of the house. Hunter thought about making his presence known but dismissed the idea. He moved into the hallway and made his way to towards the study, mindful of making as little noise as possible.

The Manor was quiet now. The last time he had been here his allies had filled the rooms. Their absence was painfully clear.

Once he entered the study, Hunter looked around. For all his books and records, it had all come to nothing. There had to be some answer – but not here.

He rummaged through his desk and pulled out paper and a pen.

*'We are in dark days. I write this hurriedly at my desk, not knowing to whom I write, but wanting my story to be known. I hope it is found by one of my kind, and in turn gives hope...*

*My name is George Astley VII, known to my friends as Hunter...*

*... I am going to find the Benandanti.'*

Hunter continued to scratch away, filling the paper with text, then folded the page when he finished. He had no idea who, if anyone, would read it; nor what help it might give, but it eased his anxiety and settled his course.

Taking one last look around, committing the room to memory, Hunter vanished.

Thrice the brinded cat hath mew'd.
Thrice and once, the hedge-pig whin'd.
Harpier cries:—'tis time! 'tis time!

# The Shadow Falls

## Witch-Hunter 3

### K. S. Marsden

## A letter from our hero...

We are in dark days. I write this hurriedly at my desk, not knowing to whom I write, but wanting my story to be known. I hope it is found by one of my kind, and in turn gives hope...

My name is George Astley VII, known to my friends as Hunter. If it matters to you, I am 28 years old, English; and in a time of peace I would be the lord of Astley Manor, near the village of Little Hanting.

But this is not a time of peace, we have been fighting the losing side of a war for the past two years. Fighting against the witches. It all started when the legendary Shadow Witch arose - a witch whose magic was without limit, a witch raised to nurse a thousand years of insult and hatred. She plunged the world into darkness so that she and the other witch kind could claw above the stricken and powerless humans, preferably with as many casualties as possible to assuage their anger.

Where do I fit in with all this? In the very centre, shouldering both the blame and the hope.

I am a witch-hunter. As was my father, and his father and so on. I am the 7th generation of witch-hunters belonging to the organisation called the Malleus Maleficarum Council, which has successfully policed and hidden magic and witches for hundreds of years. Until now.

The Shadow Witch approached me in the guise of Sophie Murphy, a beautiful, intelligent woman that I thought was an innocent that I saved and sheltered from witches. With a grating stubbornness, Sophie demanded to join the MMC and train as a witch-hunter. I was the one that allowed her into our Council. I was the one that would let her learn all our secrets. I was the one that would later fall in love with her.

She finally revealed herself as the Shadow Witch, and the first of many battles between the witches and witch-hunters was fought, in which our side was nearly decimated.

What remained of the MMC regrouped, driven by desperation against this new and unbelievable force. We had only one advantage: the Shadow Witch revealed too much about the hidden talent born into witch-hunters - into me in particular. I don't know how I do it, I cannot explain it. Some liken my talents to magic, all I know is that I am strong enough to repel witches and protect those around me, amongst other useful skills. With my new skills, we initially managed to repel the Shadow Witch and destroy her followers. She seemed to vanish for the best part of a year and, as terrible and fierce as they were, we began to beat back the witches.

Then the Shadow Witch returned, stronger than ever, and even I was helpless in her path. She systematically destroyed the witch-hunters and their allies, returning power and victory to the witches in a devastating way. Those fateful days of battle will haunt me forever, as I watched brave men and women fall at my side.

There might be witch-hunters in hiding somewhere out there, but as far as I am aware, I am the only one left.

Friendless, alone, and the most wanted man alive, I've decided it's time to learn all I can about this mysterious power I have. I am going to find the Benandanti.

**Chapter One**

The small town was near deserted. Half the people had fled, or just plain vanished. The other half sat behind their locked doors, no one ventured out once the sun set. So, no one saw the sudden appearance of a man in the rough piazza.

One moment the square was empty, the next there he stood. He was tall, well-built and had perhaps been handsome, but now his clothes were creased, his face rugged, worn and wary, and half hidden by the short, dark beard and straggly black hair.

It was a very different image than the old, relatively carefree Hunter Astley. He'd been rich, good-looking and popular.

He'd been on the run for nearly eight months, ever since the last big battle in which the witch-hunters and their allies had finally been overcome by the witches.

He hadn't dared stop anywhere for long, empty villages where no eyes could see him, or in the few dense cities that still existed where he could get lost in the crowd. He made his locations erratic and illogical, to throw off his hunters for a few peaceful hours.

Hunter had tried coming to Italy last summer, but found that wherever he went, the witches were close behind. Hunter didn't doubt that the Shadow Witch had a few spies permanently placed around here, for she knew how strongly Friuli would pull Hunter. For here was the region that had been the home to the Benandanti, centuries ago, the original anti-witches.

He eventually admitted defeat and fled to America, tracking down one lead in the library at Georgetown University; followed by Glasgow and Ulster. All he found were teasers and hints to what he truly wished to know.

As winter came around, Hunter kept his movements in the southern hemisphere. It was easier and safer than trying to find warmth and shelter – he could put no one in such danger.

But finally, spring came again, and Hunter was drawn back to Friuli. If the modern equivalent of the Benandanti existed anywhere, it would be here. It was dangerous, but Hunter had to find them, he was out of options. He'd started at the northernmost edge of Friuli and searched each town and village for hope. This one was close to the Lago di Sauris, a large landmark that allowed Hunter to gain his bearings in his speedy method of travel.

Hunter strode up to the nearest house and banged sharply on the wooden door. Dogs started to bark, but there was no sound of people.

"Per favore. Please, I need help." Hunter called out; his voice rough from disuse.

He heard the soft pad of feet and the creak of shutters. Hunter stepped back and looked at the surrounding houses.

"Please." He repeated to the dark, empty street. "I'm not a witch, I just need help. I'm looking for some people. They used to live here, many years ago. They did magic, good magic. Please."

Hunter's voice trailed off, he was used to the suspicion and wariness that now ruled every person's life. It was the way of the world under the rule of the witches. If this town couldn't help him, he'd travel to the next, and the next, persisting in his search.

"We want no magic here, signore." A warning voice came from behind a crack in a window shutter.

Hunter turned in the voice's direction. "No, I'm not here to harm you, and I'm not staying. But if you could help me by telling me anything, *anything* about the Benandanti…"

"I've never heard of them; they don't live here." The voice replied curtly.

458

Hunter frowned, it was a negative response, but at least someone was answering him - albeit through a blocked window.

"No, they might not live anywhere now. But they were in this region four hundred years ago."

"Four hundred years?" The voice spluttered. "Nobody here can help you, signore. It is too long ago. Now leave us in peace."

Hunter called out again but got no response. He even banged on the reinforced shutters but only set the dogs off again. It had been briefly promising but turned out to be less than helpful. Oh well, next village.

Hunter turned to leave the way he came when he suddenly stopped, seeing a pair of brown eyes peering around a crack in a door.

"Signore." A quiet woman's voice came. "It is true we know nothing but try the Donili monks. They have a small monastery a few kilometres south-west of here."

The door clicked shut.

"Thank you. Grazie." Hunter said quietly to the still night air.

He hadn't gotten any answers - hell, he'd hardly managed to get any questions out, but this was a start, a thread to follow. Not bad, he reflected as he left the village. Even a place as small and unimportant as this was dangerous - this close to the Benandanti rumours, it was best to travel unmarked paths and camp alone

459

and untraceable. Which meant hunkering down in the lonely forest that rose to the hills. Not a comfortable prospect, but at least the weather was mild.

At dawn Hunter was on his feet once more, set resolutely south-west, detouring only for the most stubborn natural barriers. The woman had said a few kilometres. A few. What an ill-defined description. She could mean three kilometres, while he considered it seven, or vice versa. And did she mean precisely south-west, or bearing more to the left or right? He might walk right past the home of the Donili monks, or not walk far enough. The dismal beat of his thoughts matched his steady footsteps.

He replayed the steps that had brought him here. He had thought of nothing but the Benandanti for months. The focus allowed him to block out the nightmare of last year; investigating every dusty book, every story and myth was preferable than remembering the death and violence that was behind him.

The minutes seemed to drag by, and a mere hour pushing on exhausted him, but Hunter didn't stop, the distance passed slowly but steadily. He kept a keen eye for any sign of a monastery, anything to show he was on track, but so far there had been nothing man-made, there had been no sight nor sou--

A scream pierced the peaceful countryside. Shouts followed and worse, laughter.

Hunter stopped. The sensible part of him warned caution, those screams could only mean trouble and he shouldn't endanger himself. Unfortunately, he'd already set off in pursuit of the noise, self-preservation at the back of his mind.

Drawing closer, the trees thinned to reveal a lonely little cottage. In front of the humble building a woman stood before two young children, arms held wide to shield them with her own body. The three cried and begged while a man held onto an older child, seemingly playing a tug-o-war with the boy being pulled on the other side by a laughing duo.

"Please, no." The man begged.

"You know the law." The female aggressor said with a scornful laugh. "Sacrifices must be provided."

"No, please, not my son. Take me instead."

The heartless woman shook her head smiling, finding his distress highly amusing. They all cried and begged, and some even swore and fought back; but the result was always the same, when a witch demanded a sacrifice that demand had to be met.

Hunter had seen enough.

"Release him." He shouted with all the authority he once possessed.

The two aggressors turned, unimpressed by this scruffy stranger that dared to intercede.

"Move on." The male warned. "This does not concern you."

461

"Release him." Hunter repeated. "Or I will be forced to take action."

The crying father looked between the two witches and this unknown hero; his troubled mind slow to catch up.

"No signore, you mustn't, they... they will come, they will protect us." His strange mumblings faded into a whisper and he closed his eyes briefly in a silent prayer.

The man and his comments were ignored as the witches turned to the one individual willing to stand up against them, willing to fight even.

Hunter felt that familiar spark in his mind that sensed magic. Indeed, the build up from the two witches was almost tangible. He frowned, his hand clasping the metal amulet at his throat, his whole body reaching instinctively for protection. It had been years since Hunter had first used the natural shield that he was equipped with, and now it slipped over him with an invisible, but comfortable weight.

The first wave of spells hit, designed to blind and unbalance, a typical opening move. The magic distilled uselessly in the air, leaving Hunter unaffected and the witches disturbed and confused.

Hunter sighed, soon he'd draw his gun, he'd fight to destroy these ungodly creatures. But first he needed to protect the others in case things got ugly. With a simple thought he extended the shield to protect the cowering family.

Hunter snapped to attention, his shield was blocked, he pushed again but it felt like it had come up against a solid wall. This was unsettling, in the last two years, in the endless fights and battles his shield had been battered and weakened, but never blocked.

*The spells came in from all sides, Hunter felt the shield buckle under the sheer pressure, he was half-aware of the witch-hunters at the very edge, no longer safe as his strength failed. Soon they began to fall, no longer protected from the lethal magic...*

Hunter shook his head, determined to stay in the present. Another spell dissolved against the shield. Hunter frowned, he hated blood and death and had seen enough of both to last ten lifetimes, but he duly drew his gun and steadily fired at both witches.

Hunter heard a feral snarl rip from one of the witches, but neither of them fell. Hunter froze - his aim was infallible, yet they weren't hit. Even more disturbing was the expression of confusion that was mirrored in the witches' faces. The bullets had been stopped and it was not their doing.

Beyond the sound of his own thudding pulse Hunter became aware of a low rumble of noise coming from the forest. He turned, automatically strengthening the shield about him. Out of the trees stepped two men, one grey-haired and wrinkled, the other younger than Hunter. Their eyes were closed in concentration and both chanted in low tones, the sound akin to a hum.

The older man suddenly fell silent and opened his eyes, facing the two witches. With a move of his hand there was a deep rumble and a bright flash of light. Hunter heard a scream rip from the witches, and he stumbled back, unbalanced and blinded.

It was over in a flash, Hunter felt his heart falter, then double its beat. The witches were nowhere to be seen. The father and son scrambled back to their family's embrace.

The two mysterious men turned to face Hunter, the old man locked his pale blue gaze onto Hunter and raised his hand... then faltered. His wrinkled brow creased further in a frown. He spoke quickly, but Hunter failed to follow his words, they were an Italian dialect he'd never heard before.

"Wh-what? I'm sorry, I don't understand." He stuttered breathlessly, unable to find his usual manners in this confusion.

The younger man looked at him with surprise. "Inglese." He said with some amazement, throwing a meaningful look to the elder.

"English? He says, 'you are not a witch'." The young man explained in broken English, the words flavoured with accent, while he gazed curiously at Hunter.

Hunter wavered beneath those bright blue eyes. "No... I mean, yes, I'm English. But I'm not a witch."

The older man whispered something to the young one, who nodded seriously.

"But you are using magic." He insisted, his eyes drifting along Hunter's aura, as though physically seeing the shield.

"Oh." Hunter turned his attention to his shield, reluctantly letting it drop. He was far from trusting these strangers, but felt he needed to show faith if he were to get answers. "That's not magic, it's something... different. I'm sorry, but who are you?"

"I am Marcus." The young man replied readily; a hand placed on his chest. "And my friend is Maurizio, we are Donili. And you?"

"Donili?" Hunter jumped at the word. "Of the Donili monks? But I came this way looking for you."

Marcus frowned, and relayed this to the older Maurizio, then turned back to Hunter. "And your name?" He insisted.

"Hunter Astley, a 7th gen witch-hunter with the British Malleus Maleficarum Council." Hunter replied.

Marcus hesitated at this stream of information, then repeated it to Maurizio. Hunter waited impatiently as they exchanged comments in that incomprehensible Italian, his nerves still sparking at every slight sound or movement.

"You will come with us, Signor Astley? Our council will have many questions. You have many questions also?" Marcus' voice rose, but Hunter couldn't tell whether in query or anticipation.

"Yes. Yes, of course." Hunter replied immediately, feeling truly hopeful for the first time in three months.

Maurizio, pleased with the outcome of this laboured conversation, turned to the family. The old man quickly exchanged words with the mother and father, and less quickly stood smiling as he accepted their thanks and blessings.

Marcus smiled indulgently, then hurried the older man along. They set off into the forest, trudging over the rugged terrain. Hunter, used to his above average stamina and physical ability, was surprised by Marcus, and especially the older Maurizio, who paced along swiftly and untiring. Hunter came up with mental excuses, that he was wearied from being on the run for so long, that he was further tired by the brief fight with the witches - but the truth was it was embarrassing that his breathing grew heavier and he felt sweat run down his face and neck.

Hunter stopped to take a much-needed drink from his old water bottle. He coughed and spat, feeling guiltily unlike a gentleman.

"How much further is it?" He asked his travelling companions, not quite sure what 'it' was. He took the opportunity to take a few deep breaths and kept his voice strong at least.

"Not far. One kilometre, no more than two." Marcus replied, patiently waiting for his English guest. He hesitated, obviously taking in Hunter's sweaty appearance and strained eyes.

Marcus turned and quickly fell into conversation with Maurizio. Hunter didn't even try to follow the flow of words, but he gathered from the stress in Marcus' voice that the younger man was trying to persuade the older.

Eventually Maurizio shrugged non-committedly and Marcus turned back to Hunter with a smile.

"We go the fast way - this is how we travel. Hold my arm. Trust me." Marcus said, holding out his hand invitingly, but an almost mischievous look in his eye.

Warily Hunter raised his hand. As soon as he touched the young man's forearm the world went black and Hunter felt a familiar shift.

## Chapter Two

In no time at all, the world returned, and Hunter saw an array of stone and brick buildings and heard the small crowd of people that turned to gaze calmly at their sudden appearance. Hunter, so suspicious and tense himself, noticed that people looked at him with only a vague curiosity before moving on, as though their appearance were a common thing.

Next to Hunter, Marcus turned with an expectant look.

"Do you want to sit? It is disorie- dees... *disorientante* for new people." He said, but his smile faltered as he saw Hunter show no sign of distress from this almost magical form of transport.

"No, I'm fine thank you. Where are we?" Hunter asked, brushing aside the unnecessary concern and gazing about the settlement. The buildings were strong and sturdy and defied the forest which turned the horizon green in every direction. The land sloped gently downhill in front of him and Hunter could see the shimmer of a river where the houses gave way, and further the land rose again to the next sunlit hill. "Are we still in Friuli?"

"Yes." Marcus answered, still eyeing Hunter warily. "This is the village of Donili. Come, you must meet our Abate. He is at the abbazia."

Marcus led back up the hill towards a long, low stone building that looked down on the village like a guardian. Marcus glanced again at Hunter. "You sure you ok? Most people panico after their first travel."

"It wasn't my first time." Hunter said carefully, thinking this was enough honesty. There was no need to. He didn't know how much he could trust Marcus and decided that the less he revealed about himself the better.

Hunter ignored the quizzical look from his young companion, and kept his eyes trained on the path, the last thing he wanted was to trip, fall, and look a prat. At one point, Hunter finally noticed the absence of Maurizio. But they had just reached the doors and he had no time to give the old man any further thought. Marcus rapped on the wooden doors and they were pulled open from the inside by a monk who nodded them through.

They stepped into a large courtyard. Hunter was struck by the simple beauty of the place; the sun warmed the soft brown stone, and along each side of the courtyard, shadowed walkways were marked out with pillars.

Hunter heard the pad of soft shoes across the stone quad. He turned to see another monk approach them, the man looked young and strong, and he greeted them both with quiet confidence.

"Welcome to the Abbazia di Donili, Signor Astley. My name is Biagio, if you come with me, I shall show you to the padre."

Hunter was briefly taken aback by his fluent, yet accented English and could only nod in reply, before finally coughing out a thank you.

Biagio smiled indulgently, then bowed briefly to Marcus before turning and walking away.

Hunter hesitated, not sure if he were meant to follow. He glanced at Marcus, somehow trusting this Donili monk that he met first.

Marcus tried an encouraging smile. "Perhaps I see you later, signore." The young man bowed and backed away.

Hunter frowned, he'd been deprived of company for so long, it was tempting to latch onto the first friendly face he saw. He had to remind himself that, until he had answers and his life had gained some aspect of sense again, he should remain wary and taciturn; there would be time for friendships later, if there were time at all.

Hunter gripped the straps of his rucksack and stumbled along behind Biagio, looking like any other weary traveller behind the quiet, composed monk.

Biagio led indoors and down a narrow stone corridor. He opened the last door and invited Hunter in.

Hunter didn't know what to expect, he'd been so preoccupied with the finding of a link to the Benandanti that his mind hadn't considered any further.

The room was cosy, with an upholstered bench and several soft chairs. There was a grand fireplace, that was yet unlit, and the walls were lined with shelves of books. The atmosphere of the room reminded Hunter of his own private study or drawing room at home.

There were three men sitting in the room, all were grey-haired and bore signs of age. They were in quiet conversation, but broke off at Hunter's arrival, they looked in his direction and Hunter could see that age had not dulled those sharp, shining eyes that pierced him curiously.

Next to him, Biagio made an introduction in that bizarre dialect.

One of the monks rose from their seat and replied, his gaze flitting between Hunter and Biagio the translator.

"The Abate welcomes you, Hunter Astley. Please be seated, you must have many questions. And after Maurizio's account of your meeting, we too have questions." Biagio relayed eloquently, a slight air of smugness over his own fluency.

But Hunter paid him little attention, he glanced again at the two seated monks and realised that one of them was Maurizio. So, this was where the old man had disappeared to - coming to forewarn the boss while Hunter toiled with Marcus.

Ever since he had found out about his abilities, Hunter had steadily gained more questions and no answers. But right now, he was speechless. In the awkwardness of his silence, he acted upon the invitation to sit down, sinking into one of the heavenly comfortable chairs.

The Abate sat also and spoke again.

"The Abate would like to know what brings an English gentleman to the hidden valleys of Italy?" Biagio voiced eagerly.

"I... I came looking for the Benandanti." Hunter replied, getting straight to the point.

Hunter waited impatiently for this to be relayed.

"Benandanti? It has been a long time since any sought them. They were a branch of our family that were wiped out hundreds of years ago." The Abate said via Biagio.

Hunter sat up straighter, his pulse quickening as his hopes were realised. "The Benandanti were part of the Donili?"

"Yes, they were one of the largest families. They were discovered by Europeans and were killed by their narrow-mindedness. The Europeans saw the skills that were inborn and strictly trained to protect others, but instead of seeing it as natural they accused the Benandanti of devil worship and magic and punished them.

"Thankfully, the rest of the Donili remained undiscovered, and by the grace of God, have been able to keep protecting those that ask for our help."

Hunter sat there, absorbing this new version of history. He had hoped that perhaps some of the Benandanti had survived, he could never have dreamed that the Benandanti were only a small part of something bigger, older and perhaps stronger.

"Now, I have given you an answer, it is your turn."

The Abate frowned, equally displeased with the circuitous nature of speaking through a translator. He looked directly at Hunter, "Te parle italiano?"

"Si, fluente." Hunter replied, feeling those blue eyes pierce him.

The Abate quickly dismissed Biagio, who looked disappointed at no longer being needed.

"This is easier, no?" The Abate asked in steady Italian. "I dislike using a translator, but like many of my

473

kin, I only speak the language of our fathers, and occasionally Italian."

"Si, padre." Hunter said, then couldn't help but lean forward. "But I have many things to ask."

The Abate raised a hand to stop him. "Of course, you do, but it is my turn. How else am I to ascertain if we should answer your questions, unless you answer mine?"

Behind the gentle words, Hunter saw the unyielding stubbornness of the Abate on this point, and he sat back reluctantly.

"Good. Now first, our friend Maurizio tells me you used a defensive shield similar to the Donili's. How?"

"It's a long story." Hunter sighed. "I'm a witch-hunter with the British Malleus Maleficarum Council. We discovered a long time ago that the sons and daughters of witch-hunters were born with certain advantages against witches and magic. Just small things really, they are faster, stronger, can perceive the use of magic and are immune to some spells - improving with each generation.

"I'm a 7th generation and a few years ago I was - ah - awoken to the fact that I could do *more*. I could travel anywhere in a blink; I can shield and block magic…"

Hunter broke off, there was more to it than a few tricks, his ability to shield himself and others had been a major factor in every battle. But Hunter was sure he was capable of more, there were times that things -

inexplicable things - happened; what else could it be but an unconscious use of his power. He had a sudden image of a crumbling church, dead witches half-buried under the rubble. It was a dark and terrifying scene, but if he could harness that particular power, it would surely shift the balance of power away from the witchkind.

"Are there many like you?" The Abate asked, breaking into Hunter's thoughts.

"No." Hunter replied. "I'm the only one. That's why I came to find - well, you. There's so much I need to learn. And... and for your help."

The Abate brought his hands together and looked over his steepled fingers at Hunter, his bright blue eyes very serious.

"Certamente! We dedicate our lives to helping others. But the help they receive depends on the path they are willing to take." The Abate said cryptically. The old man then frowned, an edge of suspicion in his voice when he spoke again. "Surely the help and learning you seek are the same thing?"

Hunter dropped his gaze, suddenly inspecting the dirt on his hands, before remembering he was an English gent and witch-hunter and should not fear being assertive with anyone.

"Padre, I come to you as a representative of the Malleus Maleficarum Council. It cannot have escaped your notice that we are at war against the witches. I come to ask you to help us in any way you can. Become our ally and help us drive away the shadows."

The Abate sighed, as though Hunter had confirmed his low expectations.

"No."

The single word surprised Hunter. One word, with no deliberation or uncertainty.

"No?" Hunter repeated, as though the meaning of the word eluded him. "Can't you… will you at least consider it?"

"Signor Astley, we are not fighters, we are monks, we protect life. Oh, I am sure you have what you consider valid points to argue, but on this point, I will not be moved."

"You say you protect life - then protect those worldwide that are threatened by witches. Give your protection to those that will fight for a better world." Hunter leant forward; his speech impassioned.

But the Abate looked unimpressed and did not respond to this request. Instead he turned quite calmly to the other two old men in the room.

"Forgive my selfishness brothers, in hogging all the words. Perhaps you could voice your opinions to Signor Astley's request."

Hunter blinked, looking to the other aged monks that he had near forgotten.

The unknown monk spoke first. "Whether we are the shield or the sword, we shall not enter this bloody battle. Our prayers would be ignored, and our souls scarred if we stood by and watched you and your kin killing, knowing that we were the ones that enabled such murder and massacre."

Hunter could give no reply to such an answer; how could he, he'd just been labelled a murderer. He was surprised at how forgiving the Donili sounded about witches - surely, they couldn't turn a blind eye to such an evil force. Surely, they had been fighting witches even longer than the MMC.

"How can we help those that would turn on us?" Maurizio finally spoke, "It happened once before, when your people discovered a power, they did not understand in the Benandanti. The Donili have long memories."

Hunter looked with surprise at the old monk, for some reason feeling betrayed by Maurizio's harsh and unfair prejudice. How could they hold a grudge over something that happened five hundred years ago? Back when the MMC was a very different entity, its witch-hunters narrow-minded and devout on a religious scale. The modern MMC were much more controlled, fairly ruled by strict codes and laws. But... there came a seed of doubt. Hunter flashed back to when he had discovered his own unnatural powers, he'd been torn with fear that he would be condemned, even by those he called friends, so much so that he nearly kept this huge defensive bonus a secret as he and the other witch-hunters prepared for a suicidal battle against the Shadow Witch.

"That's ridiculous." Hunter retorted with a shake of his head, arguing against his own thoughts as much as the monks' words. He took a deep breath, frustrated, and ran a hand through his straggly hair. "It's not like it was, things have changed; the whole world has changed. I've travelled so far and seen so much, if you would just listen and-"

"We believe you, Signor Astley." The Abate interrupted curtly. "Indeed, you look so tired from your travels and troubles. Perhaps you would like to rest and gather your thoughts before we speak again."

At his words, Hunter felt a wave of tiredness wash over him, and was immediately suspicious of the three monks that sat with him. Hunter frowned and fought the fatigue.

"No, I don't need to rest, I need to keep moving." He stumbled over the words, concentrating on keeping his Italian fluent. "I must keep moving... they cannot be allowed to find me. I must move on to find those that *will* help."

"No, Signor Astley, I think you need to sleep." The Abate said with quiet confidence.

And Hunter felt the darkness of unconsciousness sweep him away.

## Chapter Three

Normally Hunter's sleep was so fragmented, as he pushed himself daily beyond exhaustion. But in this forced slumber he slipped deeper and deeper.

*The colours were so bright and beautiful, as they only can be on a glorious spring day in the English countryside. The trees were in that transitional stage where the leaves gleamed green against the blossoms on the branches, waiting to fall. The sun was low and still hot, but the slight breeze was a cold reminder of the winter that was always slow to leave.*

*Hunter pushed open a small painted, wooden gate and stepped into a garden that was a half-tamed wilderness. With no control of his movements he walked up the garden path to a picturesque country cottage that inspired a vague sense of familiarity. When he reached the oak door, he opened it without hesitation, surprised at the feeling of possession that was sparked as he stepped over the threshold.*

Hunter moved through the modern interior of the old cottage, wondering whether he'd ever visited this place in his life, and why he should feel so at home.

The cottage was quiet, but as he stepped into the living room, he found that it wasn't empty. A woman was standing at the opposite end of the room, as tense and expectant as he was. She was dressed casually in jeans and a simple maroon jumper. Her dark brown hair was pulled back into a careless ponytail, and her face was so beautiful and her eyes so sharp.

Sophie, the name leapt up Hunter's throat, but he didn't utter a sound. He just stood there, stupidly still and silent. It unnerved him that, even after all this time and chaos, his heart still leapt and he felt irresistibly drawn to this woman that had seemed so special, so important to him. But still he didn't speak, he didn't trust himself.

"Hunter?"

Hunter smiled; oh, his imagination was doing a good job of representing Sophie. That voice, quiet but confident. The expression on that beautiful face, an enquiring frown that gently creased her brow, and no compassion to be seen.

"Hunter, what's wrong?" She asked, before sliding onto the settee with natural grace.

Hunter was not in complete control but sat down next to her, his eyes not leaving her face, feeling suspicion and desire in equal measure.

"You need a shave." Sophie teased, with that familiar sneer that was the closest she ever got to smiling. To make her point she ran her left hand across the side of his face, her *fingers gently stroking the coarse hair growing there. "You don't suit a beard."*

*Hunter felt an electric shock at her cool touch, and his hand flew to lay across hers. This all felt so comfortable, so familiar, Hunter experienced a sense of longing. Why couldn't he have this in his waking life, in a homey cottage with a beautiful woman.*

*He caressed her hand, his brow creased as he felt an unknown band of cold metal, then his eyes widened with understanding. A young, sharp cry rang across the room...*

Hunter woke with a start. His heart was pounding in his chest, but for once it wasn't with fear. The dream clung to him and he was disorientated as he opened his eyes. It took a few long moments for him to realise where he was - or where he should be - the last thing he remembered was that damn monk. He knew he was in a bed, with a soft mattress and light blanket, which seemed a safe place to be. Lying still, he was so wonderfully comfortable, and warm, and definitely not ready to be wide-awake. It's Sunday, Hunter thought lazily, it must be Sunday.

Quite happy not to move, Hunter ran through his dream, which was still bright and clear in his mind. He didn't often dream, and when he did his subconscious always steered clear of featuring Sophie Murphy, the human face of the Shadow Witch.

Hunter was slightly agitated by the whole happy feeling of the scene, compounded by the cry that had woken him - that cry had been one of joy, and he was pretty sure it hadn't come from either Sophie or himself.

Slowly his senses were reawakening to the world. To the bright light that filled the room, to the sound of birds outside... to the sound of another person's breathing inside.

Hunter jerked up and turned, getting twisted in the bed sheets in his rush to rise. But the haste was unnecessary. There was another narrow bed in the room, and upon it sat Marcus, legs crossed and calmly reading.

Quite unhurriedly, Marcus finished reading the page, then gently closed his book.

"I was thinking you would never wake." He said in his heavily accented English.

Hunter looked up to see the young man was only teasing.

"How long have I been asleep?"

"Twenty-four hours, signore. It is after noon." Marcus replied calmly.

Hunter swore beneath his breath and collapsed back on the bed.

Marcus smiled at the Englishman's reaction. "The Abate did not want you disturbed; he say you need rest.

He also say when you wake, I am to give you a tour and give answer to your questions."

Hunter turned his head to look at the young man. "That's very kind of you."

Marcus smiled and waited patiently as Hunter pulled himself together and traipsed off to the washroom. When Hunter came back, he was clean and alert.

"Let's go." He simply said.

The Abbazia di Donili was old and strong, and somehow warm from years of sun on the white and brown stonework. The place sprawled across the hillside on several levels; it was a long walk from the accommodation quarters where Hunter had slept, through the corridors and courtyards, all clean-cut and well-kept. There were large rooms of varying yet specific use.

Marcus kept up a running commentary of the design and use of the buildings, only pausing to search for the correct word in English, often resorting to Italian.

Hunter listened, eager for any and all information, but his attention caught every time another monk passed them by. He couldn't help being curious about the many people that lived and trained in this abbazia.

"How many monks are there?" Hunter asked, breaking Marcus' monologue.

Marcus paused, thinking for a moment. They'd reached the foot of stone steps that Marcus promptly led up. Hunter followed, and soon stepped up onto a high walkway, with the hot sun shining brightly from above, and most of the abbazia laying out before them.

"There are perhaps fifty in the abbazia, and fifty in the town. The children of the Donili join the abbazia when we have thirteen years. We train, we pray and protect. Until we leave the abbazia to marry and have our own children." Marcus spoke calmly of this organised life, he leaned casually against a stone wall and gazed down at the green courtyard below.

Hunter followed his gaze and noticed a couple of monks going calmly about their business. Hunter frowned, suddenly realising something as he looked at the young slender 'monks' with their dark hair tied back.

"There are women?" He gasped. "In a monastery?"

Marcus laughed at the Englishman's amazement. "Certamente! The Donili daughters learn with the sons. It was common for male and female to live and pray together, a long time ago."

Hunter thought back on what he knew - or what he thought he knew, of the Benandanti. They were recorded as an anti-witch breeding cult, propagating and honing the genes that allowed them to repulse witches. A good idea in theory, but Hunter couldn't imagine a less appealing life, amorously. He'd experienced a variety of women and relationships, from his childhood sweetheart whom he'd stuck with for convenience; his infatuation with Charlotte while at university, and so many meaningless dalliances. His thoughts stopped short before they arrived chronologically at Sophie, last night's dream still haunting the recesses of his mind.

"Will you have to marry one of them?" Hunter asked with a vague nod in the direction of the female Donili.

Marcus hesitated, looking at Hunter carefully. Then the young monk shrugged. "I do not know yet. I marry a Donili, or a girl from the village, or a girl from somewhere in Friuli. I do not know. Whoever I choose must be approved of by the Abate and the elders. But not for years, perhaps. I am happy training and doing my duty."

Hunter felt slightly uncomfortable. "Sorry, I didn't mean to ask something so personal."

Marcus looked away, but smiled, accepting the apology. "The Abate says to answer all your questions. You must be special, Signor Astley."

"Call me Hunter, please. And I'm not special." He said, modesty forcing him to voice the lie. Oh yes, he was very special, no matter how you looked at it.

"Hunter." Marcus repeated with a nod of his head. "It is nearly time for prayers. We will go down and join the others."

Marcus led back down to the lower level and along a stone pathway to the large church that was the head or heart of the whole abbazia. Inside the church opened up to a large, cool hall. They walked slowly between the rows of benches, and Hunter stared at the beauty of the architectural arches and the statues that stood watch. Beside him, Marcus would murmur the name of a particular saint or other; Sant Antonio; San Guiliano; San Pietro; all in hushed tones.

At the far end of the church the altar rose out of the ground, a large stone table. But behind was something to catch any man's attention. The walls were decorated in a brightly-coloured fresco. Staring up at it, Hunter could depict several suitably saintly men and women, standing with their hands placed serenely on their breast. But one picture drew his eye, a building struck by lightning.

"What-?" Hunter's voice failed as he pointed to the section of the wall bearing the image.

Marcus came up beside him and looked at the fresco. "Ah, that is importante. The old abbazia, hit by fulmini - lightning - and destroyed, in the year 1131 AD. We build again, naturalmente."

"Why should that be important?" Hunter asked quietly, not wanting to offend what they might consider vital.

But Marcus did not reply, the young monk had turned away and now bowed at the approach of another.

"Signor Astley." Came the voice of the Abate. "I hope you have enjoyed your tour, and Marcus has been helpful."

Hunter turned to see the Abate; the old monk was dressed in red and white robes, ready to lead his kin in prayer.

Hunter bowed to him, respectful of the position the man held as a representative of god. "Si padre, grazie."

The Abate looked at Hunter with an assessing gaze, his bright blue eyes very thoughtful. "Yes, we will speak properly after the service."

Hunter and Marcus both bowed as the Abate passed them by, Hunter felt his heart beat faster, harder, affected by the power of the old monk's office.

Hunter remained seated as the rest of the congregation filed out. As the church finally emptied, he got up and made his way back up to the altar to the fresco. The image of the lightning-hit church reminded him of the tower in a deck of tarot cards - a sign of disaster that overturned the old and welcomed the new. Unfortunately, Hunter could not remember whether it was a good sign or bad.

He sighed, shaking his head at his own thoughts. Tarot and other fortune-telling methods were the tools of wiccans, a laughed-at semi-religious sect that had been scorned by witches and witch-hunters alike, who had seen true magic and power. If Hunter was seeing non-existent wiccan signs, it meant that Jonathan had succeeded in educating the stubborn witch-hunter.

Hunter took a deep breath to counter the pain of the direction of his thoughts. The wiccans had suffered greatly in the new regime. They had gone one of two ways; the darker obsessives had fallen to worshipping the real witches, fawning at their feet in hope of a taste of seductive, addictive power; the harmless majority had tried to use their practices to protect against, or even overpower the witches. Hunter had even managed to become friends with some of them, had started to respect them… before the Shadow Witch and her followers killed them.

"You admire our décor, Signor Astley?"

Hunter turned, taken by surprise at the old monk's silent approach. "Si, padre. The image of the old abbazia is very interesting."

The Abate came to stand beside him, gazing calmly at the familiar pictorial representation of the Donili's history. The old monk continued in Italian. "Ah, the old abbazia. Destroyed in 1131."

"So, Marcus told me. Destroyed by lightning."

The Abate smiled sadly. "How polite of him. It was actually destroyed by magic. The monks that survived the attack went on to discover all they could about

488

witches and rebuilt the Abbazia di Donili, promising to protect the innocent people of the surrounding country. They could never have predicted that, after a few generations, certain skills would awaken within them."

"That was the origin of the Donili?" Hunter asked, amazed. The order of Donili evidently began three hundred years before the Malleus Maleficarum was set up; and they had been honing their skills since the very beginning, whereas Hunter was the first known witch-hunter in six hundred years to develop similar anti-witch power.

But that might have to do with the Donili's passive stance on witches, Hunter realised bitterly. They never brought on the outright wrath of witches that destroyed the witch-hunters' every bloodline, which was why no witch-hunter had ever reached the 7$^{th}$ generation before.

"Indeed." The Abate confirmed. "Come, let us walk in the sun before evening meal."

Without waiting for a response, the Abate led out of the church and into the courtyard. The bright spring sun was warm and blindingly low.

"I have been speaking with the other elders about what to do with you, Signor Astley." The Abate started, gazing out across the courtyard, rather than facing Hunter. "Your violent attitude towards witches, and your pride, both put you in bad stead. But the fact that you are so alike us in power enforces a certain

489

responsibility on our shoulders. Indeed, it would be preferable that you learn here and perhaps tame your temper, rather than by experimenting alone."

Hunter stood quietly beside the old monk. As his character was slighted, he felt that same pride rear up, and he couldn't help but smile at that particular truth.

"And did you reach a decision?" Hunter asked mildly. During the service, he'd used the time to assess his position. He was no longer the renowned witch-hunter with the MMC to back him; no longer was he surrounded by loyal companions that would follow his every command, even if they thought it a bad idea; no longer lord of the manor with an extensive estate. He wasn't even special compared to these monks. The Abate had proven that by so effectively and easily knocking him out yesterday. And Hunter knew that he wouldn't get his way in this place by force or argument.

"Yes." The Abate replied. "You may stay; you will train with the young monks. As long as you do not try to persuade the others with your ill-formed prejudices. Do you accept?"

Hunter hesitated, but this was likely to be the best deal he would receive.

"Si, padre." He murmured, with a bow of his head.

## Chapter Four

After breakfast the next morning, Hunter followed Marcus down another identical corridor in the sprawling abbazia, heading to his first lesson.

"Catalyn teach you, today." Marcus explained, his English slow and broken. "Manipolazione di elementi, it is basic, but necessary."

Manipulating elements? It sounded far from basic to Hunter.

Marcus noticed the look of apprehension cross Hunter's face, and he patted his new friend on the shoulder. "Catalyn is good teacher, you will see."

Hunter nodded. "So, will you be joining us?"

"No Hunter, you will join the other novices." Marcus replied, his brown eyes flashing with amusement. "I will see you at dinner."

Hunter narrowed his eyes at the younger man's comment, but opened the door, stepping into what was effectively a classroom.

And immediately stopped in his tracks.

There were half a dozen students that turned to look at him. By their fresh faces, Hunter guessed they were only thirteen at the most. Hunter half-turned, but found Marcus blocking his escape.

"Seriously?" He hissed.

Marcus grinned, not understanding the word, but understanding the sentiment perfectly. "Catalyn - un nuovo studente."

A woman in her fifties drifted over, her eyes flicking over Hunter in assessment. "You must be Signor Astley." She commented in Italian.

"Please, call me Hunter."

"Join the others please, Hunter." Catalyn gestured to the others that stood in the middle of the room. "Grazie Marcus, I shall take it from here."

Hunter's shoulders drooped and he walked over to his 'classmates' as they milled in the middle of the room with the restlessness of youth. They all looked curiously at the Englishman, their scrutiny adding to Hunter's discomfort.

"Today we will be completing the practical of yesterday's theory work." Catalyn stated in quick Italian. She paused, her eyes turning to Hunter. "Normally I have students start with earth or water manipulation. But as you join us mid-course, we will see how you cope with fire."

Catalyn held out a hand and with a mere moment's concentration, a flickering flame hovered above her palm.

"Greta, what part of the air around you is responsible for manipulation of movement, and stops you getting burnt?" Catalyn asked, as the fire moved into a ball and hovered higher.

"Um, oxygen?" The girl replied.

The rest of the class tittered, and one of the boys raised his hand.

"Carbon dioxide. Oxygen is for the manipulation of size." He rattled off, looking at Greta with superiority.

"Good Francis. Now catch." Catalyn smiled and with a flick of her fingers, the little ball of flame flew at Francis.

The boy jumped, startled; but recovered to stop the fire before it hit him. He smiled, setting it spinning in front of him, before sending it across the room to a tall girl.

The girl laughed. Hunter watched, both amazed and discomforted to watch the children play with the fire, like it was nothing more than an ordinary ball. Every ounce of his witch-hunter upbringing screamed that this was an unnatural use of magic.

Noticing his distraction, one of the novice monks sent the fireball at the outsider.

493

Hunter staggered backwards and felt the searing heat fly past his chest and combust against the wall.

"Now Luca, that wasn't very nice." Catalyn stated in a very neutral voice. "I am sorry, signore, would you like to try again?"

Hunter hesitated, not sure what was going on, nor what he was supposed to do. "I am afraid I need your instruction, Signora Catalyn."

Catalyn looked stumped for a moment, then she brought more fire to life in the palm of her hand.

"Perhaps we should try something else. Come to the table please, Signor Astley." She motioned towards the long table that was the length of the back wall. Immediately a flame flickered from one of the tall candles on it.

"Now, I want you to extinguish the flame." Catalyn stated, breaking off as she heard some of the others chuckling. "Hm, if you will excuse me."

The female monk drifted back to the group, snapping in the Donili dialect that Hunter could not follow what she had said. But from the kids' blushes, he could guess.

Hunter sighed and settled to his task. Catalyn drifted over every now and then, giving tips and advice, but the candle stayed stubbornly alight.

Hunter looked over at the teenagers, feeling a stab of jealousy when one of the youths decided to play keepy-uppy with the fiery ball.

"Luca, stop showing off." Catalyn said, although the woman smiled at the boy's antics, before turning back to Hunter.

Despite the sense of goodness that emanated from Catalyn, Hunter couldn't help feeling he was the unwilling participant of an experiment. Oh, he believed her intentions were well-meaning, but her continued scrutiny made him squirm.

Not soon enough, the lesson came to an end. Hunter thanked Catalyn and, feeling quite depressed over the whole ordeal, he made his way to the dinner hall.

Upon entering he noticed Marcus sitting with Biagio over to one side. With no better plan, he drifted over to them.

Both monks stopped their conversation and looked up to the Englishman.

"How was your lesson?" Biagio asked, managing to keep a straighter face than Marcus.

Hunter sat down next to Biagio, not saying anything.

"We exercise this afternoon. Many ages." Marcus said helpfully, not bothering to hide his amusement.

Hunter half-smiled but was already starting to regret all that was happening. For so long, finding the Benandanti meant finding answers to all of his questions. He had hoped for support, for miracles perhaps... but not this.

\*\*\*\*\*

Hunter walked through the cottage, his hand running over the familiar furniture. He made his way to the living room – as often happens in dreams, he knew who he would meet there.

A young child sat on the floor with papers around him. As Hunter entered, the boy looked up guiltily.

Hunter noticed the wet paintbrush in his hand. "Adam... what did your mother say about painting indoors?"

Hunter's fake sternness slipped further as the boy looked up, with his dark hair and hazel eyes, he was the very image of Sophie.

Hunter tutted and picked up the newspaper from the sofa. He spread the broadsheets over the carpet and stepped back, letting his son carry on. Hunter watched the young boy painting with such rapt concentration, as long as Adam was happy, that was all that mattered.

"You spoil him."

The three words were softly spoken by his ear, as two slender arms wrapped around his waist.

Hunter turned his head to glance back at Sophie, taking in her calm and composed expression, her sharp features, the challenge in her gaze.

"You shouldn't encourage him." She added.

Hunter shrugged. "It's hard not to."

Sophie sighed and rested against him, moulding to his back. They stood together quietly for what felt like an eternity, before Sophie spoke again.

"Where are you?" She asked, the words barely passing her lips when she suddenly gasped, her arms jerking.

Hunter turned and caught her, before she fell into the side table. "Sophie? Are you ok?"

Sophie looked very pale, her hazel eyes standing out brightly. She wet her lips to speak. "I don't know… it was pain, just pain." She looked at Hunter accusingly.

"It wasn't me." Hunter said. "Maybe you're not allowed to know."

Sophie pulled away from him. "Don't be ridiculous." She snapped.

"Mummy, can I have more paper?" Adam's voice broke through, the young boy looking up at his parents, the picture of innocence.

Sophie glared at Hunter once more, then pushed past him to help her son.

**Chapter Five**

It wasn't too much later when Hunter was summoned to see the Abate. He had been relaxing in the company of Biagio and Marcus, trying to learn more of the Donili dialect when the message came. Hunter was apprehensive, but obediently made his way to the common room of the senior monks.

It was the same room to which Hunter had been brought when he first arrived, but this time only the Abate was present.

"You wished to see me, padre?"

The Abate, distracted by a heavy book, looked up. "Ah, Signor Astley. Please sit down."

Hunter did so, sliding into the comfortable armchair, with a sudden feeling of déjà vu. He looked across at the padre, aside from when leading the monks in prayer, Hunter had not seen the Abate, who left the teaching of novices to the other seniors.

"Now, how are you getting on?" The Abate asked, his bright blue eyes locking on Hunter.

"Very well, thank you, padre." Hunter replied quietly, and not quite convincingly.

"Really?" The Abate asked sceptically. "Aurelio tells me that you lack attention and Catalyn says you do not connect with the other novices."

Hunter grit his teeth. So, this was why he was here, to be castigated like an overgrown schoolboy? 'I am twenty-eight years old', came the bitter thought.

Although he hadn't said a word in reply, the Abate suddenly laughed at Hunter. "Your pride and your arrogance work against you, Signor Astley. Perhaps you have been spoiled by your heroic deeds and respected image. You are too sure of yourself and cannot take criticism. Trust me, there will be a time when you are fifty, or sixty, and you will laugh at your obstinate younger self."

Hunter sat, tense and silent. Yes, he may be proud and arrogant and aware of it, but it didn't help to be laughed at.

"I do my best, padre."

The Abate waved away his pathetic response. "Perhaps your pride is attached to some of your deep-rooted beliefs. Now you are here, perhaps we can break them both. What are you?"

Hunter frowned, honestly confused. "What do you mean?"

"It is a simple question." The Abate replied with a knowing smile, then repeated, slower. "What are you?"

"A witch-hunter." Hunter said without thinking.

The Abate shook his head. "No, you choose to be a witch-hunter. It was most likely a forced decision, but you could have chosen not to hunt witches. What are you?"

Hunter shrugged, not understanding this game. "A human." He tried.

The Abate considered this before responding. "A human? Yes, you could argue that. But you aren't the same as those we call human in any ordinary sense. Hm, for example, I am Donili, a different class of human. What would you call yourself?"

"An anti-witch." Hunter replied hesitantly, voicing the term he'd often used amongst the Malleus Maleficarum Council and other witch-hunters.

"Anti-witch?" The Abate repeated. "I do not understand this term, please explain it."

When Hunter obeyed, the Abate smiled. "Anti-witch. Yes, I like this term. But to understand it fully, what is a witch?"

Hunter frowned, finding this all too patronising. But he played along, quoting almost word for word the definition that was in the modern Malleus Maleficarum - the witch-hunters' handbook. "A witch is a man or woman that can wield magic and is born of at least one witch parent. They are a sub-human species recognised as *homus maleficarum*. As such they have every appearance of being human and can cross-breed.

"A witch is born with latent powers that emerge at some time between childhood and puberty. These powers are varying in strength and use, from controlling natural forces; creating illusionary and solid threats; dominating the minds of men; and many other varied and inventive ways of undermining the natural order of a magic-free world."

"That is enough, Signor Astley." The Abate didn't look too pleased at the official MMC opinion, and to be honest, Hunter had stressed certain points, half hoping to open the Abate's eyes to the real world.

"If you want my opinion, and I know you won't like it." The Abate stated. "Anti-witches and Donili have a lot more in common with witches than normal humans."

Hunter's eyes blazed at this. "We are nothing alike. It is like comparing the Night and Day and saying they are the same because they are opposites."

He was angry at this assumption, it clashed against everything he'd ever been taught, everything he'd experienced, had learnt for himself.

*'Sounds like magic to me.'* The voice came rushing from the past, and he remembered it so clearly, how Sophie had dared to say such a thing, and his and

James' responding anger at such outrageous thinking. But Hunter finally saw it in a new light. After all, it was not he, but Sophie, that had discovered the nature of the witch-hunter's evolution into something that rivalled the witches they fought. How much had she known, there in the library, when her questions gained an extra fervour? Had she already guessed what was in store for Hunter; Sophie already binding his affections to her.

"That argument did not spare the Benandanti from persecution." The Abate's voice pulled Hunter back to the present.

"That was four hundred years ago. Things are very different now." Hunter replied, irritated by the Donili's refusal to drop this grudge.

The Abate sat back in his chair, observing Hunter. He sat silently for so long that Hunter began to think this uncomfortable meeting was over. But then the old monk spoke again.

"You are an anti-witch that chooses to hunt witches. I am a Donili that chooses to be a monk. Do you not think that witches choose their own paths also?"

"No." Hunter replied quickly and honestly. "They are inherently evil and think nothing of killing and torturing and destroying anything that displeases them. They are addicted to power, whether it is power over populace, or the power they gain internally by draining the life of a sacrifice."

The Abate nodded, considering this. "So, you have never met a witch that was good?"

"No." Hunter replied again, too quickly this time. Unbidden, his mind dredged up one figure, a witch named Beverley who had risked everything to save Hunter and James from the Shadow Witch and her followers. Even more amazing was the fact that Beverley was Sophie's mother. But dear old mum had her reasons - she feared the torment it would cause Sophie if she had to kill the man she loved.

"Witches have their reasons for everything they do - even mercy."

"Well, I think I will let you think over all we have said." The Abate said, almost affably. "I think we should have more of these debates, it is most invigorating."

Hunter, taking this as a dismissal, rose and after a courteous nod of his head he left swiftly. He did not look forward to another tête-à-tête with the Abate, he was disturbed by the awakening of old memories, and of the harsh contradictions against everything he knew in this world.

**Chapter Six**

Over the following week, Hunter did his best to learn the new role he had been set. Getting up before dawn every morning for an exercise regime that required utter control of the body and precision, Hunter had not thought that such practices were carried out this far into the western world. This was followed by breakfast and morning prayer, led by the Abate or another senior monk. The rest of the day would be devoted to understanding their skills, both theoretically and physically, only to be broken by meals and prayers. In the evenings they were free to meditate but were encouraged to read history and foreign languages.

Hunter was still irked by the fact that he trained alongside boys and girls that were ten years his junior. But soon he relaxed, comforted by having a regulated day. Also, after being put in his place by one or two of the 'juniors' that obviously possessed more skill than he did, made Hunter re-evaluate himself.

It was true that the young Donili had been training all their lives, but Hunter still felt wounded by the fact that he was the dunce of the class. He listened to the droning voices of his teachers with the same enthusiasm he'd had in those dreary Oxford lecture halls. The monks placed so much importance on theory, on the background and morals attached to every detail. And Hunter sat, impatient to test himself and improve, to get on with the whole damned reason he was here.

As the Abate had promised, he sought out Hunter again, insisting that the Englishman accompany him on a walk.

Hunter was somewhat relieved to have the excuse to get outside, the old abbazia soaked up the sun, and the air was stifling with the first heat wave of the year. The monk and the witch-hunter walked along the top of the wide walls that encased the Abbazia di Donili.

"How are you settling in, Signor Astley?" The Abate asked.

"You tell me, padre. You have your monks making reports on me." Hunter replied in a dull tone.

The Abate gave Hunter a shrewd look. "My fellow monks can tell me of your progress. They cannot tell me how you feel, George. I am guessing that you are still less than happy."

505

Hunter opened his mouth to argue but thought better of it.

"Correct me if I am wrong, but is this not where you want to be?" The Abate asked. "Why so unhappy?"

Hunter felt a flush of guilt. "No, it is padre. I am honoured that the Donili have accepted to teach me. It is just the frustration of being so inadequate compared to the others."

The Abate stopped and leaned against the parapet, looking down over his abbazia. The older man stood quietly for some time, until Hunter began to wonder whether this meeting was over.

"Naturally the Donili have tried to teach you the basics. But by all reports, you struggle with the simplest tasks."

Hunter grit his teeth, reminding himself of his previous promise of humility.

The Abate looked up to read the expression Hunter could not entirely hide. On another occasion, it might have amused the Abate; but now he was only concerned.

"You misunderstand my concern, Signor Astley. Tell me, how are you able to shield against magic?"

"I don't know, it just happens. It's a reaction that becomes an extension of me." Hunter said, thinking of how many times he had explained it to James, to the MMC, to the wiccans… he still didn't understand it, hence seeking the monks for answers.

Hunter sighed and leaned against the wall next to the Abate. "Why does that matter? Surely the Donili know both the theory and practice of such a thing. I saw Maurizio and Marcus use a shield when I first met them."

"Si, certamente. It is a useful defence we teach to all of our monks." The Abate replied. "But you never *learned*. And unless you were grossly exaggerating the part you played – you stopped a *Shadow Witch*."

Hunter shrugged, no he had never learned, per se. He had simply opened his mind to the possibilities, and there it was. After that, it was just like any muscle: the more he practised, the better his control.

"Do not shrug your shoulders at me, George. Your Shadow Witch is magic without limits, perhaps the Donili monks together could repel her."

Hunter glanced over at the Abate. Now that sounded impressive. "So, you're saying that I am powerful, even by Donili standards?" Hunter asked, both thrilled and disappointed. It was always nice for his ego to have his skills praised. But at the same time, Hunter couldn't help thinking that he had come to the Donili seeking an ally stronger than himself – one that would succeed where he had failed.

"You are as weak as a child born yesterday." The Abate replied curtly. "Except for your gift with shields and transporting yourself and others."

Hunter gazed out without taking in any of the scene. So, he was a freak here too? "Have you any theories as to why?" He asked reluctantly, not sure he wanted the answer.

"It may be a simple matter of genetic diversity." The Abate answered, his voice betraying how he was not sold on the idea of his brothers. "Your family evolved in a different country with different pressures. It is perfectly possible."

Hunter accepted this easily enough but waited to hear the rest of what the Abate had to say.

"The more fanciful of us think that your powers are linked to the Shadow Witch. She has chosen – probably unconsciously – to connect with you."

Hunter jerked straight, as though stung. "Why should what happened between Sophie and I – I mean, the Shadow Witch and myself – have any bearing on my abilities?"

The Abate smiled at the younger man's reaction. "Think, signore, you can protect yourself against magic and bullets; when you are incapacitated by loss you unlock a very destructive, but very defensive power; you can transport yourself anywhere – which is a unique ability of the Shadow, no? And Signor Astley, we must accept that you only came into your powers after you became close to Sophie."

"Yes, because she was the one who opened my mind to such an idea!" Hunter argued. He pinched the bridge of his nose, trying to stem the headache that suddenly kicked in. "So, I'm basically the Shadow Witch's toy? Are you telling me that I'm nothing like the Donili?"

"I cannot imagine you being anybody's toy, Signor Astley." The Abate replied with dry humour. The old man sighed. "I believe that as a 7th generation witch-hunter you are capable of using anti-magic, although not as naturally skilled as the modern Donili. Perhaps you are more like the Benandanti were four hundred years ago. It is just your fate to be linked with the Shadow Witch."

"Fate?" Hunter echoed.

"You do not believe in fate? That there is a bigger picture in which the threads of our lives entwine?"

"Not really, padre." Hunter answered honestly. "I like to believe that I am in charge of my own life."

"Good!" The Abate replied, surprising Hunter. "God has enough to do; we should not just sit back and let the tide of time carry us."

## Chapter Seven

After his meeting with the Abate, Hunter did his best to appear humble and accepting. Outwardly he strove to be open-minded, and as he became more adept at controlling his powers, it became easier to maintain a relaxed persona. But on the inside, he kept his stubborn streak that he was right. Perhaps if this had been a time of peace, he could have considered the possibility that witches could be forgiven. But this was a time of war, and Hunter had seen every person he'd ever been close to killed by witches, he'd seen hundreds of brave men fall, and he wasn't about to stop fighting for their cause - otherwise their deaths would have been in vain.

The Abate and his monks could be as forgiving and pacifist as they liked, it was easy for them, repelling the odd threat from their beloved Friuli home. They didn't know about the wider world in ruins - and sometimes Hunter thought they didn't care.

It was frustrating to stay in this environment, watching the days and even weeks speed by, while the world struggled on. Hunter felt guilty, in this safe haven. But it was necessary, he told himself repeatedly.

Today had been bearable, after struggling for a month, Hunter had finally succeeded in breaking through the barriers into another man's mind. After a month of straining nothingness, Hunter got a thrill from the sudden web of colour and images that brushed his own consciousness and begged him to look closer. But the Donili monks were forbidden from viewing the private thoughts of others and trained strictly to avoid such temptation. The use of the exercise was used instead to remove memories or plant ideas. Hunter had already seen both uses, without knowing it at the time. During that brief confrontation with witches in the Italian forests, Maurizio had delved into their minds and removed every trace and memory of the Donili monks, of Hunter, of the intended victim and his family; all in the space of a second before transporting them beyond the borders of the Friuli. After his own struggles, Hunter marvelled at the speed and precision of the old monk.

The second time, Hunter had been the victim. The Abate, impatient with his arguments, had invaded his mind and planted the idea that it desperately needed sleep. Hunter yawned at the mere memory of that induced slumber.

Hunter wondered, guiltily, what else could be done with such control. He knew that his teachers, the older monks, wouldn't encourage such questions. Hunter could already see the patronising smile, and the sorry shake of the head whenever he stepped out of line. But just because today's monks were spotlessly clean, unquestioning lambs, didn't mean that previous generations hadn't had such thoughts and had investigated and experimented - even if to only understand the limits better. Their writings were stored alongside many scrolls and heavy books written by the Donili over the last nine hundred years.

And Hunter had access to them. In fact, he told himself, the monks encouraged extensive reading during free time. Of course, that didn't stop him taking the precaution of reading in the privacy of his room.

He sat in front of the fire, the books and papers scattered around him. Hunter wrapped the blanket tighter around him, trying to block out the biting winter that invaded the draughty old abbazia.

Suddenly his door was flung open, the fire stuttered in the cold wash of air, and a figure stood in the doorway. Hunter started, one hand darting to the metal dog tags that hung around his neck, the other to his side, instinctively reaching for the gun he no longer wore.

"You are nervous, Hunter." The man said, unravelling the scarf from his face.

"Bloody hell, Marcus, you made me jump." Hunter gasped, looking up at his friend. "Close the damn door, it's freezing."

Marcus pushed the heavy door shut, then turned back to Hunter with an air of suspicion. "What are you doing?"

"Just reading." Hunter replied calmly, gathering a few errant sheets. "The Abate encourages us to read."

Hunter drew the open books to him with feigned innocence, but Marcus moved quickly and picked up a thin volume. His eyes darted along the written word, picking up the topic and frowning.

"I do not think he would approve of this." Marcus muttered, closing the book gently.

Hunter shrugged, gazing into the fire rather than face his friend.

"I stand by my promise not to share my unrighteous views, but I cannot change who I am or why I am here." Hunter said honestly, one hand idly tracing the heretical page. "But perhaps it would be best if you told the Abate nothing of this."

Hunter looked up at Marcus. He was sure the Abate had his monks spying on him and reporting any signs of dissent. The only question was, how far could Hunter trust Marcus. The young monk looked innocent enough.

"You really believe you are doing the right thing?" Marcus asked with a sigh. He frowned and slumped into a chair near the fire.

"Yes." Hunter replied. "If you had seen what I have seen... there would be no question. The witches are more dangerous now than they have ever been. I couldn't stop them from taking over, but I will do anything and everything I can to correct that."

Marcus sat quietly, contemplating this and more.

"How was guard duty?" Hunter asked casually, wanting to change the subject.

Although he was proving a fast learner and naturally gifted, Hunter had yet to go on a patrol with the Donili monks into the Friuli region. It was obvious that the Abate didn't trust him, that he feared Hunter would revert to his violent methods when finally confronted with his old foe.

Part of Hunter regretted this bitterly, for he longed to test his new skills for real. But deep down he knew that he could not promise to control himself.

"Quiet, no sign of witches today." Marcus replied, quite bored with a long cold day's patrol for nothing. "We think that winter has driven the witches back to the comfort of the cities, it is not likely they will roam these sparse hills and valleys."

The two men fell into silence, the only noise the cracking of the fire in the grate.

"You know, there have been so many more confrontations with witches the last few years, compared to earlier times. I was talking to my grandfather about it. I think you are right; they are stronger and more dangerous than ever."

Hunter looked up, surprised. This was the closest any Donili had come to admitting that Hunter's vision of witches had any truth. "You do? Does this... does this mean you're on my side? That you'd be willing to fight?"

Hunter's voice dropped to a whisper over these conspiratorial words. The idea of not being alone when he left the Abbazia di Donili; that he might be joined with both a friend and an ally excited him. And if Marcus were brought on side, others might follow, might open their narrow minds and take up arms. The only niggling thought was Hunter's promise to the Abate, to not try persuading his monks.

Marcus gazed down at Hunter with that familiar, condescending smile that ignored the fact that Hunter was nearly a decade older than him. "I said that I think you are right about the witch threat. That is a very big concession for me. But I will not abandon my home, my responsibilities, and my morals."

Marcus looked past Hunter to the untidy stack of scripture. "I think I should leave you this evening, before the Abate suspects me as a sympathiser to your rebellion."

The young monk stood up, grabbing his scarf from the back of the chair and left with a sorry smile. Another cold gust came through as the door opened briefly, leaving Hunter very much alone.

## Chapter Eight

After this honest exchange, Hunter and Marcus never spoke openly again on their truce. But throughout winter, when guard duty was typically quieter, Marcus began to travel further into towns with the task of meeting and blessing the citizens in his role as a Donili monk. Then he would return to the abbazia and casually tell Hunter about his day, including sharing all the news and rumours he had heard regarding witches.

It gave Hunter a safe link to the outside world, although it was sometimes hard to hear about. It seemed that now they were no longer hampered by the witch-hunters and their allies, the witches were consolidating their position, creating new laws that placed them firmly above the human populace. Each big town and city had been gifted to a particularly strong, or high-standing witch, and they were charged with controlling their borough. Hunter found out that this included providing regular sacrifices from their subjects. The witches had always performed sacrifices, boosting their powers via the draining of life from innocent victims. But now they could act without fear of discovery and persecution.

The worst part of Marcus' news was the sway in public opinion. Now the Malleus Maleficarum Council no longer existed to resist the witches, it was harder for the average person to rally against them. Hunter couldn't blame the normal people that kept their heads down, trying to salvage what they could from their new life, the survival of their families much more important than playing the hero. But it transpired that there were a few ambitious characters that did more than merely survive. They sold their souls to the devil and worked for the witches. It sickened Hunter to learn about this, he longed to be out there, stopping such weasels and unsettling the reign of the Shadow Witch. Each new story hardened Hunter's resolve. He filed them all away and gradually his anger cooled into something stronger and harder.

It became easier to appear unaffected during the day, when surrounded by the other monks, following the same patterns of learning and training. Hunter spent a lot of his time in the company of Marcus and the artistic Biagio. He was aware of the wary glances the older monks sent their way, as though the trio were rebellious youths, about to graffiti or vandalise as soon as none were looking.

Although they followed the rules and said nothing that could be remotely rebellious, there were occasional questions that came up. Biagio in particular was curious about Hunter's culture, what life was like back in England. He would ask constant questions over the towns and cities, the buildings and the lifestyle - which was alien and hard to understand for the innocent monk. Only when they came close to the subject of witches would Biagio's questions falter, his curiosity tempered by the forbidden topic of Hunter's previous career.

Yes, the days went by swiftly and fluidly, in a daze of learning and friendship. But the nights… the nights Hunter would stay up reading until his eyes could no longer focus, desperate to learn all he could, and also desperate to hold off the dreams. They did not come every night, sometimes they only came once a month, but Hunter came to crave and dread them. They were set either at the cottage or in a village, he was always accompanied by Sophie, who continued to look at him with a steady love, and a small, dark-haired boy - their son. Hunter had never seen the child that he had with Sophie, and had only heard vague reports of the Shadow Witch having a son, but in his dream the boy was fleshed out to be an active and beautiful child, who

519

looked like his mother, except with warmer Astley eyes. Adam. That was the name that rang in Hunter's mind every time he saw his son, the name that Sophie spoke out loud. And as time passed, in his dreams Hunter saw the subtle shifts as Adam slowly grew older in real time.

## Chapter Nine

"How long have you been with us, Signor Astley?"

It was a bright summer day, with the warm sun shining down on the Abbazia di Donili. Hunter stood on the high walkway, looking down the hillside to the town and the shimmering river in the distance. He closed his eyes and breathed deeply the sweet-scented breeze.

"How long have you been here?" The Abate repeated gently.

"Nineteen months, two weeks and a day." Hunter reeled off without hesitation.

It seemed such a long time, and he hated watching each day pass. But each day there was something more to learn, and he became that much stronger.

"How long do you plan to stay?" The Abate asked softly.

Hunter shrugged, "There is so much to learn, padre."

"I know." The Abate agreed. "I have dedicated my life to the Donili, and I cannot claim to know everything. But I wonder if this is where you belong..."

"You want to get rid of me?" Hunter was a little hurt that the Abate might finally be giving up on him. It was true that Hunter always had to work that little bit harder to fit in, he always had to control his temper and hide all his heretical research. It hadn't been too bad a life, until Hunter lost his close friend and almost-conspirator. Marcus had left the abbazia at the beginning of spring to marry and take his place in the village. Hunter thought back on a conversation with Marcus, only a year ago the young monk was focused on his duties and studies and had no desire to leave. But he was so young, a year could drastically change his ambitions.

The Abate gave Hunter an amused glance. "You know that is not true, my son. But I wonder, what are your plans?"

Hunter didn't reply but continued to stare out across the hills as he leaned against the sturdy stone wall. He didn't know what his plans were. During meditation and sleepless nights, he would run over scenes and scenarios, but failed to see what could ultimately work. And the longer he put it off the more daunting a prospect it became.

"You no longer speak of your old friends, your Council, your home. I fear that you are forgetting them and forgetting your reason for coming here."

Hunter sighed. "It's difficult to talk about them, they don't belong here. Anyway, I thought you wanted me to give up my old life. Congratulations, you've won."

The Abate smiled sadly. "Perhaps I did, I wanted you to abandon your violent past and adopt our ways. But I see that you are giving up everything and taking on nothing. What are you afraid of George?"

Hunter looked up, surprised by the use of his Christian name, when the Abate had never strayed from calling him Astley, and the other monks only knew him as Hunter.

"I don't know." He muttered, turning away again. "I'm afraid that the world has moved on and is beyond repair. I'm afraid that they'll think I've abandoned them. Most of all, I don't know that I can actually do anything."

Hunter fell silent, and the two men stood in the spring sunlight as the minutes drew by.

"So, if you think I don't belong here, kick me out." Hunter finally said. "Or I'll devote my life to the Donili, as a monk; or at a word from you I'll marry within the Donili and have children, I am not too old."

Hunter looked to the Abate and there was desperation in his eyes. The Abate stepped closer to Hunter and placed a frail hand on his shoulder.

"I am sure that you would make a fine monk, Signor Astley… if you could give up the inbred self-righteousness of course." The Abate suddenly smiled. "You are thirty-years-old, I am sure you do not need to be told what to do! Very well, my instruction to you is to take the first step. No one can predict the outcome, but don't let that stop you."

Hunter nodded, knowing that the Abate was only saying what he already knew.

"So, the question is, what is your first step?" The Abate asked.

Hunter took an unnecessary moment to think. "The first thing is to head home, preferably without alerting the Shadow Witch. Then I want to find my son."

"Then I suggest you go, my son. There is nothing more we can teach you. You will always be welcome back."

Then the austere Abate did something that shocked Hunter, he reached out and embraced him warmly like a son.

"Grazie, padre." Hunter managed to mumble.

## Chapter Ten

Hunter left the very next day. Now that he had made up his mind he wanted to leave before it became more painful to abandon the comforts of the Donili life. He made a few brief goodbyes amongst the monks and villagers. Hunter wished he could take Marcus, or even Biagio on this new adventure, he had become so accustomed to company and friendship and he was loathe to give it all up again.

But after a restless night's sleep; and a rushed, solitary breakfast, Hunter slung his pack of meagre possessions onto his back and closed his eyes. He had rarely thought of home for a year, but the image of Astley Manor rushed in with such strength and clarity that Hunter almost felt homesick for that brief second before he opened his eyes and the reality of the Manor overwhelmed his senses.

It was cold and dark in the sitting room in which Hunter had materialised. The brittle light of early morning seeped in at the seams of heavy drapes. Hunter's eyes grew accustomed to the dim light and he moved over to the window, peeking through a gap in the curtains. Outside the world was silent; there was no sign of life across the stretch of land that belonged to his family's ancestral estate. From the light and time of year, Hunter guessed that it was not yet 6.00am - he wondered if there were any residents still asleep above his head.

Hunter turned back to the room, there were no obvious signs of habituation; dust covered the surfaces and there was cold ash in the fireplace. Even in the darkness he could see the familiar layout of the room. He hadn't been here for two years and he felt sorry for how he'd abandoned the old place.

Astley Manor was an unusual place. For years the grand estate was owned by the very private and reserved Astley family. The residents of the local village had seen it as part of the landscape, impressive but boringly traditional. Until all hell had broken loose at the Battle of Little Hanting.

People were increasingly aware of the fact Astley Manor was filled with seven generations' worth of objects confiscated from witches, all sorts of occult and ceremonial items that could be both protective and offensive. There was also the largest privately-owned library on witchkind in the country. The information and artefacts that Hunter had at his disposal rivalled the MMC - no wonder the Council had feared his ability to work independently.

But what was most amazing about Astley Manor was the basic fact that it was still standing. The more successful a witch-hunter was, the more he and his family were targeted by revengeful witches. Families struggled to reach 5th generation status and lived in constant fear of near-inevitable destruction.

But Astley Manor stood untouched for seven generations - and it was hardly a discrete safe house.

Hunter didn't know what enchantments or miracles had been invoked by his ancestors, but no magic could penetrate the borders, and no witch could step onto the estate without having their powers stripped. And no witch would enter a witch-hunter's lair so defenceless - Hunter grudgingly marvelled at Sophie's courage in doing so for so long.

After the witch rebellion, it became the rallying point and makeshift base for witch-hunters after the fall of the Malleus Maleficarum Council. It protected them against magic, even that of the Shadow Witch. But all this protection and information wasn't enough.

Hunter still remembered the evening the witches drove the witch-hunters and their allies from the Manor. The night that Anthony Marks, the leader of the

MMC, had sacrificed himself to give the others time to escape.

Hunter didn't know if there was any organised rebellion left. And if there was, he had no idea where they were, and only a vague idea where to start looking.

Hunter heard a creak from upstairs and he tensed, his hand straying to his gun, which felt familiar even after so many months of absence in the peaceful abbazia. There were three possibilities: his charming mother had survived here alone for years; a remnant from the MMC was using the famous Astley Manor; or a witch or two were stationed here in case Hunter or his allies returned. As much as Hunter wished for someone on his side, he pessimistically assumed the worst. After all, Sophie knew him so well, she would definitely station someone here.

Hunter drew his gun and moved silently towards the ajar sitting room door, then slid into the hallway. Quickly glancing up the wide staircase, Hunter took a deep breath and purposefully slammed the door behind him. The sound was booming in the silence and echoed through the familiar corridors. Hunter heard the shuffle of feet upstairs and pressed himself into the shadows, his gun aimed steadily at the stairs.

There was the sound of feet treading slowly and carefully onto the bare boards, more than one person, trying to be silent. In the darkness of the heavily panelled hallway, Hunter detected two figures moving down the stairs. The way they moved and the fact that they carried guns echoed of witch-hunter training, making Hunter hopeful.

"Who goes there?" A voice called out.

Hunter frowned. "You first. Who are you?"

The man whipped around, staring blindly in Hunter's direction. "I am a first gen with the MMC, this property is under the Council's authority, you are trespassing. Now, who are you?"

Hunter watched as the speaker reached the bottom step and stared wide-eyed to try and detect anything in his near-blindness. Hunter, who had no trouble seeing thanks to his 7th gen status, considered bringing a little bit of light to the proceedings; but lord knows where any candles were, and he doubted that this man and his colleague would appreciate a very magical-looking but harmless ball of suspended light.

"I am not trespassing." Hunter replied quietly. "Come into the sitting room and we shall talk."

Hunter turned back to the sitting room and opened the heavy door, before promptly whisking open the curtains to allow in the strengthening morning light. He watched as two men in their thirties stepped into the room, squinting in the sudden light.

"Who-"

"I am Hunter Astley, 7th gen, lord of this manor." Hunter said quickly, cutting across the inevitable question.

The two men stood staring gormlessly at Hunter. They obviously hadn't expected that answer.

"Do you, ah, have any ID?" One man managed to choke out.

Hunter laughed, suddenly released from tension and amused at how things were playing out.

"I haven't had identification on me for years - an unfortunate result from being constantly on the move and not wanting to be known, of course." He smiled, oh yes, how handy would that be, if he were caught by enemies that could quickly check his passport to discover who he was. "But if you won't take my word, go to the portrait room. Unfortunately, I don't have one, but if you look at my father's I am sure that you will see the family resemblance."

The two men continued to stand there, looking nonplussed. But one eventually managed to speak.

"We thought you were dead." He breathed. "After the battle of Salisbury Plain, we thought none had survived."

So, it suddenly made sense, why they looked at Hunter like a ghost. He supposed that it was a natural assumption, especially as Hunter had no way to contact any surviving MMC, even if he had thought it safe to do so.

"I am very much alive and well, I've just been off the radar. But who are you, gentlemen?"

"Shaun Williams, 1st gen." The first man replied.

"Jack Lowe, 1st gen." The second man added. "We're part of the MMC, stationed here to defend Astley Manor and its contents for the good of the Council."

"So, the MMC still stands? I feared there would be no organised resistance. Where are they based? Not here, obviously."

"They're currently at a secure base within travelling distance." Shaun Williams replied obscurely.

"I think I should go to them." Hunter suddenly decided; he was likeliest to learn what he needed to know from the MMC directly. "Where are they located?"

The two witch-hunters exchanged a look.

"Sorry sir, we aren't authorised to disclose that." Jack Lowe said formally, "But we can take you."

Hunter paused, considering this offer. He would prefer to blink straight there rather than spend potentially hours in a car. But he doubted he could learn where the MMC were located without breaching the privacy of the witch-hunters' minds. Plus, as he thought about it, blinking and suddenly materialising inside the anti-witch headquarters might not be the most sensible entrance.

"Very well." Hunter said with a brief nod of agreement.

The witch-hunters shared a brief conversation, with Jack taking the task of driving Hunter, and Shaun staying to keep charge of the manor. Jack left the room to get the car ready, leaving Shaun with Hunter. Shaun stood uncertainly, obviously in awe of the legendary 7th gen, returned-from-the-dead, Hunter.

"We're not really supposed to leave only one guard on duty. I mean, we're due to return to base when the next team relieve us, but I'm guessing you'd rather go now, sir." Shaun rambled on.

"It's fine." Hunter cut across, something else on his mind. "Mr Williams, can I ask... do you know anything of my mother? Is she still here?"

Shaun hesitated. "I don't know for certain, sir, but I think Mrs Astley is in MMC care."

Hunter found it hard to believe that his proud and fierce little mother (who had very little respect for witch-hunters) would give up her family home, no matter what the danger. And Shaun's flimsy answer did nothing to comfort him.

Outside there was the rumble of an engine, and Hunter went out towards the drive to find what looked like an old army jeep. Jack Lowe was already sat at the wheel and eyed Hunter curiously as he hopped into the passenger seat.

Jack coaxed the old jeep forward and they crunched over the gravel until they got to the long drive. Hunter looked out at the beautiful, familiar landscape that was his estate. They passed through the village of Little Hanting, a picturesque place that Hunter had always taken for granted.

Hunter sighed, watching the scene pass by - too slowly for his liking. Hunter tried to surreptitiously glance at the speedometer. He frowned as he saw the needle wavering over the 45mph mark.

"Sorry." Jack suddenly apologised.

"What for?" Hunter asked, looking up at the older man. Closer to, Hunter could tell that his initial guess of mid-thirties was a bit young. Jack looked closer to his late-forties, or even early-fifties.

Jack looked back, unconvinced with Hunter's innocence. He nodded to the dashboard. "I'm sure it's slower than what you're used to, but it's MMC rules. Diesel is rationed, so we have to drive conservatively. Not that this old piece of crap could go fast anyway."

"It's fine. It's faster than walking." Hunter replied unconvincingly. What would be faster and more fuel economic would be to blink over there.

They drifted back to an uncomfortable silence that allowed Hunter too much thinking space.

"So… how long have you been a witch-hunter?"

"Nearly two years." Jack replied shortly. The older man glanced unnecessarily in the mirror, and his grip tightened on the wheel. "I joined the MMC after I lost my son to the witches. He was a witch-hunter, see. Fell at Salisbury Plain."

"I'm sorry." Hunter mumbled.

"He was only twenty-year-old, he said he'd save the world or die trying." Jack smiled bitterly at his late son's bravado. "Maybe you met him? Darren. Darren Lowe?"

Hunter saw the gleam of hope in Jack's face, the hope that his son lived on in one more memory, and he felt sorry for letting him down.

"I'm sorry, I didn't." Hunter replied quietly. "There were... so many men and women at Salisbury Plain. I wish I could say I knew him."

"It's ok." Jack mumbled, to himself. "It's ok."

## Chapter Eleven

The jeep rumbled on for over an hour, until Jack nodded and spoke up.

"Nearly there."

Hunter looked out at the surrounding countryside but saw no sign of life. Jack swung the jeep off the main road and down a private track. Hunter finally saw an old barbed wire fence running around what looked like an airfield. Across the cracked tarmac were a couple of derelict hangars.

"Just... wait and see." Jack said, watching Hunter's expression with amusement. Jack drove straight into the hangar and parked the jeep alongside several vehicles of similar antiquity.

"This way." He jumped out of the driver's seat and led the way to an internal concrete bunker. Jack pushed back his sleeves and grabbed the handle of a small iron door, with a grunt he managed to drag it open wide enough for them to enter.

"After you, just mind your step."

Hunter frowned and stepped into the dark. Immediately before him was a set of steps leading down, faintly lit from far below. Hunter had taken a few steps when he heard the door clang shut behind him, blocking out all daylight.

"The MMC has gone underground. Literally." Jack said as he squeezed past to lead the way.

The faint light grew stronger as they neared the bottom, until they came to its source - a single oil lamp next to another door. Jack paused to pull out a key and quietly opened up.

On the other side there was more light provided by extra lamps. Hunter could see a desk set up with a man and woman quietly discussing some dreary matter. They both looked up at Jack and Hunter's entrance.

"ID?" The woman asked automatically.

"Jack Lowe, 1st gen." Jack replied, handing over an old driving licence.

"Lowe." The woman mused, glancing down at the desk. "You're not due to return for another week. Is there a problem?"

"Not exactly. I had to escort someone here." Jack said. Hunter had the strange feeling that Jack was relishing the moment. "Mr Hunter Astley."

The effect was immediate and a little unnerving for Hunter. The expression on the woman and man's face were identical. Hunter doubted if they could have looked more shocked if Jack had brought along the Shadow Witch, or even Father Christmas.

"H-Hunter? Astley?" The woman gasped. Her eyes flicked over Hunter hungrily, matching the actual person to the name.

She suddenly turned to the man standing gawping behind her. "Go - tell the Council. Go now."

The man staggered away then, with one more disbelieving look at Hunter, he broke into a run and disappeared down the far end of the corridor.

"Um, radios don't work, so the fastest way to send a message is with a runner." The woman explained.

"I know, I remember." Hunter said with a smile.

The woman blushed and looked rather breathless; Hunter wondered whether it was his sudden appearance that caused this reaction, or was his old charm still in perfect working order? It would be flattering if it were the latter.

"Y-you're really him, Hunter Astley?" The woman breathed. "I never thought... I've heard so much about you, we all have-"

Jack coughed in the background, breaking the woman's rambling.

"Oh, sorry. Why don't I take you through to the Council?" She offered with a glowing smile.

"It's ok Lesley, I know the way." Jack said softly to the woman. He clapped Hunter on his back. "Come on, it's this way."

Hunter politely bid the woman goodbye then followed Jack down the corridor.

The underground base was like a warren with numerous corridors and rooms, Hunter could only marvel at the scope of it. As they walked along the empty corridors gradually filled with the faces of people wanting to see Hunter with their own eyes. Obviously gossip and rumours still travelled fast. He heard his name being passed in whispered voices and he felt the energy and excitement that was connected to it.

There was the sound of hurried footsteps and Hunter saw several people rushing towards them. One man pushed in front, limping heavily, but smiling widely.

"It is you! How the hell?!" He laughed and grabbed Hunter, wanting physical confirmation. "You are a bloody miracle."

It took a second for Hunter's brain to process that the person before him was someone he knew. "Toby? Christ, I never expected - I thought you were dead!"

"Likewise, Hunter, likewise."

"It's good to see you again, Mr Astley." A reserved voice broke through.

Hunter looked past his old friend Toby to see another familiar face. "Sergeant Dawkins? It's good to see you too."

"Actually, it's General now." Dawkins commented with a wry smile. "Not that that matters here."

Hunter took a moment to look at his old acquaintances. They looked so worn and aged since he'd last seen them, they had obviously had a rough time these last couple of years, and Hunter felt guilty over his own safe life.

"So, where have you been?" Toby asked.

"Ahm..." Hunter hesitated, aware of all the keen eyes and ears in this cramped corridor. Even after all he'd done, and all he'd learnt, he was still uncomfortable sharing information on his almost-magical abilities. Especially to strangers. And especially in the official witch-hunter base.

There were obviously stories told about him, but Hunter didn't know how accurate they were.

Dawkins accurately read the hesitation. "Come through to the Council rooms, Mr Astley."

It was a relief for Hunter to follow the General to a quiet, empty room. It was lit by the yellow light of an oil lamp on the wall, casting shadows from the table and chairs.

Toby limped over to a chair and dragged it out, dropping into it heavily. Hunter sat opposite him, glancing enquiringly at the leg that stuck out stiffly.

"Broke my leg pretty bad." Toby explained, hitting his thigh with frustration. "Got caught by witches a week before Salisbury Plain - was so mangled I missed the mission. Two years and I'm still limping."

Hunter shook his head, "I still can't believe you're alive! I thought all witch-hunters over the 2nd gen status had been hunted down - especially those unlucky enough to have met the Shadow Witch during her time undercover."

Names and faces of those that had been on the list of the Shadow Witch came to mind; Brian Lloyd, Matt and Dave Marshall... James Bennett. They had made the mistake of making themselves known to Sophie Murphy. Toby Robson, as a 4th gen was also on the list and it was a miracle that he'd survived.

"I can't explain it, I've been lucky." Toby said with a shrug. "Besides, you're still alive and kicking, surely you top every list!"

"Yes, how did you survive?" General Dawkins broke in, the army man leaning against the table. "Where have you been, and why?"

Hunter glanced briefly at Dawkins, before staring resolutely at the wall. "I thought there was no one left. I saw the last of our men fall before I resolved to leave to continue the fight. I was on the run for months, trying to shake any followers."

Hunter paused, taking a deep breath. "You both know what I'm capable of, well I went to find the Benandanti..."

Hunter went on to tell of his meeting with the Donili and explained all the time he'd spent with them and all he had learnt.

## Chapter Twelve

"So, you've finally returned to us?" Dawkins asked after Hunter had finished.

"I had to find out what was going on." Hunter replied, somewhat off-topic, not wanting to admit that re-joining the MMC wasn't on his list of priorities.

"What do you want to know?" Asked Toby.

"Everything." Hunter said with a shrug. "What's the current status of the MMC and its allies. Even what the witches have achieved - I've been out of it for so long."

"Well, the witches are consolidating their position, so we're busy protecting our last strongholds and trying to find their weaknesses. It's not easy. You're right about the MMC, we've hardly any real witch-hunters left, most of the people here are 1st gens. As for the army, well…"

Toby broke off and looked to Dawkins, allowing the General to take over.

"The army is split in two." Dawkins sighed. "The majority are with us, integrated as 1st gen witch-hunters. But there is still a standing British Army - working for the person running Britain."

"The Royal family?" Hunter asked, vaguely hopeful.

"In a secure location in Scotland." Toby said with a shake of his head. "I'm afraid our country's leader is the Shadow Witch and her council."

"That's not good." Hunter muttered.

"No, it's not." Dawkins agreed. "Look, I have rounds to do. Can I leave this to you, Toby?"

Toby assented and the General left with a brief goodbye.

Hunter stared at the closed door. "I remember him being a lot more fun."

"We all were." Toby said bleakly. "Colin was the natural successor after General Hayworth, but he still feels like he has to prove it."

Hunter looked about him at the bland room. "So, what is this place?"

"An abandoned RAF base. We can only guess why there's such an extensive underground run, we can't find any record of its existence - it was either above top-secret, or completely forgotten. It's a miracle we found the place." Toby explained. "We've been using this place for nearly a year now. I miss windows and daylight, but at least it's safe."

"How can it be safe against witches? How can you put the MMC in danger by staying still so long?" Hunter felt his temper rising, angry at his old friend's complacency. Hunter didn't think he had to tell Toby of all people how the witches had chased them out of Astley Manor; out of their bases in Manchester and Newcastle.

"Relax Hunter, it's ok." Toby said, smirking at Hunter's expression. "The witches won't find us here."

"How? How can you know that?" He demanded.

"It's... hard to explain." Toby said with a sigh. "You wouldn't understand unless you saw it for yourself. Then again, I'd love to see what she says to you."

"You are not making any sense at all Toby." Hunter said curtly, very aware that the other witch-hunter was laughing at him.

"Come with me." Toby said, suddenly standing and hobbling to the door.

Toby walked down the corridor with a pronounced limp, and Hunter could feel his excitement.

"I'm going to introduce you to someone very special, Mythanwy Elspeth Lughnasa - but everyone calls her Mel." Toby explained. "She's not a witch, as far as we can tell, but I want you to keep an open mind."

"This isn't filling me with confidence." Hunter warned. "Nor is it explaining anything."

"Look, Mel is… Mel. She found this place, swore it was safe." Toby said, gesturing vaguely with one hand. "And don't look at me like that, Hunter. You just have to meet her to understand. She's very truthful, I don't think she knows how to lie, actually."

Hunter frowned, not liking this, but said nothing as he followed Toby through the warren of corridors and doors. They eventually stopped at a door guarded by a witch-hunter, as they approached, he nodded them through, closing the door behind them.

The room was exactly like the one they had just left, except there was a sofa along one wall, with a neat stack of folded bedding beside it. A table took up most of the space of the room, and at it a young woman was sitting alone, with pale blonde hair held back with a blue ribbon. When she looked up, it was with big blue eyes, and seeing her guests she smiled widely.

"Hi Dave!" She gushed, jumping up eagerly.

Toby, smiling in fond response to her enthusiasm, turned to Hunter and explained quickly and quietly. "We don't know who Dave is, she calls all men Dave."

Then he turned back to the girl. "Hello Mel, it's nice to see you again. But my name is Toby, remember. Now, I have someone I'd like you to meet, Mel, this is my good friend Hunter."

Hunter felt his scepticism suspended as he faced the mysterious Mel. It was hard to tell her age, she must have been at least twenty years old, but her open and innocent expression made her look younger. She wore a pale blue blouse, and knee-length white skirt; her outfit was modest and old-fashioned. Mel's face lit up as she saw Hunter.

"George!" She gushed, then pouted. "You're late."

Hunter saw that Toby was as confused as he was. So much for every man being called Dave, he could only assume someone had told Mel about his rarely-used Christian name.

"I'm sorry I'm late, Mel." Hunter said slowly, "I didn't mean to be."

Mel smiled again, obviously satisfied with his apology. She stepped up close to him, her blonde head barely reaching his shoulder. Mel reached out and gently placed one small, cool hand in his. She bit her lip and rocked up on her toes, so very excited that he was here.

"Sit down, sit down, we shall have tea and cake and all things nice." Mel rambled on, drawing Hunter to the table and chairs.

Mel danced around the table, making sure her two guests were seated before skipping to the door and yanking it open.

"Hello Dave." She trilled to the witch-hunter on sentry. "We're having a tea party. Can you bring the tea? Mother doesn't let me use the kettle; she says I'm clumsy."

"Sure thing Mel." The witch-hunter chuckled, and to Hunter's surprise, the guard left to fetch tea.

"Is she sane?" Hunter whispered to Toby.

Toby shrugged in response, smiling and relaxed. "It doesn't matter." He murmured back.

"Rustle, rustle, little mouse." Mel suddenly popped up between them, joining in the whispering. "We shall have our party, but quietly, quietly, for papa is working and cannot be disturbed."

"Mel?" Toby said, trying to gently get her attention. "Hunter wants to know about this place, why it's safe from witches."

Mel frowned, as she obviously tried to work out who Hunter was. Finally, she looked at Hunter with a vague understanding.

"Georgie Porgie, pudding and pie; killed the witches, made them cry. When the truth came out to play, Georgie Porgie ran away."

"That's very nice Mel, but we came to talk about this place. Be a good girl and tell Hunter."

Mel beamed at Toby with her bright blue eyes and white smile. "Yes, I am a good girl, I always eat my greens and brush my teeth before bed. But witchy-witches aren't always good; sometimes they stay up past their bedtimes, or spill blood on the floor." Mel looked momentarily scandalised at the thought. "Naughty red stains make mother so angry."

Mel got to her feet and moved about the small room, almost with a dancing step, she tilted her head to skywards.

"Starlight, star bright, first star I see tonight-"

"Mel, that's the ceiling." Toby interrupted with the first sign of impatience. "And it's daytime."

"They can hear me." Mel promised. "But the witches can't. Their ears are deaf, their eyes are blind they cannot see, they have not found their specs with me. And in their hidey-holes, the mice are safe and have tea."

As if on cue, the door opened and a witch-hunter entered, carrying a tray of tea. Hunter enjoyed the sight, having been without this very British custom for so long. He leant forward to share a private word with Toby. "You know, I'm not too keen on being referred to as a mouse."

"Me neither." Toby concurred. "But it's just her way of seeing the world."

Mel acted the good little hostess and served the tea, before sitting next to Toby. She gazed unflinchingly at Hunter with those strange, innocent eyes.

"Mel, how do you know that you are right?" Hunter asked carefully.

"I..." Mel hesitated, looking uncomfortable. "I open the book and read the words where no lies can be written. But not everyone likes it. People are scared of me and shoo me away."

Mel took a sip of tea and beamed again, her moods so very changeable, but also infectious. "But Dave is nice to me, and I have so many friends here."

## Chapter Thirteen

They left shortly afterwards. In the narrow corridor, Hunter found himself wishing he was outside, just to be able to breathe again.

"She's something, isn't she?" Toby asked casually.

Hunter shook his head in disbelief, struggling to find words. "Definitely. I mean... all that nonsense. At least, it seems like nonsense except I felt like she was trying to communicate something to us."

Toby smiled wryly at his friend's attempts to understand. "You see what I mean though, once you hear her you cannot doubt her honesty."

"I know, you're right, I don't think she can lie." Hunter said, pausing and looking back down the corridor. "She's so innocent, childlike even. Yet enigmatic - I swear I'd do anything to keep her safe."

"Don't worry, she has that effect on everyone." Toby said, almost guiltily. "Just be careful. She's an emissary of the truth. The Truth. Something beyond good and evil, right and wrong. She can be dangerous."

"Dangerous? But you told me to trust her."

"I told you to trust what she says to be true, nothing more." Toby countered.

Hunter sighed, finding this all a little bit hard to assimilate. "So that's why she has a guard, to keep everyone safe? She's effectively a prisoner?"

"No, no, the guard is to keep *her* safe, and to keep track of who sees her." Toby hurried to explain. "We could never keep her prisoner. She comes and goes as she pleases."

"Isn't that a risk to security?" Hunter asked.

Toby sighed. "We tried to force her to stay once, she got upset and refused to talk to anyone for days. Then one evening she'd vanished, we couldn't tell how, but she wasn't on base and no one had seen her leave. She turned up a week later, as happy and chirpy as though the whole thing hadn't happened."

Toby saw the doubtful look on Hunter's face. "I know, it sounds bloody dodgy, but there's nothing we can do."

Hunter sat in council with half a dozen witch-hunters. The only people he recognised were Toby Robson and General Colin Dawkins. The rest were senior members of the MMC, though none were more than a 1st gen status.

Hunter sat there, listening to them go over the boring finer details of missions he had no knowledge of. He'd never been a fan of fine detail, of paperwork and dull updates; Hunter used to give such menial tasks to his right-hand man, a very capable 1st gen called James Bennett.

"So, Mr Astley." A stern woman addressed him, "To get straight to the point, what are your intentions? Are you here to help? To assume a role of leadership?"

Hunter felt all eyes descend on him. "I'm not here to take over."

"Then you're here to work for us?" The woman asked doubtfully. "From what we hear of the stories, you don't follow orders very well."

"Theresa…" Toby warned in a low voice.

"No, it's ok." Hunter said, knowing that his past unease with authority was bound to arise. "But that was then, and this is now. I'll be here to help, I'll do what I can, and I will be here to advise, but sometimes I'll have to go my own way."

"You sound like you already have something planned." One man voiced.

Hunter looked round the table, eyeing each member of this Council. He wondered how much to share, how much to keep back.

"The Shadow Witch has a young son." Hunter said, then stopped.

"Devil's spawn." One voice spat.

Hunter looked round with surprise.

"Enough, Mr Andrews, we don't need those common rumours." Toby said, stepping in to mediate again. He then turned to Hunter to explain. "The child was probably conceived during a ritual, but most whisper that his father is the devil himself."

Hunter felt frozen inside, as he wondered how much his old friend knew, or had guessed. More worrying was how everyone would react when the truth inevitably came out. But he would put off that unsavoury moment for as long as possible.

"You have a plan concerning this witch-child?" The woman, Theresa asked.

"I'm going to kidnap him." Hunter said calmly.

The room was deadly silent as the shock statement set in, then suddenly it erupted. Several chairs scraped back, and six voices all clamoured and argued. Hunter sat quietly, patiently waiting for them all to finish their indistinguishable rants, many expletives filling the air.

"Are you finished?" Hunter asked mildly.

"Hunter, you can't be serious." Dawkins said, still standing and leaning across the table to make his point. "Even if such a thing were possible, why would you do it?"

"Surely you can see that we could use him as leverage." Hunter lied. "And if the boy has even half the Shadow Witch's power, he could be very useful. He's still young enough to influence."

Hunter felt a stab of guilt, for lying to these people, and for even daring to say such cruel plans. But all he wanted was his son, safely with him before any real offensives began. If he had to tell a few falsehoods and bend a few rules, so be it.

"It can't be done. Such a mission would be suicide." One witch-hunter argued, struggling to keep his cool.

"I hate to disagree, but I know that I could do it. All I need to know is where the boy is." Hunter spoke with such certainty and authority that the others were momentarily cowed.

"We shall consider giving our permission, Mr Astley." Theresa said coldly, motioning towards the door.

"You're crazy, you know that?"

Hunter was sitting on the floor in the corridor outside the council rooms, he didn't care about the cold or discomfort, he actually liked the distraction. He raised his head out of his hands as he was spoken to. The Council were behind a closed door deliberating his fate. All except Toby, who stood staring at Hunter with sheer amazement. Good old Toby, just like he always had been, he never got mad, even when Hunter contemplated insanity. Would the rest of the Council think he was crazy? Most likely, but they still might let him go ahead with this mission. Not that it mattered how they voted; Hunter had already made his mind up.

"You're crazy." Toby reiterated.

"I'm just doing what I have to do." Hunter replied calmly. "Shouldn't you be with the Council fighting my corner?"

Toby sighed and dropped in down onto the floor next to him, inelegant and awkward. "Dawkins will deliver my vote. As if the others don't know already. I'm a witch-hunter through and through. The legendary Hunter Astley turns up and wants to lead a suicidal mission, I'm in."

"I don't know about legendary." Hunter said with a crooked smile. "And I'm not leading anyone, I'm going alone."

"You can't! I-"

"You are not coming." Hunter said firmly. "I know what you're capable of Toby, you know I respect you, but I can't risk you slowing me down."

At this the amiable Toby swore beneath his breath and cast a dark look down at his bad leg, cursing it. "Fine. Fine, we have others that can go."

"A group of 1st gens?" Hunter asked bitterly. "No thanks."

"They're the best we have." Toby replied in a half-hearted argument.

"I'm not taking 1st gens into the Shadow Witch's lair." Hunter said adamantly. The last thing he wanted was a bunch of ill-trained, noisy and slow wannabe witch-hunters botching his one and only chance to get his son.

"You used to trust 1st gens." Toby said quietly, then glanced anxiously at Hunter. "I'm sorry about your team. And about James, he was a good man."

Hunter tensed, waiting for the familiar lurch of grief and guilt that came whenever he thought of the people that he had lived and worked with for so long. It had been General Hayworth and Anthony Marks that had put them together; Maria, the unflappable Ian, sweet little Alannah, and of course James. They were all ghosts now.

James had been there when Sophie Murphy had appeared on the scene. James and Sophie had never gotten along, and that combined with his friendship with Hunter and his unique authority with the MMC had made James an obvious target. Hunter would always regret not being able to save him in the end.

The Council door flew open, interrupting the uncomfortable silence. General Colin Dawkins walked out unsmiling and went straight over to Hunter.

"You've still got a strong influence, Hunter. You have permission to go." Dawkins said, strangely cold.

## Chapter Fourteen

Hunter didn't waste any time. He insisted on going that night, before the Council changed their mind. Dressed in black, with a balaclava to hand, he felt himself slip into the mode where his actions were reflexive. It felt reassuringly good that it came back so easily after so long.

Even though he was going into the witches' den alone, Hunter left the Warren with ten witch-hunters. They broke the surface and travelled in the cloudy darkness for a couple of miles. It was part of the agreement that Hunter would not blink directly in and out of the safe headquarters in case he could be followed. They made their way across the silent countryside, scrambling over fences and brushing through fields of high grass, Hunter's trousers becoming cold and damp as he strode through.

Eventually one of the witch-hunters called out, marking this spot as a safe distance from the Warren.

While the others checked the safety of the designated area, Hunter did a self-inventory, then pulled up his hood. He touched the metal dog-tags around his neck for luck, tucking them inside his shirt. Then he was gone.

One second, he was standing in the middle of a dark field, the next he was stood in the middle of a dark field, only a change in direction of the wind to confirm his change of location. Hunter looked up to see an extensive scattering of stars across a very clear sky. He looked about to get his bearings, and saw a building hunched in the darkness to the west.

Hunter moved quickly, every nerve tingling, ready to sense guards or traps in the darkness. The house began to loom as he drew nearer, a great black block against the inky, starred sky. Several windows were filled with warm yellow light that flooded out weakly into the grounds.

Hunter sat in the shadows, listening intently, looking, feeling. He was pretty sure most of the house was sleeping, with only those on guard duty awake. He heard the quiet buzz of conversation of two people in the entrance hall. He thought he heard the shuffle of feet that might mean more security pacing corridors.

Hunter moved closer, then crouched by the door. He closed his eyes and opened his mind, reaching out to the two witches in the hall. It was too easy, to break into their minds and distract them. Witches were unprepared to defend against magic, for who would use such skills against them?

Hunter carefully opened the door and slipped inside soundlessly. The two witches stood there, strangely vacant in their expressions as Hunter drifted by. Once he was out of sight Hunter released them, and they took up their conversation, none the wiser that any time had passed.

Hunter headed upstairs, crouching silently in the shadows whenever a guard passed close. He held his breath when one walked particularly close by, he then darted across the corridor as soon as they had gone. Following his gut, his instincts, his heart; whatever it was that drew him along, Hunter slipped into the nursery.

Even in the darkness, Hunter could see the mess of toys strewn across the room. He heard a half-noise and turned to see a female witch rising from a chair. Hunter barely had time to feel panic, before he met her gaze. The witch's eyes fluttered closed and her body slumped. Hunter dashed forward to catch her before she hit the ground with a thud and laid her sleeping self down softly.

He should kill her now, while she was defenceless. After all she'd seen him (balaclava or not), and all his witch-hunter training demanded it. The knife in his belt felt heavy and demanding, but Hunter reluctantly turned away. He wasn't here to fight and kill, he only wanted his son.

The witch had been sitting next to a door, and Hunter opened it, letting himself into the night nursery. There was a small bed in the middle of the room, and there, oh there in the pale sheets was a small, dark-haired boy.

Hunter drifted closer to him; his eyes locked on his son. He looked so peaceful and so beautiful as he slept.

Hunter paused as he sensed something else, a gentle breath and steady pulse, a rhythm of life that was so painfully familiar to him. Not here, but in the next room, just beyond that wall, he was certain Sophie slept.

He'd not been this close to her since the battle of Salisbury Plain, when he had tried to bind her powers; and she had killed his friends before vanishing. Hunter felt a physical blow at this revelation, that the Shadow Witch was mere feet away.

Hunter's pulse stuttered as he heard a distinct change in Sophie's sleep, as if she too, were disturbed by their closeness. Fearing his time was running out, Hunter scooped up his son from his bed. He felt the little boy stir in his arms, and an alarm went off in his head.

Hunter held his son close and thought of the meeting point. It only took a moment before he felt the cold breeze cut through his clothes, and in the cloudy darkness he could see men carrying lamps as they moved in towards him.

The boy cried in his arms, squirming to get out of his hold, and punctuating with high-pitched screams. Hunter put him down before he dropped the struggling boy, setting him on his feet. The boy staggered away from Hunter; his face frozen with fear having been dragged from sleep to be surrounded by strange men. Adam's cries were continuous, and the other men shouted to one another over the noise, hardly helping to calm the poor witch-child.

Hunter pulled off his balaclava and bobbed down, holding out his arms. "Adam, Adam, it's me."

The boy suddenly stopped crying at the sound of his voice and turned.

"Daddy!" He shrieked, then threw himself into Hunter's arms.

"It's ok." Hunter mumbled into Adam's hair, holding him tightly. "It's ok, no one's going to hurt you."

After a minute or two, it dawned on Hunter that the rest of the world was silent. He looked up to see a ring of horrified eyes gazing down at him.

## Chapter Fifteen

The reaction of the Council to the news that Adam was Hunter's son was everything Hunter had predicted. They were initially silenced by shock and disbelief, and more than a little disgust. This was swiftly followed by anger.

Hunter didn't know what they were angrier about - the fact that their shining hero had taken the enemy to bed and fathered a son; or the fact that Hunter had lied about his motives in reclaiming Adam. But it all faded into the background as Hunter revelled in knowing his son for the first time. Adam was exactly how Hunter imagined he would be; exactly how he appeared in his dreams. A dark-haired, bright-eyed little boy with a ready smile. Hunter wondered how anyone could think Adam was evil or the son of the devil.

What was amazing was that from the very first moment Adam had seen him in the middle of that field, the boy had recognised Hunter as his daddy and had clung possessively to him. Hunter tried to discover the reason for this and had tentatively asked Adam how he knew. But the little boy had shook his head, not understanding the question. Hunter didn't push the point, but just enjoyed spending the next few days playing games and telling stories in the privacy of the quarters the Malleus Maleficarum Council gave him. Well, it wasn't exactly a generously given homely quarters, it was more similar to a minimal-comfort house arrest while the Council debated Hunter's punishment and future with the MMC.

Hunter knew that he could take Adam and blink them both far away at any time, but for now he was content to stay as the MMC's 'prisoner' in an attempt to mend those hastily burnt bridges.

Adam didn't mind being cooped up, there was so much to preoccupy a four-year-old mind. He had a very definite sense of games one should play with a father, and it seemed as though the little boy had saved them all up in anticipation of this meeting.

It was on the third day of their seclusion finally came to an end. The door opened and Mel ran in, heading straight for Adam and descending upon him with a great bear hug. Hunter raised a brow but didn't say anything as he heard his son giggling at the sudden attack.

"She's been waiting to do that for days."

Hunter looked up to see Toby enter in a more dignified fashion and close the door behind him.

"So, I offered to bring her after you'd settled in." Toby added, sitting on the sofa next to Hunter with a sigh.

"You look tired."

"Molly's ill." Toby shrugged, then realised that Hunter probably didn't remember who Molly was. "My daughter. She's got a bit of a fever and kept us up all night."

Toby smiled bitterly and nodded to Adam. "You've got all that to look forward to, you know."

"Did you know?" Hunter asked.

Toby sat silently for a while. He understood exactly what Hunter was asking. "I had my suspicions. It seemed like too much of a coincidence for Adam not to be your son. But I didn't want to say anything, and then it seemed that everyone who knew the Shadow Witch as Sophie Murphy had gone, and there was no point in saying anything."

Hunter sat there, digesting this. Toby was one of the few people that knew Hunter and Sophie had been a couple. But at Toby's words, Hunter realised that Sophie Murphy was no longer recognised as a beautiful, intelligent woman that he had fallen in love with; people only knew the terrifying and unlimited power of the Shadow Witch.

"And the Council?"

"Are pretty pissed off right now." Toby said, smiling as he watched the childlike Mel bob down to talk to Adam. "You have a talent for frustrating authority, Hunter. You provide a unique advantage against the witches, but the Council wonder whether you're worth the trouble."

Hunter smiled bitterly. "Déjà vu." He muttered.

Toby laughed at this, obviously thinking the same thing. Once, before all chaos had broken loose, Toby had brought the news to Hunter that the Malleus Maleficarum Council were turning against him in what amounted to a political struggle.

"Speaking of which, what happened to Halbrook?" Hunter asked. Gareth Halbrook had long been a thorn in Hunter's side.

"That cockroach is still alive, as far as I know." Toby said, not meeting Hunter's gaze. "He survived Salisbury, but hasn't been seen since."

They were distracted from their conjecture by Adam running up to them with his hand outstretched.

"Look, daddy, Mel gave me a pet!" The boy said excitedly. "He's called Incy."

Hunter looked down and inhaled sharply at the sight of a large spider in Adam's little hand. His eyes snapped up to Mel, who was sitting silent and serene in the middle of the floor, obviously pleased with her present.

"A spider?" Hunter asked with exasperation. "Fine. Why don't you get Mel to teach it tricks?"

Adam grinned, and held Incy carefully close to his chest as he took it back to the ever-smiling Mel. There was a knock at the door and Hunter looked up to see a very sober face pop round the door.

"Excuse me, Mr Astley, the Council want to see you."

Hunter glanced at Toby and sighed. Here they went again. "Can you watch Adam for me?" Hunter asked, not wanting to take his little lad before the Council, and not trusting him in the care of anyone else.

"Sure thing, mate." Toby said, looking across at Adam and Mel, content in their games with Incy.

Hunter got to his feet, already weary at the thought of what the Council might throw at him next. But he obediently followed the messenger out of the room and through the Warren. The man was silent and was either unable or unwilling to answer Hunter's questions.

They carried on walking until they reached the stairs that led to the exit. Hunter went up them, frowning at what might cause the Council to hold an outdoor meeting.

It was only mid-afternoon, and it was a reasonably fine day, with pale grey clouds covering the sky with a few brief breaks of sun.

Hunter marched across the fields to the same location they had used the night he had abducted Adam. His sharp eyes focussed on the group of people in the centre of the field. A few Council members stood off to one side, deep in discussion. The rest of the witch-hunters formed a wide circle, all standing to attention, their guns aimed at a single female figure within. The woman stood with her back to Hunter, but there was something familiar about the dark brown hair that was lifted by a passing breeze, and the tall, elegant figure.

"Ladies, gentlemen, what's going on?" Hunter asked as he drew close to the Council members.

He was fixed with several pairs of cold eyes.

"We have taken a prisoner. And she demands to speak with you." Theresa explained, her voice miraculously calm and even.

Hunter glanced again at the woman that required such a heavy guard. He automatically began to walk in a slow, wide circle outside of the witch-hunters, slowly bringing himself into the eye line of the prisoner. Hunter was aware of the Council falling into step behind him, but they were the least of his worries when he finally faced the woman.

"Bev?"

"Good afternoon, Hunter. It's been a while." The woman replied civilly.

Dear god, Beverley Murphy, the mother of the Shadow Witch, and one of the last people that Hunter wanted to see. Hunter felt his pulse speed, and he was very aware of the audience he had for this special reunion.

"It has. Must be four years now." Hunter replied conversationally. Had it really been four years? He remembered the last time he had seen Bev like it was yesterday. When she had been playing the messenger, bringing news of Adam's birth. "What brings you here?"

Bev smiled coolly at his weak questioning, as though he couldn't guess. "The Shadow Witch sent me, to ask you to return her son."

Hunter stood with his arms folded across his chest as he swiftly processed the information behind the words. "She knew it was me?"

"Of course, who else could have done it - would have dared do it? Even after all this time, Sophie still recognised your work." Bev replied.

Hunter stood quietly, his initial worry that he should be so easily recognisable was dwarfed by the thrill of hearing someone else say Her name aloud. Oh boy, that was wrong.

"And she expects us to just give him back? And everyone stays friends?" Hunter said bitterly.

Bev sighed, annoyed by his attitude, and clearly unmoved by the many guns aimed directly at her. "It is her right; she is his mother."

"And I am his father." Hunter returned swiftly, ignoring the tenseness, ground teeth and dirty looks from the other witch-hunters. "Adam stays with me."

Hunter grimaced at what might come with this stubbornness. He had to know what was coming, and only Bev Murphy could answer him. The main question was, would she be forthcoming, and would she be truthful.

"Now tell me Bev, how did you find us, and how many more are coming."

Bev eyed the gathered witch-hunters with an assessing gaze. She seemed to be weighing her options. "Our intelligence showed this area to be void of witchcraft. It was an educated guess that your base would be somewhere in the region. I have been wandering for two days in hope of crossing paths with a patrol. As for how many - the Shadow Witch sent me alone. For now."

Hunter nodded as he assimilated this information, and took a step back, turning to the Council members. "What now, sirs?"

General Dawkins watched Bev carefully, fixing the witch with a scrutinising gaze. "She'll be taken into custody and held until we arrange a trial. She'll be given a chance to offer information for leniency."

A bitter lump rose in Hunter's throat. He could not imagine Bev being put through whatever strict trial had been developed in these harsh times. But he nodded again, he might as well agree with the Council for now.

The witch-hunters moved in to escort the witch under guard into the cell-like rooms in the Warren.

Hunter stepped back, out of the attention of every man. His dark brown eyes fixed on Bev with a sudden intensity, as his thoughts reached out to brush across the surface of hers. Bev's eyes widened with shock and she glanced at Hunter as she was led past.

*'I will meet you later. You are under my protection.'*

Bev's expression hardened, and she gave an imperceptible nod.

"So, you recognise this witch?" Dawkins asked, his voice coloured with disgust as he watched the witch walk past them.

Hunter frowned as his eyes lingered on Bev. Yes, he knew her. He was suddenly assailed with the memories of meeting Ms. Murphy, it had been a fine summer's day when he, Sophie and James Bennett had landed on her doorstep by chance. She had seemed like any other mother; welcoming, but cautious of the men that accompanied her daughter. Hunter almost smiled as he remembered how Bev had warned him off Sophie - he had initially thought her over-protective, but he now saw that she had been trying to protect him.

Hunter nodded in response to Dawkin's question.

And the General looked unsatisfied with his answer. "And what of her? You crossed paths and you failed to kill her? What is her position with the witches?"

Hunter grimaced at the General's presumption. Obviously, it must be expected that he killed any witch he met. It was only a few years ago that it had been common practise to imprison witches and bind their powers. But all that had changed when the Shadow Witch had opened the prisons and returned the witches' powers, and the witch-hunters had suffered for their previous leniency.

"I didn't know that Bev was a witch - she was one of the bound when I met her. She was the Shadow Witch's point of contact when she was undercover - a liaison to the other witches." Hunter replied convincingly. It sounded like the truth and was believable. Hunter wasn't about to tell this frankly austere Colin Dawkins that Bev was Sophie's mother.

"And when I was held prisoner at the witches' headquarters, she was-" Hunter broke off. He'd been about to say that she was the one to help him escape, when he suddenly realised that this Council might see him in Bev's debt. "-she was a mediator in the group, I'm not surprised that she should be sent."

Hunter ignored Dawkin's sceptical look and turned to walk back towards the Warren. The rest of the Council fell into step, the party finally deserting the field.

"So, what do we do about the boy?" One asked.

Hunter felt anger flare up. The boy - his son. He was annoyed at how narrow and close-minded these people were; they wouldn't even call Adam by his name.

"I don't know. We knew he could be a beacon for the Shadow Witch to find us. But it might be worth it if he shows some real power." General Dawkins replied, cold and logical. He turned to Hunter. "Does he?"

Hunter didn't reply immediately. He knew that he'd promised the Council a chance to have a mini-witch with all the power of his mother, but he wondered, did Adam's anti-witch paternity cancel out Sophie's power? "No, not yet anyway. It's perfectly normal for witches not to display power until puberty."

"So, we may have to wait ten years!" The Council member, Theresa, stressed. "Ten years of danger for a flimsy promise of power - is it worth it?"

"Depends on how you see it." Hunter replied warningly.

He stopped walking, glaring at the Council members. How could they talk about such a sweet, innocent boy like that? Hunter turned his mind to Adam, playing in their quarters. It was so tempting to blink away from these fools and back to his son. But Hunter stopped himself. It would only upset the Council more if he started blinking about the place. And maybe it would be better if he did not draw any further attention to that particular ability for a while.

Hunter walked on again, striding out so that he did not have to walk with the Council. He just wanted to get back to his rooms. Hunter was not stopped as he entered the Warren, and no one crossed his path as he made his way through the dim and confusing corridors towards his comfortable prison.

Hunter flinched as he threw the door open with unintended force. Three faces stared up at him.

Toby stood up, frowning. "What's happened?"

Hunter closed the door behind him with more care. "Look, can you stay here for another half hour? I have to go somewhere, and I can't let the others know."

Confusion and suspicion clouded Toby's face at this request. "I have no idea what you're talking about, Hunter."

"Look, Toby, I swear that I will explain everything later. But I need to go. Now. I just need you to hang around, and if anyone comes in, tell them I'm - I'm in the bathroom. I'll be listening for that one. Thanks mate, I owe you."

Hunter clapped Toby on the shoulder. Toby opened his mouth to respond, but it was too late, Hunter had already blinked out.

Hunter took a deep breath as he left, he always got dizzy when he had to guess where he was travelling. He locked onto Bev and pulled himself through the cold and dark. When he opened his eyes, Bev was staring at him calmly. Of course, for a woman that had

573

seen frequent miracles from her daughter, to have a man materialise in her cell must mean nothing.

"Hi... are you ok?" Hunter asked weakly. He looked about the small room that had nothing in it, no chair nor table wasted on this witch. Hunter glanced at the door and reached out with his mind until he confirmed the presence of two witch-hunters standing guard outside.

"I am a prisoner to our ruthless enemy. But other than that, I am fine." Bev said bitterly, automatically keeping her voice low. "You are taking a risk."

Hunter shrugged; some risks were worth it. "Why did Sophie send you?"

"To get her son back. My grandson." Bev replied, finding the answer obvious.

"No, I meant, why you? Sending her own mother into the lion's den. I haven't told the Council, by the way, they think you are a regular witch."

Bev didn't respond immediately; she folded her arms protectively in front of her. "She sent me because she knew that I was the one witch that you would listen to. And also... because she can afford to lose me."

Bev looked sharply at Hunter, her green eyes glinting with a pain that had hardened over time. "She never forgave me for what I did, for daring to steal her powers to save you and your friend. And I think... I think she suspects the other part I played."

Hunter frowned at Bev's words. "What part would that be?"

Bev dropped her gaze, her fingers twisting together as she fortified herself. "How... how do you think Brian Lloyd found out about the return of the Shadow Witch?"

Brian Lloyd had been a highly-respected 5th gen witch-hunter; he had been Hunter's own trainer after his father died. Brian had been Sophie's trainer when she pretended to be a fresh recruit. Until the Shadow Witch had killed him for getting too close to the truth.

Hunter felt the breath knocked out of him at the realisation of what Bev was admitting. "The papers; that was you?"

He opened his mouth to speak but stopped. Sophie had noticed Brian disappearing every couple of weeks but had assumed he had a woman to visit.

"Brian didn't know who I was." Bev said quietly. "He did not know I was Sophie's mother, there was no reason to connect us. I feared what Sophie would do, and I had to warn somebody. Amongst the witches, Brian Lloyd was a famous witch-hunter."

Hunter took a deep breath. "Well, I suppose that explains why Brian hid his research so far north..."

Bev tucked her dark hair behind her ear. "Yes, though I wish he hadn't. From then on Sophie has been suspicious of me and my motives. A crack in our relationship that the more ambitious in the Witches council have played upon. Shortly after I brought you news of Adam's birth, I was stripped of all trust and respect and reduced to being a face, frequently ignored in her house. I became no more than a carer for Adam.

"This is my chance to redeem myself. It has been made clear to me that if I do not return with Adam, I should not return at all." Bev sighed, resigned to her fate, then spoke again beneath her breath. "Yet if I do return victorious, they will all question how I persuaded you to give him up."

"Bev, I'm sorry." Hunter replied quietly. He had never considered what consequences her lenience might yield. He almost felt guilty for what had happened. "How can Sophie treat you like that?"

Bev looked directly at him, with no shame. "It's not so much Sophie these days, as the other witches at council. My daughter is little more than a figurehead, now that the witches have what they want. There to cow the populace while the council are the real power."

Bev shook her head at her own daughter's place. "After all those years of hatred, of wanting revenge... I don't think Sophie ever gave serious thought to what would happen afterwards."

Hunter stood quietly, feeling pity towards his old lover; and then disturbed that he should so naturally feel sorry for the bane of his life.

"So please, give Sophie her son back. Adam is all she has in this world."

"Likewise, Bev, likewise." Hunter muttered, feeling that he had much less than Sophie at this point.

"But she is distraught, you have not seen her! She fears what the witch-hunters will do to a half-witch child."

"I would never let any harm come to him." Hunter replied, hurt that Bev thought he would ever let that happen. "Why shouldn't she trust me with my own son? I am the good guy after all."

Bev smiled bitterly at the honest answer that she left unspoken. She gently shook her head. "You are the enemy Hunter, capable of atrocities in a time of war. And even without that, Sophie would never put her trust is paternal affection!"

"But…" Hunter stopped; Bev's comment made him pause. What did she mean by paternal affection? His brow creased beneath this little mystery. "What do you mean?"

"Sophie never told you? Why she hates witch-hunters. Why she distrusts men, you above all?" Bev replied quietly, musing over an old torment. "Because-"

Hunter suddenly jumped. He heard Toby saying his name, as clearly as though he stood beside him, though he remained in another part of the Warren. This mystery would have to wait.

"I have to go; I don't want them to know I'm here." He explained, then blinked out.

Hunter was in a small dark room, and through the door he could hear Toby talking. Hunter reached out, fumbling in the dark until he found a chain. The toilet flushed and Hunter opened the door into the main room of his quarters.

Adam and Mel were still sat in the middle of the floor, and Toby sprawled comfortably on the sofa. All just as Hunter had left them. Except for the fourth person in the room.

Hunter looked towards Colin Dawkins, who stood near the door, wearing that seemingly permanent sceptical expression.

"Can I help you, General?" Hunter asked mildly.

Dawkins didn't reply immediately but took in the scene suspiciously. "I came to see if you were alright."

"To check up on me, you mean." Hunter corrected, suddenly tired with the pretence of friendship and deciding to jump straight to the point.

Dawkins made a half-hearted effort at being affronted at Hunter's assumption, then just shrugged.

"Can you blame me? You knew that witch by name." Dawkins said coldly. "You're hiding something Hunter; you had a familiarity with that witch. I saw your concern over what we might do with her."

Hunter stood silently, not sure how to respond to this. Even if he denied it, the obvious lie would throw fuel on the fire of suspicion. Hunter gazed at Dawkins, trying to work him out. Had he been too eager to presume that a familiar face meant a friend and ally in these times? He realised that Dawkins had been cool, even negative, ever since he arrived at the Warren.

"Look, Colin, is there something I have done? For I thought we were friends, you and I?" Hunter asked quietly and sincerely.

The General smiled bitterly and shifted his weight. "You jump to conclusions, Hunter. I was never in this to be anyone's friend. I followed orders from General Hayworth, regardless of my own opinion." Dawkins shook his head and paced away with restless energy. "He saw something in you that he was willing to die for, but forgive me, for I see nothing."

"I'm not asking you to die." Hunter responded, a subtle anger and distress colouring his tone. But the General continued as though he had not heard him.

"I see nothing, save a power that is unpredictable and limited in its use. I see the person that wields it as a man lacking all sense of duty, who thinks himself free of all the restraints and rules of our society, a man that can *beget a son* by the enemy! And a man that, when we go for that hard push, will probably run and hide again in the Italian hills."

Dawkins voice grew colder throughout his rant, and he glared at Hunter with a finally unveiled revulsion. The General stood for a moment more, then wrenched the door open, suddenly leaving the room.

Hunter and Toby were left speechless in his wake. The only sound came from Mel, who was singing quietly…

*"Fuchs, du hast die Gans gestshlen, Gib sie wieder her!"*

Hunter frowned at what he recognised to be a German nursery rhyme; he was quickly learning to not be surprised by anything Mel might do. But her little voice did make him shiver.

*Hunter pushed the cottage door open and struggled through, his sports bag slung over his shoulder.*

*"Sophie, I'm home." He called out, aware of the noise of the television that floated through from the living room.*

*There was the sound of thumping feet, quickly followed by the appearance of Adam, all black hair and pale skin and very big bright eyes as he greeted his father.*

*"Daddy!" He squealed, promptly throwing himself at Hunter and clinging fiercely to his legs.*

*"Hey little man, I brought a visitor too." Hunter said, giving Adam an awkward hug, while trying to keep his sports bag balanced. Hunter shuffled down the hallway, to let his guest in, hampered by his son.*

*Another man came limping in behind Hunter, his eyes gleamed at the sight of his favourite little boy. "Hey up, mate."*

*"Uncle James!" Adam shouted, immediately releasing his father and barrelling into James, his noisy hug quickly followed by ear-splitting laughter.*

Hunter chuckled, not sure who was the biggest kid, and he turned away to see Sophie hovering in the doorway. She was always more reserved when James was around. Hunter dropped his bag and walked over to her, kissing her in greeting. She pulled away and looked pointedly at the floor.

"I hope you're going to clean that mud up, Hunter. How was rugby?" Sophie dragged her cold hazel eyes from the mess on the floor and looked directly at Hunter, a deep need in her gaze that almost distracted him.

"It could've gone worse. We only lost by six points. But I had to take James for stitches afterwards."

In the hallway, James kicked off his shoes and, holding a giggling Adam upside-down, he pushed past his hosts into the living room. He tilted his head as he passed, showing off the red area above his brow. "I still say I didn't need stitches - a plaster would've done. Nowt a cuppa tea can't fix, anyway."

Sophie sighed, rolling her eyes at the Yorkshire man. From the very first time they'd met, Sophie and James had never gotten along. But she moved grudgingly into the kitchen. Hunter paused to untie his boots and kick them off; from the living room he could hear the cartoons on the television, and the sound of Adam laughing at James' funny accent. From the kitchen he could hear the clink of mugs being set out, and he could just imagine Sophie's expression.

Obedient to his heart, Hunter walked into the kitchen and wrapped his arms around his Sophie, he breathed in the scent of her hair as he murmured a few choice words in her ear.

Sophie took a shuddering breath, savouring the moment. But as the kettle boiled, she pulled away from Hunter's arms and played the perfect hostess, taking through the steaming hot tea for Hunter and James, just as she used to back in Astley Manor, back before all the madness. Hunter followed her like a shadow through into the living room. Adam was quieter now and sat on the floor in front of his Uncle James. James turned to accept his mug of tea and Hunter could see fresh blood on his face, seeping out from the stitches, much more than he expected. A red drip rolled down James' cheek, and the Yorkshireman caught it before it dropped onto the clean sofa.

"Why are you always bleeding when I see you these days?" Hunter said with exasperation. But half of his consciousness tore away with sudden fear, his eyes were fixed on the wound on James' face, the bruises on his arms and legs, all of which became large and glaring under Hunter's scrutiny. James' eyes looked back at Hunter, empty.

"I'm sorry I couldn't save you." Hunter murmured. Then awoke, bathed in cold sweat.

## Chapter Sixteen

More than anything, Hunter wanted to see Bev again, to ask her more about the danger they were in, to ask her what she had meant before. But he could not risk it, the Council were more alert than ever, and Colin Dawkin's enmity had thrown him.

The next day Hunter was summoned to the Council again. He came, reluctantly leaving Adam in the care of Toby's wife, Claire Robinson. Claire had looked less than thrilled at the prospect of babysitting the half-witch child but had agreed for her husband's sake.

When Hunter arrived at the Council's rooms, he found them all seated about the long table, awaiting his arrival.

"Ah, Mr Astley." Theresa greeted warmly, looking up as he entered. "I'm glad you could join us. There are certain matters in which we require your help. One in particular, actually."

She motioned for Hunter to join them at the table, and a folder of hand-written documents was pushed towards him. He flicked through them, some pages stirring a certain familiarity in him, although on a whole they made no sense.

"After your disappearance we claimed Astley Manor and its extensive collection for the good of the Malleus Maleficarum Council."

Hunter looked up at this, a flash of anger that anyone should take what belonged to him and his family. Theresa gave him a sympathetic look, then continued.

"We found documents, arranged and researched, pertaining to this Shadow Witch, and one we did not know existed in 1940. We wondered if there might be some information about the last one, how she was contained, how she was released, that might aid us now. Of course, your documents were incomplete, but they did point to a German source. The Council decided to send a small party of witch-hunters to investigate this source. Yesterday we received word that they have failed and been killed."

There were shared murmurs of condolences and regret from the Council members. But they all fell silent again.

"I hope you understand our predicament, Mr Astley. Good men and women have given their lives trying to discover a weakness in the Shadow Witch, and I do not want their sacrifice to have been in vain. Yet travel between the UK and the rest of Europe is slow; communication is slower still."

Theresa fell silent, and Hunter sat there with a vague impression that this was where he came in.

"And what do you want from me?" He asked hesitantly.

"You can travel anywhere, can you not?" A man to his right asked.

"Yes." Hunter replied slowly. "Well, as far as I can tell."

"Well then, you could be in Germany at a moment's notice." The man continued. "And find out what we all need to know."

"I know you no longer follow Council orders." Theresa added, noticing Hunter's reluctant expression. "But this could be the breakthrough, the information that you came back for. Also, you can see it as repaying our help in recovering your son. And you needn't do this alone, you'll have the best witch-hunters with you."

Hunter grimaced. "I can't take anyone else-"

"Nonsense." Colin Dawkins interjected coolly, the first time he had spoken. "I've seen you transport a whole bloody army when the need arose for it - and travelled with you myself I might add."

Hunter waited for Dawkins to finish and did his best not to fix him with a scathing look. "Thank you, General. But I did not mean I was physically incapable, just morally. I can't risk a group of unprotected first generations, no matter how good they are." Hunter had expected some resistance or argument against his statement, but instead he was met with silent, knowing stares.

"We thought you might say that. And perhaps you are right, anyone would be in double the danger if you were around them, and we should not inflict that on any first generation." Theresa agreed. "Which is why we've assigned a higher gen to you."

Hunter wavered; he had not expected to win that argument so easily. Then he froze. A higher gen? "Not Toby!" He blurted out, shocked at the idea that his invalid friend might be dragged into this.

"I wish." Toby grunted. "But thanks for the vote of confidence."

"No, not Toby." Theresa replied with a vein of amusement in her voice. "A sixth gen, due back at the Warren today. We will send them along to your quarters once they are briefed."

Theresa nodded at the file beneath Hunter's fingers. "You had best spend your time memorising that. We expect you to leave as soon as possible."

*****

Hunter was sat in his room, trying to wrap his head around the documents before him. It was stodgy reading material and jumped from English to German (and even a piece in Russian); and his concentration was not aided by Adam and his new best friend Mel, equally jumping between games and quiet time, where Mel tried to teach Adam German.

*"Wo ist vater? Es ist der vater! Wo ist mutter? Es ist der mutt-"*

"Mel-" Hunter snapped, then immediately felt guilty beneath her hurt blue gaze. "Sorry Mel, it's just you are disturbing me, and I have to…"

"Ok, George." Mel mumbled, looking away, obviously not forgiving him easily this time.

Hunter thought back to the last time Mel had come around, and something suddenly struck him. "Mel… did you know that I was going to Germany?"

*"Sonst wird dich der Jäger holen, mit dem Schießgewehr…"* Mel murmured tunefully, still not facing him. "Or the Hunter will fetch you, with his gun."

Hunter leant forward, about to speak when there was a sharp knock at the door. Hunter jumped, and cursed his nerves, before going to open the door.

"Toby, come in." He said, unsurprised, standing aside for his friend.

But before Toby could limp in, a blonde girl pushed through impatiently. Hunter watched in shock as she took a blatant gander about the room and then turned to him with an assessing blue gaze.

"So, this is the famous Hunter Astley?" She remarked in a ringing American accent. "I thought you'd be taller."

Hunter opened his mouth to reply but found himself dumbstruck.

Toby (biting back a smirk) nodded to the new girl. "Hunter, this is Kris Davies-"

"Kris-*ten*." The girl stressed.

"Sorry, Kristen. Kristen Davies, 6th gen. She'll be accompanying you to Germany." Toby finished.

Still short on words, Hunter held out his hand to shake, a gesture Kristen ignored.

"So, it's true then? You can, like, just blink and be there?" Kristen asked, her blue eyes bright and excited at the thought. "But I mean, it just sounds magical."

"Ahm." Hunter managed a non-committal sound, as he let his arm drop back by his side.

"The Council suggests meeting in the field and setting off at dawn tomorrow." Toby interjected helpfully.

"Dawn?!" Kristen scoffed. "What's wrong with you people? Instantaneous travel at our disposal and we can't sleep in 'til a reasonable hour? Whatever. I'm gonna go crash."

The girl sighed heavily and without any further explanation she left the room.

Hunter stood there baffled. "That was... interesting."

Toby chuckled. "Oh, you have no idea mate."

*****

The Warren had quietened down for the night, as those within settled for sleep. Hunter watched silently as Adam slept soundly on the fold-out cot, looking ever so peaceful as he dreamt.

Hunter knew that it might be days before he saw his son again - longer if things went wrong. He also felt that tonight would be his last chance to finish a certain conversation. Hunter sighed, not wanting to leave Adam alone, but knowing that he had to, so as not to draw attention. He closed his eyes, the blackness enveloping him tightly, and when he opened them again, he was in the small cell-like room, the faint light from an oil lamp showing that addition of a camp bed someone must have dragged in. Hunter walked over and gently touched the sleeping Bev's shoulder.

The woman awoke with a start, snatching back from Hunter, eyeing him fearfully. But after a moment, she managed to calm herself.

"What are you doing here?" She hissed, brushing her long dark hair out of her eyes, to see him better.

Hunter frowned as he looked at her, something about her had changed, her very aura altered. "They...

they bound your powers?" He asked hesitantly, referring to the old witch-hunter practise of binding a witch's powers with the use on an artefact that would then be catalogued and stored. A practise that ended when the Shadow Witch had broken the key and released every bound witch in the world, to wreak havoc and revenge.

Bev sighed, looking weaker and older than she had just a day ago. "At least they let me live. Not that it matters, nothing does now. My magical heritage has never brought anything but trouble."

Hunter could only feel pity for this woman that was a shadow of her former, proud self. He moved to sit on the single, hard wooden chair in the room.

"You once told me that you could have been the next Shadow Witch. What happened?"

Bev looked at him with a faint smile. "You have a good memory."

She sat quietly on the camp bed, pulling the coarse covers snugly about her. Bev gazed at Hunter for a while, as though assessing whether or not to be honest with him. But then she shrugged. After all, she had already admitted that nothing really mattered anymore.

"I remember when they first approached me - the witches. It was my 30th birthday when they just turned up. They said that they were heir hunters, trying to find the descendent of Sara Murray. They asked a lot of questions, many I didn't understand, but seemed satisfied with my answers. When I asked what I was due to inherit, they turned to one another and became conspiratorial. They told me what they were - witches - I didn't believe them of course, so they cast a few showy spells to make their point. They told me what I was, what I could become. But I... I was wary. Up until that point I knew who I was, I was happy with my simple life and didn't want to take on their fight and their cause.

"They perhaps read my reluctance, but their eyes lit up with an intense greed when my daughter suddenly walked in. Sophie was thirteen and very angry back then. Always in trouble at school, disrespectful and challenging authority."

Hunter was caught by this little insight to Sophie's youth. Up until then he had never considered what she had been like as a girl, but her mother's description sounded very believable, that she had always been proud. Hunter half-smiled at his thoughts, and kept silent, not interrupting Bev's story.

"I hoped that it was just teenage rebellion, a passing phase. But I didn't trust the way those witches looked at her, and I forbade them from approaching Sophie until she was at least sixteen. Much good it did. Soon after, Sophie changed, becoming quieter and more secretive. She'd always been proud, but she became almost arrogant. I was in a difficult position. I couldn't come down hard on her, because I knew that would just push her straight to the witches, and I wanted to keep some influence over her, make sure she kept even a fragment of humanity and morality.

"Then when she was sixteen, they gave her another witch's power, a small taste of what she was to gain. And Sophie was hooked. Then finally when she was nineteen, news came through that the Shadow Witch's power was to be returned. And... well, you know the rest." Bev finished, her voice hollow and eyes empty, as though she had nothing left to live for. But then a small spark was remembered. "How's Adam?"

Hunter hesitated, still absorbing Bev's little story. "He's fine, reasonably settled and happy. I, ah, didn't tell him you were here."

Bev blinked, but slowly nodded. "Of course, no need to upset him." She mumbled, more to herself than to Hunter.

"You said that Sophie would never put her trust in paternal affection, or men at all." Hunter reminded quietly, gently pushing for information.

"Well, she hardly had a good role model." Bev almost snapped, then fell silent again.

"I'm sorry, Sophie never mentioned her father, I don't know..." Hunter replied, suddenly embarrassed at how little he knew about the woman he had claimed to love.

Bev stared at him with that assessing gaze again, then eventually sighed. "Sophie's father wasn't there, because..."

Bev broke off and looked away, into the darkness as her eyes gleamed with an old hurt. But after a minute's composure she spoke again, quieter this time. "When I was sixteen years old I... I was raped by my boyfriend. Sophie was the result of that rape, but I kept her, and I loved her. I thought to keep her parentage from her, but secrets have a habit of coming out in the end. She grew very angry, and she blames you. Your family anyway."

Bev broke off, gazing curiously at Hunter, bemused at how things worked out. "As she sees it, if my grandmother, Sara Murray, had not been forced to strip her descendants of power to save them from George Astley V and others like him, then there would have been no way that a mere mortal man could... could..."

"Bev... I didn't know." Hunter choked out after this shock confession. "I'm so sorry."

Bev waved a hand dismissively. "Oh, *I* don't blame you. It's in the past, and after all, I got my Sophie. Yes, I have learnt to come to terms with it."

"But Sophie?" Hunter asked gingerly.

"Sophie is still torn between hating your family and loving you." Bev replied with a smile. "And she got her revenge. After the witches delivered the Shadow power to her. Her father was the first person she killed."

Hunter sat in quiet shock. He could just imagine that sinful father taking a lone walk, when suddenly the shadows came to ensnare him and there - there would be the daughter he knew nothing of, a fierce and beautiful woman, driven by hate and vengeance.

"I…" Hunter tried to start talking but found his voice unwilling. He coughed and began again. "I'm leaving in the morning on a mission. I'll hopefully be back within the week, and I will return. We will talk again."

Bev half-smiled, her tired hazel eyes locked on Hunter as he rose from his chair. Her gaze did not falter as he stood there in the middle of her cell. And then suddenly he vanished, and Bev was left staring into space.

## Chapter Seventeen

It was a grey and dismal dawn, with wispy mist-like rain clinging to their hair and clothes. Hunter stood in the middle of the field, with Kristen beside him. The girl yawned, and huffed, and stamped her feet against the cold, making her displeasure against this early departure very clear indeed.

Hunter was a little more awake, although he'd hardly slept after last night's revelations. Instead he'd stared unseeingly at Adam as he slept, watching how peaceful his son was. Although he didn't want to admit it, even to himself, Hunter feared that Bev's confessions would bring another dream upon him, tangible and real, and having the pain of seeing Sophie and understanding her a little better.

During those sleepless hours, Hunter had allowed his mind to turn over those dreams. They were disturbingly real - he remembered the panic he had felt after the first dream, last year at the Abbazio di Donili. The Sophie in his dreams was the Sophie he remembered, but he still couldn't explain how the Adam of his unconscious imagination matched the real Adam perfectly. The location had confused him for a while - why would their pretty family picture not be situated at his Astley Manor? But finally, the realisation dawned on him that they were at Beverley Murphy's cottage near Keswick.

But dreams were dreams, and no real answers came, though his mind ran over and over it.

"Are we going or what?" Kristen snapped, fed up with waiting in the cold.

Hunter blinked, dragging himself back to the present. "Yes, yes." He muttered.

At that moment Toby limped forward, hand outstretched. "Good luck, Hunter."

Hunter shook his hand. "Thanks. And you'll…"

"Look after Adam, yes I promise." He confirmed with a reassuring smile. His wife Claire wasn't fantastically happy with the arrangement, but she was slowly accepting that Adam was a sweet and innocent young boy, despite his unorthodox parentage.

Happy that his son would be in safe hands Hunter swung his backpack over his shoulder and stepped back, holding his hand out to Kristen. The girl took it nonchalantly, but Hunter smiled at the cold sweat on her palm that she could not hide. With a nod to the Council members, they vanished.

Hunter opened his eyes to a wooded area.

"Woah, shit." Kristen exclaimed, staggering back as her knees buckled.

"Steady." Hunter murmured, "Maybe you should sit down."

He frowned at how pale she was looking. Kristen obediently lowered herself to the ground shakily and stuck her head between her knees with a groan.

"Ugh, god, is it always like that?" She moaned.

"Only the first few times. You get used to it pretty fast." Hunter answered, remembering how his previous team had adapted. He crouched in front of her, waiting patiently for her to recover.

Kristen groaned again, obviously dismayed at the idea of doing it again. But she finally lifted her head and flicked her blonde hair back over her shoulder.

"Where are we? Why is it so bright?" She moaned, squinting against the unexpected light.

"We're a few hours north of Berlin, in the Bioshärenreservat Schorfheide Chorin, I used to holiday near here. And it's light because we're an hour ahead of where we just set off from. Hence why we set off so early." Hunter replied patiently, relieved that she was recovering quickly. His method of transport affected people differently. Hunter remembered the first person he'd blinked away, a young and still-optimistic Colin Dawkins - the then-sergeant had been pale and winded, but not as dizzy as poor Kristen. Now that Hunter knew that she was ok, he couldn't help but find her reaction amusing.

"We'll, ah, start trekking to civilisation once you're feeling up to it." Hunter added, smiling bitterly that he should be hampered by this witch-hunter the Council promised wouldn't slow him down.

"Nah, I'm good, I'm ok." Kristen argued, and got back to her feet, looking a little pale, but very determined.

Hunter watched her carefully, but just shrugged his backpack straight and began to walk due south. Kristen kept up with him without complaint, occasionally having to jog every few steps to keep up with Hunter's longer stride. They kept marching until the trees dropped away and the morning sun beat down on them, and then continued still over the varying terrain. They kept away from roads and settlements as much as possible. After an unrelenting pace for two hours, Hunter had to admit that he was impressed with Kristen's fitness, the girl wasn't flagging. Of course, maybe that had something to do with her 6th gen status. By the 6th generation, a witch-hunter had earned a little extra strength and stamina beyond the average man. Hunter glanced at the blonde girl again, curious at how a 6th gen could have survived the witches' purge of any and (almost) all witch-hunters above a 2nd gen status.

Hunter moved to ask her, but Kristen opened her mouth instead.

"What? Do I look funny to you?" She asked toughly, as she caught the older guy staring at her again. "Or maybe you're thinking something else. Bet it's been a while since you saw a woman, cooped up in that monastery?"

Hunter raised a brow at the girl's attitude and laughed when she actually had the cheek to wink at him. "No, I promise I wasn't thinking that, not that I wouldn't be flattered, you're a very pretty young... I mean."

Hunter broke off and kept his head down, marching along. What the hell was wrong with him, once upon a time he had been the most charming young man, he'd been able to banter and tease with any number of women. Kristen had just caught him off guard.

Hunter coughed and brought his thoughts back to where they'd jumped from. "For your information, the Abbazia de Donili was home to men and women. No, I was wondering how you are, well, alive? How did you survive, being a 6th gen?"

Kristen walked along quietly for a couple of minutes, trying to coordinate an answer that made sense. "Just luck, I guess. I was never registered with the American Malleus Maleficarum Council, so I slipped under the net."

Hunter continued to stare at her, trying to work her out, until he nearly tripped. "But how? Forgive me, but surely your MMC would pounce at the chance of having a 6<sup>th</sup> gen working for them. And if they're anything like the UK Council, they keep stringent records of all witch-hunter bloodlines, whether they join or not."

"Yeah, you're right, except they didn't know about me." Kristen replied, a little smugly. "My mom fell in love with this English witch-hunter that saved her, and she stayed with him for a while. But it didn't work out, so she moved back to America and didn't know she was pregnant with me. I didn't even know what I was until I was a teenager, and I started getting these headaches and it was obvious I was different from everyone else. Mom finally had to tell me about my father and all about witches. I mean it freaked me out, seriously. But I was even more scared of the idea of this Malleus Maleficarum Council coming along and taking control of me."

Hunter nodded, in silent agreement with her comment. He'd never been keen on the politics and double nature associated with any council.

"I couldn't ignore it though, when I realised the headaches was my mind detecting magic, so I worked rogue, just small stuff, not alerting the MMC. Then that night came, when everything just crashed, and the world was turned upside down. I knew it was witches, and I felt guilty as I watched the MMC destroyed and I couldn't do anything to stop it. The witches set themselves up as authority figures and began to hunt down all the witch-hunters listed with the MMC. I wasn't on the list, but I wasn't about to hang around doing nothing. I joined in a few rebellions, but with only 1st gen hunters it was pretty desperate, especially fighting those average witches. I realised that I would be more useful fighting the epicentre, so decided to follow the rumours of the Shadow Witch to the UK. Jumped on a boat to Spain, then travelled up Europe, keeping out of trouble best I could. I finally met your MMC last year and have been working with them since. They were pretty happy to get a 6th gen. Took them no convincing after I mentioned my father's name, either."

Hunter listened quietly and stopped to grab his water canteen. He offered it to Kristen first, before taking a drink himself. "And who is your father?"

"Brian Lloyd." Kristen replied, with a tilt of her head.

Hunter choked on his drink, spluttering so water dribbled down his chin. He gasped and wiped his sleeve inelegantly across his mouth. "What?" He rasped, his eyes red and watery.

"Mm, guess you've heard of him then." Kristen replied innocently, although a mischievous smile touched her lips. "Turns out he was something of a hero."

"You're *Brian's daughter*?" He stressed, trying to take in this bizarre turn.

Kristen nodded slowly; eyeing Hunter like he was an imbecile.

"But…" Hunter frowned, he thought he'd known Brian. How could he not know that he had a daughter? "Brian was my mentor, after my dad died, he taught me almost everything I know. And I thought I knew him - he never mentioned you."

"He didn't know about me." Kristen said with a shrug. "You really knew him?"

"Yeah, as well as anyone." Hunter replied. "He was this big, stubborn, fierce man with impossible standards, but he was loyal and one of the best damn witch-hunters we had. He was world-famous amongst witch-hunters, you should have seen how many people honoured him after his death. He, ah, was killed by the Shadow Witch."

"I know, your MMC told me, when I first came, half hoping to meet the father I never knew. But they also told me that he was the one that uncovered the Shadow Witch and made sure the world was ready for her." Kristen said, quieter now, as she thought about the greatness of this mystery father figure that had lumbered her with these gifts and the duty that was bound to them.

"He did." Hunter confirmed. It had indeed been Brian that had put together the clues and worked out that the Shadow Witch was returning. Or so Hunter had thought; that conversation with Bev made Hunter look at things in a different light.

And now here was his daughter. Hunter gazed at her again, with new eyes. Kristen looked nothing like Brian Lloyd, but Hunter thought he saw some of his stubbornness and hopefully his courage.

He smiled and tucked away the canteen, picking up the pace again, as they headed for Berlin. Kristen walked alongside him, quite pleased with herself.

"So, you know you're a 7th gen and have all these extra gifts... does that mean if I have a kid, they'll be the same?" Kristen asked.

Hunter thought for a moment. "I don't know, I guess so. But there have been so few 6th gens and I'm the first known 7th gen that I can't promise they would." Hunter looked resolutely ahead. The Abate had thought 7th gens special, but only on the first step to being truly evolved anti-witches. Was it truly only Sophie that made Hunter more than that?

"Well... I know how to make it much more possible." Kristen replied, nudging Hunter with her shoulder as they walked together. "You know, if you ever fancy it."

Hunter laughed, "You don't give up do you?" He shook his head, he had to admit that Kristen was pretty, but this was hardly an appropriate time for flirting.

Plus, now all he could think was this was Brian's daughter…

## Chapter Eighteen

It was nearing evening by the time the city of Berlin was finally in sight. They had trekked for near twelve hours. Kristen had been energetic and chatty for the first six hours, but after they took a brief midday stop, she became quieter, her fewer comments taking on a sarcastic and annoyed edge. Hunter didn't rise to her jibes, but just kept walking. Yet even his legs were beginning to burn, and he cursed the fact that he'd decided to be overly cautious in where they transported to. He told himself that it was still a shorter journey than if they'd had to travel by normal means from England, but that was little comfort.

Hunter looked up at the quiet streets as they walked into Berlin, he took a deep breath, but said nothing and the two witch-hunters continued to march in silence up the tarmac roads of the outer boroughs. It was eerily quiet, in this once heavily populated area, that there was so little noise. Once there would have been television and music rolling out of the houses and flats. There would have been the constant background noise of people talking, children laughing and playing. The roads filled with the constant drone of vehicles rumbling through. But the cars stood as unused relics at the curb, no more technology threw out noise, and the children and families alike stayed quiet behind their doors. Hunter and Kristen passed a few pedestrians, people that kept their heads down and hurried home before dark.

The atmosphere was enough to make Hunter and Kristen only whisper sparse words as they kept walking. Hunter kept a sharp eye out for the street signs, following the directions from the file he had memorised last night. Glauben Strasse was the address he had been given. Glauben Strasse, Glauben Strasse, the name of the street pounded in his head in time with his footsteps.

Eventually they came to the road. It was unremarkable, the same as every other in the estates that clustered about Berlin. Hunter glanced over his shoulder to visually check that they were not being followed, while his other senses stretched out to confirm it. Satisfied that they were alone, he led the way to the house number he had been given and rapped sharply.

Hunter could hear someone shuffling towards the door; followed by a pause that dragged out for several long moments.

"Wer sind sie?" *Who are you?* A voice came out bluntly, muffled by the door.

"Herr Holtzmann?" Hunter said, leaning in towards the door so he did not have to raise his voice, he then continued to give the barest of their background.

At the mention of the MMC, the man gasped and unlocked the several bolts on the door and pulled it open. He stood before them as an older gentleman in his sixties, but with sharp eyes that took in their faces, then checked the street was empty before ushering them into the narrow hallway.

"Danke, Herr Holtzmann." Hunter murmured as he stepped through, the dim hallway was losing the daylight and was relying on the old oil lamp that was set on a side table. "Ich bin Herr Hunter Astley, und das ist Frau Kris Davies."

"Kris-*ten*." Kristen hissed.

"You came! And much quicker than I had anticipated, I only sent the message to your Council a month ago." Herr Holtzmann said, still gazing at their faces with an unsettling intensity.

"We knew the importance of this assignment and came as quickly as possible, Herr Holtzmann." Hunter replied, quickly skating over just *how* they had travelled so quickly. "The last British witch-hunters stayed with you, ja? Do you have any of their documents or information?"

"Please, call me Max." Holtzmann insisted, then paused, putting his thoughts into words. "Unfortunately, no, your witch-hunters were very careful not to share any details with me, for their safety and mine. Over the six months they were here, they never brought papers home, never spoke of their work. I knew that they were researching the background of the Shadow Witch and looking for her weaknesses, but nothing more."

Hunter inwardly sagged, that they had travelled so far for this. "Is there no one else that helped them; that could help us? The German Council?"

Max shrugged. "Our Council is not as strong as yours, and they have moved their base away from Berlin in an attempt to survive the persecution of witch-hunters. Berlin is reigned over by the witches and we are left to cope as best we can. But I know that your men had a contact, an important one, at the Reichstag."

"Ok, well that's a start." Kristen said, the first words she'd spoken. "Let's go there."

Hunter looked at her with askance, worrying that this was just the first of many silly blonde comments he might have to deal with. "Kristen, do you know what the Reichstag is?"

"Sure, it's the old parliamentary seat of Berlin, now used as the witches' headquarters, locally known as the

Witches Rat, home of the most powerful witches in Germany, currently headed by a female witch called Laura Kuhn." She replied with a haughty flick of her blonde hair, and a challenging look in her flashing eyes. "I'm not as dumb as I look."

Hunter sighed, looking back to Max. "Are you sure there are no other contacts or leads we could take?" He asked. Hunter was not a coward, but if he could avoid walking into the epicentre of witches in Germany, then he would.

"No." Max replied immediately and confidently. He had had a month to think about what the British witch-hunters could do, after his friends had been killed.

Hunter shrugged. "Fine, then yes Kristen, we're going to the Reichstag."

Max smiled sadly at the young people before him, that were so ready to go into danger, just like the last poor souls. "You are both welcome to stay tonight, Herr Astley, Frau Davies; and seek the contact tomorrow in the safety of daylight."

"Danke." Hunter replied, accepting the offer. He was tired after the trek and if he needed to rest, he was positive that 6th gen Kristen would be feeling twice as bad.

Max showed them to the spare room, where several mattresses covered most of the floor, the blankets and pillows all clean and set aside since their last users needed them no longer. Max hesitated at the door; from the thin coating of dust, it looked like he never came in this room, still full of the memories of the British witch-hunters that had been his friends. Max disappeared into the house, eventually coming back with a modest tray of food for the two witch-hunters.

Hunter sat down on the furthest mattress and helped himself to the bread and cold meat that Max had brought them. Expecting that Kristen would settle likewise, he raised a brow when she came over and sat beside him, picking off his plate. He had to admit that he did enjoy the warmth and comfort as she leant against his arm, and the very scent of her. Kristen was right, it had been a long time...

"Kristen." Hunter warned coldly.

The girl sighed, sitting up straight, and eyeing him undecidedly. "What? I'm not hurting anyone."

"We're working." Hunter replied, getting to his feet to put a little more distance between them.

Kristen gave a crooked smile, and her eyes gleamed with a mischief that Hunter recognised from his own youth. "Technically, we're not working until tomorrow."

Kristen's smile faltered as she saw that she wasn't winning. She wrapped her arms about her knees and looked innocently up at Hunter. "You know, if you don't find me attractive, you could just say, I wouldn't be offended, promise."

"It's not that, it's…" Hunter paused, wondering how to phrase it. "I've got a bit of a psycho ex, and I don't want to get you in any trouble."

"Come on, how can any ex of yours cause trouble for 6th and 7th gen witch-hunters?" Kristen said with a yawn, and without waiting for a reply she lay down and tried to sleep, with the happy knowledge that Hunter at least found her attractive, by his own omission.

Hunter stood staring at Kristen as she settled, then realised that the American had been away during the whole realisation that Hunter and the Shadow Witch had been a couple and had a child; and he and Kristen had probably left before she had chance to hear the Warren gossip. Poor girl. Hunter sighed and dropped down onto the mattress furthest from Kristen

As he closed his eyes, he realised that he was far too tired to hold back the inevitable dream.

*Hunter was lumbered with a heavy satchel and he was glad to dump it in the hallway when he reached home. It had been a long day and he was weary. He kicked off his shoes without unlacing them and shrugged off his coat, hanging it on the coat stand before trudging through to the living room. Sophie was curled up on one half of the settee, quietly reading, but she looked up as he entered.*

*Without a word, Hunter collapsed on the settee next to her, giving a small sigh of contentment at the soft seat. Sophie*

rested her book and continued to gaze curiously at him, wondering what on earth could be troubling him.

When it became apparent that he wasn't going to say anything, she finally spoke. "Hard day at work?"

"Hmm, about average these days." Hunter replied in a monotone voice.

"Anything interesting happen?" Sophie enquired with a too-perfect innocence.

Hunter turned his head against the back cushion, to gaze at his dear Sophie, who did not fool him one bit. There was not a chance that he was going to let her hear anything of value, whether this was magic, a dream, a delusion or any other kind of madness. "No. Same old, same old. Though we've had a new girl start. Very annoying. Very American."

"Very pretty?" Sophie asked, jumping straight to what she considered important.

"Don't know, didn't really notice." Hunter replied.

"That's a yes then." Sophie replied with a chuckle, amused at Hunter's attempt to not give the wrong answer. She turned back to her book, convincingly uninterested with this new girl. "What's her name?"

"Oh no, no." Hunter replied, "You're not learning that. All I need to do is give you a name, and doubtless you'll track her down. I haven't forgotten Gabriella, and neither have her family. All we did was flirt and you had to go in there with your curses…"

Poor Gabriella, Hunter thought. An innocent girl from the Donili village that hadn't known that her innocent

612

flirting would bring on the wrath of the Shadow Witch. There had been no solid proof of witchcraft or foul play after the accident, but Hunter was convinced that it was too much of a coincidence.

"I don't know what you mean." Sophie replied airily, turning the page of her book.

## Chapter Nineteen

The Reichstag was an impressive building set in the centre of Berlin. Hunter, Kristen and Max stood in the shadows of the Sheidemannstraße, looking out at the building. People moved with business-like haste to and fro in front of the Reichstag, in fact only the lack of tourists distinguished it from pre-witch Berlin.

"There is Herr Beerbaum." Max muttered, nodding to one gentleman who marched past in a fine suit. "Calls himself Bürgermeister der Leute - Mayor to the People, the ambitious arschloch. Beerbaum is not a witch but is one of their main supporters.

"There is Frau and Herr Shaudt, they are witches on the lower council." Max continued, pointing out another couple who walked into the Reichstag. "The Witches Rat is made up of the lower and upper council. From what I gathered; your witch-hunters had a contact in the upper council. How do you propose to get in touch with them?"

Hunter looked up at the daunting Reichstag, the morning sun glinting fiercely off the glass dome. "I was thinking of walking up and asking." He replied unconvincingly.

"That's a shit plan, Hunter." Kristen said with half a laugh, unsure whether he was joking or not.

"Look, the last guys took six months to find this contact, we don't have that long, we need this source now. We need to let that contact know we're here." Hunter argued quietly.

"So, what you got in mind?" Kristen prompted.

Hunter paused, gazing at the young, energetic witch-hunter. "You trust me?"

Kristen shrugged. "Sure, why not."

"I'm going to hand myself in, be the bait to draw out the contact." Hunter said simply.

Kristen thought about it for a moment, then nodded. "OK, I'm in."

Hunter smiled at her willingness. He fleetingly considered trying to talk her out of it, but figured it was pointless. He'd never been able to counter the stubbornness of those that aided him: Toby; Marcus; James; even Sophie. Hunter always seemed to attract the most iron-willed people.

"You are going through with this?" Max asked with exasperation. "You are crazy, you both are!"

Hunter turned to the old man. "Max, thank you for your help over the last year, the British Malleus Maleficarum Council are in your debt. But you need to go home now and forget all about us.

Hunter held out his hand, and when Max took it to shake, the old man froze in shock. Hunter looked deeper into those bright eyes and pushed further until he could sense the presence of thought...

The two men stood there for no more than a minute, when Hunter finally let Max go. Max stood for a moment, disorientated, then wandered away.

"What did you just do?" Kristen asked quietly.

"Altered his memory, removed everything to do with the MMC." Hunter muttered, shaking his head to get rid of the ghost of another man's memory.

"Huh, one of your party tricks?" Kristen asked warily.

"Something like that." Hunter replied. "It's for his own safety, and ours - I don't want to leave a trail."

Cutting off the moral argument he was sure was brewing, Hunter led across the street straight up to the Reichstag. There were two armed guards at the main door, and they eyed Hunter and Kristen warily as it became apparent that these two people weren't passing by.

"Guten morgen." Hunter called out as he climbed the first few wide steps. "We'd like to see the Witches Rat."

"You have appointment?" One guard asked.

"No, but they'll want to see us, we're witch-hunters." Hunter replied helpfully.

The effect was immediate. The guards both aimed their guns at the unwelcome visitors. The first guard snapped at Hunter and Kristen to raise their hands, while the second shouted the alarm in frantic German. Hunter glanced at Kristen and raised his hands as half a dozen armed guards came running out. Their force was well-trained. Four men secured the two dangerous witch-hunters and marched them inside, while the others carried the bags and weapons, they had taken from them.

The Reichstag wasn't designed for holding prisoners, but Hunter and Kristen found themselves thrown into a room with small, high windows, and the door locked behind them.

"What happens now?" Kristen asked, rubbing her arms where the guards had held her.

Hunter walked calmly about the room, which seemed to have no real function. "We wait." He replied, feeling a certain déjà vu. This wasn't the first time he'd walked into a witch headquarters, unarmed. It was a miracle he was still alive.

Time passed slowly, the two witch-hunters sat in silence, afraid to say anything prying ears might hear or deduce. Hunter paced the room at first, testing the defences. A powerful witch had put a block over every window. But after years of fighting the Shadow Witch and developing his own powers, he could read the flaws of this comparatively average magic. It was a relief to know that there was nothing physically stopping Hunter from leaving at any point.

By the time the door eventually opened again, Hunter was beginning to feel offended at how low a threat and a priority he and Kristen obviously poised to the witches. Two people appeared at the door, Henric Beerbaum, whom Max had pointed out earlier, hovered with dark flickering eyes that Hunter immediately distrusted. He had the air of a man that had done well at the expense of others. It made Hunter seethe - it was weasels like this that made the fight so much harder.

The second figure stood before Beerbaum radiating power that sang in tune with the defences that Hunter had been probing earlier. The female witch stood staring at the captives; her eyes narrowed.

"Why are two British witch-hunters seeking the Witches Rat?" She asked in fluent English.

"We came to find out what happened to our friends." Hunter replied conversationally.

The witch hesitated, not sure how to take this very calm man. "The six we caught nosing around last month? They were arrested and executed, which is the fate of any witch-hunter we find." She spoke slowly, clarifying the unfortunate position of the two new witch-hunters that were so ridiculously stupid as to hand themselves in. No wonder the witches had won, if this was an example of their enemy.

"Yes, but before that, we believe that they had an inside contact at the Reichstag." Hunter replied, casually pushing aside the threat.

The witch froze, shocked by this announcement. In her silence, Beerbaum shook his head and simply said, "Impossible."

"Nothing is impossible, trust me." Hunter replied dryly.

"Why are you telling us this?" The witch asked suspiciously.

"Because we think that this contact has important information."

The witch hesitated again, and Beerbaum took the opportunity to add another snide comment. "You are hardly in a position to make use of any such information."

The witch suddenly came out of her daze and snapped at Beerbaum in rapid German. The man replied with false humility, then without notice they both left, the door being closed and locked behind them.

The two witch-hunters stood in silent contemplation for a long moment, then Kristen stepped up, looking imploringly at Hunter.

"What the hell was that Hunter?" She fumed. "Are there any other secrets you want to share with them? No, don't shush me Hunter!"

"Be careful using names, we don't know who's listening." Hunter hissed, his paranoia kicking in. He didn't mind taking on a building full of witches, but if they worked out exactly who they held captive, the Shadow Witch wouldn't be far away, and Hunter wasn't ready for that.

"Of course, I told them. What do you think the witches are going to do now they know there's a traitor in their midst?" Hunter explained. "They'll hunt them out - doing our work for us and getting a result much faster."

"It's risky though, what if they kill them before we can do anything?" Kristen asked quietly, unsettled by being the sensible one.

Hunter shrugged. "Trust me." He knew he was being rash, but he was already nervous after one day away from Adam.

*****

Barely ten minutes had passed when the witch returned, alone this time.

"Frau Kuhn wants to see you." She said calmly.

The witch looked between the two witch-hunters and with a sigh she raised a hand. Hunter suddenly felt his wrists drawn together behind his back, as though ropes pulled tight. He struggled against the unnatural feeling, but his elbows felt like they were about to pop under the strain. Hunter glanced back and saw Kristen struggling likewise. Hunter concentrated on the vein of magic around him, he could sense the strength and the weakness, and he knew he could break it –

"Come quietly and you will not be hurt." The witch said with mild amusement at their plight, not knowing that Hunter was a mere breath away from breaking her bonds. But Hunter remained passive, turning to Kristen and meeting her fierce gaze he nodded, not saying anything but hoping she took his lead.

The young witch-hunter visibly relaxed before his eyes. Hunter always found it unsettling when people trusted him unquestioningly; it was a big responsibility on his shoulders. But it sure as hell made it easier to get through the tasks ahead when there were no arguments or lengthy explanations to waste time on.

"Move." The witch snapped, pointing through the open door.

Hunter led the way; Kristen close behind him and their captor bringing up the rear. Hunter grimaced, suddenly struck by the realisation it wasn't his first time bound and captive in a witches' headquarters. Only this time he doubted there would be a miracle rescue, as there had been by Bev Murphy. Oh well, the plan had seemed like a good idea this morning.

The witch-hunters walked obediently down a dark corridor of the Reichstag, before finally reaching a set of double doors. The witch pushed past them and knocked.

"Ja?"

At the sharp female voice, the witch pushed the doors open and nodded Hunter and Kristen through. Hunter walked in, immediately taking in the scene. The room was an office, official and almost clinical in appearance. Photos of previously important people adorned the walls, along with the German flag.

And at the broad, polished desk, a woman sat, looking up expectantly. Frau Laura Kuhn, the strongest and most feared witch in Germany. She was an attractive woman in her mid-forties, her light brown hair scraped back in a severe bun and shocking blue eyes locked fiercely on the witch-hunters. Frau Kuhn rose from her desk and walked over to the bound witch-hunters, assessing them with a detached, impersonal gaze.

Hunter saw Kristen flinch as Kuhn drew near, and as the witch passed him, he shivered at the strength of magic that rolled off her. It took every effort on Hunter's part not to raise his shield against her. He didn't doubt for a second, she'd be able to read it and work out who he was.

"You seek a spy in our ranks." Frau Kuhn snapped in rapid German, no question in her voice. "You will tell me everything, their name, other sources."

"We cannot." Hunter replied mildly, looking back at the witch that had brought them.

Kuhn followed his gaze and paused as she regarded her colleague. "Danke Erica, you may leave."

The witch nodded and left immediately, trusting that her boss could handle the two bound witch-hunters.

As soon as the door closed, Hunter felt a bubble of magic rise about the room, it was thick and cloying and Hunter guessed it was to keep what was said in this room firmly private.

"What are you and the Amerikaner here for?" Frau Kuhn demanded.

Hunter paused, thinking how to play this. Kristen leant towards him; her curiosity caught by "Amerikaner".

"She wants to know why we're here." Hunter muttered, translating quickly.

"Well why don't you tell her." Kristen replied quietly, rolling her eyes. She then turned to the witch and spoke louder, enunciating each word. "We are here to find out about the Shadow Witch."

Frau Kuhn looked scathingly at the blonde witch-hunter, then spoke in clear English. "I am German, I am not deaf."

She then looked at Hunter, obviously marking him as the brains of this operation. "You are fools, you follow your friends' fate by coming here."

"Yes, that has already been pointed out, thank you." Hunter replied politely.

Kuhn shook her head and walked back to her desk. She held her hand over a drawer and closed her eyes. A moment later there was an audible click, and Kuhn opened the drawer and pulled out a thick sheaf of paper. She immediately held it out to the witch-hunters.

"Yes, me. Although I may have to find a scapegoat if I am to keep my position." Kuhn mused. "Well, make what you will of it." She snapped back to attention and thrust the papers in Hunter's direction.

Hunter looked down, momentarily shocked into silence, but then wet his lips to speak. "Ahm, perhaps you could be so kind as to remove our bonds." He commented, straining against the magical restraint at his wrists.

Frau Kuhn smiled. "Remove it yourself, Astley."

Hunter froze, then immediately raised his shield, not needing to hide it would seem. "You know?"

Kuhn did not reply straight away; her eyes followed the lines of his shield and as she read the strength of it, she looked mildly impressed. "Yes, Herr Beerbaum did not take long to work it out – you are quite famous, Hunter Astley."

While she spoke, Hunter broke the magic that bound his wrists with a simple channel of thought, then freed Kristen.

"So, what does this mean?" Hunter asked warily.

It means that the Shadow Witch is on her way, and I cannot help you." Frau Kuhn replied sadly. "Our Burgermeister has likely contacted her people already, the ambitious little pig. The house will be sealed, and I doubt even you, Herr Astley, can break out, when it is designed to trap you in."

"But... you are the most powerful witch in Germany." Kristen broke in. "Can't you do something?"

"Against the Shadow Witch? I highly doubt it." Kuhn replied, a frown creasing her brow. "And if I tried, I would be revealed as a traitor, and would lose my place. And then who would curb the violence against my people? Who knows what monster my successor might be?"

Frau Kuhn walked away from them, looking at one of the large windows, yet not seeing the stretch of green and grey ahead. "I was happy with life before the Shadow Witch. Since her rise, Germany has been in ruins, the average person treated as nothing more than cattle. As the most powerful witch I was offered this position and took it in the hope I could make life easier. But I have to hide my own husband for fear he will be targeted, and I have to counter the malicious moves of some witches and people like Beerbaum. I have thought about finding equally sympathetic witches, but it is too dangerous. And then the witch-hunters came, and I felt new hope... until they were caught by the others. And now you."

Hunter was left silenced by her confession.

"You have to hide your husband?" Kristen echoed.

Frau Kuhn half-turned from the window. "He's not a witch, just a normal man. Under the new regime I am permitted to... take up with such a person to procreate. But to love such a man would be frowned upon indeed. Albert's very existence is hidden, and I have to answer to Laura Kuhn twenty times a day instead of Frau Gren as I long to be."

Kuhn walked back to the witch-hunters, looking much weakened, even though her magic still rolled off in powerful waves. "Please don't reveal any of this when She comes for you. I'm trusting you to find a way."

Hunter tightened his hold on the folder and nodded.

Kuhn took a deep breath and composed herself. "I'll take you back to the holding room. Good luck. And remember – once we are outside this room, we are not shielded from eavesdroppers."

Hunter and Kristen exchanged a look, neither feeling confident at this point. But Laura Kuhn opened the door, shattering the bubble of privacy. The witch looked suddenly fierce and daunting; all softness washed away once more.

## Chapter Twenty

Back in the holding room, Hunter stood, waiting for the sound of footsteps on the other side to fade completely before he turned to Kristen. "Ready to leave?"

"Hell yes." She replied with a dramatic sigh. She eagerly grabbed his hand and closed her eyes, prepared for the pulling, rushing sensation that… didn't come.

Kristen opened one eye, then seeing the same room, she opened the other. "Hunter?"

Hunter was pale and panicked. Shit. He tried again, but nothing, he was completely blocked. Shit. Even with Kuhn's warning he had arrogantly assumed he could still get out.

"I can't…" He gasped, his eyes roving skywards as his senses pushed out. They were met by a wall of magic infinitely more complex and stronger than the other witch's defence. And Hunter could read the pattern of the magic, it was as familiar to him as his own.

"The Shadow Witch. She's trapped us, I can't find a way out." Hunter said, dropping Kristen's hand, guilty at the fate he had sealed for her. "She's coming."

The two witch-hunters stood in a shocked and fearful silence. Hunter became gradually aware of a quiet voice singing, akin to a radio far away.

> "...Alle Leut', alle Leut' geh'n jetzt nach Haus'
> Grosse Leut', kleine Leut',
> Dicke Leut', dünne Leut'"

"Mel." Hunter suddenly blurted out, remembering where he had heard it before. As soon as he spoke, the singing stopped.

"Hi George." That familiar chirpy voice came out.

Hunter turned and, beyond all comprehension, Mel walked over to him. She still looked like an innocent angel, wearing a modest pale blue dress and a white cardigan. Her pale blonde hair was held back with a white headband.

Hunter stood gaping, wondering if this was madness, or his desperate imagination. But Kristen moved closer to him, her eyes locked on the strange girl.

"Mel, what are you doing here?" Hunter asked, remaining tense and defensive.

"You're not glad to see me." Mel replied, faltering at her friend's less than friendly welcome. "Adam was worried about his daddy, he wanted me to make sure you are OK."

Hunter noticed that Kristen looked at him oddly, and he realised that he hadn't told her about his son.

"Yes, I am glad to see you, of course I am Mel." Hunter replied, remembering how easily hurt this immature girl was. "But Mel, how... did you get in here?"

Mel paused, her brow furrowing in confusion. "I don't understand."

Hunter took a deep breath to calm himself. Getting frustrated at Mel wasn't going to help.

"That's OK Mel. But are you able to come and go as you like? Just like in the Warren?"

Mel bit her lip but nodded slowly.

Hunter took another breath to calm the nerves that threatened to overwhelm him. The Shadow Witch was close, she was so very close, and Hunter didn't want to meet her just yet.

"And can you take Kristen and me with you?" Hunter asked quietly.

"Of course, George, if that's what you want." Mel replied, taking a moment to work out who Kristen was. She must be the other girl, the one with the blonde hair that was so much yellower than Mel's. Mel fiddled with a lock of her own hair, contemplating which was prettier...

Hunter noticed the imperceptible changes in the room around him, the background noises seemed muffled and the shadows thickened.

"Excellent." Hunter stated, desperate to hurry this up, they were definitely out of time. "Then let's go, altogether, right now."

Hunter held out his hand to Mel, who looked completely confused by his haste, but obediently slid her delicate little hand into his, her cool fingers curling firmly around his. In his other hand, Hunter grasped the papers Frau Kuhn had given him, and held out his arm so Kristen could grip his wrist. Hunter nodded to Mel, who looked at him strangely for a moment, her blue eyes hypnotic.

Then she let go of his hand and Hunter blinked, the atmosphere had changed, the air was cooler and fresher. He finally dragged his eyes from Mel's and looked around, noticing the change of scene, the shelves of books that covered the walls, the old cushioned chairs arranged informally in the middle.

From one of these chairs, a man rose. A man with silver-grey hair and loose robes. A man that Hunter recognised in a way that suddenly calmed him.

"Padre!" Hunter strode over to him, taking his hand as an old friend.

"Signor Astley? But how?" The Abate looked thoroughly puzzled by the sudden appearance of his old pupil, especially in the heart of the Abbazia which was protected from such magical entrances. But his sharp grey eyes moved over Hunter's companions, and when they settled on Mel, he took a sharp intake of breath. "Begone demon, you are not welcome here."

Hunter frowned at the fierceness of this good Abate and glanced between the old man and Mel.

"Padre?" Hunter squeezed the Abate's hand, hoping to stimulate a response, but when none was gained, he dropped his grip and stood there helplessly. In the silence, the need to be an English gentleman reasserted itself. "Padre, may I introduce Miss Kristen Davies, a 6th gen witch-hunter. And Miss Mythanwy Elspeth Lughnasa, who, well, rescued me not a minute ago."

Hunter finished speaking and continued to watch the Abate. He had never seen such disgust on the old man's face.

"Better to die than be in debt to a thing like that. Make her leave, she is not welcome in these walls." The Abate seethed.

And Mel, who was being spoken of so ill, paid the old man no attention, she was far too preoccupied playing with Kristen's ponytail, seeing how her golden hair played in the light in comparison to Mel's. Poor Kristen, who had never had the pleasure of meeting

Mel and had only heard about her, merely shrugged at one more bizarre chapter today, and stood patiently.

"Padre, please." Hunter began but trailed off. He could see the stubbornness of the Abate's stance and knew they would have to do as directed. "OK, we're going."

Hunter gestured to the girls to follow and made his way to the study door.

"You may return, once she is gone." The Abate added in a choked voice.

Hunter barely acknowledged his words and walked out with Kristen and Mel trailing after him.

"What was that about?" Kristen hissed as they walked out into the courtyard towards the main gate.

Hunter shook his head. "I don't know. I'll try and find out." He said, truly worried over his old mentor's reaction.

Hunter stopped as they stepped out of the Abbazia. The rest of the Donili village lay out before them, beautiful and peaceful in the early afternoon sun. Hunter quickly decided on a plan of action and led the two girls down to the village until they came to a small and newly-built cottage, the light wood barely touched by weather. Hunter rapped on the door and waited for an answer.

After only a minute the front door opened and a young man with a head of thick black hair looked out. His eyes lit up the moment they landed on Hunter, and with a loud laugh he flung the door open and hugged his friend without reserve.

"Hi Marcus, how's married life?" Hunter gasped at the strength of the hug and forced his friend back to arm's length to get a proper look at him.

"It is good, good, Hunter." Marcus blushed at his polite enquiry, then looked to the two blonde girls. "Would you like to come in?"

Hunter accepted and the trio went into the house. It was small, but it was obvious that Marcus was proud of it, and Hunter praised it accordingly.

Marcus' new wife came through at the sound of visitors to see if anyone cared for a drink.

"Ah Marissa, you are more beautiful than ever." Hunter greeted, happy at Marcus and Marissa's blissful little life. And a little envious too.

"Marcus, I have a meeting with the Abate. Would it be OK if my friends stayed here until I return?" Hunter asked.

"Of course." Marcus replied without question.

Hunter smiled and pulled Kristen aside in the small room. "Can you keep an eye on Mel? And here, look after these, see if you can find anything."

Hunter held out the folder they had gone through so much for, and Kristen took it with a determined little nod.

"I won't be long." He said, then ducked out of the room.

Back at the Abbazia, Hunter knocked on the study and, not waiting for an answer, entered. The Abate was seated in his chair once more, and looked up expectantly as Hunter walked in.

Hunter looked at his old mentor with a certain disbelief. How could this man have reacted so rudely to one that Hunter considered a friend?

"Hunter, it is good to see you. You look well." The Abate suddenly said, his voice hollow as he knew what would come from his predictable, rebellious student.

"No. No niceties. Why were you so rude to Mel?" Hunter demanded.

"A creature such as she is not welcome in this Abbazia." The Abate repeated slowly and quietly. "Do you not know what manner of abomination it is?"

Hunter paused, having no idea where this was going. He barely knew Mel, and he definitely didn't understand her. But whatever she was, she was here to help. "I realise that she is far from a normal human being, but surely you of all people can accept her, padre. Or were your lectures on leniency and acceptance so narrow-mindedly reserved for witches?"

"And I will not understand how you can vehemently hate witches and defend her!" The Abate snapped, showing his first flare of temper. The old man took a breath and calmed himself. "But you do not know what she is. And I will not be the one to enlighten you. Just be aware Hunter, do not trust her."

Hunter turned away, bloody frustrated. This was the second time he had been warned not to trust Mel, but what was so bad about her?

"Forgive me padre, but I will trust her and anyone else who helps me against the witches."

The Abate froze at this. He opened his mouth to speak, but it was long moments before the words managed to come out. "She... is helping against the witches?"

Hunter looked at the Abate, wondering what caused him such surprise. "Of course."

The Abate stood up and walked over to a bookshelf and raised his hand to take a book, before hesitating and pulling back.

"No, no, I should consult the others." He muttered in the Donili dialect, then looked up, remembering Hunter's presence. "Well? Go, back to your friends, back to England or wherever you're needed."

Hunter frowned at the bluntness of the Abate, but as the older man remained flustered and worried, Hunter backed away, having no answers and more confused than ever.

Hunter walked slowly down the hill, back towards Marcus' house. His thoughts were heavy. How could an innocent little thing like Mel possibly worry the trained and skilled Donili monks?

Hunter reached the house and let himself in. The young couple, Marcus and Marissa, sat in the main room, awkwardly shy hosts. Kristen sat silently; the papers still clasped firmly in both hands. And Mel? Mel sat with a vague smile, softly humming.

"Hunter!" Marcus jumped up at the return of his friend. "How was the Abate? Your friend Kristen explained his unusual behaviour."

Hunter shrugged, not quite sure how to start explaining what was going on.

Marcus saw his hesitation and confusion and quickly spoke again to cover it. "You will stay for dinner, yes? And you can tell me everything then."

Hunter smiled and accepted, although a part of him was ready to leave this peaceful place and return to the stress of the Warren. And return to his son. But there was a pressing matter that had to be dealt with now, his brown eyes returned to Mel, and he inwardly sighed.

"Mel, may I have a word please? In private?"

"Of course, George!" Mel replied gaily, immediately springing to her feet. The blonde girl followed Hunter outside with the eagerness and affection of a puppy.

In the quiet sprawling village of Donili, Hunter took Mel's hand and they strolled in the pleasant afternoon sun.

"Mel… who sent you?" Hunter asked.

"Adam did." Mel replied, frowning that she had to repeat herself. "He was worried about you."

637

"No, I don't mean today. I meant, who sent you to the witch-hunters?" Hunter persisted.

"You… you don't want me? Will you send me away?" Mel asked, her voice cracking with pain.

"No, of course I won't send you away Mel. But I need to know who sent you." Hunter pressed.

But Mel was shaking her head and biting her lip. "We wanted to help. I want to help. Everyone is so nice, and I have so many friends."

"Who is 'we'?" Hunter asked gently.

Mel's wide blue eyes caught him again. "The one who sends me and waits for you to ask for help."

"And who might that be?"

Mel let go of Hunter's hand and started humming and swaying to her own tune.

"Mel, please tell me." Hunter continued softly, knowing that one firm word could have her crying again.

And little Mel turned back to him with a dazzling smile, and started to recite:

"Lucy, satan sataniel,

Fall to earth my fallen angel;

Little fire and little light,

Morning star no longer bright."


The world stilled as she spoke, a cloud passing over the sun, causing everything to be a little duller. No birds could be heard and even the wind dropped. Hunter shivered with a sudden chill.

Then the moment passed, and Hunter's senses returned to the world that still went on regardless. And dear Mel was still smiling so openly at him.

"Right." Hunter said, needing to break the silence with something. "And he wants to help me?"

Mel nodded. "Yes, but you need to ask him for help, otherwise he cannot interfere."

Hunter frowned, hoping that this was one of the times Mel was being cryptic. She couldn't mean what he thought she meant. "Cannot interfere? Except from sending you, of course."

"No silly, I wasn't meant to help." Mel chided him. "But everyone was so nice, I wanted to."

Hunter took a deep breath, completely lost at this point. Were they really having a nice chat about the Devil? Satan, Lucifer, whatever you wanted to call him.

Years of studying the occult – both MMC sources, and the woefully misled public information – and in many witches went hand in hand with the Devil. Literally. In the older texts they were said to invoke him, allow him passage into our world. They were said to fornicate with him and suckle his familiars. Of course, such reports died away over time, as the world became less superstitious and more cynical. Even in the MMC reports and lectures, over time the focus had shifted from the religious implications to the purely physical and scientific. Oh, how they had all moved on, and progressed, and yet here Hunter stood, discussing Lucifer.

"Ahm, Mel, isn't he generally on the witches' side?" Hunter asked hesitantly, not really wanting to encourage this vein of madness.

Mel shook her head, her blonde ponytail flicking wildly. "He made them, representatives of the Devil on earth, and asked only for their lifelong worship. But the naughty witches neglect him. He is forgotten in the shadows, and his familiars starve and perish. Poor Lucy."

Hunter shook his head, unable to think at this point.

Mel smiled sympathetically and slipped her small hand back into his. "Shall we go back? I am sure dinner is nearly ready, and we must help set the table."

## Chapter Twenty-one

Returning to Marcus' house, there was the smell of rich stew and fresh bread. Mel hurried ahead, as eager and carefree as ever. Hunter walked slowly, more than a little dazed by their conversation.

Kristen frowned at his expression and pressed him for an explanation. But Hunter shook his head, he didn't want to speak of it at all, and would never bring mention of the Devil inside his friend's house. Instead Hunter turned his attention to the folder that Kristen still clung to defensively.

"Did you find anything?" Hunter asked.

"Nothing new. A lot of it didn't make sense. And quite a bit is in German." Kristen replied, readily relinquishing the folder to someone that might make more out of it.

Hunter took it and sat down, flicking through the first few pages. Kristen hovered over his shoulder, leaning in uncomfortably close, hoping to learn something.

"This is just a letter from the 40's from a scientist, Herr Braun." Hunter muttered, moving it aside. He'd already seen a copy of the letter years ago – an experiment involving witches, hunters and the Nazi party. To create a Shadow Witch.

But beneath it, there was a report he'd not seen. It followed the initial trials and reported a more successful attempt at cracking the ancient spell that bound the Shadow Witch's powers. The scientists and gathered witches had followed an old ritual and mass sacrifice, which resulted in the artefact giving off a wave of energy. But unfortunately, they were at a loss where in the world the Shadow Witch had awoken. Ah, Hunter knew the answer to that. He wondered what it must have been like for Sara Murray, in the middle of England, to wake up suddenly imbued with limitless powers and no explanation, and no help.

"Are you staying the night?" Marcus asked after dinner. He was ever the kind host but was uncomfortably aware of how cramped his little house would be with so many guests.

Hunter hesitated. It was so tempting to stay just one evening in this sanctuary and put off the danger and drama that was to come. But he shook his head. "I need to get back."

One bright-eyed little boy came fiercely to the front of all thoughts. Adam would not forgive him for lingering.

Deciding there was nothing to be gained by waiting any longer, Hunter led his two companions outside (he considered it rude to just disappear from Marcus' living room), and with a wistful look up the hill at the Abbazia, they vanished.

Back in the Warren, Hunter went immediately to Toby's room. The Council could wait for their report until after Hunter had seen his son.

He knocked on the door and waited. It was wrenched open by a pale looking Toby, who gazed at Hunter with such worried eyes, that Hunter felt his blood freeze.

"What's happened?" Hunter demanded, pushing his way into the room, desperate to see his son safe and well.

But there was nothing to fear, Adam was sitting on the bed, surrounded by toy ponies, playing with a girl of about five or six, that Hunter immediately took to be Molly, Toby's daughter.

"Daddy!" Adam squealed, propelling himself into Hunter's arms.

Returning the hug, Hunter looked enquiringly at Toby, who still hovered by the door, wearing a worried expression.

"It's – it's the witch, Beverley." Toby started. "The Council took her; I don't know where."

"What?" Hunter snapped.

"They tried to take Adam too." Toby now hurried to say before Hunter blew up. "But we refused to hand him over. But Bev – there was nothing I could do to stop them."

Hunter stood dazed, overwhelmed with gratitude to his old friend for keeping his son safe; and predictably furious with the Council.

"Christ, Hunter, be honest with me. Bev is *her* mother, isn't she?" Toby suddenly said, breaking through Hunter's thoughts.

Hunter frowned, sure that they'd been careful with that particular secret. "How…?"

"Well... your familiarity with her. And they look alike. Also, it made sense to send the boy's family to retrieve him."

Hunter was amazed. "You're not bad at piecing these things together."

Toby shrugged, very much aware of his ability to read between the lines.

Hunter stood still for only a moment longer, then turned and stormed out of the room.

"Watch Adam." He shouted back at Toby.

"Don't do anything rash, Hunter." Toby shouted down the corridor, then sighed, knowing it was futile.

Hunter marched down to the Council rooms, banging his fist against the door. Without waiting for a response, he threw the doors open and barged in.

There were only three Council members there. General Dawkins, Theresa, and Reynolds. They all sat sociably at the table, nursing cups of tea, talking of insignificant things. And they all looked up at the unannounced intrusion of the witch-hunter.

"Mr Astley, you're back." Theresa said, looking impressed at his swift return. "Did you find anything?"

"Where is Bev? Where is the witch?" He demanded, ignoring Theresa's question.

The Council members exchanged a glance and Hunter felt the atmosphere cool.

"That is no business of yours." General Dawkins replied without looking at him.

"Don't start that shit." Hunter warned. "Tell me what you've done, or I'll..."

Dawkins stood up suddenly, squaring up to Hunter in an attempt at intimidation that Hunter was far from impressed by.

"Or you'll do what, Astley? Defy us, again?"

Hunter exhaled slowly, his eyes never flinching from Dawkin's gaze. He eventually replied, his voice low and all the more threatening. "Maybe I will. Maybe I will take what I learnt in Berlin and leave you with nothing. Maybe I'll take Kristen and Toby with me, and let you fight this with just your 1st gens. Or maybe I'll see how many of them want to join me too."

Hunter saw doubt creep into Dawkin's eyes. Oh, the General knew well enough the power and influence Hunter had over other witch-hunters. Hadn't he seen for himself how the Warren had become excited by their hero's return. But then his gaze hardened again.

"You wouldn't dare." He snarled. "We all know that's not your style – you'd rather run away alone than take on the responsibility of others. After all, didn't your actions kill your last team!"

Just as Hunter was about to snap, Theresa stood up.

"Gentlemen, enough! General Dawkins sit back down. And Mr Astley, please calm down." Theresa kept a solid gaze on them until they both did as they were told, then turned to Hunter.

"The witch had nothing more to offer us, so she has been taken to a secure location."

Hunter hesitated, processing this. "A secure location? Where is more secure than the Warren?"

"The Warren is designed to be a base, a home for witch-hunters. We do not have the facilities to keep that sort of prisoner here."

Hunter snorted at the idea, these rooms were solid, the doors and bolts heavy duty, and the corridors filled with trained men and women. What threat could a bound witch pose.

"Fine. Then where is she?" He demanded.

"As I said, it is none of your business." Dawkins said snidely from the table.

"Hunter." Theresa stepped between them again before anything happened. "We cannot tell you; I wish we could. But you are a front-line fighter and we cannot risk you being captured with that sort of information in your head."

Theresa reached out awkwardly to grasp his arm in some sort of sympathetic hold. "I'm sorry…"

Hunter shrugged away from her and backed towards the door.

There was a cough from the forgotten Reynolds, who sat uncomfortably watching the scene. "What about your find in Berlin?"

Hunter glanced at him, looking slightly dazed by the change of topic. "Um, Kristen has it all, she'll bring it by."

And then he left, with the unsettling thought that the Council had almost taken his son – and would equally refuse to tell him anything.

## Chapter Twenty-two

*Hunter walked into the familiar cottage with a feeling of trepidation. Everything was as it should be, except for Sophie. She stood, awaiting him in the living room, a look of despair about her.*

*Hunter moved towards her, only for Sophie to step back.*

*"Don't." He pleaded softly, holding out a hand to her tense, half-wild form.*

*"I can't." She stressed, twisting, almost writhing against the rigid pose she dictated for herself. "I can't do it anymore. This is just a fantasy in which I've allowed myself to be human – to allow myself to believe I am human."*

*"I don't know what this is, but it's not a fantasy that I love you, and if I could choose any life it would be this." Hunter continued in soft tones, taking a careful step towards his Sophie.*

*But she staggered back again, shaking her head, her eyes dark with pain. "Yesterday... was so close. I was relieved that you escaped. But these chances have run out. The next time we will meet, and I cannot be restrained by love, or desire for a life that was never ours."*

*Sophie finally moved towards Hunter; her hand outstretched. Hunter blinked and looked down as she dropped a small object into his hand. He took a deep shuddering breath as he saw her gold wedding band in his palm.*

*Hunter opened his eyes to the dark room in which he lay. A single tear rolled down his face and fell onto his pillow.*

*The war was swiftly coming back in their direction, he knew it. Their little respite, if that was what it could be called, was over. And he wasn't looking forward to what was coming.*

*He'd been into battle before, many times. He knew he wasn't a coward, he did not fear for his own life, but he dreaded the loss of others, people he had started to grow fond of and felt responsible for.*

It was around 7am, and Hunter had only been awake for half an hour, but still lay in bed, too miserable to move. There was the sudden unwelcome sound of someone kicking the door open. Hunter watched with one lazy eye as Kristen walked in, precariously balancing a tray with what looked suspiciously like breakfast.

Hunter noticed Adam sit bolt upright in the small bed on the other side of the room.

"Hey kiddo, I got orange juice and toast." Kristen greeted the little boy, setting the tray down on the only table in the room.

Adam hesitated, tempted by the breakfast, but wary of the strange lady. The little boy looked over at his father for permission.

Hunter could only groan. "What are you doing, Kristen?"

"Bringing breakfast." She replied innocently. "Think of it as thanks for saving my life."

Hunter sat up in bed, looking his usual ruffled morning mess, with extra dark circles under the eyes today. "Technically, I didn't save your life, Mel did."

"OK, then think of it as punishment for putting my life at risk." Kristen shrugged, and helped herself to a piece of toast. "It's all a ruse, anyway."

The girl then proceeded to sit on the foot of Hunter's bed. Hunter immediately pulled his feet back and got out of bed, wary of where this might go, and what the forward Miss Davies might do, even with Adam in the room. He walked over to the tray and helped himself to what was supposed to be coffee, but it was the best they had in this time of war. Hunter took one sip and grimaced at the bitter taste, then handed a cup of orange juice to Adam before finally returning his attention to Kristen.

"OK, what do you want?"

Kristen played with her toast, in no rush to answer. "To clear one or two things up. I heard some stuff since we got back."

Hunter froze, wondering what 'stuff' she might have uncovered. But he stayed silent as the girl finished her toast and continued without further prompting.

"Psycho ex, huh? Understatement." Kristen said with a smile that was caught between cruel and disbelieving. "Now that really is the actual cliché of sleeping with the enemy."

Hunter glanced sharply towards Adam, feeling very protective of the innocent little boy, that didn't deserve to hear people slander his mother.

"Kristen, outside." Hunter ordered with a curt nod of his head. Without waiting for her, he marched out into the cold corridor. Hunter frowned, he wished he'd put some shoes on, his feet were bloody freezing.

"Say whatever you want to me, but I would appreciate it if you watch your tongue around my son." Hunter said as Kristen came to join him, more than a hint of a threat in his voice. He leaned past her to pull the door shut, leaving Adam to have his breakfast in peace.

Kristen's blue eyes darted back in the direction of the room. "Then it's true? He's really her son? I thought, and kinda hoped it was just a rumour."

Hunter stood silently, he'd quickly become used to such shock and disgust from the witch-hunters, ever since they had found out.

"How?" Kristen asked, then blushed. "I mean, I know *how*, but how could you?"

Hunter shrugged; it was nearly impossible to explain to these people that were already so biased.

"For a year before the Shadow Witch emerged, we knew her as Sophie Murphy. She was a friend, a colleague, and yes, for a while a lover. Long enough for Adam to be conceived. There was no reason to suspect her of being a witch."

"Is it true you used some bullshit about the boy being a possible offensive weapon to get the Council to agree with kidnapping him, rather than tell them the truth?" Kristen asked, hardly convinced, but jumping to her next train of thought anyway.

Hunter smiled bitterly at the recent memory. "Yes. They would never have understood. Half of them still don't. Besides, it could still be true, I have no way of predicting what Adam might become. But it would involve waiting for him to reach puberty before we get a clue. Although if I'm honest, I don't think we have that long."

Kristen narrowed her eyes at his final comment. "Is it really that bad?"

"It's starting to feel just like it did before Salisbury Plain." Hunter sighed, referring back to the last decisive battle; when almost all the witch-hunters and their supporters were wiped out.

Kristen wrapped her arms about herself, suddenly cold. "Well, what are you going to do?" She asked, her eyes fixing his again.

Hunter hesitated. "I'm going to fight alongside the witch-hunters…"

"No, I mean, what are *you* going to do? You have-" Kristen broke off, glancing down the corridor before continuing in a much quieter voice. "You have powers no one else can dream of; a half-witch, half-eighth gen son; a blonde demon; and an army of magic monks."

Hunter looked at her, utter shock robbing him of his ability to speak. How did she know?

Kristen shrugged, seemingly reading his mind. "I had a nice chat with Mel and Marcus, just to find out where they sided in this whole thing. You've got a lot of powerful friends, Hunter. And y'know, it makes me wonder why you're content to be just a number on the battlefield, when you have all that behind you."

Hunter sighed. "I don't have any miracles up my sleeve." He replied weakly. But he recognised a kick up the arse when he saw one.

"Fine. Can you get your hands on the Berlin papers?" He asked, waiting for her to nod. "Then meet me here when you have them. Bring Mel if you see her before I do."

653

Kristen nodded, and without another word sauntered off down the corridor. Hunter watched her go, then returned to his room. Adam had finished his breakfast and was currently hiding under his father's bed – the giggling gave him away. Hunter smiled, and played along for a minute, loudly exclaiming that his son had vanished. All the while he pulled on his day clothes. Once he was fully dressed, he bobbed down, and pulled his screaming and kicking son from under the bed.

"Found you! Now get dressed Adam." Hunter said, pulling clothes out of the drawers and helping his son into them. "We're going to visit Uncle Toby-"

"And Molly!" Adam interjected; his voice muffled beneath his jumper.

"And Molly." Hunter agreed. "Then we're going to a very special place."

Hunter took Adam's hand and led the way down the corridor to Toby's room and knocked. He figured it was unnecessary to drag his son along for this part of business, but after the Council had nearly taken him, he was loathe to let the little boy out of his sight.

Toby answered the door within a couple of minutes, still looking quite groggy at this time of the morning.

"Hunter? What-"

Hunter smiled and, taking that as an invitation, let himself in. Adam immediately let go of his hand and took the opportunity to run and jump onto the still sleeping Molly's bed.

"Hi Toby, sorry to bother you so early, but I've just come to let you know I'm leaving." Hunter said, getting straight to the point.

Toby stood there speechless. "What? You – you're leaving? Why? What's the plan?"

"There's no established plan yet. I've just got to go and do what I can to bring the Shadow down. I'll be taking Adam with me. Oh, and Kristen too." Hunter explained, realising it didn't contain much of an explanation

Toby frowned, his mind obviously a little sluggish this morning, and hurrying to catch up. "Fine. Give me an hour to sort things out here, and I'll come."

Hunter knew he'd say something like that. He sighed at the reckless loyalty he seemed to gain from so many good men and women.

"You can't come." Hunter replied firmly.

Toby paused, for once in his life looking angry. "You're taking Kristen. Perhaps you find the girl you've known ten minutes more useful than me. Well tough shit Hunter, I'm not getting left behind this time."

Hunter hesitated, truthfully as an able-bodied 6th gen, Kristen was likely to prove more useful on whatever this mission was, rather than a crippled 3rd gen. But Hunter would rather die than admit this to Toby.

"You can't come." Hunter repeated gently. "I need someone I can trust to represent me here. Due to my unfortunate little clash with Dawkins, more than a few people will assume that I'm a coward and doing a runner, or that I am fracturing the MMC and rebelling. They need to know that I'm doing this for them, and that I'll be with them on the front line when it comes to the fight."

Toby still looked stubbornly furious, but his shoulders started to sag as his resolve wavered. "I don't like it."

"I know. Thanks Toby." Hunter replied, motioning to Adam that it was time to go. "Trust me, when it comes to that big fight, you're the guy I'll want next to me."

"What, so you can spend more time protecting me?" Toby retorted as Hunter and Adam left.

Upon returning to their room, they packed all of their meagre belongings into a couple of bags.

"Dad, can I take Incy?" Adam asked, having finished collecting the few toys and books that Molly had grown bored with and donated to the younger boy.

Hunter winced at the mention of the spider but conceded. If Adam could find him.

There was a knock at the door, and before Hunter had a chance to answer it, his visitors let themselves in. He was suddenly joined by his two blonde accomplices. Mel drifted in, beaming at her young friend Adam, and obviously delighted at the idea of a little trip. Kristen walked in behind her, smiling knowingly. She waved a thick folder at Hunter, who looked impressed.

"Already? That was quick work."

Kristen shrugged. "Pretty minimal security, they trust everyone in the Warren."

Hunter looked around. Everything seemed ready. There was no time like the present.

"Hold hands." He instructed, slinging his bag over his shoulder, and taking his son's hand.

Mel held onto Adam, Kristen held onto Mel, and nodded to Hunter.

Hunter took a deep breath and closed his eyes, thinking firmly of his destination, an image so strong in his mind that he knew he was there before he opened his eyes. It was a beautiful summer morning, to be stood in the English countryside, in front of one of the grandest houses in the county. Hunter looked up at the old building and squeezed Adam's hand.

"This is Astley Manor, where I grew up. And one day, it will be your house." Hunter explained, introducing his young son to the family estate.

"Wow, so this is the famous Astley Manor?" Kristen said, apparently in awe of the place she had obviously heard about. "So, this means you're like, a Lord or something?"

Hunter gave her a withering glare. "Why don't you all come in?"

Hunter led the way up to the main door and on into the entrance hall. "I'll give you the full tour later. But for now, let's just say that Astley Manor was built in the last half of the nineteenth century by George Astley II. It has many witch-repellent spells and devices built into the very foundations – no witch can enter without being stripped of their powers. It is also the home of the most extensive witch-related library in the world – which we will be taking full advantage of."

Just as Hunter finished speaking, two men appeared behind him, their guns held steadily towards them. Hunter turned around, unsurprised by their presence.

"Ah, Jack, Shaun, how good to see you both again. Don't worry, these people are guests of my house."

The two men stood silently, sharing a glance as they tried to work out what to do next. The Council didn't have protocol for this.

"Now, you're probably wondering what to do." Hunter added helpfully. "To be honest, you're best reporting this to headquarters and awaiting orders. Or you could help us find what we're looking for, so we can defeat the witches."

The two men, still suspicious, lowered their guns.

"Sir," Jack began, hesitantly. "There is something you should be aware of..."

Before Jack had a chance to explain, the something, or rather someone, became apparent.

"All this noise, this early in a morning is uncalled for. On a Sunday too! Why, if you had any shame-" The arrogant female voice stopped suddenly, as the person came down the stairs and saw who had blustered in.

'Oh no.' Hunter thought. He'd much rather face demons and witches. He watched warily as the petite figure made her way down the stairs. Dressed in black, with her make-up flawless as ever, looking as though the war had not touched her.

"George?" Even her monosyllable enquiry sounded harsh. "So, you came back then."

Her cold grey eyes swept over the small group, assessing the visitors unforgivingly.

"Mother, it's good to see you, no one would tell me where you were." Hunter replied, suddenly guilty that he hadn't done more to find her sooner.

"Well." Mrs Astley began huffily. "Your witch-hunter rebels came and claimed Astley Manor for 'the cause' in your absence. They stuck me in some poky community building."

She exhaled her displeasure. "But I heard you had returned, and there was no longer any legal reason they had to hold me. But to think that I have no right to live in my own home without my son's approval is appalling."

"I'm sorry you had to go through that, mother." Hunter replied, his guilt increasing. "I had no idea that would happen when I left."

"Well, you did leave. Gallivanting off and having a fine old time, just like your father, I'm sure. While I stay behind and try to make the best of the neglect." Mrs Astley paused, finally acknowledging the rest of the group. "And you bring a party back as always. You seem incapable of acting alone George."

Hunter looked to his small group of friends, feeling regret again that he should drag them into his misfortunes. "Mother, may I present Miss Kristen Davies and Miss Mythanwy Elspeth Lughnasa."

"Pleased to meet you, ma'am." Kristen said, more polite than Hunter had ever known her, obviously wary of the petite battle-axe before her.

Kristen held out her hand, but Mrs Astley just let it hang there, looking with disdain at the girl. "Oh no, George, not an American. Too gaudy and pretty, and nowhere near as elegant as the last one. And your other friend keeps rather quiet. Modesty is a virtue, but extreme shyness a curse. And look at her, one can hardly tell her age she dresses such a lamb!"

Kristen's mouth was agape at the criticisms that were thrown her way, and poor little Mel pressed closer to Hunter.

"She scares me." Mel breathed, making Hunter smile that an accomplice of Lucifer should fear his mother.

"And who is the boy?" Mrs Astley demanded, speeding along the introductions.

Hunter gave Adam's hand a reassuring squeeze before replying. "Mother, this is Adam – your grandson."

And finally, Hunter got to witness his mother being shocked into silence. Mrs Astley stood there, her normally pale cheeks fading to white and her thin lips opening and closing as she tried to comprehend this.

"No, but... how is this?" The normally articulate Mrs Astley was at a loss.

"He's mine and Sophie's son." Hunter answered softly. Then he looked down at Adam. "Say hello to your Grandmother Astley."

But the little boy clammed up, and faced with his daunting grandmother, he squeezed harder on his father's hand and shuffled to hide behind Hunter.

Mrs Astley pressed her fingers to her lips, looking quite choked up. "Finally, a grandchild. One I can help raise right this time."

Hunter frowned at this; he knew that his mother had long craved a grandchild – she had been less than subtle in her hints for years. But there was no way he was letting that poisonous woman near Adam – with his contradicting parentage the boy already had enough issues.

"Sir?" A male voice cut in, and Hunter turned to Jack as he spoke up, looking both nervous and amused by the exchange. "Sorry to interrupt, but you said you were here looking for something."

Hunter blinked, oh yes, back to business. It was almost a relief to turn his attention from his mother, back to the imminent witch threat.

"Right, I need to finish translating a few newly acquired papers. Kristen, I'll show you to the archives, bring up everything you can find from Old George, my grandfather, especially pertaining to the 1940s. Mel, can you go to my family's collection of artefacts – see if there's anything you recognise as useful that we might have mislabelled."

Hunter looked up to Jack and Shaun. "Gentlemen, if you wouldn't mind aiding the ladies."

Shaun stepped forward, introducing himself to Kristen and Mel and offering to show them the way. Jack gave Hunter one last look, then followed the trio towards the library.

And so, Hunter was left alone with his son, and his mother. Mrs Astley stood quietly; her eyes fixed on her grandson. Then suddenly she clapped her hands together.

"Well, I suppose I should start with tea and coffee for everyone while they work."

Hunter looked at her warily. Mrs Astley was infamous for being a cold hostess, and this out of character offer made Hunter start. "Mother…" He began but was quickly cut off.

"With Charles gone, we can hardly offer hospitality as we once did, but it will have to suffice." Mrs Astley mused aloud, then feeling quite determined, she headed off in the direction of the kitchen.

For a few minutes, Hunter was left alone with his son in the entrance hall of his old home. He stood and breathed in deeply, taking in the familiarity of this house that seemed to awaken, as Hunter's party began to move through it, and the cheerful atmosphere recognised the return of the master of the house, and the young heir.

## Chapter Twenty-three

Hunter had been sitting in the study for a couple of hours, poking over the Berlin papers. He was slowly beginning to piece together what Laura Kuhn had found so important. But it was hard to concentrate while his mother hovered in the room.

Oh, she was silent, Hunter had never known her to be so quiet; Mrs Astley was rapt with delight with Adam's existence. Well, at least she did not seem disturbed by the fact that his mother was a witch, which was a refreshing change. No, for once it was the other way around, with Adam feeling quite unsettled by her unwavering attention.

As Mrs Astley sighed contentedly once more, Hunter snapped, slamming his pencil on the desk.

"Mother, perhaps another round of coffee is in order. And you should probably assign our guests rooms for later." He suggested, hinting heavily that she should make herself busy.

Mrs Astley looked towards him; her gaze steely again, now that it had been torn from her grandson.

"If you wish to be alone, you only had to say, George. I do not know why you insist on treating me like an idiot." Mrs Astley stood up and brushed her black skirt into neat lines. "I shall see to lunch, as I doubt anyone else has cared to plan it."

Hunter looked at her sceptically. "But you can't cook, mother."

Mrs Astley raised a neatly plucked eyebrow at his comment. "You would be surprised, my son, what I have had to learn these past few years." Mrs Astley said without modesty.

Hunter stared down at the book in front of him, taking in none of the words as his mind ticked over. "Where is Charles?"

Mrs Astley didn't reply immediately, but took the time to straighten the cuffs on her blouse. "He died. Last autumn. Not that you care, of course. You did such a good job of abandoning us."

"Mother, I-" Hunter stopped, aware that he had no excuse for his past choices. Charles had been a loyal part of the household for as long as Hunter could remember and had been a source of company for his unpopular mother. "I'm sorry, I thought you were safer without me. How did they get to him?"

Mrs Astley blinked in surprise. "Not everything comes down to witches, George. Charles had lung cancer. I thought he had pneumonia that would not shift. He only told me the doctors had diagnosed him with cancer months later, near the end. He said that he did not want to cause any unnecessary hurt or fuss." Mrs Astley gave a wistful smile.

Hunter sat silently, noting his own pang of grief and, shockingly, sympathy for his mother. Mrs Astley had depended on Charles for years, and Hunter had often wondered about their friendship.

Mrs Astley took a single glance in her son's direction and tutted at the emotions that he was daring to feel. "I do hope that isn't pity your feeling, George."

Content that she had made her point, Hunter's mother picked up their empty mugs and made her way out of the study.

Hunter shook his head, while he waited for the stuffy feeling to leave the room. When it didn't seem keen to clear, he decided he needed to stretch his legs. With a sigh, and a creak of the antique chair, he got to his feet. Hunter held his hand out to his son, and together they headed to the library.

Inside, Kristen and Shaun were ensconced at a desk, their heads close together over a stack of papers. Before Hunter had a chance to ask what had them so riveted, the opposite door opened and Mel danced through from the cellar, Jack following more calmly, carrying a few bits and pieces from the famous Astley collection.

Jack looked sheepishly up at Hunter, the older man excited to be able to handle the artefacts they had previously guarded and treated with near reverence.

"Did you find something?" Hunter asked hopefully.

Mel smiled brightly, her blue eyes shining. "So many pretty somethings, some we thought lost long ago!"

"But anything useful, Mel?" Hunter tried again, focusing his question.

"Oh, nothing as useful as that." Mel answered, pointing vaguely towards Hunter. "But some of these will protect against strong magic."

Hunter nodded, then paused and rewound over what she had just said. "Wait, you mean they're not as useful as me?"

That was interesting; both exciting and frightening that a demon should value his ability to shield others above these amulets and trinkets he'd been taught to respect.

But that wasn't what Mel had in mind. She giggled, and playfully smacked his arm.

"No, silly. That." Mel reached up and pulled at the dog tags Hunter perpetually wore, until they slipped out of his shirt and were visible for all to see.

Hunter wrapped his hand around the familiar piece and raised it for inspection. Nope, they looked the same as they always had; a soldier's old dog tags that Hunter had worn for as long as he could remember. "Why do you say that Mel?"

Mel's eyes narrowed as she tried to work out why her friend George didn't understand his own history. "They belonged to your grandfather, when he was a young man, fighting a world war."

"Really?" Hunter mumbled. He wondered how it could be that he had never known this; had never asked. He had always assumed that it was just one of many protective amulets owned by the Astleys.

"Uh-huh, and then his witchy lover put her super-strong spell on it. She was super-strong, after all, sweet little Sara."

When Mel stopped speaking, Hunter was aware how deathly quiet it was in the library. No one spoke and no one moved.

Hunter coughed, trying to find his voice. "Sara? As in Sara Murray?"

Mel brightened up at his recognition. "Oh, so you know her? She is lovely. We tried to send her a familiar, but she'd popped her clogs before she had chance to meet it."

Hunter stood silently, staring out unseeingly. Then he snapped back to attention and shook his head.

"That's crazy." He snapped.

Feeling a familiar wave of anger and frustration threaten to rise up, Hunter turned and left the room.

Everyone else was left in awkwardness, sharing embarrassed glances with one another that they should have witnessed this.

Without a real destination in mind, Hunter ended up on the first-floor corridor. He paced up and down it a couple of times, the familiar portraits of his ancestors silent in the background.

Eventually he stopped at his grandfather's. It was the second to last, with the final one belonging to Hunter's father, "Young" George Astley. Beyond that was a space that always hinted that a portrait of Hunter would join the others, but he had always put it off.

He took a deep breath and looked up at his grandfather's likeness. Hunter hardly remembered him from real life, he'd died when Hunter was a young boy. But from what Hunter gathered, Old George was an unremarkably average man (when one ignored the witch-hunting occupation). People liked him, although he wasn't exceptionally outgoing. He was giving and charitable, without being overly kind. Old George had not married until he was in his forties; and by all accounts it was a pleasant marriage, with the production of a single son.

In fact, as far as Hunter could work out, the only remarkable thing that Old George did was to defeat a Shadow Witch. And now thanks to Mel, even that was in question.

Hunter sighed, his right hand moving instinctively to the dog tags at his chest. Had they really belonged to his grandfather? He looked up at the portrait of Old George. There was something at his neck, but it was hard to tell at this angle.

Hunter glanced guiltily down the corridor, then reached up and unhooked the painting, lifting it down from the wall. On closer inspection, the brush strokes only revealed a hint of grey tucked into Old George's shirt. It could be anything, and Hunter knew it was only his desire to see his dog tags that made his eyes depict and translate the image. He moved to return the painting, when something else caught his eye.

Hunter frowned. Now that the painting was no longer on the wall, he could see a rectangular shape carved into the plaster. Hunter put his grandfather's portrait down gently. Then he reached up and traced the groove,

Hunter shook his head and sighed. It couldn't be this obvious, could it?

He searched his pockets and pulled out his battered old pocketknife. He ran the blade through the groove and felt little resistance; then he twisted it until the small panel shifted and fell obediently into his hand.

Hunter looked down at the wedge of wood and plaster, then turned his attention back to the wall. Someone had made a nice little hidey-hole, only big enough for the book that was nestled within.

Hunter pulled it out; it was a notebook, looking very unimpressive with its unadorned navy cover. Hunter flicked through the pages that were filled with tight black handwriting that looked very familiar.

Hunter finally settled on the first page. It was clearly dated November 1948 in the top right corner.

"By the hand of George Astley V.

"It is three years since the death of the Shadow Witch, and I am finally fulfilling my promise to write down all of my dealings with Ms Sara Murray."

Hunter's heart beat faster. It was here. How long had he been looking for his grandfather's account of the 1940's Shadow, and mad Old George had hidden it in the bloody wall!

Hunter looked down the corridor, but all remained silent, no one had followed him here. He looked about for a nearby chair; and seeing none he sat down on the floor, his back against the wall and his knees propped up in front of him. Hunter opened the seventy-year-old notebook again.

## Chapter Twenty-four

*In the summer of 1939, I was seventeen years old, and the only son and heir of George Astley IV, the famed witch-hunter. My older sister Elizabeth is married and living a life away from the witch-hunting madness. She always was the sensible one. I felt that my life was always planned before me – I would follow my father, of course, and look after the Manor when my time came.*

*But that year was to upset everything. In summer, I met the most beautiful girl I had ever known. Although, perhaps less girl, and more grown woman. Sara Murray was twenty-one years of age, and the mother of a two-year-old daughter. She came to Little Hanting to stay with her uncle's family. 'So, the countryside could improve her health,' was the official story. But the village is small, and secrets are not easily kept, and shortly after her arrival it was widely known* that she had been sent because her parents could no longer bear the shame of a child born out of wedlock.

As you can imagine, my own parents discouraged all association with her, and forbade any romantic inclinations I might feel. Stuffy, antiquated pair that they are. Of course, it did not put me off from seeking her company. Over that summer we became good friends, and I discovered that Sara was not only beautiful, with her bright green eyes and rich brown hair; she was also smart and sweet and funny.

I confess that I was quite in love with her within a month of knowing her. For who could not love such a kind and honest lady. Indeed, several of the young men in the village sought to court her, despite her sins of the past. But she declined them gently, wishing for nothing more than friendship. And friendship I readily gave, rather than be cast out of her acquaintance.

Sara was always a very sensitive person, she became uneasy when foul weather arose, and would shake with fear at bad premonitions. She had an uncanny ability to see future events, although the visions often didn't make sense until it actually came to pass. I attributed it to mundane wiccan skills, because I could never sense a hint of magic around her.

That autumn she became worried to the point of being ill, but so did the rest of the country. It was no surprise when we fell back into war with Germany, tensions had been building for so long that it had been a question of 'when', not 'if'. It didn't alter life much in Little Hanting; we were too far from any city or place of interest.

*Personally, I was itching to help, but had to wait until the following summer to be old enough to volunteer. Sara begged me to wait another year, but she seemed resigned to the fact that I would go immediately. Her objections were so mild, that it was actually comforting – I was becoming so used to trusting her future sight – had she seen my death she would have tried harder.*

*I will not go into my time at war, this account is on one focus only, and I do not need to raise any more painful ghosts. It was a year until I returned home, and I arrived to find Little Hanting showing signs of war. Many homes had taken in children from London, and many of the women had joined together to manufacture uniforms on top of their daily chores.*

*When I met Sara, there was a little awkwardness after twelve months apart; but that soon melted, and we were close friends once more. I could tell that something was upsetting her, and after many attempts to distract me, pleading that it was trivial, Sara finally confessed that she felt something was coming. And it was coming for her. When I pressed for more information, she shook her head, swearing that was all she knew.*

*I only had a month's leave and was due to re-join my squadron. When I went to the train station, Sara came to say goodbye, her daughter Beth walking confidently next to her now. I made a big fuss of Beth, as always, and promised to bring something back for her. And to Sara, I wanted so desperately to tell her that I loved her, that I would come back to her. But her eyes willed me silent, we both already knew. I had to suffice with a polite kiss to her hand, and then boarded the train and was away.*

*I would be away longer this time. I spent a lot of time in Africa in 1942. Summer flew by without a break, as did autumn. Hallowe'en came around, not that the army celebrate such a random festival, but as a witch-hunter I always acknowledged it. I wondered if my father and other witch-hunters were kept busy back in Britain. The war had disrupted so much, even the witches were quiet this time last year. And of course, thinking of home always made me think of Sara, and little Beth. I had decided now that they would be my family, regardless of any scandal that might arise. The next time I was home I would ask Sara to be my wife.*

*And then I heard her voice. At first, I thought it just a fragment of a memory as I thought of her, but then it came again.*

*'George, help me.' It was as clear as though she were standing beside me. I looked about the tent to see if anyone else had heard a female voice, but only I was alert, no one moved from their books or broke their low conversations.*

"*I thought I must be going mad, but I heard her again, her voice worried and pleading, and somehow I knew it was real and that I had to get home immediately. Thankfully my superior is a member of the Malleus Maleficarum Council (senior in army rank, though from a lesser family of witch-hunters) and he readily accepted that urgent matters of witchcraft called me home – and oh how I would curse that my little lie would become true.*

*The five days it took me to get home were the longest of my life. I took connecting cargo flights, followed by a bus to London, before finally a train that would take me within five miles of Little Hanting. I don't think I spoke one more word than necessary on the whole trip, only fretted over what I might find.*

*I arrived in early evening and went directly to Sara's house. It seemed deserted and lacking all life, but a couple of minutes after I knocked, the door opened to reveal a very pale Sara. Her green eyes locked onto me, the panic in them clear. She led me into the lounge, where Beth sat by the fire, quietly reading a new picture book.*

*As soon as we sat down, Sara's emotions overcame her, and tears fell as she retold all that had happened of late. On Hallowe'en, she had been in the house alone with Beth, making up scary stories, and fashioning a witch's cloak for her daughter from spare clothes, nothing unusual at all. And then she was suddenly speared by pain and ambushed by deafening voices chanting. Sara collapsed, and when she came to, she was aware of Beth sitting next to her, sobbing. Sara comforted her child, reassuring her daughter that she was fine, when she noticed that the fire and the lights had gone out. But even as she thought of relighting them, the fire in the grate burst into life.*

*Sara was always so logical; I can well believe she tried to find other reasons and causes. But the truth made itself clear when she merely thought of changing the blown lightbulb, and she found herself in the kitchen. Beth's scream at the* mother's disappearance drew Sara's attention back to the living room, and with her attention her physical self followed. In a moment she was kneeling, cuddling and reassuring her daughter once more.

And then she called for me, sent her fear across continents, and bade me return. Which I did dutifully.

After telling her story, she began to shake, and I held her until the panic left her. We both knew what she had become – I could almost see the magic roll off her; and Sara had heard enough of my tales of witches to be beyond any doubt herself. The big question was how this had occurred, and more importantly what we were going to do about it.

Thankfully my parents were in Scotland, making an annual visit to family there; with my father out of the way there was not another witch-hunter for miles around, so Sara was safe from the immediate threat of detection. Long-term solutions evaded me. I mentioned that we could bind her powers, like any other witch. Sara readily agreed, but when I placed the amulet on her skin it swelled with her energy and shattered. I had never seen such power before. And I had a feeling that we would not be able to contain it 'til we knew how it had formed.

I interrogated Sara over her history, her family. I broke down every tiny detail of what had happened lately and found nothing. There was nothing to explain what had happened to her. We spent hours trawling through my family's library – set up by my grandfather, it is considered the vastest in the country. It was here that one term kept cropping up when we researched powerful witches - the Shadow Witch. Magic without limits. It had been over five hundred years since the last one, for all we knew Sara was her descendent. But we were no closer to knowing why it had suddenly awoken now.

And then one day we had company. A small coven of three witches had felt Sara's simmering power from across the county and had come to Astley Manor to seek it. They came right up to the door, and I could feel their magic railing against the protective amulets there. But no defence is impenetrable, and I knew it was only a matter of time before they broke through. I ordered Sara to stay hidden and went out to meet them.

They did not back down when confronted with a witch-hunter, and swiftly one died at my hand. But the other two bore down on me fiercely, when suddenly they were blown back by a wave of power I was beginning to recognise. Shaking, I turned to see Sara standing at the open door, an unfamiliar and furious look on her face. But she snapped out of her trance and was nervous and worried once more; and guilt entered her green eyes as I checked the witches and found them dead. One had a broken neck from their fall, the other looked as though a heart attack had claimed them.

Sara was highly distressed that she had brought danger to my home, and swore that no witch would ever set foot on my land again. I felt her power rise up and ripple out, although it would not be until much later that I would understand what she had done.

*Sara became very unsettled and insisted on leaving Little Hanting. I tried to talk her into staying, even moving into Astley Manor. I tried to persuade her that I could talk my father round to trusting her, but even as I said it, I knew I would struggle, my father was very much of the old code of witch-hunters. Perhaps it was wise she left, that we kept this secret between the two of us only. I found her a cottage in the unspoilt countryside to the North, out of range of any witch-hunter.*

*While she settled into her new home, my research was going nowhere, and in the end, I had to approach the MMC and use their connections to dig further on what might have caused this change in Sara. It was more rumour than fact that the Nazis had been experimenting with the occult. It was so slight, but the only lead I had. Germany was probably the least safe place to be right now, but if I waited, I feared the trail would go cold, or be destroyed completely by this terrible war.*

*I went to visit Sara before I left for the continent. She was less than happy about the danger I was putting myself in for her. While I was there, she begged to be able to do one small thing – she took my dog tags, and I could feel the familiar build of her magic. The dog tags glowed for a moment, before returning to their unimpressive state. She gave them back to me, explaining that they would protect me. I was not fully convinced, but I would accept anything from her.*

*I returned to my post in North Africa. I started my journey from there, a journey that would take over a year. It* was a frustratingly slow process, but they were dangerous and difficult times. Eventually in the summer of 1944 I arrived in Berlin. We had been told that we had won the battle, but all I saw when I arrived was destruction. Berlin echoed London in the Blitz, the survivors moving around quietly, their faces drawn. Apart from the children, somehow children can find joy, however slight.

I cautiously approached the German MMC under the guise of a German soldier that wished to join them as a 1st gen. The MMC is an establishment over five hundred years old and has withstood more wars and disasters than I'd care to mention but has always maintained a detachment and its own strict code. But I was not going to risk revealing who I really was – I might put my trust in the MMC, but I could not forget the years our countries had spent fighting.

They accepted me with relative ease – I believe they were struggling to recruit young men with the cost of war to young lives. The British MMC had even started to accept women (as long as they were the daughter of a witch-hunter and naturally gifted) to swell their ranks, something previously rare and strongly dissuaded.

The German MMC put me with a 3rd gen, Herr Magnus Becholsteim, who was ten years my senior. Magnus was a good enough man, and under other circumstances I believe we could have been friends. He was very proud of his skills and for the month I was with him I had to force myself to be slow and clumsy in everything I did, knowing as I did so that I could easily outmatch him and most of the witch-hunters

Germany had to offer. By day we would 'train' and revise over old cases; by night we would relax and over a few drinks Magnus would regale me with stories of his great and daring deeds. I took them with a pinch of salt, but it was during these quiet evenings that I finally learnt a little more.

Magnus was telling me about his time training when he was younger, at the feet of the Herr Ancles (who I will confirm was known worldwide as one of the best in our era), and Magnus spoke of a fellow apprentice Herr Hartmann, a 2nd gen that Magnus took great joy in teasing with his own, greater inborn skills. I asked out of politeness rather than true interest, if they still kept in touch, but Magnus' reply intrigued me.

He initially shrugged and said that Hartmann ended up transferring his loyalties from the MMC to the Nazi Party and fell in with a bad crowd. Sensing that he had my interest in this bit of scandal he smirked over his brandy glass and gave me the whole story. I shall not waste time and paper with his possibly exaggerated tale, but give a brief account:

After joining the Nazi Party, Hartmann became convinced that the MMC could contribute more, their knowledge and their artefacts. The MMC was not going to be persuaded to take sides in a war, but Hartmann ended up being poached by a Herr Richter to join a faction that experimented with the occult. Magnus couldn't confirm what Hartmann might have achieved, but there were strong rumours of mass sacrifices and the co-operation of a certain witch (later caught and executed – Herr Brawn).

*Magnus was vague about having any idea where Hartmann was at present, but I was convinced that the German MMC was as stringent as we were about keeping track of potential witch-hunters, regardless of whether they'd turned their back on the MMC, or not.*

*It took two more weeks of snooping through the MMC's files, while pretending I was doing the dull background and paperwork for my trainer, but I finally found the last known location of Hartmann. I told Magnus that my mother had fallen ill, and that I needed to return home, giving me a week at least before anyone became suspicious enough to track me.*

*I set off to the North of Germany, to find Hartmann where he worked in a secure compound. I followed him one evening to his civilian home and I waited for morning, and when he left for work, I broke into his house. I spent that day meticulously going through everything.*

*I found a few letters in his desk from Braun and Richter, pertaining to past and present experiments. I found a drawer marked 'Failures', which held several artefacts. But no clear answer. So, I waited for Hartmann to return home.*

*As soon as he walked through the door, I grappled with him. I am not proud to say that the man had to be beat into submission. I questioned him over the mass sacrifices and his work around Hallowe'en 1942. He wasn't very forthcoming with words, but his eyes moved to the drawer I had searched earlier. With a little more persuasion, he confessed about the dagger, which he had smuggled from the MMC in Berlin, that his colleague Braun swore held immeasurable power.*

They just had to find the right witch and the correct volume of sacrifices. He told me that at one Hallowe'en it changed. They broke the spell binding the dagger, and nothing happened. They were just left with an old, blunt dagger with no special qualities. He claimed that despite the disappointment, it was not unusual for their experiments to fail, and he always took his failures home as a memento and reminder.

I took the dagger, and a handful of his letters. For a moment I thought that I should kill him, but he was an outcast of the MMC, and knew nothing of my identity; and I had seen enough death to last a lifetime. I knocked him unconscious and left immediately.

My journey back to England was frustratingly slow, when I knew I had completed my goal and longed to see Sara again. I returned by Christmas 1944, and went straight to Sara's cottage. With her uncanny foresight she knew that I was coming and had dinner almost done by the time I arrived.

I slept for a day, exhausted and finally safe enough to relax for the first time in nearly two years. When I was conscious and finally refreshed, I took about a week to relay everything I had seen and done. There was a lot to tell, and my story had to wait for when Beth was at school or asleep. She had grown so much since I last saw her, but Beth was still excited to see me and seldom left my side.

I stayed with them for Christmas and the New Year, then finally started to plan to head back to Astley Manor to further research the dagger. Sara came to my room to help me pack, and curiously picked the dagger up. I remember her face as she looked at it – confusion and contemplation written across her pretty features.

"You realise there's writing here." She said, wondering why I had not mentioned it to her before, I looked over at the blade that I had carried for months, but saw the same dull, plain metal with no inscriptions. But Sara went on to insist there was 'By Her Hand Only' written there.

I went home, this thought plaguing me. I ignored the fuss my parents made at my return and went right back to researching answers. The only thing I found was an old and questionable bit of information that I was not willing to share. But in the end, I didn't have to. Sara sent me a message to see her immediately.

I dutifully set off for her cottage once more and had scarcely entered the door when she revealed that she had been having vivid dreams ever since touching the dagger. She started to tell me about them, and my heart dropped, they echoed precisely what I had learnt. That the last Shadow Witch had been infatuated with a mortal man, who was killed by her fellow witches. She had grown so distressed over what she had created that she had killed herself rather than subject the world to her power any longer.

Sara swore that she would do the same. That was the first and only time we ever argued, voices raised and Sara looking fiercely angry. She, trying to destroy her life, and I trying to save it. Sara tried to make me understand how tense and frightening her life was, trying to hide from witches and hunters alike. How even Beth was afraid of her when strange things happened. And I- I could not give up on the woman I loved when I had been to hell and back to save her.

I stormed out that day, furious that she should take the easy way out. And how I regret that was the last time I saw her.

A couple of days later, the dagger was missing from its drawer, and in its place a note.

'Dear George,

By the time you read this, it shall be too late to stop me, I know what has to be done.

Please know that I have always loved you, and I don't know how I would have gotten through these last few years without you. How I wish things were different and the curse had fallen on any but me. But it has, and I can't let the temptation of the power I could wield push this damaged world any closer to destruction.

As for Beth, I hope she remembers that I love her, but my last use of magic will be that she and her children will be bound from powers themselves. I would not wish them to be persecuted by the MMC.

I am sorry to rip her from your life also, but I think she is safer where none know her, or me. A distant cousin with whom I am friendly is to adopt her. There are so many parentless children after this war, it will not be suspicious.

There is one thing I ask: something tells me that the Shadow will rise again, and I see it involving the Astley family once more. They will need to know the truth, when the *time is right – will you write an honest account of all that has occurred?*

*With all my heart,*

*Sara*

## Chapter Twenty-five

Hunter held the original letter that had been folded and inserted in the pages of the small notebook. The writing was delicate and very different to the hand that had gone before it. He looked back at the book and flicked through the rest of the pages but found nothing.

Old George must have considered his story told, either that or he didn't have the will to go on. It put his life in a different perspective. Hunter had thought him relatively dull, except for his one shining achievement of killing a Shadow Witch. An achievement that was now overturned. No wonder he hadn't liked talking about it; Hunter had thought he was just being modest.

Hunter closed the book and turned it over in his hands, brushing off the last of the dust from the navy covers.

"Hunter?"

Hunter sighed as he heard his name in that cautious tone everyone seemed to adopt around him.

"Hunter, we were worried where you got to." Kristen said, walking up to him. "Well, we were all worried, but then Mel started teaching Adam Gaelic or something, so they're happy."

Hunter looked up at Kristen, dragging himself firmly back into the present.

"Did you find something?" Kristen asked, looking at the notebook she was sure Hunter did not have before.

Hunter held up the offending article.

Kristen nodded, her eyes narrowing at the very plain little book in his hands, wondering if that was the source of Hunter's current weirdness.

"And?" She prompted.

Hunter took a deep breath as he thought over what he had learnt, of Old George and everything he had gone through for the woman he loved, he thought of the history and connection that had been hidden...

"It tells of how to kill a Shadow Witch." Hunter finally replied in a low voice. He eventually pushed himself up off the floor and stood on numb legs. He looked at the offending item in his hands, weighing his options. He didn't want to share what he'd read, it felt personal; but he also didn't want to seem like he was keeping secrets from the people that were risking everything to follow him. With a sigh, Hunter handed

Kristen the book, then without a word he started to walk back down the corridor.

Kristen looked at him, her blue eyes wide with curiosity. She looked down at the book that had been shoved into her hands, and then flicked through a few of the pages, scanning what was written.

"Hunter, wait!" She called, jogging to catch up with him, wanting to keep him on his own for a little longer. She grabbed his arm, yanking to insist that he stay. "So... Mel was telling the truth? About your grandfather and the witch?"

Hunter stopped, reluctant to meet Kristen's eye, he shrugged. "Isn't she always telling the truth?"

Kristen paused for a moment. "Good point."

Hunter used her hesitation to pull away again.

"Hunter... do you want to talk about it?" Kristen asked, uncertain.

Hunter stood still, hovering between what he wanted to say, and what was polite to say. He took a deep breath and turned back to Kristen, a half-attempt of a bitter smile on his lips. "Talk about what? That it's in my genes to fall in love with a Shadow Witch? Or that my whole family's history is a lie; and our right to persecute witches suddenly questionable? No, I don't want to talk."

Kristen blushed at Hunter's little outburst, feeling embarrassed on his behalf. And feeling uncomfortable at the prospect of bringing up a certain something. "So, if they were lovers, does that mean you're related to… um, Sophie?"

Hunter looked at her sharply, surprised to hear anyone use Sophie's name; and also, a little disgusted at the insinuation.

"No!" He snapped. "Old George loved Sara, but they were nothing more than friends. Sara had a daughter with another man before they met."

"Alright." Kristen replied calmly, tapping her long nails against the hard cover of the notebook, trying to think of a polite way out. "I'll… um, add this to the rest of our sources."

Kristen pushed past Hunter and hurried away, back to the library.

## Chapter Twenty-six

Later that evening, when everyone else had retired to their rooms, Hunter sat alone in the drawing room. Despite it being summer, a fire crackled in the grate, for extra light and to try and push back the interminable chill of this big old house. Hunter nursed a glass tumbler of whisky – he couldn't remember the last time he'd had whisky, being on the run had left no time for a drink, and the Donili had favoured wine only. To be honest, he was surprised that his personal stock hadn't been raided in his absence.

He took a sip of the amber liquid and gazed into the flames of the fire. He thought again over what he had learnt today, and his mood didn't improve. He felt like his grandfather had lied to him, betrayed him. Old George had led Hunter and everyone else to believe that he had killed a serious threat. The truth was just depressing.

Hunter sighed and silently cursed Old George and Sara. By the sounds of it, they were doing what was right at the time. But surely this was not the outcome they had wanted. For such a smart woman with allegedly accurate foresight, Sara Murray had done a shite job in saving the world from the power of a Shadow. She'd only managed to postpone it for seventy years. And she'd foolishly allowed her death to spark a fierce desire for revenge in her great-granddaughter.

Hunter wondered what Sophie would make of all this. She would probably think that he was making it all up for some hidden reason.

Hunter heard the soft pad of bare feet in the hallway. He glanced up briefly to see Kristen opening the door, then returned to his comfortable haze of whisky and thoughts.

"Is this for anyone?" Kristen asked, nodding to the bottle on the table next to him. Not waiting for an answer, she poured herself a generous portion.

Kristen tried a couple of times to strike up light conversation – on the history of the house, or Mel's newest piece of randomness. But Hunter was proving an unwilling companion, his answers short and uninterested. Eventually things dissolved into silence, both of them drinking wordlessly.

The small carriage clock on the mantelpiece chimed eleven times, claiming Kristen's attention.

"Well, I suppose I better head upstairs." She announced, and then knocked back the rest of her whisky. Kristen looked at Hunter, her eyes bright. "Care to join me?"

Hunter looked up at Kristen. Her proposition came as no surprise. And of course, he would politely turn her down. He should turn her down.

Hunter didn't reply immediately, instead his eyes lingered on the young woman in front of him. He couldn't deny that she was attractive, her features delicate, but far from weak; her blonde hair falling in soft waves past her shoulders. His eyes travelled down, appreciating the simple t-shirt and jeans that showed off her womanly curves and narrow waist.

Noticing Hunter's new focus, Kristen opened her mouth to come out with some witty barb, but then she thought better of it. She set down her empty glass, then removed Hunter's from his hand. The faint chink of the glass being set down on the table was the only sound.

Kristen felt a familiar lick of desire, along with an unfamiliar tension that rose through her as she moved closer and wordlessly straddled Hunter's lap.

Hunter watched her careful and precise movements. He breathed deep as her scent enveloped him, and his hand came up to catch the back of her neck and pull her into a desperate kiss. Kristen's heart began to race, as she tasted the whisky on his warm mouth. She kissed back hungrily, her teeth grazing against his lower lip.

When they eventually pulled apart, their eyes met, equally dilated with passion. Hunter felt his own pulse demanding more, and he watched Kristen as she gave a mischievous half-smile.

Kristen pulled her t-shirt up and over her head, revealing the pale, toned body that Hunter had occasionally speculated about. A black bra stood out against her milky skin, and her curves were emphasised. Her breasts rose and fell with her quick, shallow breathing. Kristen leant down and caught his lips again, moaning into the kiss as Hunter's hands dug firmly into her thighs, pulling her closer.

"Wait." Hunter breathed, then spoke stronger. "Stop."

Kristen froze. That hadn't been what she had been waiting to hear. She caught Hunter's eye. "Seriously?"

"We shouldn't do this. It's neither the time nor place." Hunter muttered, pushing the semi-naked girl off his lap so he could stand up.

"This is exactly the time and place – we live in dangerous times; can you promise we'll still be safe tomorrow? And you can't go back to pretending you don't want me." Kristen snapped.

Seeing that Hunter wasn't going to reply, and even less likely to reignite the mood, Kristen silently swore and reached for her discarded top. She pulled it back on, embarrassed that she had to do so in this manner.

Her eyes flashed dangerously in Hunter's direction. "Did you forget how to use your dick in that monastery? Or is it still her? You know it's pretty twisted if you're still in love with her."

Hunter took a deep breath, and tried to argue, to deny it, but the words died in his throat.

"That's it, isn't it?" Kristen asked, her voice and her sweet blue eyes filling with pain. "She should mean nothing to you. You had what – a fling for a few months, *years* ago. Get over it."

"I wouldn't expect you to understand." Hunter replied, smoothing down his appearance, and careful not to catch her eye.

But Kristen was determined to get his attention one last time. She walked straight up to him, her fierce gaze meeting his.

"Just remember Hunter, that whatever you *think* you feel for her, we will fight, and we will kill her. Just as she will strive to kill you." And with that, she turned on her heel and left.

Hunter watched her go and continued to stand silently while he listened to her light steps up the staircase and across the landing. When he was confident that Kristen was in her room, he finally moved.

Hunter only thought of his warm bed now but made a stop by Adam's room. It was the first time the boy had slept alone since he had been kidnapped. Having always shared a room with either Hunter, or Molly.

Hunter paused at Adam's door. Upon hearing nothing, he quietly opened it, letting in a stream of faint light. Hunter felt a vibration, similar to magic, but too faint to make out. He frowned but was suddenly distracted by his stirring son.

Adam rolled over, and seeing someone in his doorway, he sat bolt upright. "Daddy?"

"Yes, it's me." Hunter replied gently. "Were you having a bad dream?"

Adam rubbed his eyes and didn't even try to hide his yawn. "No. You woke Incy." His little voice sounded surprisingly accusing.

"Sorry, I'll not do it again." Hunter replied, confused by the random comment, and thinking that he should perhaps limit Mel's influence. "Go back to sleep, Adam."

Hunter watched as his young son obediently lay down, cuddling close an old bear Mrs Astley had dug out. Hunter smiled briefly, recognising the teddy from his own childhood. Trying not to make a sound, Hunter gently closed the door, and made his way to his own bed.

## Chapter Twenty-seven

The next morning Hunter woke up disorientated. He lay still, his eyes flicking from the high ceiling, to the long dark drapes, and the antique furniture. He'd not slept in this room for years, but it hadn't changed. It all echoed back to a time when things had been normal – well, more normal.

Hunter wished he could freeze things now, something telling him that from here on, things would only get worse. But he could already hear the rest of the house stirring, and reluctantly got up. Hunter winced at the whisky hangover that casually reminded him that his body was out of practice imbibing his old levels of alcohol.

When he made his way downstairs, the smell of fresh coffee was already wafting out of the kitchen – and thankfully Jack had gotten to the task of producing drinkable coffee, before Mrs Astley could delight them with another pot of tar.

Hunter didn't say much to the motley bunch that crowded into the kitchen. Discussing their next step over breakfast, while still half asleep was not the best plan. But finally, after his second cup of coffee, Hunter called for his team's attention. His team – it felt strange ever acknowledging it again. He took a deep breath and pushed back the memories of sitting in this kitchen with James, Maria, Ian and Alannah. Even Sophie once upon a time. Now was not the time for emotions or weakness.

"We've got a lot of work to do. We know how to kill the Shadow Witch, which is a big step in the right direction, but it won't win us this war. The whole world is at war with the witchkind. Oh, I know Britain will bear the brunt of it, being the home of the Shadow Witch and her Council, and they may crumble without her. But we have the rest of the world to contend with.

"We need to co-ordinate with our foreign allies, with other witch-hunters, and even witches like Laura Kuhn, if any exist." Hunter broke off, hardly believing what he was suggesting: an alliance with witches. Padre would be so proud that this stubborn Astley was finally opening his mind to the possibility of good witches. "So, we need to get Marcus, and any other Donili I can persuade to help with transport.

"And… we're going to America. Five years ago, the witches used a machine to bring down civilisation. Let's see if we can restore it." Hunter tried to sound more convincing than he felt, and his gaze finally drifted to Miss Davies.

Kristen looked a little nonplussed at his attention. "I hope you're not waiting for me to drop critical information here, Hunter. I'm from New York; I only ever went to D.C. on a school trip in eighth grade. And I was never part of their MMC."

Hunter waited for her to finish, then shrugged. "Ok… does that mean that you don't want to go?"

Kristen opened her mouth to retort, then closed it again, her eyes narrowing at him in a silent warning instead.

"Thought as much." Hunter muttered, choosing to ignore her look.

Jack glanced between the two witch-hunters, suspicious at their sudden hostility.

Hunter sighed and suggested that they should inventory and pack everything they had found, so they could take it back to the MMC at a moment's notice. He also asked that they start making a list of potential allies while Hunter sought the Donili.

The chairs scraped back as everyone rose, ready to leave their impromptu meeting in the kitchen. Poor Shaun was nominated to clean up, and everybody else made a quick exit.

Jack stood in the hallway beside Hunter. The older man looked questioningly to his 'leader'. "What if the Abate refuses to help - are you willing to fracture the Donili?"

Hunter shrugged, not the most persuasive argument. It had already crossed his mind many times over the last two years that, if he asked for help and the Abate denied him, what path was there for him to take? Could he betray the man that had trained him; to whom he had sworn not to force his views on others? There was no satisfactory outcome, and Hunter felt a knot of anxiety that the time had come to find out.

"I only give the monks the option to help us. It is on them to take it." Hunter finally said, not entirely convinced himself.

"And, ah, what's happening with you and Kristen?" Jack asked, nodding towards the library where Miss Davies had disappeared. "Things looked a little tense."

Hunter grimaced. He hardly knew Jack and wasn't about to unload his personal grievances on him. But he must have looked somewhat embarrassed because Jack suddenly smirked.

"Look Jack, it's..." Hunter began, but trailed off, having no idea what he was going to say.

Jack put his hands up defensively. "Hey, forget I said anything." He gave a small chuckle and walked away.

## Chapter Twenty-eight

It was still morning when Hunter and Adam suddenly materialised in the Donili Village. The villagers barely spared them a glance, so used were they to the monks appearing.

Hunter walked up to the abbazia, Adam holding his hand tightly, looking around in wonder. Adam had wanted to come with his daddy and, as the trip was perfectly safe, Hunter had agreed immediately. To be honest, he didn't like the idea of leaving his son in his mother's care; and he was wary of encouraging any further influence from Mel.

The Italian sun was already hot on their backs as they walked up the hill to the Abbazia di Donili.

Hunter and Adam were unhindered as they entered the large gate and headed towards the Abate's rooms.

A few of the monks watched them curiously as they passed, but then returned to their daily tasks.

"Si, entrare." The Abate called after Hunter knocked.

Hunter smiled encouragingly at his son, then pushed the heavy door open.

The Abate was sat in the window seat, a heavy tome on his lap, and the window open to encourage the morning breeze.

"Ah, Signor Astley, another visit so soon, I am honoured." The old man said politely, though his blue eyes carried his questions.

"The honour is mine, padre." Hunter replied formally. "Things have, ah, progressed quickly since last we spoke."

The Abate gently closed his book and placed his hands upon it. "Go on."

"The witches are stirring and preparing for war. I can feel it; the fragile peace vibrates and is ready to splinter."

"Very poetic. Perhaps you have missed a calling in life." The Abate replied drily. "And what is your purpose in coming here?"

Hunter took a deep breath. "To ask what I once asked before: for help. I know that you will not fight or defend, but I beg you to consider helping us reach out to our allies. We have no way of communicating quickly with them – I can't be everywhere at once."

The Abate sat, silently considering this request, then finally nodded. "I will bring this up with the other monks in a meeting this afternoon. You may attend it, but you will not have permission to speak. Is there anything else you wish to tell me?"

Hunter hesitated, thinking over the discovery of his grandfather's notebook. He weighed up getting the Donili's help regarding the knife, but the cost of sharing Old George's attachment to the old Shadow Witch.

"There's a dagger we need to locate. It is from the time of the original Shadow Witch and has the engraving 'By Her Hand Only' on the blade." Hunter finally admitted, carefully leaving out the how and why they came to this information. "We believe it can bind the power of a Shadow. And kill one."

The Abate looked a little worried at the mention of a weapon against their enemy. One with the strength to bind her? Why did the old man suspect that Hunter was more likely to take the kill option?

"I vaguely recall a mention of this dagger in our historical archives... I shall have to find the particular parchment before I start misquoting it." The Abate replied. "Now, let me account you with all that we have discovered since you were last here."

The Abate glanced down to Adam, hesitating. "This is your son, I take it. Does he understand Italian?"

"Yes, this is Adam, padre. And he does not know Italian. Just English. And some German... and Celtic – it's a long story."

The Abate nodded. "Then I may speak freely without upsetting him. Biagio has been trawling through the libraries, day and night, in the hope to find some obscure information that may help you. There was a child mentioned, one from two enemies – and he shall become a leader in a united world."

Hunter tightened his grip on Adam's hand. He had previously voiced that Adam could prove important, but that had been to appease the Council so that he could keep his son safe. Hunter wasn't sure if he liked his speculations being confirmed. He'd much rather let Adam be normal and lead a safe and happy life.

"You never made mention of this before." Hunter said accusingly. He had never kept his son a secret from the monks, and it struck him as odd that they had never brought it up in the year and a half that he had lived here.

The Abate gave an understanding smile. "It is written in the scriptures of San Fiedro, who was known to see portents and futures with persuasive accuracy. But the Donili do not hold with the questionable prophecies and such. It was only Biagio who thought to look through the dusty, unpopular parchments."

Hunter gave a brief smile and felt a little relieved. He was not one to believe in prophecies, but he thought of his young son at his side. Young being the important word. How could a four-year-old boy become a leader? How would the years play out until he was old enough?

"He's just a kid. Does it say how?" Hunter asked weakly.

The Abate made a non-committal gesture. "It is vague. You may read the original source; they have been set aside for you."

Hunter looked down at Adam, who appeared bored by these two grown-ups who talked in unknown words. He didn't want his son in danger – he would make this a safer world for him first.

"Thank you, padre. We will head to the library now."

The Abate held up a hand to stop him. "There is something else."

Hunter looked to the old monk, the Abate's usually serene expression betrayed his concern.

"Something worse?" Hunter asked warily.

"Perhaps worse, but definitely more solid." The Abate glanced over to Adam, before looking to Hunter again. "It is about the demon you brought here..."

Hunter suddenly bristled at how the leader of the Donili was so prejudiced against Mel. "I told you before, she is here to help, and I am happy to accept it."

A rush of breath hissed through the Abate's clenched teeth. "Be careful how you say that. There are some powers that will twist an oath and hold it against you. But Signor Astley, do you know why she helps you?"

Hunter shook his head. "Mel is free to do as she pleases. From the sound of it, her boss wants more balance between the witches and the rest of the world, to reassert his control."

"And you believe that?" The Abate asked, then ploughed on without waiting for an answer. "I must ask, Signor, does she show interest in your son?"

"Well she…" Hunter broke off, thinking of the past few weeks. Mel had been spending time with him, Hunter. But he could not deny that the blonde girl was fascinated by Adam. Surely that was natural and innocent, as she seemed half a child herself. "She… why?"

The Abate sighed, relieved that his former pupil wasn't defending the demon blindly. When it came to this mysterious Mel, even the Donili were unsure what she was capable of.

"I have discussed her with the other elders, and our strongest theory is that she is here to claim Adam for her master. You say that Lucifer wants balance and control. What better control than to have the loyalty of an exceptionally powerful being from childhood?"

Hunter stood, dazed by what the Abate was proposing. "Mel wouldn't – she couldn't do that." He argued feebly.

"I hope you are right." The Abate replied gently.

Hunter turned down the wrong corridor as he went to the library, and had to turn back, a flash of embarrassment at his mistake. His mind was still firmly fixed on what the Abate had said. Demons, and prophecies, and greatness. It all seemed far-reaching. But then again, if someone had told him five years ago that the world would fall to ruin, and witch-hunters would use magic, he would have thought it equally unlikely.

When they finally made it to the library, Hunter received a warm welcome from Biagio. The young monk seemed as taken with Adam as everyone else, and immediately knelt down to introduce himself to the boy.

"Biagio, the Abate said you had set aside some articles for me." Hunter pressed straight to the point.

A look of concern crossed Biagio's face, but the monk covered it so quickly with his usual smile that Hunter wondered if he had been mistaken.

"Of course, I shall show you to my desk." Biagio replied, then looked back to Adam. "And while your father reads, perhaps you will teach me more English, giovane."

Hunter clapped Biagio on the back. "Teach him Italian instead, he has been learning every other language!"

Hunter was led over to a large table, where there were scrolls and papers as promised. After Adam and Biagio drifted away in the library to give him space, Hunter began to sort through what was before him. He could sense how old some of these scrolls were, and handled them slowly and carefully, despite his desire to pull out what he needed from them.

His head had started to ache from processing the handwriting and translating the various Italian dialects. Then something finally caught his attention – a scroll dictated by San Fiedro – that was the name of the seer that the Abate had mentioned, was it not?

Hunter read through the whole, confusing piece. San Fiedro had been a rambler, and most of this did not apply to Hunter. He went back and re-read the section that seemed related to them. And read it again to make sure that he had translated it correctly.

The information was hard to take in; the Abate had been careful in what he had left out!

Hunter sat there looking very dazed when Biagio returned to tell him it was time for dinner. Upon seeing his friend, Biagio could tell what he had read, and stood there silently, waiting for Hunter to say something.

Hunter forced the words out. "The child shall be an orphan of war." Hunter looked up to Biagio, hoping the monk would correct him. "I'm not supposed to survive this?"

"It could be translated differently. Metaphorically, instead of literally." Biagio translated. "Seers are notoriously misleading, hence why the Donili do not put stock in their words."

Hunter gave a bitter laugh at Biagio's attempt. "And yet the Abate thought it solid enough information for me to read."

Hunter sighed, glancing around the room. "Where is Adam?"

"Playing football with the younger monks." Biagio replied. "They shall meet us in the dinner hall."

Hunter tried to smile at the amusing image of the monks playing football (some of them were rather good) with his small son, but he found it hard to be even remotely happy right now.

Death did not scare him. Long ago he came to terms with the fact that he would die relatively young. It was part of being a witch-hunter. And there had been countless times when he had thought that his time had come, only for a last-minute rescue, or lucky distraction, to allow him one more day. He had proven that he was brave, time and again.

So why was this so hard to take? A random hint from a long-dead stranger?

Hunter sighed and decided to treat it with the same scepticism that the Donili bore it. He re-rolled the parchment and left it on the pile, then followed Biagio to dine with the others.

Dinner was a regular, pleasant affair, and was followed by the migration of the senior monks to the meeting room to the left of the great hall.

After leaving Adam once more in the care of Biagio, Hunter slipped into the back of the room. No one acknowledged his presence as he sat quietly as requested.

The Abate stood at the head of the long table and glanced briefly to Hunter before he began to speak.

"My brothers, we have observed over the last few years the increase of witch infringements, and we have done our duty defending Friuli. But there have been rumblings amongst our ranks that we should take a wider concern.

"There is evidence that the witches are gearing up for another war on those that refuse them. Signor Astley comes again to request our help. Now we must decide whether to break our oaths and restrictions; or sit idly by while many lives are lost."

The Abate looked around the group, meeting each monk's eyes, before settling his gaze on Hunter, with a ghost of a smile.

Hunter near held his breath, and the realisation of the Abate's words sent a shiver through him. The Abate was taking his side! His pulse began to race with the excitement of possibility now. But Hunter forced himself to remain passive on the surface as the rest of the monks had their say.

It was a blur of discussion with gentle debate. A couple of the oldest monks clung to the tradition and what was known, but the majority followed the Abate's lead after a few arguments that seemed more perfunctory than anything else.

The meeting quickly moved onto the practicalities, the Abate laid down the rules of those that could help – only adept students that were of age would be given the option.

After the main point of discussion, the Abate opened the floor to other topics, but the monks were too distracted and eager to get on with rallying their students to be able to think of anything else. Everyone departed, leaving the Abate and Hunter alone.

"Padre... how can I thank you?" Hunter asked, a grin splitting across his features.

The Abate dismissed his thanks with a wave of his hand. "It is necessary, Signor Astley. As much as I have come to care for you, it is not just for you that I do this. There are countless lives at risk – it would lie heavy with me if I stood by and watched and forced the others to stand by me."

The Abate walked down the room and sat closer to Hunter. "So, what are your plans?"

Hunter took a moment to work out the best way to explain. "Five years ago, the witches used a device to knock out technology. I'm going to find it and reverse it, to bring us back out of the dark ages. But it also occurred to me that if this device could cast a global spell, then it might also be used to block magic. If you could spare some Donili, we could experiment with-"

"No." The Abate interrupted. The old monk looked towards Hunter with calm curiosity.

Hunter was surprised how yet again the Abate could so firmly dismiss an idea without consideration. "But padre, just think – we could remove magic forever."

The Abate clasped his hands in front of him, and again thought how to get through to his passionate student.

"You have come to the conclusion that witches can choose to be good, or bad, no? When you win this war, as I believe you will, would you leave all witches defenceless? There will be many desires for revenge that will not end with battle – every man and woman who is called a witch will suffer. You will start a new witch craze. I say, let them keep their magic and allow them to govern themselves. I would also say, do not voice your plan with this device with anyone – others might think it worth the attempt." The Abate gave a knowing smile. "Not that you have ever heeded my advice before, Signor Astley."

Hunter sat quietly, taking this in.

"Now, you shall return home and turn plans into actions." The Abate added.

Hunter stood up to leave but paused. "Padre... I read the San Fiedro papers. Do you think there is any truth in them?"

The Abate smiled a little sadly. "I believe that if I were to prophesise a female pope it would happen. Not in my lifetime, or for a thousand years perhaps. But it will happen; will people say it is because a Donili monk predicted it so? San Fiedro could mean you, Sophie and Adam; or he could be predicting the reunion between North and South Korea. If you want to live a long and happy life with your son – go do that, prove it is nothing to do with you."

Hunter took a deep breath, trying to let the logic of the Abate's words reassure him.

"You are the most stubborn man I know, George." The Abate added with affection. "Personally, I truly believe that you would ignore the grim reaper himself, if it did not suit you. I believe that whatever happens will be your choice."

### Chapter Twenty-nine

Hunter and Kristen appeared in one of Washington's many parks, startling a young couple from their midnight tryst.

"I think we ruined someone's romantic ambitions." Kristen muttered bitterly.

Hunter ignored her comment, and watched the couple walk away, the guy casting suspicious glances back over his shoulder. But the guy eventually accepted that Hunter and Kristen must have always been there, and he had just been distracted – because people appearing out of nowhere was impossible.

Kristen glanced around their surroundings, as she straightened her cuffs and rechecked her weapons. "Welcome to America."

"I've been before." Hunter admitted, looking guilty. "When I was on the run a couple of years ago, I went everywhere. Which included breaking into Georgetown University."

Kristen looked at him, aghast. "You broke into a uni? Why?"

Hunter shrugged. "To see their research on witches and the Benandanti. Why would anyone else break in?"

"Most people would get a library card and go during opening hours."

Hunter sighed. "What a boring option."

He turned and led in towards the city. Even without lights, the Washington monument held its own, dark against the horizon, allowing Hunter to gain his bearings. He pulled out a DC roadmap, checking their best route from here.

Washington's MMC headquarters had been in the countryside when it had been built a couple of hundred years ago; but was surrounded by the inevitable expansion of suburbs. Hunter and Kristen jogged along, two inconspicuous figures in black.

"Remember the plan?" Hunter asked as they drew closer to their target.

Kristen looked at him sceptically. "'Keep quiet and don't get seen' is not a very professional plan. Did you have anything else to add?"

"We can't get any intel on what to expect, so we need to use the time-honoured technique of improvising. We find the device and destroy it." Hunter replied, thinking aloud.

Despite the dozen questions she wished to ask, Kristen just nodded. Her hands flitted from the protective charm at her neck, to check the knives and guns for the umpteenth time. "Let's get this over with, then."

Hunter stopped in the shadows, a hundred yards from the front gate of the old headquarters. There was a gatehouse, well-lit, with at least one guard. Beyond that, the drive leading to the house was wide and open, with nowhere to hide from any prying eyes.

Hunter wouldn't take that route unless there was no other option. He motioned silently for Kristen to follow him. He kept a safe distance and followed the perimeter round.

The grounds were extensive, and Hunter noticed the stately house disappearing behind the wall. He stopped, listening carefully. He couldn't hear anyone near. This would have to do.

After legging Kristen up, Hunter pulled himself over the wall. He quickly dropped into the darkness on the other side. They kept low as they made their way across the grounds to the big white stone building.

There was the low murmur of voices of the guards on duty. Hunter knelt in the shadow of the doorway and sent his mind out until he felt two others. They hesitated in their chat as they felt the presence of something, but before they could act upon their suspicions, Hunter pushed the desire to sleep deep into their conscious. Within a minute they had already settled into a deep and stable sleep.

"Neat trick." Kristen breathed into his ear.

"Are you impressed, Miss Davies?" Hunter asked as he unlocked the door, to reveal two slumped guards.

Kristen shrugged. "Maybe." She admitted as she pushed past Hunter, stepping over the inert bodies and slowly drew out her knife. The witch-hunter looked about warily.

"A lot of magic in this place. Can you find the right source?" She asked Hunter.

Hunter took a deep breath and concentrated again. He felt the same as Kristen, the oppressive wave of magic from many witches; but as he focussed, he could feel the different patterns, including one that was terribly familiar.

"This way." He murmured, nodding where the corridor led off to the right.

They moved slowly through the house, their senses stretching out as they moved deeper into enemy territory.

Kristen had moved in front but hesitated as she felt magic ahead. Hunter stopped beside her to feel the steady throb of power.

"The machine?" Kristen murmured warily, her blue eyes taking in the darkness before them.

Hunter let his senses range out, then shook his head. "No, a shield." He replied, his eyes following the shape of it.

Kristen looked on more blindly. She rummaged in her pocket to pull out a coin. Before Hunter could stop her, she tossed it down the corridor. The penny flashed as it flew unhindered through the air and clattered against the wooden floor.

"It's not a solid barrier." Kristen commented.

Hunter cast her a warning look. "What if that had set off an alarm?"

"I kinda wish it had – we could spend more time killing witches and less time sneaking around." Kristen checked her gun for the hundredth time, then moved hesitantly forward. She had only gone two steps when she stopped again.

"Hunter, I can't get through." She said, her voice rising slightly as the only hint of her stress. Kristen pressed her hand firmly against an invisible wall, frowning as it didn't shift, then pressed her shoulder against it and shoved with all her weight.

Hunter stepped up beside her, his hand raised. But he felt nothing and was able to step further down the corridor.

Kristen let out a disappointed sound.

"It appears the shield is selective. I'm guessing it blocks anyone without magic – witches can come and go as they please."

"That's great." Kristen snapped. "Can you get the blasted thing down and let me through?"

Hunter looked at the shield from this side; the rhythm of the magic had the same familiarity as that of the machine. "This is the work of the Shadow Witch. It could take hours to find a weakness – if there was even one to be found."

"You can't just leave me here." Kristen hissed.

"We don't have much choice. I'll destroy the machine and be back here before you know it." Hunter promised.

"You better be. I'm giving you fifteen minutes Hunter, then I won't be held responsible for my actions."

Hunter silently swore but seeing how futile it would be getting into an argument with Kristen right now, he set off further into the house. There was the steady thrum of power that led him on. The machine. Hunter and the rest of the British MMC knew so little about it, save that the Americans had been experimenting with what they had commandeered from witches, rather than storing or destroying it.

Hunter followed his senses to the bowels of the house. What had originally been built as extensive cellars had been converted into storage rooms by the American MMC. He moved past the shelves of tempting artefacts, and on towards the source of the pulsing power.

It didn't look impressive, a dark cabinet that came about waist high. Hunter felt along the wooden edges, looking for the opening. His hands spread over the pentagonal top, and prised it lose.

The inside shimmered silver and pearl. There were five mirrors on the inner panels, all reflecting a twisted glass block that hovered in the centre.

It was not quite the 'machine' that Hunter had been expecting. But he could scarce breathe from the thick waves of magic that emanated from such a simple thing. He stepped back to get a better view of it. A part of him had hoped there would simply be a plug to pull, or a switch to flip.

Hunter looked at the glass centre, he could read the rhythm of magic clearly – although the amplification was purely Sophie's work, the basis was someone else's. Something that could be changed, or broken.

Hunter's fingers drummed against the edge of the cabinet. He could change the function of the machine. Standing over it, here and now, he could see how easy it would be for him to alter the basics. It wouldn't be long before it pulsed out with anti-witch power that would leave the witches defenceless.

The thought had barely taken place, but Hunter could already feel the guilt weigh heavy upon him. He couldn't do that to individuals like Laura Kuhn and Bev Murphy. Damn the Donili for messing with his moral compass!

Before he could change his mind, Hunter grasped the glass. It felt surprisingly cold against his skin as he lifted it out of the mirrored case. He threw it to the ground and watched it shatter. The magic in the room immediately shrunk back.

Just as Hunter thought that felt a little too easy, a wave of power exploded out, knocking him off balance. Hunter scrambled back to his feet, his head pounding with the alarm that refused to stop.

Hunter retraced his steps, hurrying back out of the basement level, listening for the sound of alerted witches above the drone of the alarm.

Hunter jogged up the stairs and back along the landing.

"Kristen." He hissed, seeing no sign of the blasted woman.

At that moment a figure turned the corner at the far end of the corridor. The unknown woman froze in shock at the sight of the intruder, then she raised her hand. Hunter could feel offensive magic building up and pulled his shield around him.

Suddenly Kristen jumped out from the shadow of a doorway, her arm wrapping around the witch's neck and tightening. The witch struggled, her hands clawing at Kristen's sleeve, but eventually her eyes fluttered shut.

"You were supposed to keep out of trouble." Hunter snapped.

"Yeah, well you left me in a house overrun with witches." Kristen countered. She bent down to pick the unconscious witch up by the arms. "Help me put her with the other one."

Hunter stooped to pick up the witch's legs, and they lugged her towards the nearest broom closet.

Hunter looked down at the second slumped figure, a young male witch.

"You've been busy."

"I know, as I said-"

"I'm sorry." Hunter interrupted before she could start again. "But let's get out of here before all hell breaks loose."

"You should have thought of that before setting of that blasted alarm." Kristen snapped, but willingly followed Hunter as they made their way through the maze of corridors.

They made it all the way to the back door, when Hunter suddenly stopped, Kristen slamming into the back of him.

Three people blocked the way, one of them kneeling down to check the pulse of the two witches Hunter had knocked out earlier. They immediately locked onto the trespassers; Hunter could feel the build of magic as two of them prepared to cast. The third was apparently human and pulled out a gun instead.

Hunter reached for Kristen's hand, ready to blink them out of here; but the American had other ideas and pushed past him, barrelling towards the new enemy.

Hunter swore beneath his breath, pulling his shield up just in time to catch the opening spells of the witches. He felt the magic dissipate in the air but had no time to work out what game the witches were playing as he went for the gunman. He knocked the gun aside as a shot fired, mercifully wide; then twisted the man's arm until he dropped it.

Hunter looked coldly into the eyes of the weak human, disgusted that any person could choose to serve the witches that were intent of stamping down the world. But he was still human, and Hunter couldn't bring himself to kill him. A swift blow to the temple made the man crumple to the ground, unconscious, but alive.

Hunter turned to see Kristen dispatching the second witch.

"Don't you remember your training – hit the gunman first."

Kristen raised a brow. "Sorry, I was preoccupied."

Before he could make a retort, Kristen stepped away the bodies and out into the cool night air. She darted across the dark lawn, Hunter following close behind her. The house was really beginning to stir, each window quickly becoming lit.

He paused at the wall, listening for any out-lying guards; but everybody seemed to be converging on the house.

Realising that Kristen had already climbed the boundary wall and was ahead of him

Hunter followed Kristen as she ran back to the park, his 7th gen night-sight easily keeping track of her figure in the dark. He felt the adrenaline rush washing over him. It had been a success – one major advantage removed from the witches. Hunter again felt the regret that he couldn't do more to completely overturn it, but he had sworn a promise to the Donili.

Up ahead, Kristin shouted to hurry him up, as she ran on towards a still, silvery surface.

Hunter caught up to her as she reached the partially man-made lake, a lonely pier casting a shadow over it, and a lake house hunkered on its edge.

Kristen jumped up the porch steps and pushed open the door. The place was abandoned, everything of value stripped out long ago. Such a shame for a fine husk of a building.

"Now, why did we have to run all the way out here?" Hunter asked, hovering in the doorway.

"Sorry, adrenaline rush." Kristen said, her blush showing in the dark. "It was either run here, or… ahm. So, a friend told me about this place and I suddenly wanted to come see it."

Kristen pushed a lock of blonde hair behind her ear and looked about the immediate vicinity. "Not quite how he described it."

Hunter stepped into the bare room. "It's not the worst place I've seen."

So much of the world ruined – all manner of thugs and thieves taking advantage of the discord. But also, surprisingly, the same discord had given so many normal people the spark to step up and shine brighter as they defended their home, their neighbourhood, even their country.

Hunter walked up to Kristen, not thinking, only knowing that he had grown accustomed to being comforted by her presence. Perhaps it was because she was a very capable $6^{th}$ gen – he didn't have to worry about her, she could take care of herself. Or perhaps it was because she was a link to his past, the daughter of his mentor; although he never looked at Brian in the same way.

There was nothing wrong with putting a friendly hand on her shoulder, but Hunter frowned as Kristen winced away from his touch.

"You're hurt?" He voiced. "Why didn't you say?"

Kristen bit her lip. "It's nothing; a scratch. I'll patch it up when we get back."

"Nonsense, come outside so I can see it better." Hunter insisted.

Outside, the full moon was distant in the night sky, its faint light making out the clean shapes.

Hunter walked towards the lake, picking a spot to sit where they were free from shadows. He looked up expectantly to Kristen, then patted the ground beside him. "Sit down, let me see your shoulder."

Kristen hovered next to him, then obediently sat down, with her back to Hunter. She gingerly pulled her jumper over her head, revealing her pale skin and blood-stained tank top. "See, it's nothing."

Hunter tutted, looking over the gash across her shoulder blade. It wasn't deep and most the bleeding has already stopped, but Hunter was sure that didn't make it any less painful.

"Hold still." He murmured. Hunter lightly pressed his fingers about the wound, then closed his eyes and focussed on what the Donili had managed to teach him.

After a minute's silence, Kristen squirmed, trying to see over her shoulder. "What are you doing? I've bandages in my pack if you've forgotten them."

"Shush and sit still." Hunter repeated. "I'm knitting the wound closed."

"One of your tricks?" Kristen asked as she sat straight again.

Hunter sighed. "Yes, one of my tricks." He admitted quietly. Hunter concentrated again on her injury. It was not difficult, even for the relatively unskilled Hunter. He remembered the headaches and sickness he felt

726

when he had tried to heal worse wounds than this. Healing Kristen's gash caused no detrimental effect to himself.

Hunter opened his eyes, happy that the work was done. He went into his pack to find an antiseptic wipe, cleaning away the blood from her shoulder blade. The skin beneath was pink and tender, but no sign of the injury.

"Nifty trick, I'll have to remember it." Kristen said. She sighed with satisfaction and pulled her blonde hair out of the way of Hunter's gentle touch. "If I'd known this was all it would take to get some attention from you, I would have let a witch stab me earlier."

Hunter smiled at her comment, as he leant forward and kissed her bare shoulder, earning a gasp from Miss Davies.

"Y-you're not going to spoil the moment and say we're heading home now?" Kristen asked, a hint of hurt beneath her voice.

"Not just yet." Hunter murmured, pulling her closer.

## Chapter Thirty

"You're back, finally." Jack remarked, not hiding his relief. "How did it go? Were you successful?"

Hunter reluctantly let go of Kristen's hand and moved to sit down in the comfy seats by the fireplace.

"Yes, it worked out better than I could have hoped." Hunter stated, his eyes following Kristen as she sat across from him. A mischievous smirk crossed her lips, but the American didn't say a word.

Jack caught the look and glanced between the two, his suspicions raised.

"Brilliant." Shaun crowed. The young man immediately picked up the house phone. He put the receiver to his ear and his face dropped. "It's still not working."

Hunter shrugged. "Magic will no longer interfere with technology. But we have five years of disuse to contend with. It could take months, or even years to repair the deficit."

Shaun replaced the phone in its cradle and looked to Jack for support. "So, this won't help us in this war?"

Hunter ignored the confused look Kristen was trying to get across to him. "No, it likely will not. Unless the news of it can be used to put the witches off their stride."

"You need to think long-term, Shaun." Jack said in support of Hunter vocally, although he looked far from convinced.

Hunter sighed. "I'm absolutely knackered. I wanted to see my son before I crash. Where is Adam?"

Shaun snapped out of his daze of disappointment. "He and Mel are in Mrs Astley's quarters."

Hunter stopped in his movements. "I'm sorry, Mel is in my mother's rooms?"

"Um, yeah." Shaun confirmed. "Mrs Astley invited her after breakfast. I think she thinks Mel is a nanny."

Hunter swore beneath his breath and got to his feet; there were far too many things wrong in that picture.

Hunter made his way up the main staircase but stopped as he heard footsteps behind him. He turned to see Kristen catch up with him.

"Kristen?"

"Why did we do it, Hunter?" She asked, her blue eyes hard and demanding.

"Can you be a little more specific?"

Kristen blushed, but didn't drop her gaze. "Why did we destroy the witches' device now? Why not just wait for the war to be over?"

Hunter took a step down, coming closer to Kristen. He reached out and gently brushed his fingers against her waist, a crackle of electricity went between them and he wasn't about to deny it.

"You didn't enjoy Washington?" He asked in a low voice.

Kristen leant in closer, her eyes closing and her soft lips parting – but then she snapped out of it and batted Hunter's hand away.

"Don't try and distract me, Hunter. There's something you're not telling us."

"There's plenty I'm not telling you, I'm sure." Hunter replied wearily. "It may take months to start fixing even the basics, but the sooner we get the ball rolling the better."

Not to mention that Hunter couldn't guarantee that he would be around after the war to destroy the machine. The Donili's prophecy hung heavy above him, as much as he tried to logically deny it.

"Now, if you don't mind, I'm off to face my mother." Hunter added, moving up the staircase again. "You're welcome to come."

Hunter saw that doubt cloud Kristen's face from the very idea of being voluntarily in Mrs Astley's presence.

"No, I thought not." Hunter muttered beneath his breath, a little disappointed that he had to deal with his mother by himself.

As Hunter walked along the corridor to his mother's quarters, he could hear piano music drifting out, beautiful in its simplicity.

Hunter pushed the door open to see Mel sitting at his mother's gleaming Bösendorfer piano. Mrs Astley sat on the large leather settee, Adam beside her, a book open on his lap.

Mrs Astley looked calmly up at the interruption. "Oh George, you're back. Only gone for one night, this time?" The woman huffed. "You take after your father, swanning off and returning when it suits. Having a fine old time, I daresay."

Hunter had heard this too many times to let it wind him up. "I told you yesterday, mother, I went to Washington DC to destroy that American machine. We can bring back technology now."

"Why bother." Mrs Astley said dismissively. "The world is better without it."

Hunter didn't know whether to smile or groan. It was too much to expect any sort of praise or concern from his mother.

"Miss Myfanwy plays quite well." Mrs Astley commented, decidedly changing the topic of conversation. "But then, I always find that those with special needs have talent that surpasses the rest of us."

"Mother! Mel does not have special needs. She is…" Hunter broke off. What could he tell his mother, that Mel was a demon, a servant of Satan? And worse, that Mel found Mrs Astley scarier than her master?

"I do wish you would see people for what they are, George. No wonder that Sophie girl duped you." Mrs Astley remarked, glancing down at Adam, her gaze softening. She clearly didn't care what had gone wrong with her son and Sophie, when the outcome had given her a grandson.

Hunter felt distinctly nauseous. "Right I need to get some sleep. Adam, are you ok staying with Grandma Astley?"

Adam scrunched up his face. "But it's only lunch time, daddy!"

"I know, I know, I'm sorry." Hunter said quickly, some amusement slipping through the fatigue. "If you would like, I can ask Shaun to practise football with you again."

Adam sat thinking about it, pulling the big old book close about his chest. Hunter could see the familiar early edition of 'Winnie the Pooh' – obviously Mrs Astley was playing the doting grandmother.

"Later." Adam decided, opening his book again. "Night, dad."

## Chapter Thirty-one

That night, Hunter was in a deep and dreamless sleep when he was suddenly awoken by a flying child.

"Dad, dad! A monk is here!" Adam shouted, bouncing erratically on the bed, his bony knee hitting Hunter's stomach and making him groan.

Not happy with how slow his father was reacting, Adam grabbed the spare pillow and hit him as hard as his young arms could manage.

"I'm awake, I'm awake!" Hunter protested, pinning his son's arms down before the boy could take another swing.

"What time is it?" Hunter croaked, glancing at the curtain-covered windows. There was hardly any light coming through the gaps, so he guessed it was ridiculously early.

"Adam, why are you up this early?" Hunter asked, more out of exasperation than any real desire for an answer. "How did you know one of the monks had arrived – you were supposed to be in bed."

"Incy saw him in the living room, he woke me up and told me."

Hunter groaned. He was definitely restricting how much time Adam spent with Mel from now on. Something – some missing link, nagged at his subconscious, but Hunter wasn't awake enough to pay it attention.

"Right, how about an early breakfast?" Hunter threw his duvet over Adam's head and took a moment to pull on his slippers and dressing gown to keep away the chill that permeated through Astley Manor even in summer.

"Yes!" Came Adam's muffled reply, as he shuffled out of the duvet and off the bed. "Can I have Coco Pops? Jack found some and said I can have them."

Hunter and Adam made their way downstairs, the old house was dark and still sleeping. They stopped at the living room, which was illuminated by the crackling fire someone had helpfully lit. There, as Adam had promised, a familiar monk stood. Marcus was inspecting the bookshelf as he waited, his eyes drifting over the British classics.

"Marcus, you're here early." Hunter said pointedly.

"I did not want to miss you, Hunter." The monk said, looking a little sheepish. "I did not know your routine. But you did not have to get up, I wait."

"Adam told me you were here." Hunter explained. "C'mon, kitchen. Coffee."

Hunter yawned and led the way to the kitchen. Adam ran ahead and began rummaging in the cupboards, triumphantly pulling out a bright box of cereal.

Hunter went to get a bowl, but his son snatched it from him. "I can do it." Adam insisted.

Hunter smiled, reluctantly letting his son make his own breakfast, images of the potential mess the Coco Pops would make. He turned to build a fire in the aga and tried to get a match to light. Hunter heard Marcus chuckle behind him, and a fire sprung up in front of him, causing Hunter to fall back onto his arse.

"That's cheating." Hunter stated. "I never managed to learn that trick."

"Hmm, it is strange." Marcus replied, suddenly serious. "That you can shield an army, but you cannot light a fire."

"Yes, thanks – the senior monks enjoyed pointing that out." Hunter sighed at the hours spent in theory and practice as he tried and failed to learn something even the youngest monks could do; and the following, in-depth discussions about possible reasons and solutions. It had all made Hunter's head ache; he had never done well with finicky detail. That had always been James' job.

"At least I finally learnt how to make that hovering light." Hunter said defensively, to stop the natural progression of where his thoughts were leading.

"So, this is Adam." Marcus said as Hunter put a pot on the stove. "It is nice to meet you, signorino. I have heard a lot. Biagio ti ha insegnato italiano, sì?"

"Biagio!" Adam started through a mouthful of Coco Pops. "Abbiamo giocato a calico."

"Incredibile." Marcus glanced at Hunter. "Your son has a talent for languages."

Hunter handed a mug of hot coffee to his friend. That was an understatement, to be honest, it worried Hunter a little that his son picked up so much so easily. "Anyway, I thought you two had met earlier this morning? Adam was *supposed* to be in bed."

Marcus looked confused. "You are mistaken, Hunter. I see no one this morning."

"But he…" Hunter broke off, frowning. It was too early to work anything out. "What brings you here, Marcus?"

"The Abate wanted to send a message. I volunteered." Marcus replied, pulling a face as he took a sip of the bitter coffee. "He says well done with the… the… macchina."

"Sorry, it's the best we've got." Hunter mentioned, very much aware that he needed to restock his pantry. "Is the Abate and the Donili ready to spread the word?"

"They already do it, Hunter. My wife is with your MMC as we speak. Biagio has gone to Frau Kuhn. Luis to South Africa; Anna to America... The list is long, most of the monks have decided to help you."

"Marissa is with my MMC?" Hunter echoed, worried at the idea of sweet innocent Marissa dealing with General Dawkins. "Will she be safe? They won't confuse her for a witch; or view her in ill light because of the connection with me?"

"Marissa can take care of herself." Marcus said with a slow smile as he thought of his love. "We have agreed to meet at the Abbazia de Donili in one week to discuss the next step."

The talk drifted conversationally over life in Donili for the next hour or so. Adam, after his early and exciting start, was falling asleep where he sat, so Hunter picked him up and carried him to the living room, laying him on the settee.

Hunter had made a second round of coffee, and he and Marcus sat in amiable silence by the time the rest of the house stirred. Hunter always liked to hear footsteps and voices filling his house. The Manor, for all that it made him feel at home, could also make him feel cut off from the rest of the world.

Marcus flinched beside him, and Hunter looked up to see Mel enter the room. He could not blame the monk for feeling a tad uncomfortable with a demon around.

Then something clicked.

"Mel, can I speak with you outside?" Hunter said, his voice cold as he tried to keep his temper in check.

Hunter pushed past a dazed-looking Shaun and ignored Kristen as she shouted his name. Hunter threw open the front door and stalked out into the courtyard, the gravel crunching underfoot. Hunter squinted in the bright sun and ignored the beauty of the countryside around him.

Mel followed him, her plimsole-covered feet were feather light and making hardly any noise.

Hunter stopped in his tracks and turned to face her. Her blue eyes were wide, and she looked so innocent in her white summer dress. Hunter pushed aside that instinct to trust and protect her.

"Mel, what is Incy?" He snapped.

Mel looked bemused at Hunter's ignorance. "He's a spider, George."

"Is he a familiar?"

The world was silent, the wind stilled, and the morning chorus of birds quietened. A familiar. Hunter felt sick mentioning it.

The silence seemed to stretch on.

"Yes." Mel whispered.

738

"You gave my son a familiar!" Hunter roared, his calm breaking. "You gave my four-year-old son a fu-"

"Hunter!" Kristen shouted as she jogged over to them. She looked between Hunter and Mel, hardly believing that Hunter was losing his temper with her. "What the hell is going on?"

"Adam's pet spider is a familiar." Hunter said with disgust.

Kristen paused. "Have you given her chance to explain?"

"No, but-"

"Then don't be so damned hasty." Kristen turned to Mel. "Mel, why did you give Incy to Adam?"

"For protection." Mel said simply, watching as Hunter started to pace in front of her, the energy of his anger almost palpable.

"Is it dangerous?" Kristen asked, forcing herself to keep her attention on Mel. "Will it hurt Adam?"

Mel looked shocked that she would even ask. "No! Incy is there to protect and serve Adam."

Hunter just grunted and kept pacing.

Kristen put her hand on Mel's shoulder. "Mel, why don't you go have breakfast while I have a chat with Hunter."

After taking a moment to work out who Hunter was, Mel turned and went back to the house with all the appearance of a kicked puppy.

"Why are you defending her?" Hunter snapped after Mel had retreated.

"Uh, maybe because I don't need you losing it and accidently blowing something up. Plus, it would be pretty dumb to piss off a demon. And I'm sure it's not as bad as you're making out."

Hunter stopped his pacing and glared at Kristen. He hated that she had made two very good points; and one that was way off the mark.

"I suppose I shouldn't expect you to understand, Miss Davies. You were never educated; you couldn't know what it means."

Kristen nodded, her lips pursed, then reached out and slapped Hunter across the face hard enough to make his head snap back.

Hunter staggered back, surprised. "Ouch!" That was the hardest a woman had ever slapped him, but then again, he'd never been slapped by a 6th gen witch-hunter.

"Be glad that's all you're getting. I don't need you, or anyone, accusing me of being uneducated. I have a GPA of 4.0 and I have the benefit of not being brainwashed by your Malleus Maleficarum prejudices."

"You don't understand." Hunter forced himself to be reasonable. "A familiar is a devil-spawned creature that feeds off witches to survive."

Kristen rolled her eyes. "It's a symbiotic partnership – in return the witch gets a loyal servant. I have done the reading, Hunter."

Hunter swore beneath his breath and stalked away towards the expansive Astley grounds.

Kristen jogged to catch up with his longer strides. "What's really upsetting you Hunter? That Incy's a familiar? Because you've been perfectly fine and accepting that Mel's a demon. Or is it because it further points out that Adam's a witch!"

Hunter stopped. He didn't want Kristen to be right, but he couldn't deny the pang of guilt in his stomach.

Kristen walked round to face him, then stepped closer, her hands running up his muscled arms, her head resting on his chest. Hunter felt the warmth and comfort of her, it felt right.

Kristen tilted her head back to look at him. "There is no rulebook on what to expect where Adam is concerned. Just don't take it out on others." She rose onto her toes and pressed a gentle kiss to his lips.

Hunter responded by pulling her tighter against him. "I'll try. Can I rely on you to step in and distract me when it goes wrong?"

Kristen looked up at him, a blush colouring her cheeks. "I think I can handle that. Come on, let's get back inside, I want to catch up with Marcus."

Kristen slipped her hand into Hunter's and he let her lead him across the long grass. Hunter still wasn't happy, but the initial shock had passed. He wondered if there was any way of guaranteeing Mel was telling the truth, rather than relying on instinct.

As they came back to the front of the house, Hunter glanced warily at the living room windows and surreptitiously dropped Kristen's hand.

She immediately turned to give him a questioning look.

"Sorry. I'm not ready... for 'us' to be public." He explained weakly.

"Way to charm a girl, Hunter." Kristen snapped, her patience suddenly fraying. "And just so you know – most of them have already guessed."

Kristen turned in her heel and marched through the heavy front door, making it slam back on its hinges.

Hunter's old womanising ego savagely kicked him in the head. But it was too late to change how badly that had come out and he had enough to worry about without adding Kristen to the list.

As he walked into the living room, he saw that Adam was awake now. Probably due to the numerous adults gathered awkwardly, waiting for Hunter to return.

"Adam, come with me." Hunter said quietly, nodding to the corridor.

"It wasn't me!" He replied quickly; his big hazel eyes worried.

Hunter smiled. "Nothing's wrong. Just come on, it's secret."

The boy jumped down from the settee and pushed past Shaun to get to join his father.

Hunter didn't go far, leading his son to the empty library. He closed the door firmly behind him, then turned to face the boy.

"Adam, does Incy ever bite you?"

"Yes – but it doesn't hurt daddy!" Adam answered, looking very worried again. "You won't make me get rid of him, will you? Because he's mine. And Mel – Mel says it's normal."

Hunter took a deep breath, reminding himself to stay calm. He couldn't believe Mel would tell his son that; normal – how the hell did Mel know what was normal!

"Adam, show me where Incy bites you." Hunter requested.

Adam hesitated, then rolled up his trouser leg. "There." He pointed to the back of his right calf.

Hunter knelt down and ran his thumb over the area that Adam indicated. His flesh paled and flashed back pink where pressure was applied. Apart from one spot the size of a penny; it stayed pale and did not change colour, because there were no capillaries to do the job.

The witches' spot. The site on a witch's body where their familiar fed; reputed not to bleed; and one of the signs that medieval 'witch-prickers' used to identify and persecute witches. Hunter knew enough of the history and anatomy attached to the spot, and the truth was that Kristen was right – it was yet another reminder that his son was a witch.

"Daddy, I miss mummy." Adam said as his father's silence continued. "She'd let me keep Incy."

Hunter sighed in defeat. "You can keep the spider, Adam."

The boy sat quietly for a minute. "When's mummy coming?"

Hunter hesitated, it was not a conversation he wanted to get into, how could he tell a four-year-old that his mother was a baddie on the other side? He wondered how Sophie had managed up to now. Hunter had no proof, but his gut feeling told him that Sophie had never painted him as the bad guy in Adam's eyes.

"We'll see her soon, Adam. Soon." He finally answered, honestly enough.

## Chapter Thirty-two

Hunter tried to concentrate, but throughout his conversation with Marcus and for the rest of the day, his mind kept coming back to Mel. He felt unsettled that he had allowed this demon such unlimited access to his son. When he put it in such stark terms, Hunter could hardly believe it; he had been so quick to trust Mel. Despite every logic, and the warning from the abate, he had continued to accept that she was here to help.

By that evening, Hunter decided that he had to do something. He quietly asked Mel to join him in the library; as an afterthought, he asked Kristen to come too.

The little blonde demon walked into the library with her usual, skipping step, then turned to face Hunter with those big, curious blue eyes.

Hunter waited for Kristen to come in and perch on the nearest table. He closed the door and slowly turned back to Mel.

"Mel... you are my friend, yes?" He asked hesitantly.

"Of course, George." Mel replied, smiling at the easy question.

"I want to be your friend; I want to trust you. But I don't trust your boss." Hunter said, getting straight to the point.

Mel pouted at what she considered unnecessary worry. "Luci is only trying to-"

"Trying to help, yes, I know." Hunter cut in. "When we were in Donili, you said that you weren't supposed to help us. What were you supposed to do?"

Mel chewed her lip, swaying slightly where she stood. "I was supposed to watch. I was supposed to keep the witch-hunters safe until you came. I... I was supposed to stay unseen, but everyone was so nice. I hadn't had friends before."

"So, does that mean you don't have to do everything Lucifer says?" Hunter asked. "You can choose to disobey?"

Mel continued to look uncomfortable. "He doesn't control me. I won't be punished as long as everything happens as it should."

Hunter shivered at the very idea that he was playing into the hands of the devil. "What about Adam? What did Lucifer ask you to do for him?"

Mel blinked in surprise, thinking it obvious. "He asked me to give him a familiar."

"Is that everything?"

Mel was startled by the harshness of Hunter's voice. She nodded. "I am here for you George, not Adam."

Hunter glanced at Kristen, hoping that she would jump in if she thought he was being too harsh, but the American just gazed calmly towards the two of them.

"Mel, you said that you could read the truth. Really look at what your boss is doing and tell me that he isn't interested in Adam." Hunter insisted. "Tell me that there isn't a possibility that he will try and claim Adam."

Mel looked away, her unease growing. When she turned back to Hunter, there were tears in her eyes. "Yes."

Hunter heard Kristen move from her table. He gave a bitter smile, a silent promise that he wasn't about to lose his temper again.

"And he will use you to get to him." Hunter said, resignation in his voice. "Mel, I can't let that happen. I need you to make a choice. You have to stop working for Lucifer, you have to reject him and all his future plans. Or you have to leave and never come back."

"Y-you don't want me?" Mel stuttered.

Hunter sighed, his heart breaking at the sight of the distraught and innocent Mel. "We all want you to stay, Mel. But I can't risk Adam."

"H-he'll hurt me."

Kristen stepped up and hugged the poor girl. "I'm so sorry, Mel. This is for the best. Why don't you sleep on it and let us know tomorrow?"

Mel shook her head. "No, no, I don't need to wait. I choose my friends; I will always choose my friends."

*****

The following afternoon, Hunter and his accomplices were sitting in the garden.

"Your English countryside is as beautiful as you say, Hunter." Marcus remarked, glancing curiously at his host. "But this… is this the normale build-up to a war?"

"I don't know what you're talking about." Hunter replied innocently, as he took in the scene. Mel and Kristen sat on the lawn, Mel busy threading daisies into Kristen's hair; Shaun was racing Adam around Mrs Astley's geraniums. Jack sat reading, occasionally looking up from his book to smirk at his younger colleague.

"I don't think this war has any precedent for comparison – unless we go back to the Middle Ages and my records get sketchy that far in the past."

Marcus frowned at the long words and waited for Hunter to repeat his meaning in Italian.

748

Hunter added more. "These men and women... and demons... they are going to fight with us. I shan't deny them time to relax and enjoy themselves. Besides, don't you know how rare it is for a British summer not to be accompanied by rain?"

Marcus smiled and shook his head but gazed contentedly across the grounds of the Astley estate. The once controlled lawns and hedges looking slightly wild, and all the more beautiful for it.

"I see why you fight, if you come home to this." Marcus observed. Suddenly the monk sat a little straighter, turning his gaze to the house. Marcus relaxed again and smiled. "You have a guest."

Hunter grimaced, wondering whose arrival could amuse Marcus. He really did not want his mother coming out to join them. Mrs Astley would only complain over the state of her garden.

He looked up and was very pleased and surprised to see Biagio walking over to them instead.

"Biagio! I didn't know you were coming."

"Yes, the Abate has given me permission to come here before the official meeting in Donili. Your mother told me you were out here." Biagio replied, faltering a little at the mention of Mrs Astley. "She is... very pleasant."

Hunter recognised the faltering, almost questioning pitch of his statement. "What did she say to you?"

"That I have good diction, for a foreigner." Biagio answered. "Is this good?"

"Yes, that's positively a compliment."

"Better than I got." Marcus contested. "'Dressed inappropriately for my station,' and 'they should insist on foreigners knowing good English before they are allowed to visit'."

"Please take a seat, Biagio, and tell us why you are really here." Hunter said before things could get silly.

Biagio did so and looked rather pleased with himself. "Well, as you know, I have been to see Frau Kuhn. She sends her best wishes, Giorgio, and wanted me to convey that no harm came to her after your escape. Actually, she was so impressed that you managed to escape, that she is confident in strengthening the alliance between you!"

Hunter sat up a little straighter – there was an unexpected bonus. When Hunter had escaped with Mel and Kristen, he had been consumed with relief that they had avoided the Shadow Witch; it had not occurred to him that they could have inspired any great opinion.

"Frau Kuhn explained that there was an artefact that belonged to Germany. Something that was stolen long ago. The British witches recently returned it to the Witches Rat as an emblem of peace and unity." Biagio went on, savouring every last word and moment of anticipation until his audience looked ready to hit him.

The monk went into his satchel and pulled out an object wrapped in black silk. Putting it down on the garden table deferentially, Biagio began to fold back the covering.

Hunter's breath caught in his throat and he could not tear his eyes away from the object.

Biagio coughed to get their attention, obviously pleased with their reactions. "Frau Kuhn expressed that if this knife was to belong to anyone, it would belong to you, Giorgio."

Hunter leant forward in his seat and reached out until his fingers brushed the black silk – he dared not touch the knife itself. It did not look how he had imagined it would, a blunt and chipped relic that betrayed the many years of its existence. The narrow grey blade gleamed in the bright summer sun, and the handle was ivory and simple in fashion. He could not see the words 'For Her Hand Only' etched into it, not on this side anyway.

"The Abate consented that this was a gift for you, from Frau Kuhn, and therefore removes responsibility of this item from the Donili."

Hunter looked up at Biagio, trying to work out the Abate's true meaning.

Biagio sighed, having hoped that his more flowery expression would be satisfactory. "Padre said that he agrees the knife belongs with you. He wished for you to have it before the Donili meeting, so the other elders could not interfere with what is a morally grey area."

Hunter slowly let out his breath. Here it was, the one known thing that could end the life of a Shadow Witch. He looked for a certain someone, wanting it verified.

"Mel?"

Hearing her name, Mel stopped plaiting Kristen's hair and danced over to the garden table.

Hunter noticed how both monks shrank back at the arrival of the little blonde girl. Hunter still hadn't forgiven her over the familiar, but he couldn't understand how the monks were so naturally repulsed by Mel.

"Mel, can you tell me anything about this?"

Mel looked down at the table and immediately her normally carefree expression froze. It was the first time Hunter had seen her look fearful.

"It… it is Sabine's, the weapon of the Shadow Witch." Mel answered in a small voice. "When she wields it, it will always claim it's victim. Wiccans and witches, monks and demons…"

"And demons?" Biagio echoed with unnecessary interest.

"It was a gift to Sabine, the gift of death." Mel said quietly.

"From Lucifer?" Hunter asked, filled with distaste that the blade was from Mel's boss.

Mel slowly nodded. "She was given the gift of death because we knew one day, a hundred years after the witch-craze started, Sabine would grow weary of life. She fell in love with a mortal man, and after he died, she had the one tool that could allow her to join him."

Obviously, content with her part, Mel left and drifted back to where Kristen sat, the American alert and eavesdropping.

"Why do I feel that every time I get one answer, I get a hundred new questions." Hunter muttered, looking at the dagger.

"I concur. I am not happy with the ambiguity of her answers." Biagio added. At the looks he received from Hunter and Marcus, Biagio turned sheepish. "I do not like what I do not know."

"Well, get back to the Abate and inform him on our new mysteries." Hunter said with a grim smile.

Biagio bowed his head. "I shall see you at the meeting in a few days."

"You're not staying for dinner, Biagio? My mother will be disappointed."

Biagio suddenly looked worried at the prospect of upsetting Mrs Astley.

"Go Biagio, I will make your excuses." Hunter insisted.

Nobody particularly enjoyed Mrs Astley's company, but the feeling was normally mutual. Mrs Astley often didn't like or approve of those she was forced to spend time with. Hunter didn't know if he felt sorrier for Biagio for potentially having his mother's favour.

## Chapter Thirty-three

The morning of the meeting, Hunter blinked over to Donili Village, taking Adam and Kristen with him. Mel travelled using her own method; and Marcus brought along Shaun, who had dropped blatant hints that he wanted to come.

Jack and Mrs Astley had also been invited in the end, but Hunter's mother refused to make a trip abroad on so little notice; and Jack selflessly decided to stay so there was at least one witch-hunter at the Manor. Not that he thought any witch or demon would be brave enough to take on Mrs Astley.

Donili Village was as bright and beautiful as ever, the green of the surrounding forest, and the glint of the nearby lake. The Abbazia stood out on the top of the hill, ruling over the landscape.

Hunter briefly stopped by to let them know of his arrival, then headed to Marcus' house to await the midday meeting.

He didn't know what would happen at the meeting, or what to expect. Impatience burned through his veins, so instead of stopping when he reached his friend's house, Hunter kept going, breaking into a jog.

When Hunter heard another set of footsteps join his, he started to run.

Donili Village was soon left behind, and the track became narrower as it entered the trees. It was simply a blur of green as Hunter ran down the track that weaved between the great trunks. It was not long before the glinting lake could be seen, and Hunter only stopped when he was at the water's edge. He looked out over the peaceful and familiar scene, while he rolled the tenseness out of his shoulders and stretched his stiff limbs.

"Hey Hunter, not running back to England, are you?" Kristen called out as she slowed to a jog and stopped beside him. "You can really run."

Hunter glanced over to her, not sure if he wanted company. "Thank you, Miss Davies. I had already noticed."

Kristen snorted at his lack of humility, making Hunter soften a little.

"You almost kept up." He offered.

"Shut up, we both know that's a lie." Kristen said with a laugh. "You know, I always thought being a 6<sup>th</sup> gen was pretty awesome, but just a few weeks with you and I'm feeling disgustingly average instead. I wish I had been born a generation later."

Hunter inwardly sighed at her comments – yes, it was just a lucky chance of birth that had given him these powers. Would that he had been born someone else, someone average and non-influential.

"I'm going for a run, want to come?"

Kristen looked at him warily. "How far?"

"Just a lap of the lake."

Kristen smiled at the challenge and took the track to the right.

Hunter watched her disappear into the trees and gave her a ten second head-start, before following her. Kristen may not be as fast as Hunter, but she was easily as nimble as him, not slowing down as she darted between the trees and raced on.

Hunter felt his own pulse start to beat faster, his breathing coarse from the exertion. They had gone over a third of the way round when Hunter finally caught up with her.

"So... why the run... this morning?" Kristen asked between breaths, not breaking stride.

"I had too much energy." Hunter answered. "I couldn't risk getting frustrated by something stupid at the meeting later and potentially hitting someone."

"Well... Colin Dawkins is gonna be there, I'll understand if you want to hit him anyway." Kristen answered, flashing Hunter a mischievous look before concentrating on the path ahead. "What's his beef with you anyway?"

"Pass." Hunter replied. He honestly couldn't think why the now-General always reacted with hostility towards him.

"You know, there are better ways to expend energy." Kristen said, glancing over her shoulder at Hunter.

Before he had a chance to react, Kristen put on the brakes and threw her weight into her shoulder. When Hunter collided with her, she quickly spun him off balance and let the momentum carry them both down.

Hunter grunted as he hit the ground, his hands quickly found Kristen's waist, but he didn't hurry to push her away.

"I think I like your method of distraction."

"I thought you might." Kristen said with a satisfied smirk, before she kissed him.

## Chapter Thirty-four

The meeting took place in the Abbazia. Hunter and Kristen were ushered into the auditorium where Hunter had once had lessons alongside the young monks. The seats rose in tiered levels on all four sides, so that all could see, and be seen.

The room thrummed with energy, filled with more people than Hunter had imagined. Besides the monks, there were some he recognised – Colin and Theresa, supporting the British MMC; David and Terry from the Australian MMC; Annette and her little assistant from France. And Laura Kuhn. Hunter paused, shocked that the witch should be present. Laura looked up, recognition in her eyes, but before they could greet each other, they were called to take their seats.

"Benvenuto, signore e signori." The Abate took the floor, calmly taking in the crowd with his grey eyes. "Primo, if you do not understand Italian, your assigned Donili monk will translate."

Hunter lowered his head to Kristen's and quickly translated for her. A flash of annoyance crossed her face, and Hunter could only hope that she would be satisfied with his relay of the meeting.

The Abate waited for the murmured conversations to die down, then continued in rapid Italian. "You are all welcome to the first meeting of witch-hunters, witches and wiccans alike."

There was a lull as his words were translated, then the hall erupted. People were on their feet, most looking betrayed, and many looking angry.

Hunter got the impression that the Donili had been less than forthcoming on what this meeting would entail. He looked down at the Abate, who wore that same amused expression he always had at Hunter's outbursts.

"Silenzio!" The Abate finally shouted. "The Abbazia will play a neutral ground for all parties at this and future meetings. As long as you are within these walls no magic will work, and no violence will be tolerated."

As he translated this to Kristen, Hunter wondered if 'no magic' was supposed to include Mel. He'd witnessed the blonde demon break the Donili rules before; it would be a shame if she popped up now and ruined padre's speech. Hunter bit back a smile and forced himself not to think of Mel, in case that was all it took to summon her.

"This is the future, ladies and gentlemen. Where the Malleus Maleficarum and the Witches Council unite as equals to govern themselves." The Abate continued. "Finer details can be worked out in your own countries once the war is won."

The Abate went on to discuss each country, calling on every representative. Each comment and description was brief, but it still took two hours to complete the hall.

Hunter sat and quietly translated throughout, noting how the stories were all so familiar. Everyone was on the verge of rebelling and only needed the final push. Even the witches were alert and ready for the chance to change things.

Luckily Hunter was not the only British MMC representative, and General Dawkins keenly took the spotlight. Colin said his piece, and Hunter wondered how he'd never noticed what a pompous arse he was. Huh, probably because he'd previously considered Colin a friend, when the soldier had obviously only been humouring him while General Hayworth was in charge.

Hunter was snapped out of his train of thought by a sharp elbow from Miss Davies. He looked accusingly at the American – surely, she didn't need Dawkins translating.

Kristen nodded to the Abate in response, and Hunter suddenly noticed that all focus was on him.

"Signor Astley, if you please?"

"What?"

"Our mission in Washington." Kristen hissed.

"Oh right." Hunter muttered, getting stiffly to his feet. The run this morning followed by sitting still for two hours was not a good idea.

"As you all know, five years ago the witches used a device from the American MMC to disrupt technology to set us all at a disadvantage. I thought you may all like to know that it has been disabled. Everything is still a long way from being restored, but this is more proof that things are moving in our favour." Hunter finished and sat down.

The hall was filled with murmured translations which were followed by expressions of polite interest. Not quite the reaction Hunter had hoped for.

"Jeez, what have you gotta do to impress people around here?" Kristen muttered beside him.

On the floor, the Abate held his hands up for attention.

"I am sure there is much more to say." The Abate continued in Italian. "And the Abbazia di Donili is open to all of you, if you wish to stay the rest of the day. But

762

you must bring the battle back to those that delight in murder and sin. I recommend making a stand at the next full moon. Delaying will likely help no one."

The room became a buzz of voices again, and the Abate waited patiently for his audience to settle again.

"The longer we wait the more chance the Shadow Witch and her council will have to discover our plans. We cannot give them time to corrupt this alliance between hunters and witches."

The Abate paused and Hunter was surprised to see a flash of uncertainty cross the older man's features. The Abate glanced to where the other senior monks sat.

"As many of you have been told, the Donili's interference was only going to extend to playing the messenger and neutral party in this conflict. But we have decided to go one step further."

Despite the crowded hall, the Abate's eyes found Hunter's.

"To reduce the lives lost and to ensure a swift conclusion to the war, the Donili monks will be joining you on the front line; we will block unfriendly magic."

Hunter felt his pulse race. The Donili had changed their minds! It was only Kristen's hand on his arm that stopped him from getting up from his seat as the shock of excitement flooded through him.

Anything was possible now.

## Chapter Thirty-five

The sun had set, and it was proving to be a warm autumn evening.

News had filtered through to the witches that an opposing force was massing. The spies were all running home with the same information – that the witch-hunters had somehow managed to pull together numbers not seen since Salisbury Plains.

The Shadow Witch was hardly concerned. They had crushed them before; they would crush them again. And this time, she would put an end to Hunter Astley.

The other witches on the council had sent a wiccan servant to help her get ready for the battle. The Shadow Witch looked down at her now as she laced up the sturdy black boots. The Shadow Witch, the most powerful witch for a thousand years, hardly needed a servant to help her dress.

She glanced to her right, to where her full-length mirror stood. Sophie took in the dark circles under her eyes and the drained, pale look despite her summer tan. She pushed back a lock of dark brown hair that had already fallen out of her plait. Sophie was quite sure the rest of the witches didn't notice how worn she looked these days; ever since Adam had been taken, she had not slept and had travelled across the world at the slightest hint of his presence.

As the days had turned into weeks, she had only become more desperate. She could not understand how she was unable to find him, she very much doubted that Hunter had the power to block her son from her. Oh, she was certain that Adam was *with* Hunter, but it made her worry over who else was involved; who had managed to shield Adam from *her*.

Upon hearing the news that the pathetic remnants of the witch-hunters were rallying against the witches, Sophie was determined to face them. After all, wherever the witch-hunters went, Hunter would surely be involved.

She swallowed down the lump that rose in her throat as she thought of Hunter. She wasn't still in love with him; for the sake of her kin, she couldn't be. Sophie had been plagued by dreams that had allowed her fantasies and delusions to live. But no more. She had to remember that this was George 'Hunter' Astley, killer of witches; the man that dared to kidnap her innocent son.

She thought back to the many times she had given him the opportunity to see sense, to put aside the conflict and live peacefully with her. How many times had this leniency cost her, Sophie's reputation and influence amongst the witches had never been lower. She would not give Hunter the chance again.

"Is there anything else, ma'am?"

Sophie was brought back to the present by the timid voice. She glanced over at the wiccan that now stood with her eyes deferentially lowered. Sophie exhaled, trying not to show the distaste she felt for this woman. For all wiccans; the grasping, leeching creatures. She had punished enough of them over the last few years; an example had to be made of those that dared to use magic that did not belong to them.

"No, leave me." Sophie snapped.

The middle-aged woman bobbed her head and darted out. Sophie let out a small scream of exasperation; she could already feel the adrenaline for the forthcoming battle flooding her system. She would kill Hunter; reclaim her son; and then she wouldn't stop until she had beaten down the opposition in the witches' council. It was time they acknowledged who she was – not just some figurehead – but a leader who answered to no man.

*****

Darkness fell over the British countryside; and with it came the witches.

They came out of the shadows like an endless sea, until they filled the valley. On the opposing slope, a mundane army was awaiting them.

The Shadow Witch looked up, her enemy had gone for the higher ground, traditionally an advantage. Her frown deepened; let them cling onto any hope they liked, they would be dead by morning.

"Let Hunter Astley come forward." She called out, her hazel eyes scanning the faces of the mob before her.

Nobody moved. The Shadow Witch hissed her disapproval and turned back to her fellow witches. It didn't matter, Hunter might be hiding amongst the ranks – probably with his new little girlfriend – but she knew him; Hunter wouldn't let people die on his behalf. No, he was the hero, he would come to meet her. As she passed the senior witches of the council, she gave the signal.

The witches around her began casting, the air suddenly thick with magic. Sophie took a deep breath, taking pride in the strength of her allies; allowing their magic to flow softly over her skin, building her confidence. Then she turned to face her enemies and all hell broke loose.

Her army surged forward, racing to meet the witch-hunters that stood frozen on the slope. The distance closed and the magic flooded out before them.

Sophie faltered in her stride as she saw the spells dissipate against a solid barrier. Hunter. The ghost of a smile passed her face as she brought out her own destructive power, aiming it into the masses. Sophie watched as her magic buckled the shield – poor Hunter must be distracted; it was hardly up to his usual strength. Without any further concern, Sophie pushed anew. Shouts and cries rose up around her, the metallic tang of blood filtered into the air.

There was an explosion to her left, close enough for Sophie to feel the heat of it against her bare face. She squinted against the brief brightness and focused on finding Hunter. The person projecting the shield was close and Sophie pushed forward, only delayed by one brave soldier that barrelled into her from the side. Sophie ducked under his clumsy attack and in one smooth motion, spun the man off balance and brought up her knife, letting the unlucky man crumpled to the ground.

Leaving the other witches to do the damage, Sophie pressed on with single-minded determination. She brought her magic close about her, a moment more and she could throw everything she had at Hunter to try and catch him off guard...

But Hunter was not there.

The source of the shield was a grey-haired man, no taller than Sophie. He was dressed in a simple black linen outfit and moved like a man half his age. Sophie stood frozen, lost as to who this man was.

'The Benandanti; he has found the Benandanti.' No sooner had the revelation crossed her mind, the mysterious man turned to face her. His shockingly blue eyes observing her.

"Buonasera Sophie."

"You know me?" She asked. Nobody called her that anymore; enemies and allies alike only saw the Shadow Witch.

The Benandanti hesitated, and Sophie could sense him trying to strengthen his shield as her witches renewed their attack. His focus was then only for her. He bowed his head in acquiescence.

"Signor Astley has told me much about you."

Sophie's frown hardened, but she kept control of the thrashing emotions within. How dare Hunter discuss her with anyone, he had given up that right.

Sophie took a deep breath, ignoring the chaos around her. "Where is Astley? Tell me and I will let you live; I will let you return to Italy and carry on your peaceful existence."

Before the old man could reply, a noise rose up above the din of battle, a horn. The very simple note was taken up across the stretch of the battlefield and even though it was mundane, Sophie couldn't help but be unsettled.

"What mischief is this?" She demanded.

The Benandanti smiled gently. "It is the new world. Embrace it, Sophie, for all our sakes'."

Sophie felt a fracture in the magic around her and spun round. It took her a moment to work out what was the cause – it could not be happening! But suddenly, witches were fighting witches. There were patches of rebellion spread across the valley; a third of her forces were suddenly turning on the others, pinning them in against the witch-hunters on the opposing slope. Sophie's eyes tore wildly across the scene – how could they betray her? How could they betray everything they had sacrificed so much for?

This was Hunter's doing – she did not know how, but Sophie was adamant he was behind it. That no-good, deceitful bastard had somehow decided that he would work with witches now. Why not years ago, when she had offered him everything? How could he refuse her then, force the world to make war; then think that this was the right course?

Suddenly overwhelmed with the new targets she wished to punish, Sophie turned back to the Benandanti, who stood calmly observing her.

"Where is Hunter?" She snapped, her calm façade breaking.

When the old man did not answer, Sophie raised her hand, her magic seeping out and curling around the man's throat. She could feel his attempts at blocking it, his pitiful shield designed for lesser witches. Sophie gazed on dispassionately as the man began to gasp as she slowly constricted his airways.

"He's... he's not..."

Sophie sighed and released him just enough for the old man to speak properly.

"He's not here. He never was. Even without him, your side has been beaten, Sophie." The Benandanti's blue eyes glinted. "You have a choice. You must choose to stay and fight, or to go to him. He is in the church hall in the next village – but only for the duration of the battle – after that, he will disappear again."

Sophie released the man, letting him slump to his knees. So, Hunter was playing the coward. She let out a scream of frustration, her magic exploding out with force, knocking over every witch-hunter, witch and monk in her path. Leaving them motionless on the grass, Sophie wrapped her shadows around her and vanished.

## Chapter Thirty-six

Hunter paced the room, the little ball of light that hovered above his head moved with him, back and forth across the ceiling.

"Will you please stand still?" Kristen begged, from where she perched on an old desk. "Or at least make your light thing stay still – it's giving me a headache, bobbing all over the place!"

Hunter looked across at the girl. "Sorry." He muttered, shoving his hands in his pockets and forcing himself to be still. "I'm just... not used to not doing anything."

Hunter thought of the men and women out there. They were protected more effectively by the Donili than Hunter could have ever managed. The 'good' witches had switched to their side, giving them overwhelming odds. Hunter could already see how it would play out – their enemies would realise the futile situation and flee, or they would make an heroic last stand and be cut down.

Hunter didn't want to be cocky, but the truth was that as long as the Shadow Witch was subdued, his side could not lose.

"George Astley, the famous witch-hunter. Are you nervous?" Kristen asked in wonder. "Proof that you're only as flawed and human as the rest of us?"

Hunter tried to raise a weak smile at her ribbing. "I've never been bait before."

"Don't worry, everything will go to plan. Your witchy lover will be here as soon as she realises you're not with the others."

Hunter felt his palms sweat at the very thought. "You don't have to stay for this, Kristen. It'll be safer if you leave."

"And you don't have to do this alone." Kristen said, re-stating an earlier argument. "But I want a reward when all this is finished. Two weeks in the South of France – just you, me and Adam."

The shadows in the room started to thicken and congeal. She was coming.

Hunter rested his hand close to his gun, and Kristen got to her feet, moving closer to his side.

The Shadow Witch appeared, the shadows hugging her elegant frame. Her sharp features were framed by her dark brown hair, which continued in waves down her back. For a moment she looked beautiful.

And then a moment later her hazel eyes snapped onto Hunter and every fibre of her being echoed her anger.

"You bastard. How could you do this Hunter?!" Sophie fought to find words, her hands clenching by her sides.

"The battle is over. You've lost." Hunter replied, sounding official to feign calm.

The Shadow Witch looked nonplussed at his statement. "What...? Where is my *SON*?" She screamed. A wave of magic rolled off her, so powerful it blasted Hunter and Kristen from their feet.

Hunter grunted in pain and caught his breath while he sat in an ungainly heap.

"You think that you were dangerous when my witches killed Charlotte? When they killed James?" Sophie growled, looking down at Hunter. "That is nothing, *nothing*, compared to what you have unlocked in me by taking my son. Not even your anti-magic can stand against it."

Sophie raised her hand and Hunter felt the air leave his lungs and he gasped frantically at nothingness.

"Give Adam back to me and I shall show mercy. If not, I will tear this world apart looking for him. Not even your Benandanti monks will be able to stop me."

"D-Donili." Hunter gasped, then realised that Sophie had allowed him to breath to respond. "Donili monks. If you are going to defy and kill them, at least call them by their true name."

"Where is Adam?" Sophie hissed, the threat of her magic welling up for another attack.

"I will take you to him." Hunter said rapidly, still on his knees before her. "On the condition that you are bound. We can be human; we can live together in the cottage in Keswick – I know you've seen it too."

Sophie paused, her eyes glazing over. "That's nothing but a dream, however you engineered it."

Hunter shook his head. "It was not my doing." He thought back to the dreams that had invaded his sleep for the past two years. He had always believed they were real, that he shared them with Sophie, that she was behind them. If not Sophie, then who?

"I seem to remember giving you the same option, more than once. You always refused, insisting that you were on the 'right' side." Sophie replied, her cracking voice betraying how close she was to losing this calm façade. "But look at you now Hunter, uniting with witches, despite all your protestations and morals. What were all those deaths and battles for? You disgust me."

"I'm making a better world." Hunter said humbly, then raised his voice. "For our son; for the people that deserve to be treated as more than cattle and sacrifices;

and yes, for the witchkind that are peaceful and want to join that future."

Sophie laughed, but Hunter could sense the hum of power focussing in on him, ready to rip him apart, should Hunter answer wrong. "In this you describe one person perfectly. Let me ask you this Hunter: *where is my mother?*"

Hunter's gut twisted at the question. Sophie read the answer in his expression and her calm broke. Her scream was a wall of sound that made Hunter cower on the ground.

Then suddenly the scream stopped with a grunt of pain.

Kristen, forgotten in the background, slowly moved away from Sophie, her bloody hand leaving the dagger hilt-deep in her torso.

Sophie looked down disbelievingly. She weakly smiled and closed her eyes, wavering a little in her stance. The woman took three measured breaths, then yanked the knife from her stomach with a scream. The pain dropped her to her knees, but then she gave a bitter laugh, and slowly stood up.

"So, this is the American girl. She is pretty, you're right. Consider me jealous." Sophie flipped the knife in her hand and, spinning quickly to face Kristen, drove the blade deep into her belly.

Kristen's eyes widened and she staggered back until she hit the wall.

"Kristen!" Hunter cried, jumping to his feet.

Sophie held up a hand to stop him. "You will say your goodbyes, and then you will join me." She said coldly.

The shadows in the room thickened and began to curl around her once more.

Hunter stood paralyzed, watching as Sophie left. A whimper from Kristen snapped him out of his daze, and he rushed to where the girl half-lay, slumped against the wall.

"What the hell did you do that for?" Hunter snapped, gingerly moving her blood-stained top away from the wound.

"Well you clearly weren't gonna do it." Kristen said, hissing sharply at the pain of each movement. "And I confess, I got a little jealous, all that talk of happy families."

"And look where it got you. 'By Her Hand Only' Kristen." Hunter said, exasperated. "You could never have killed her. And now…"

"And now I'm the one dying." Kristen finished, very matter-of-fact.

Hunter wanted to deny it, to tell her it would all be fine. "It must always claim it's victim, just like Mel warned: the gift of death."

"T-that's all very well, Hunter. Now do you think you can take this thing out of me?" Kristen grimaced. "It really hurts."

"If I do that you will bleed to death quickly."

Kristen rolled her eyes at his statement. "Die quickly; die slowly; I'm still dead Hunter."

Hunter took a deep breath and obediently pulled the knife out of her with a swift movement. The blade clattered to the floor beside them.

"I'm sorry." Hunter took her hand as he knelt next to her. "I am so sorry for all of this."

Kristen smiled weakly, her skin looking greyer by the second. "I have no regrets. I got to meet you. And I get to die a hero, like my father."

Hunter felt his eyes burn. This was unfair, she was too young, and she shouldn't die for his mistakes. "I wish things had been different – this war, the Shadow Witch rising up. You would always be the one I was meant to meet. You still would have come to England to find your father. Brian would have tried to keep you as far away from me as possible, as any sensible father would…"

Hunter's thoughts followed the alternative life they could have led. He was struck again by how cruel fate was – it should be him dying instead.

Hunter's heart skipped a beat as the realisation hit him. Hunter reached out and put a hand over her wound. Kristen gave a small whimper, barely audible.

"Kristen, I want you to watch over Adam. Let him know I loved him." Hunter stated, confident that he was making a better world for his son.

Through her waning consciousness, Kristen stirred, understanding something serious was happening, something she would not like.

Hunter closed his eyes and focussed on the wound. His power was repelled as it stayed greedily open.

Hunter took a deep breath and opened himself to the curse, the remnants of ancient magic felt the presence of a willing victim and slid happily along into this new vessel. Hunter shuddered in pain, the focussed again on Kristen. This time her wound closed as easily as the practice sessions with the Donili; her flesh knitting together to leave a very sore red scar across her stomach.

Hunter had to steady himself as he felt a wave of dizziness. It was hitting hard and fast, he had to get out of here.

Kristen stirred and weakly grabbed his sleeve. "No." She mumbled.

Hunter grabbed the chain at his neck and pulled it away. He stared at the dog tags in his hand, they had protected him for so many years. He pressed them into Kristen's hand.

"See that Adam gets these. And… ask Toby and Claire to raise him. Don't let my mother get her claws into him."

Hunter leant down and kissed Kristen's forehead, then blinked away.

## Chapter Thirty-seven

Hunter instinctively followed Sophie. The witch purposefully kept her shields down, and he slipped easily into the space next to her.

Long grass swayed in a sweet-smelling breeze, and the rising sun highlighted the hilly landscape.

Hunter took shallow breaths, careful not to aggravate his new wound. He glanced down; glad he was wearing black. His stomach was already queasy, and he didn't want to see the red stain spread.

"I used to come out here when I was a girl." Sophie said, her voice reflective. "This was always my escape, no one bothered me here."

The witch sighed and turned back to Hunter. She was wearing a mask of calm again, but Hunter could see the unsettled light in her eyes. "Where is my son Hunter? Last chance, or I will kill you."

"You won't kill me." Hunter said calmly.

Sophie looked at him with more than a hint of disdain. "I have killed hundreds of witch-hunters."

"But you won't kill me." Hunter repeated. "You have had every chance these past few years. But you always held back – for God's sake, Sophie, you even rescued me on one occasion."

Sophie grew paler as he spoke. "So, you think I will hold back again, simply because I love you?" She argued, then realised what she had said. "Loved you. You're still living in a dream, Hunter."

"Love, self-preservation; whatever works." Hunter replied with a shrug. "You and I are connected Sophie; in a way I don't think either of us can truly explain. We are linked. You suspected it when you tried to kill me four years ago, when all that pain rebounded onto you. And every time since then, when I have nearly died, you were there. The time I nearly suffocated from trying to blink to close to your army – I bet you felt that too. I don't think you will directly kill me."

Hunter felt the energy drain out of him as he spoke, so he slowly sat down, not caring about the dew soaking into his trousers. "And I bet you feel exhausted now, but can't explain why"

Sophie looked down at Hunter like he was a child, her lips pressed in a firm line of disapproval. "Of course, I'm exhausted – I have been fighting this battle whilst you've been hiding away with your tart!"

"I found out how Sara Murray died." Hunter suddenly stated, wanting to shift the focus away from Kristen.

"Killed by your grandfather, I know." Sophie snapped, frowning at the swift change in topic.

Hunter shook his head. "No, she was actually friends with Old George; and he loved her, would never have hurt her. Not that he could have. It turns out that the only way for a Shadow Witch to die is if she uses her own dagger to take her life."

"The dagger... you're lying." Sophie protested.

"The gift of death – by her hand only." Hunter quoted. "I have a letter written by your great-grandmother as proof. It is in the Manor."

Sophie hissed through her teeth. "I bet you would just love to get me inside the Manor. Block my powers, never let me out again, is that the grand plan Hunter?"

"No... we're never seeing the Manor again." He replied with a pained grimace.

Sophie stopped and finally paid attention to him. She slowly knelt beside him, and then gently reached out for Hunter's hand. Her breath hitched as she saw the red stain on his palm, and she felt his black jumper to confirm the source.

"You... you..." Sophie stuttered, her pale face blanching further. "You gave your life for that American bitch? You kill us both to save her? Do you have any idea what you have done?!"

"You inflicted the blow, I just took... took advantage of it." Hunter said, quiet in response to her anger. His hand resting gently on top of hers. "I am making a better world for our son."

Sophie snatched her hand away and without a thought, slapped him. "And you think that makes it alright? You think I'm going to lie down and accept it! Bastard!"

She lashed out again and after the first blow, Hunter tried to stop her. He wrapped his arms about her, struggling as she flailed wildly.

He grunted in pain as Sophie's knee connected with his thigh – clearly aiming for something more painful.

"Change it." Sophie demanded, her voice rough from screaming.

"I can't." Hunter murmured. "It's too late."

"Adam..." Sophie's body shook and she made the conscious effort to sit beside Hunter with what was left of her grace.

"He'll be fine. Toby and Claire will look after him, as though he were their own." Hunter said, his eyes drifting shut as he imagined his son's bright future. "He will grow up in a world where the two sides of him can be at peace. The monks will see to his training when he's older..."

"And we'll just fade." Sophie said, bitterness clinging to her voice.

"No, not fade; we will exist forever." Hunter replied, his breaths becoming shallower. "No one will ever find us here."

Hunter tilted his head to look up. The misty, pastel clouds were tinged with pink, and the sun was just starting to creep over the horizon. The barren, rolling hills still dark against the sunrise.

He smiled. "A new day."

## Chapter Thirty-eight

Kristen awoke to find herself alone. As she sat up, she felt very sore, but very much alive. As the events of last night hit her, she broke into tearful sobs, curling back up on the floor as she waited for the shock to pass.

Eventually she got back to her feet, wavering a little, but knowing that she had to find the others. Kristen squinted in the bright sunlight that flooded through the windows, a piercing headache from the suffocating build-up of magic in this room. She had to get out.

Kristen stumbled outside, taking deep breaths as she waited for her head to clear. The summer sun beat down, warming her cold limbs, but as she tried to walk, she fell to her knees on the gravelled path. Faced with the challenge of trying to get back to the MMC, Kristen silently cursed Hunter for blinking them here – he should have insisted she drive over if the bastard had been planning on leaving her.

As her thoughts strayed to him, emotion welled up in her throat. Kristen bit it down and concentrated on the basics, of breathing and her dubious balance.

"Mel." She mumbled, then through her head back to shout. "Mel!"

There was the soft sway of a white summer dress beside her as the demon silently appeared. "Yes, Kristen?"

Mel knelt down, her usually carefree expression clouded with concern, as her blue eyes took in the signs of damage to her friend. For once, she seemed at a loss for what to say. Biting her lip, she pulled out a handkerchief and wiped some of the drying blood from Kristen's face.

"He- he's gone." Kristen gasped.

"I know." Mel said quietly.

"Is there anything you can do?" Kristen begged.

Mel put her finger on Kristen's lips to shush her. "Don't let Lucy hear; George said he wasn't allowed to help."

"I don't-" Kristen took a deep breath and blinked back fresh tears. Hunter and the Donili monks had all advised against invoking the devil. But Kristen wondered if it might not be worth it, to bring Hunter back, especially when it was her fault he had gone. Her hand strayed to her stomach, which was tender to the touch.

"I need to get back to the others." Kristen said, before she could be further tempted. "Can you take me to them, please?"

Mel smiled and placed her hand on Kristen's shoulder...

The battleground looked like organised chaos. Those that were able-bodied helped the injured in a makeshift hospital. Some had the unwelcome but necessary task of retrieving the dead, working in pairs as they gently laid the fallen in a line to be identified.

There were not many dead; it looked like the Donili had done their duty well, in discouraging the witches. Then when the rebel witches had switched sides, their once-comrades must have followed suit or scarpered. Fighting on would have been martyrdom.

Kristen got to her feet, taking in the scene. There was still the throb of magic in the air, but it was quickly diluting into the open space. Kristen's headache was becoming a much more mundane thing, no longer a signal that her witch-hunter side should be on high alert.

Kristen spotted a group of men and women surveying the field, and as they moved along, she recognised the distinctive limp of Toby Robson. Ignoring the aching pain and complaints her body was making, Kristen started to move towards them. Mel moved with her, supporting her with a surprising strength.

Toby saw them and immediately looked past the girls for their friend. "Hunter?"

Kristen shook her head. "He and the Shad- Sophie – they're gone. Hunter asked if you would take on Adam." Kristen blurted out, stating the important stuff before her emotions got the better of her again.

Toby froze, his face blanching of colour. "How are we going to do this without him?"

**The new world**

Theresa straightened her jacket as she stood up. "It is an honour to welcome you all to the first meeting of the new Malleus Maleficarum Council. It has been decided that from this day on the MMC will enforce the new laws that give witches the same rights and responsibilities as other civilians."

She paused and looked about the room, taking in the new faces alongside the familiar. "The Council itself will have two representatives from the witchkind…"

Those that gathered were clearly uncomfortable. It had only been a few weeks since the final battle and tensions were still high.

There were many more important things to do in rebuilding the world. Just when there had become a new normal, the equilibrium had shifted again.

The country was busy rebuilding. There were plans for housing and power, for simple things they had all taken for granted before the war.

The Council had agreed that they needed to establish the basics before they could move forward.

The witches had a whole manifest of new rules, as to what they could and could not do. To what influence they were allowed to have. Sacrifices and all other means of unnaturally gaining power were banned. Theresa had the unhappy task of laying down the new laws. She looked around the witches in the council; some had been more vocal than others in their disagreement. She imagined there would be months, or even years before they established real peace and understanding.

The changes the witch-hunters had to bear were equally drastic in Theresa's eyes. They had to open up their operation to the scrutiny of everybody.

The meeting drew to a close with more questions arising than were answered. Theresa picked up her leather briefcase and made her way outside.

The autumn rain had a chill to it, but she turned down her taxi in favour of the walk. She needed it. Theresa turned up the collar on her coat and made her way across the grey courtyard, pausing at a plaque by the main gate.

It was completely blank, the inscription yet to be decided upon.

Honestly, Theresa preferred at as it currently was. She murmured a prayer to the many lost over the last few years. Just considering those she had personally known – the list was too long. She only hoped she did them proud.

Theresa shivered, chilled by the ghosts more than the rain. With one last glance at the plaque, she moved on, to walk the streets of London, to finally go home.

## Epilogue

Two dark-haired children were rolling over in a heap when the boy suddenly vanished.

"No fair, that's cheating Adam." The girl called out, getting to her feet. She was twelve years old and her lanky limbs had an adolescent awkwardness about them.

Adam, at eleven, was half a foot shorter. He reappeared behind Molly, pinning his arms around her.

"Is not. In a real fight, we have to use everything we've got."

Molly struggled, trying to get free, her face reddening as she tried to resist the temptation to throw her head back and break the younger kid's nose.

"Auntie Kristen?" Molly pleaded.

Their trainer and referee looked up from the book she was reading beside their makeshift training grounds in the garden.

"Adam, let go of Molly." Kristen said, giving him a look to say she wasn't joking. "You are both here to improve, and neither of you is going to get faster or stronger if you keep disappearing mid-fight."

Kristen sighed. Since Mel had taught Adam how to blink for a seventh birthday present, Adam too frequently chose to use his power to get out of many things. More than once, his foster-father had tried to ground him and, instead of staying in his room, Adam would blink away to the beach. Usually taking Molly with him.

"Save your tricks for when you're fighting as a real witch-hunter."

Adam pouted, hating when his auntie labelled his gifts as mere 'tricks'. But he obediently let go of Molly.

Molly rubbed her arms. "I heard Macclemore Senior saying that we shouldn't be called witch-hunters anymore. That it's not politically correct." Molly stated in a grown-up voice.

Kristen snorted. "Sure, whatever."

"You don't think so? I mean, it does discriminate." She said, chancing a glance at Adam. It was no secret that he was half-witch, even if that half had been bound when his mother died.

Kristen shrugged. "It's just a name. Besides, 'witch-hunter; witch-hunter-hunter; and all-round-paranormal-police' is a bit of a mouthful."

Molly and Adam laughed at the face their cool Auntie Kristen pulled.

"Enough, start again. No cheating." Kristen announced.

Molly grinned at Adam, and before the younger boy could move, she flipped him and pinned him to the ground with her knees.

"You ok, little bro?" She asked, batting her eyelashes innocently.

Adam squirmed, then dropped his head back on the ground in defeat.

"You might be bigger and stronger than me now, but just wait. This summer I'm joining the Donili and they're gonna teach me everything."

Molly pushed herself off. "Good, I can't wait to get rid of you, loser." She held out her hand to help him up. Honestly, she was going to miss him. A lot. They had grown up together as one big, dysfunctional family.

But everything was about to change. Adam would go to the Donili and Molly would be starting apprentice duties with the MMC when she turned thirteen in autumn. Who knew when they'd next see each other.

Kristen noticed the flash of depression in Molly's soft brown eyes. "Hey, maybe your dad will take you all on holiday to Friuli for Christmas."

Molly snorted. "Yeah right, he's too busy on the Council these days."

Kristen tried to smile, but it was easily seen through.

There was a part of Toby that had never recovered from the injury that had ended his career in the field. Now he threw himself into his work as an important Council member. Survivors' guilt, they all had their fair share of it, Kristen thought as her hand idly traced the scar across her stomach.

"Ok you two." Kristen said, snapping back to the present. "Again."

Other books by K.S. Marsden:

**Witch-Hunter** ~ *Now available in audiobook*
The Shadow Rises (Witch-Hunter #1)
The Shadow Reigns (Witch-Hunter #2)
The Shadow Falls (Witch-Hunter #3)

Witch-Hunter trilogy box-set

**Witch-Hunter Prequels**
James: Witch-Hunter (#0.5)
Sophie: Witch-Hunter (#0.5)
Kristen: Witch-Hunter (#2.5) ~ coming 2021

**Enchena**
The Lost Soul: Book 1 of Enchena
The Oracle: Book 2 of Enchena

**Northern Witch**
Winter Trials (Northern Witch #1)
Awaken (Northern Witch #2)
The Breaking (Northern Witch #3)
Summer Sin (Northern Witch #4)

\*\*\*\*\*

Read on for a first look at the prequel **Sophie: Witch-Hunter.**

Find out about everyone's favourite cold-hearted bitch, and how she became the Shadow Witch…

# SOPHIE: WITCH-HUNTER
## K.S. MARSDEN

### Chapter One

The cold, dead ashes rose into the air with each footstep. The fire had long since burnt out, leaving nothing but the bare bones of the village. She walked slowly, admiring her work. A little arson was beneath her, but she had to admit, there was an artistic beauty in destruction.

The distinct sound of sobbing rose from the silence. She turned to witness a solitary figure hunched over the remains of someone he must have loved.

The man looked up as she approached. He was young and had perhaps been handsome, but fresh burns and welts made him unsightly.

The man took a sharp breath as he realised who she was, then pointed and began to shout, "Shadow! Shadow!"

She sighed, taking a knife from her belt. No one ever called her by her name anymore. Sabine...

"Sophie!"

Sophie snapped out of her daydream and turned her attention to Mr Gill.

Her maths teacher frowned, as he pointed sharply at the board. "Perhaps you could answer the equation, if it's not too much trouble?"

Sophie sighed, Mr Gill was always trying to catch her out, it was always unfair. She was generally rude and never paid attention, but it didn't give him the right to be an arse.

Her hazel eyes flicked up to the simple equation that was giving her classmates so much trouble: the answer was nine.

"Forty-two." She replied out loud.

Mr Gill stood looking more smug than normal, amused that she was finally wrong. "And how did you work that out?"

"Douglas Adams. Forty-two is the answer to everything, which makes your lessons pointless, don't you think?"

There were a few raised brows in her direction, but no one even broke a smile. Either nobody here was a Hitchhiker fan, or they were too scared to potentially upset the ice queen.

Sophie turned her attention back to her teacher, realising he was threatening her with disembowelment, detention, or something similar.

It was torture that she had to sit here and put up with so much crap from these mere mortals that didn't matter in the bigger picture. It was only a matter of days until Sophie's sixteenth birthday, when she could finally stop pretending that she was human; when she could embrace her birthright.

She was a witch.

Not just an ordinary witch, either. Sophie was a Shadow, a rare creature that hadn't been seen in centuries, and was magic without limit. Or at least, she would be when her council finally found out how to unlock her powers. For more than two long years, Sophie had been led along with promises and tantalising hints. Now, it would finally be hers, and she could almost taste the power.

She wondered what her classmates would do if they knew. Would they treat her with the respect she deserved, knowing that she could destroy them with a word? Or would they laugh at her? The over-saturation of witchcraft in media made them a joke. Who would fear the truth, when it was so much easier to tease the freak that thought themselves a witch.

Unconsciously, Sophie's gaze drifted to her classmate, Izzy. A real freak in the making. The only way that humans could access magic was by training in Wicca and following their codes. Izzy skipped that, and thought she could be a witch, just because she wore black and liked candles. You could practically smell the incense sticking to her.

Sophie's thoughts were broken by the ring of the final bell. Ignoring the red-faced Mr Gill, Sophie grabbed her stuff and headed out.

The sky was grey and the rain trickled down. Pulling up her hood, Sophie turned away from the school bus and headed towards the car that was parked on the corner every Wednesday.

"How was school?" Lynette asked, as she did every week.

Sophie shrugged. "It was fine."

She stared unseeingly out of the car window, idly playing with a lock of her dark brown hair. "Mr Gill is close to cracking. We don't need him causing trouble. You might need to speed up his next dose."

Lynette frowned, glancing over to the teenager. "I wonder who's making him crack... Sophie, potions are not to be taken for granted."

Sophie sighed and tilted her head back. "What is the point of teaching me how to make potions that will blur the memory, if I'm not allowed to use them?"

Lynette ignored her, turning down a private road, the twisting driveway shadowed by overgrown bushes and gnarled trees. It dissuaded the locals from investigating any further; and most of them had half-forgotten Thorne House even existed.

The overhanging branches gave way, leading to the beautiful, old Georgian house. It had been built by the Thorne family in the 1800's, but had been uninhabited for decades.

Lynette and her small group of companions had spent the last two years making the house habitable and homely again. Two years since they'd found Sophie, and moved to the humdrum town of Keswick to watch over her. 'A guard of honour' Basil always said. He was always a little pompous, which was why Sophie tried to spend as little time as possible with him.

Lynette pulled into the new garage that had just been built this summer, and they both made their way into the warmth of the kitchen.

Lynette tied back her long, blonde hair, then wrapped a pinny around her slender waist. "OK smart arse, what's the first thing you should do before starting any potion?"

Sophie mirrored Lynette, and picked her own apron. "I should make sure the four elements are at hand, to give the potion strength and balance." She rattled off, trying not to roll her eyes.

Lynette had been drilling the basics into her for so long, Sophie didn't think she could forget them, even if she wanted to. Sophie was already pulling out the candle and matches from the drawer, as Lynette watched on. A bowl of water and a potted plant, and she was ready.

Sophie had argued against the necessity of such things when she first started her lessons, thinking it all a little cliché and magicky. Lynette had looked ready to throw a bowl at her head, and tersely explained that all myths and wiccan practices stemmed from fact.

"Which herbs are the active ingredient in a memory-altering potion?" Lynette asked, after Sophie had all of her tools assembled.

"Orchid, thistle, cinquefoil, anise and lilac can all be used to improve the memory. Any can be used to overdose and cause the brainwaves to reset." Sophie answered, idly picking at her sleeve. "Thistle is the best bet for this area and time of year."

A few minutes later, and the concoction was bubbling happily away in the pewter pot.

"How's your mum?" Lynette asked while they waited.

Sophie sighed, looking towards the grey, rain-streaked window. "Do we have to talk about that?"

Lynette pursed her lips, gazing at the girl with bright eyes, free from wrinkles. She might only look a few years older than Sophie, but Sophie knew that she was actually old enough to be her grandmother. Or at the very least, an interfering older aunt. Which explained the maternal streak.

"You shouldn't keep shunning her."

Sophie rolled her eyes back to the blonde woman. "She's the one that wants me to ignore my birthright, she wants to keep everything witch-related away from me."

"Oh Sophie, you'll never get rid of us." Lynette replied, as she refolded a tea-towel. "I know you won't listen to me on this, but one day you'll want your mum at your side. After all, everything she is doing is simply what she thinks is the best for you."

Sophie was glad to hear the crunch of tyres, marking an arrival that would halt this conversation. Her heart dropped when she realised who had come.

Lynette offered her an apologetic glance, as the door opened and Basil swept in.

Everything about Basil Effington-Smythe made Sophie's skin crawl. She had to fight the desire to punch him in the face, every time he opened his odious mouth. It was unfortunate that Basil had a secure position with the witches' council, and was effectively in charge of protecting Sophie, and preparing her for her duty.

"Mrs Cutter, how are things proceeding?" Basil asked, skipping the pleasantries.

"Very well." Lynette answered.

Basil's gaze fixed on her, his disapproval emanating from him.

"Sir." Lynette reluctantly added.

Basil turned to look at Sophie, his blue eyes watery and weak. She always found his gaze cool and impersonal, as though he was only looking at the title of the Shadow Witch, where Sophie was an unfortunate attachment.

"Miss Murphy."

"Mr Effington-Smythe." Sophie replied, equally cold.

Basil chewed over her attitude, his thin lips pursed.

"Preparations are going well for your birthday party this weekend." Basil said, looking barely interested. "The witches' council will attend, and we've received communication from foreign councils. It looks like it will be an impressive affair, I am bringing in extra security..."

"And what of my present?" Sophie cut in, before Basil could regale them any more with his hard work and achievements. "Will you be delivering my power?"

"Of course." Basil declared, with a dismissive wave of his hand. "I am arranging for you to have further tutors, who can teach you more than herbwifery."

His cold gaze shifted to Lynette, and for a moment Sophie feared they would take away her steady friend and confidante.

Sophie could sense Lynette's frustration. The older woman had to bite her tongue, as Basil was her superior. Luckily, Sophie had no such issue to hold her back.

"Lynette stays." Sophie said, her voice wavering.

"We'll see." Basil mused. "Her skills might be better used elsewhere."

"Lynette stays." Sophie repeated, firmer this time.

The male witch was stumped. He was so used to winning arguments, and getting his own way. Sophie could almost see the cogs turning, as Basil weighed up the pros and cons of losing this battle.

"As you wish, Miss Murphy. Mrs Cutter makes such little contribution to the witches' cause, I don't think there's any harm in her staying on at Thorne House, for a little longer." Basil announced, as though it had been his idea all along.

Sophie rolled her eyes at the casual insults Basil managed to throw in at every opportunity, but held her tongue; she was getting exactly what she wanted. It shouldn't surprise her really, this weekend she would finally access her magic, and would be the most powerful witch in history. Perhaps it was his sense of survival that persuaded Basil to concede to her.

*****

Later that evening, Lynette stopped the car at the end of Sophie's street, far enough away so they couldn't be spotted from her house.

Lynette turned the engine off and faced Sophie, a worried look on her face.

"Are you inviting your mum to the party on Saturday?"

"What? No!" Sophie unbuckled her seat belt. "She's made it perfectly clear that she wants nothing to do with witches."

"Sophie… this is an important time for you, I think your mum would like to be a part of it."

"I'll think about it." Sophie said, unconvincingly. She knew that she'd do no such thing, and she wasn't fooling Lynette either.

Before Lynette could nag her any further, Sophie hurried to leave the car.

It was a typical English autumn evening: dark, cold, and a threat of rain in the air. Sophie breathed it in, letting the chill run through her thin jacket. She always had to take a moment to calm herself and check her mental defences, before she went home.

Home was such a warm word for the four walls that trapped Sophie with her non-witch mother. Their cottage was cute and traditional on the outside, but once inside, it was very modern. The décor was sleek and sharp lines. The only cosy touch was her mum's favourite sofa, the tired, red couch added a little faded colour.

Bev Murphy was currently curled up on the sofa, with a book and a tartan blanket on her lap. Her head snapped up at her daughter's entrance. Sophie hated how alike they looked, with the same dark hair and striking eyes; the only difference the frown lines that were becoming a permanent feature on Bev's otherwise youthful-looking face.

"Sophie? Have you had a good day?" Her mum asked.

"Yeah." Sophie replied briefly, as she shrugged her coat off.

"There's dinner in the oven..."

"I'm not hungry." Sophie muttered, keeping her head down and heading to her room.

"Sophie, I think-"

Sophie slammed the door shut, cutting off the rest of that sentence.

## Chapter Two

The next morning, Sophie got up early, hoping to miss her mum.

Unfortunately, the older woman was up, dressed for a day at the office, sipping at her coffee in the kitchen. "Morning," Bev greeted, with a forced lightness that fooled no one.

"Morning." Sophie echoed, as she got her breakfast, her eyes firmly fixed on the tiled floor.

"I thought we could do something this weekend, for your birthday. Maybe go shopping, or out for dinner?" Her mum suggested. "You could invite some friends."

Friends? Sophie almost snorted at the idea. She didn't have friends, she had nothing to do with the other students at school. Besides, the witches were more co-conspirators than chums.

"I've got plans. I'm going out with my 'friends'." Sophie replied, forcing the full sentences out. "I'll be late tonight, I'm doing a double kick-boxing session."

"Maybe you could invite your kick-boxing buddies along at the weekend." Bev persisted. Clearly, if she couldn't go, she wanted to make sure that some normal humans were in attendance.

Sophie couldn't help the flicker of amusement at the idea, and what the witches might think. Not that she would be extending an invitation – Sophie enjoyed kick-boxing, it was a great way to vent her frustration. Socialising was the last thing on Sophie's mind; she'd not spoken more than two words to the other class-goers.

*****

Sophie was summoned to Thorne House at midday on Saturday. She arrived to find the place a hive of activity, with unfamiliar people moving furniture, creating room for a dance floor.

Sophie could hear clattering in the kitchen, and didn't dare trespass.

"Sophie!" Lynette called from the first-floor landing. "Up here, dear."

Sophie made her way upstairs and was swept into one of the grand bedrooms.

"What's happening?" Sophie asked, as soon as she had chance.

"We have to get you ready for tonight." Lynette replied, with her usual air of innocence.

Sophie frowned. "That's six hours away. Besides, my dress is at home."

"Tonight is... it's important to make the best impression. There will be a lot of powerful witches attending." Lynette stressed. "We thought it would be best if we get you ready."

"We?" Sophie echoed, "This sounds like Basil's idea."

"He might have suggested it, but I picked the dress." Lynette pushed Sophie onto a padded stool in front of an elegant mahogany dresser.

"Still, isn't this a bit excessive?" Sophie argued, eyeing the various beauty products and tools of torture. She'd always thought she was prettier than average, and it was insulting that Lynette thought she needed all of this.

"I have to make you look like a witch."

Sophie looked in the mirror, to see Lynette's reflection. Even though the woman was much older than her, she didn't look it, and had a natural glow of beauty about her.

"Why are all witches beautiful?" Sophie asked, suddenly curious. Even Basil, who was one of the ugliest people Sophie knew, was handsome on the outside.

Lynette picked up Sophie's hand and started to apply a cool cream that felt quite nice.

"Magic is a part of our lives, it is woven into everything we do. We wield it in spells, but it also responds to our subconscious desires." Lynette explained.

Sophie raised a sceptic brow. "So, witches use magic to look better? And stay young?"

Lynette chuckled, "No, nothing so active. It responds to a witch's vanity. It's probably hard for someone as young and pretty as you to understand, but I challenge you to find anyone in the world who hasn't been concerned about their looks or wrinkles at some point in their lives."

"It sounds like a waste of magic." Sophie muttered.

"We're not always in control of our power. It's an instinctive thing – can you always control breathing? Or blinking?" Lynette asked, brandishing a cuticle file.

Sophie fell silent, allowing Lynette to carry out her ministrations.

Time ticked by, as Sophie's hair was also attacked. Lynette had finally put the finishing touches to her make-up, and Sophie looked in the mirror. As much as she didn't want to care, she liked how she looked. The make-up was done naturally, and her hair fell in gentle, perfect curls.

Lynette smiled at her expression, as she pulled out a floor-length dress that was a rich crimson.

"That's red." Sophie stated warily, thinking of her safe black dress at home.

"Of course, it's time to be more adventurous."

*****

Sophie stood at the top of the staircase, feeling a wave of nerves. It was one thing to know about the witches, it was quite another to see them en masse.

For once, Basil hadn't been exaggerating. Thorne House was full of more people than Sophie thought possible. They mingled and chattered above the background of classical music.

All fell silent when they noticed Sophie, and all eyes turned her way. Lynette squeezed her hand in a show of silent support.

"Ah, Miss Murphy!" Basil trilled, beckoning her to join him.

Unable to see any way to escape, Sophie made her way downstairs.

"Miss Murphy, this is Frau Kuhn, from the German council." Basil introduced, positively bristling with excitement.

"A pleasure to meet you." The woman greeted in excellent English.

Sophie nodded, unable to summon a smile.

Basil didn't seem to notice, taking her arm and steering her through the crowd. He continued to introduce her to the 'important' people.

Names and faces became a blur, as these witches gazed at Sophie with scepticism, or gushed over her in a fawning manner. A couple of over-excited witches even bowed in respect. Sophie didn't know how to feel about it. She had been schooled for years that she would be the one to lead the witches to a shining new future, but to see the respect these strangers held was oddly disconnected. None of this seemed to matter until Sophie's power of the Shadow was unlocked.

As soon as there was a lull, Sophie leaned in towards Basil. "And my power?"

Basil's society smile froze for a moment, he patted her hand reassuringly. "All in good time, my dear. Ah, you must meet Reynolds. Reynolds!"

Basil's call summoned a male witch from the throng.

Sophie felt her breath hitch and her pulse start to race at the mere sight of him. It was unfair that witches in general were beautiful, but this man was ridiculous.

Tall, with black hair and designer stubble, his dark brown eyes sparked with intelligence. His expensive suit was perfectly tailored to his slim, athletic frame.

"Miss Murphy, may I introduce Tristan Reynolds. He will be assisting with your education from now on. He is one of our most promising witches in the fight against the witch-hunters; he will be teaching you offensive spells."

Sophie felt the heat of a rare blush rise to her cheeks, and she was glad for the layers of make-up Lynette had insisted upon.

Tristan Reynolds eyed her coolly, then tilted his head. "A pleasure, Miss Murphy."

Damn, even his voice was attractive, but Sophie could sense the insincerity of his words, which helped bring everything back into perspective. She wasn't some silly girl, to be distracted by looks; she was to be the Shadow Witch.

*****

810

Sophie had never been to a formal party, but she always imagined it would involve ball gowns, suits and lots of political talk.

Of course, there were less-than-subtle differences with this witches' party. The talk often centred on the fight against the vile witch-hunters, and as the evening wore on, some witches started to show off their party tricks.

After only witnessing magic in an educational role, as part of her training, Sophie was surprised to see witches using it frivolously. It was hypnotic, watching the flares of fire curl into living creatures which performed for their owners. Or the witches that played with water and light, to make crystalline rainbows scatter across the ceiling.

Sophie felt her first real pull of belonging. These were her people, who embraced their magical inheritance and would not be cowed by the witch-hunters snapping at their heels.

It was nearly midnight when Basil appeared at her side again.

"Miss Murphy, it's time for your gift."

Sophie felt a rush of adrenaline. "You found out how to unlock it?" She asked breathlessly. She had to admit that she'd already assumed that he'd failed. Again.

Basil gave another false smile, and led her outside. The gardens were beautiful tonight, with lights hovering in the air, providing warmth against the autumn chill.

Right now, though, Sophie didn't care if she was standing in this gorgeous venue, or alone on a barren moor. All that mattered was Basil giving her what she was due.

She spotted Lynette ahead, with a witch she didn't recognise. The strange woman knelt as Sophie approached.

"Sh-shadow, I am honoured." She stuttered.

Sophie looked around, a strange feeling of foreboding creeping up her spine. "What's happening?"

"In light of everything you are to become, the witches' council have decided that the sooner you have powers, the better. Think of it as the next level of training, to prepare you for the full power of the Shadow."

Sophie's heart dropped. She knew it, she'd got her hopes up and they'd failed again.

Her eyes lowered to the woman who still knelt before her, her auburn hair shining in the witch-light.

"Stand up, Mary." Basil snapped.

The woman obediently rose, graceful in her ballgown. She had pale skin and a pretty scattering of freckles. Her green eyes lifted briefly to meet Sophie's, then shyly dropped again.

"I am most honoured to have been chosen." She said breathlessly.

"What-?"

Sophie's question was cut off by Basil.

"Mary has agreed to transfer her powers to you. Mary, hand."

The woman obediently held out her hand to Basil. She shivered as a knife was produced and cut into the pale flesh of her palm.

Sophie's eyes widened at the bright red blood that began to drip onto the floor between them. Panic froze her to the spot, but Sophie finally tore her gaze away from the blood, towards her mentor Lynette.

The older woman looked a little paler than usual, but nodded in encouragement.

"Your hand, Miss Murphy." Basil commanded, holding the bloody knife.

Cautiously, Sophie held her hand out. She bit back a cry of pain as he cut her palm, and placed a white crystal in it.

Mary moved her bleeding hand over Sophie's. When they touched Sophie felt a rush of something new, unknown, and completely breathtaking.

Sophie drew in a shuddering breath; overcome with light-headedness, her balance faltered. As her knees buckled, she felt a pair of strong hands guide her to a chair.

"Easy, Miss Murphy." Tristan's deep voice murmured.

Sophie opened her eyes and gasped. There was an aura rolling off everyone. Deep, rich colours pulsed with every heartbeat.

There was pressure on her hand, and Sophie saw Lynette looking at her with a familiar worry. For the first time, Sophie saw her power, radiating in soft blue waves. The natural part of Lynette that Sophie had been blind to, with her human eyes.

"Are you alright, Sophie?" Lynette asked quietly.

"I had no idea…" Sophie said, her voice breaking.

She looked out over the garden and could see the layers of spells woven together. Her eyes raised to the night sky and the very stars seemed to sing in high, cold tones.

Basil broke into her circle of awareness, his aura pulsing a sick yellow colour that felt strong, yet brittle. "We need to network. Everyone will be thrilled to witness your first taste of power."

"No." Lynette said, more forceful than Sophie had ever witnessed. "She's done enough tonight, she's not your performing monkey."

"But think of the opportunity…" Basil started to argue.

Lynette stood firm, "Sophie needs to rest, and get used to her new powers."

Sophie felt hands lifting her from her seat. "Come on, sweetie, I'll get you to your room." Lynette cooed in her ear.

Sophie let herself be guided back inside Thorne House, but recoiled at the doorway. The masses of witches and their conflicting auras were a deafening mess that made her head hurt, and her knees buckled again.

"Allow me." A deep voice broke through.

Sophie's sense of balance lurched as she was lifted off her feet and carried. She took a deep, shuddering breath to try and regain some control. She should be offended by this; she wasn't some flimsy damsel in distress. She raised her eyes and saw Tristan's firm jawline, and the powerful grey magic that seeped out of him.

Maybe she'd say something later.

### Sophie's story is available in ebook and paperback.